VIRTUAL BLUE

R. J. SULLIVAN

Dedicated to Monica A. Felver-Kellogg, the "first fan" of Blue and R.J. Sullivan.

ACKNOWLEDGMENTS_

ORIGINAL 2013 NOTES, ACKNOWLEDGEMENTS, THANKS, AND OTHER STUFF YOU CAN SKIP.

ARGH! THERE BE SPOILERS AHEAD! Virtual Blue is a direct sequel to Haunting Blue. I've done my best to ensure that this novel stands alone while minimizing "spoilers." Still, I could not avoid referencing several key plot-points from Haunting Blue.

The character of Skye MacLeod is the creative property of E. Chris Garrison. Used with permission. https://sillyhatbooks.com/

THANKS AS ALWAYS TO TEAM R.J.:

My critique group INKlers: Judith Phelps Bastin, Rodney Carlstrom, Becky and John Dockery, Bill Larson, and Kathy Watness.

Nikki Howard for making room for a second-favorite author, and for being "Maxine" last summer. Monica Kellogg for your ALL CAPS AND EXCLAMATION POINTS!!!!!

TCQ: Michael West, John F. Allen and E. Chris Garrison, for your ongoing friendship, comments, and always being in my corner. John provided the image of the Baalina Rune.

Nicole Rinaldi for over five years of "research" as my online gaming pal, for being my EMT resource, and for composing one great and one (intentionally) awful poem for Chapter One: Smart Girl and Loneliness.

Noel Rinaldi Williams for continuous, ongoing, awesome marketing art.

Debra Holland, always and forever Editor Prime. "It's not a dream anymore."

Seventh Star: Stephen Zimmer who puts it out there 24/7, Amanda DeBord, the red pen of power, and artist extraordinaire Bonnie Wasson who literally makes me look awesome.

None of it would matter without my family: Linda "Mrs. R.J." Sullivan for always......yeah, that about covers it, and our three nerds in the making, Amanda, Cindy and Steven.
And Mom, Dad, Mike, Hariette, and Hannah. I love you.

2020

Danielle Muething for bringing her incredible narration skills to my audiobook adaptations. And, in the case of Virtual Blue, reading from the manuscript and documenting typos and other errors for me.

Bryan Donihue for helping me through the republishing nightmare... er... process.

CHAPTER ONE

"Fiona?"

"Mom?"

A voice, silent for two years, stirred Fiona into a vortex of confusion.

"Fiona, you must help him. He needs you."

Fiona stood in the living room of the home she and her mother had lived in for three months.

Her mother sat on the white leather couch, her shoulders slumped in obvious fatigue. She gazed at the cream-colored carpet, lines on her face visible from drained emotion.

"Mom, you're alive!" Joy surged through her, but a gnawing coldness in her stomach told her she was kidding herself.

She dropped onto the couch and wrapped her arms around her mother. "I'm sorry. I'm sorry. It's my fault you died. If I hadn't left, Gunther couldn't have..." Overwhelmed, tears fell from Fiona's face and soaked into the soft shoulder of her mother's blouse.

"It's not your fault, sweetie. It was my time. Now, listen; I can only stay for a little while."

A comforting, oddly cool hand patted the back of Fiona's head.

"No!" Fiona locked her arms around her mother. "Last time I

walked out of this room, I said we'd make up for lost time. Then you died."

Tender fingers caressed Fiona's arm. "It's okay, baby. Don't mourn me. I watch you from a good place."

"Mommy, please don't go."

"I had to come to you, to warn you. A great evil—even greater than Gunther—is about to be unleashed. You must go to Chip and stop it."

"No, Mom. Chip can't help. Chip's just as much to blame. If he hadn't messed with Gunther's ghost..." Not entirely true, but after two years of replaying that night, she still couldn't help but blame him...and herself. "If he hadn't gone searching for that money, trying to clear his father's name..." Another sob clogged her throat. Fiona trembled, wanting nothing more than to spend the rest of their precious moments together locked in an embrace, enjoying total silence. Something they never did when her mother still lived.

Her mother leaned forward and pressed a gentle kiss on her forehead.

Fiona's heart glowed. She drew a shaky breath. She remembered that the last time she'd talked to her mother, Fiona had kissed her on the cheek, with no idea it would be a final goodbye.

"Chip did nothing, my dear. But he stands in the path of a great evil that will destroy him if you don't help."

Head reeling, Fiona hugged her mother tighter. "Chip asked me to visit him for Thanksgiving break. I wanted to stay with Dad here in New York, instead."

"You've been ignoring all of Chip's invitations the last few months," the specter scolded.

"Mom..."

"Chip needs you, Blue, and if you're truly honest with yourself, you need him, too. Now, more than ever."

Fiona couldn't speak, shocked that her mother used Chip's special endearment for her, after her blue, spiked hair. She'd never told her mother about the nickname. There hadn't been time.

Fiona broke their embrace and crossed her arms over her chest. "If I see Chip, it'll be to break things off. I've thought about it a long time, and I don't want to be in the relationship anymore."

"Fiona, I've forgiven him. Why can't you?" Her mother's tone changed to the impatient negotiator Fiona had known all-too-well. Her mother apparently caught herself. "Fine, dear. Do what you must. Just get on the plane and get back to Indiana. Or you'll most certainly regret it."

———

"Fiona!"

A masculine voice startled her awake. Her eyes snapped open to focus on her dad's face. She drew in a breath, and a hand touched her shoulder.

"No!" She couldn't stop the cry from escaping her lips.

"Fiona, honey, it's okay."

Fiona's pajama top stuck to her, sweaty under the thin quilt, but the familiar smell of her dad's aftershave made her sit up and lean into his strong shoulder.

I'm here, not in Perionne. She glanced around the bright white walls of her bedroom in the spacious condominium her dad owned in upstate New York. Johnny Depp as Jack Sparrow winked back at her from one wall; framed prints of *Starry Night* and *The Scream* decorated another.

I'm home.

Blinking through the disheveled hair in her eyes, she pulled him to her in a hug.

He hesitated, then wrapped an arm around her waist and patted her on the back.

She understood his discomfort. She usually remained stiff during these offerings of love from the father who'd been unavailable most of her life. It was a minor miracle they could find any way to connect after missing so much time.

Her dad's concerned voice rumbled in her ear. "Do you remember your dream?"

Fiona nodded against his shoulder and told a partial truth. "I was dreaming about...her."

His grip became less tenuous and more caressing. "I'm sorry, Fiona. I know how you still miss her."

Fiona pulled away and wiped tears from her face, not wanting to offer more detail. "I'm not sure I'll ever get over it."

Her dad nodded and rose, his awkwardness apparent. "Come down when you're ready. I have breakfast waiting."

Several minutes later, showered, dressed, and, feeling more like herself, Fiona padded lightly down the spiral staircase to the great room. In the open kitchen, her dad stood with his back to her, holding a spatula over a pan and facing the stove while projecting calm confidence. She eyed the stack of pancakes on a plate near his elbow.

Fiona hopped into a stool at the breakfast bar and waited, drumming her fingers on the countertop. "Pancakes? What did I do to deserve this special treat?" On most weekends, her father diligently manned the stove to coax up his special pancakes. During the week...not so much.

He turned and placed the loaded plate next to hers. "I have a late morning, but I'll probably be at the office into the evening tonight. I was hoping you had a little time, as well. Besides, after the night you had, I thought you needed a little pampering."

Fiona picked up a fork and stabbed the top four with unguarded enthusiasm. She grinned, grabbed the syrup bottle, and dribbled syrup over the stack of cakes on her plate. "I always have time for pancakes," she teased. Though she had rounded out a bit since high school, she still thought she looked too skinny.

Her dad tipped a carafe of chilled orange juice from the middle of the breakfast bar and poured some into a glass. He slid onto the stool next to her and filled his plate.

"This works out well," Fiona said, not looking up. "I need to talk to you about something. I made a decision this morning, and I'm not sure what you're going to think."

He reached for a mug of steaming coffee and raised an eyebrow in mock concern. "Oh? Are we going to have a confrontation?"

Fiona giggled. They argued rarely, and when they did, they usually settled disagreements by talking it out–a refreshing change for Fiona after the years of intense fights with her mom.

Fiona took a deep breath and decided to just say it. "I think it'd be best if I spent Thanksgiving in Indiana this year. With Chip. Rather than going to Perionne, he's staying at his house in Bloomington. Thought I'd join him for a few days and let him show me around the IU campus."

"Oh?" Her dad took a long sip from his coffee. "I'd hoped that we would spend a few more holidays together before your boyfriends took up all your time."

An unspoken *we've had so few* hung between them.

Only last year, Fiona learned that her dad hadn't willingly stayed away while she grew up. When he'd first rejected her mother's offer to move to New York to be near him, her mother had placed a trumped-up restraining order against him. Only after her death did he feel he could come back into his daughter's life. Fiona finished her senior year of high school in Perionne, living with Chip and his father, and then moved with her dad out to New York.

"I know. And it's not what you think." As his other eyebrow rose, she stopped herself. "Okay, okay, it *is* what you think. Sort of. But I've made another decision. I'm going to break up with Chip. And I can't email him or text message him. We've been together over two years, and we've been through a lot. I need to talk it out and make it right. I owe him that much."

Her dad wiped a napkin across his face. "I know a lot of this is new to me, but I imagine that every father is torn between secretly wanting his daughter to swear off boys and join a convent, and to find some sort of balance between what's cool and what's safe. Chip's been a strong, stabilizing influence on you, but I've been concerned about you for a long time."

Fiona swallowed a mouthful, wondering what was coming next.

"Do you have any friends at school? Good friends?"

An embarrassed flush burned over her face. "I do okay," she said, shifting in her seat. She couldn't even explain it to herself, but friends hadn't been a big priority her first year in college.

"Listen, it's not that I don't appreciate having you here. But you know if you want to live on campus, you're welcome to at any time."

"It's a ten-minute ride by subway, Dad. Living on campus doesn't make sense."

"And that's also a great excuse to stay away from campus life...I've been concerned that this long-distance relationship has been an ongoing reason for you to turn away from the people around you. You have a boyfriend, but you never see him, so you're free to ignore all social activities for the next four years and come home every night to study or watch DVDs with your dad."

"I know, Dad. I just had to realize it for myself." As her father's words struck home, hurt stabbed at her. "Hey, are you saying you don't like watching movies with me?"

Her dad chuckled and rose from his seat. He placed an arm around her shoulders, pulling her close. "I love watching movies with you, Fiona. I just want you to be happy. And you're old enough to decide for yourself where you can go for Thanksgiving. You work it out and do what you have to do. But I still get you for Christmas, deal?"

Fiona hugged her father close. "Deal."

They separated, and he bent to retrieve his leather briefcase. "What are your plans today?"

Fiona looked down at her orange juice. "Um...well, I have Writing 201 at 10:30, Algebra 3 this afternoon, and...a classmate is coming over to study with me."

"Is this classmate of the male or female persuasion?"

"Um..."

The eyebrows crept up again.

Fiona giggled. "Male, and it's not what you think."

Her father drew out an exaggerated exhale. "Lucky for you I happened to schedule a late day for myself."

"It's *really* not what you think!"

"Shouldn't you get rid of one boyfriend before you invite another boy into the house? Or is that sort of thinking old-fashioned?"

"Daaa-aaad!" She played along. "He's in my lit class."

"And you can't study in the library?"

Fiona folded her arms across her chest. "As it happens, I *thought* you were going to be here, so everything would've been fine."

"All right, all right, you can meet him here. But if he wants to take you out to Starbucks, I'd be okay with that." He leaned over and kissed her forehead. "Have a good day. I love you."

"Love you, too."

The door shut, and Fiona hugged herself, shaking off a sudden chill.

———

AFTER CLASSES, Fiona raced home to get the house ready, telling herself the arrival of Drew Allamand didn't mean anything.

She'd met Drew last year in Introduction to Poetry. They'd been clustered with about ten other writing majors in the same workshop classes. Throughout the year, study group invitations had piled up, each rejected in their turn. By winter, these had morphed into "Friday night party at Gwen's" and "poetry reading at Drew's." She'd started the semester excusing herself from a *CSI* season premiere party.

Last year, all she wanted was to be left alone.

And now?

As the doorbell rang, she wiped clammy hands across her jeans, and, not for the first time, wondered what the hell she was doing. Why had she finally invited a classmate—a decidedly cute classmate—to her home?

Trying to calm the butterflies in her stomach, she opened the door.

Drew, dressed in a blue T-shirt and faded jeans, grinned at her. Waves of dirty-blond hair curtained his boyish face. He held a compact plastic folder in one hand. "Hi, Fiona." He reached one arm out to hug her.

Startled at the familiarity, Fiona stepped back, then caught herself and leaned into his friendly, brief embrace.

Drew walked through the door, amusement flashing in his cool green eyes. "Good to finally see you outside of class. Nobody would believe it when I said I was coming over today."

Wow, has it gotten that obvious? Fiona led Drew to the couch next to the coffee table stacked with her textbooks. "I know. You've all been very patient, and I've been ignoring you." She sat on the couch, motioning an invitation at the spot next to her.

Drew dropped down and slumped against the cushions. "No, it's cool. It's just, you know, we're all in this together. Gwen wants to see more of you, and the others, too. But, hey," Drew shrugged. "I told them you'll show up when you're ready, and not before."

Glad for his understanding, she tried to explain. "I had...a rough senior year. In high school, I mean."

"Your mom died, I heard. Gwen mentioned something about it."

A laugh escaped Fiona, and she fought a sudden urge to leave the room. "I doubt Gwen knows the half of it." She looked at the coffee table and picked up the massive Norton Reader. "Want to start with this?"

"Hell, no."

The frankness of his reply splashed like cold water on her face. She looked into piercing green eyes. "What?"

"You're a poetry major, right?"

"Yeah."

"Well, so am I. Let's see 'em, Fiona. Show me your poems."

A rush of excitement flushed through her.

Drew waved the plastic folder in his hand. "I'll show you mine if you--"

Fiona giggled. "Don't be a cornball. Stay right there." She stood and raced toward the stairs. She could feel his gaze follow her up the spiral stairwell. She returned a few seconds later, grasping her own zippered portfolio.

Drew took the offered folder and looked at the first piece in the stack, called "American Idol Finalist," a poem she'd penned shortly after the move to Perionne. She noted Drew's intake of breath during the last stanza—a pleased reaction he couldn't fake.

"Wow. That's terrific, Fiona. So much anger, and yet focused into such a cutting observation about media and sexism. I love it."

"Yeah, thanks." Fiona felt herself flush from the praise. "There's a whole story behind it, as well. My English teacher wanted to fail me after reading that, until a friend intervened and busted him, more or less."

"Sounds like a good friend to have." Drew's voice held the hint of a question.

"Yeah. Chip, he's...a guy I was seeing back in Indiana. A long time ago." She stared down at the carpet, feeling ashamed as the lie spilled from her mouth.

Drew turned the page, this time reading a borderline-rant Fiona had penned shortly after breaking up with Joey, her—she could admit now—loser boyfriend.

Smart girl.
Slick guy.
Coffee bar nights.
Poetry under starlight.
She gave her heart away.

Stoned stare.
Stupid, crazy fights.
She's barely out of sight,
He gave her heart away.

Fiona waited for Drew to take in the words.

The pause extended much longer than it would have taken to read the poem. Drew lowered the paper and seemed to retreat into himself for over a minute. Finally, his gaze turned to her, as if seeing her for the first time. "This is also incredible."

Heat crept into her cheeks.

"You have a beautiful soul, Fiona. You should bring these to one of our poetry-reading gatherings."

Fiona shrugged. "I know. I wanted to, I just... well, you know how poetry is. You sort of expose your innermost self to everyone."

Drew nodded. "I know. Believe me, I understand. But that's the magic of it, as well." He flipped through the pages and stopped at an assignment piece from last spring. The red B- still showed at the top.

Loneliness
An empty, gaping hole.
It's so deep, so dark.

Clawing your way to the light.
Your fingers become so raw.

Heartache so strong,
You just stop existing.

Is it possible to go on?

Drew's gaze scanned across the first few lines.

A different sort of embarrassment flushed over her. "That's...kind of unfinished. I mean, I turned it in, but I couldn't..." She trailed off. *I couldn't do it, and I wrote crap. I guess there's nothing more to say about that.*

"Huh." Drew couldn't hide the disappointment in his voice. "Is this about another boyfriend?"

"No, my..." She stopped, not sure she wanted to go there with this relative stranger.

Another pause before Drew spoke again. "Not bad. Missing something, though. Maybe if you keep working on it. We can brainstorm some time."

Fiona smiled, trying to contain her welling attraction. "I'd like that."

Drew flipped pages and read another recent assignment. Without comment, he turned more pages, read, then skimmed more still. With a deep sigh, he closed the portfolio and turned to look at her, a somber expression on his face. "It's worse than I thought."

"What?" Panic broke her reverie.

"You." Drew extended his index finger and tapped her upper sternum.

She froze, unsure how to respond to a skewed act of both familiarity and respect.

"You're dying inside. At least, your inner poet is dying, isn't it?"

His words made her ache. "My inner poet definitely took an ass-kicking last year." She offered a sad smile. "And yeah, I've been a little lost."

Drew finished her thought. "And that's why you've stayed away from us."

Fiona processed his words, trying to find an honest answer. "My mom...she didn't just die. She was murdered. We had unresolved problems between us, and then just like *that*..." she snapped her fingers. "...she was gone."

"Oh, my God, I'm so sorry." Drew crossed himself. "You must have been devastated."

Surprised by his response, she downplayed the moment. "Let's just say I've had my share of therapy in the last couple years." She thought back to her appointments with sympathetic Dr. Churchill and how the therapist tried to help her refocus the blame away from herself and onto Gunther, where it belonged.

But because the incident involved a ghost, Fiona couldn't completely confide in the doctor without the risk of being diagnosed with schizophrenia. So, stuck with a secret she couldn't disclose, Fiona sorted through some of her issues, especially her feelings for Chip, on her own.

Or have I?

Drew leaned close, and for the first time, Fiona realized his arm had slipped behind her shoulders. *When did that happen?*

"I like the poet I see on those first pages," he whispered. His words bridged the space between them. "I like her a lot. You should let us help you."

Fiona swallowed. "I want to."

"*I* want to help you, if you'll let me."

She tipped her head up toward him. "I'd like that."

His lips touched hers.

She responded hungrily.

He deepened the kiss.

Her back arched from her need, her toes curling. She reached up and stroked the back of his head.

What a kiss!

They separated moments later, the air filled with their mutual gasps.

Guilt slammed her. Nausea churned in the pit of her stomach, and she knew this was wrong.

He leaned in for another kiss.

"No. No, Drew, we need to stop." She placed a hand on his shoulder, pressing gently, hoping she wouldn't have to use more force.

To her relief, he leaned back into the couch. "It's okay." He took a deep breath. "It was pretty intense for me, too. I didn't mean to push."

Fiona shook her head. "No, it's not that. I like you. And I'm okay with what happened. It sort of helped me confirm something. But right now, the words my father said this morning are going through my mind. I need to get rid of one boyfriend before I take on another."

A palpable silence hung between them before he responded. "Yeah, you might have mentioned the boyfriend part." His tone chilled, and his eyes flashed anger.

"I'm leaving next week to visit him over Thanksgiving weekend."

"And that's supposed to make me feel better...how?" A touch of amusement cut through the coolness in his voice.

Fiona grabbed Drew's arm, noting the hard muscle under her fingers. "No, listen. Chip and I...we've been in this sort of long-distance non-relationship for over a year now. He's special to me, but...I need to end it and move on. But properly, face to face, without any side baggage."

"You mean me?" Drew's voice carried a hint of anger. "I'm the side baggage? Nice."

"Be fair, Drew." Anger crept into her own response. "This just happened. You caught me off guard." *I will not be bullied into feeling guilty.* "You and I haven't talked. You didn't ask me out. Yes, it would be convenient for me to tell him I met someone else, but that's not true. Chip and I...we imploded months ago. He just doesn't see it, and I do. I need to make him understand we're no good for each other. That's what's fair and right. For him. For everyone." She let the moment linger before adding, "Including you. And a week from now, we can figure out what..." she waved a hand in the air, her mind failing to conjure an appropriate word. "We can figure out what...this...is. If anything."

Drew wiped his hands over his face. "I've been kind of watching you for over a year, hoping you'd come out of your shell."

"Oh." She didn't know what to say. Blood pounded in her ears.

Drew nodded. "Look, I dated around a bit last year. Gwen and I went out a few times. And others." He stopped himself. "God, that sounds worse, doesn't it?"

The moment of tension ended in a burst of mutual laughter.

Drew dabbed at his eyes. "You do have that whole 'girl of mystery' aura going for you. Nothing scary, though. So I've been interested on and off." Drew pulled his arm from around her and clapped his hands together. "All I'm trying to say is: do what you have to do, and we'll talk. No pressure, I promise."

Fiona offered a smile. "Good. Now, I have two other requests."

Drew grinned, and his face reflected his amusement. "Uh, oh, are you one of those demanding women?"

Fiona reached up and stroked his cheek. "First, I want to see *your* poems. Secondly, maybe we can get some *real* studying done in the next couple hours and get ready for that test."

Drew smiled. "Done."

———

A COUPLE HOURS LATER, after receiving a sedate kiss goodnight, Fiona shut the door. She returned to the couch, curling her knees up and holding her folder of poems in her lap.

As her reaction to Drew's presence faded, she swallowed back a tear and clutched the folder to her chest. *He's right. My inner poet is dying.*

Marda Mercedes descended the basement steps and stood before the shrine.

Though they'd resided in the half-duplex for over five months, she still thought of the off-campus house as their temporary base of operations.

Marda chose her team of three specialists from hundreds of candidates. All were Sisters in high standing amongst the dozens of covens of Baalina scattered across the Midwest. Baalina grew these pockets, beginning with her first follower, whose name was lost to ancient history. The cult grew as Baalina drew each woman who'd heard her voice and led them to Her worshippers.

Within the covens, Baalina's chosen ones enjoyed the peace of sanctuary isolated from all other influences. Christians throughout history despised the Sisters and worked tirelessly to destroy them. When found, they called them out as witches and enacted punishment accordingly.

And yet, it was the Wiccans who'd rejected Baalina's worshippers most strongly. Wiccans who rejected the concept of demons in the flesh and mocked the practices of the Sisterhood. In some cases, it was the coordinated efforts of Wiccans that broke many of Baalina's most promising candidates away from the Sisterhood.

Over the last few months, Marda had enjoyed isolation and sanctuary in the company of her two most loyal lieutenants, the so-called Terror Twins, Cyndi and Vanessa. Cyn and Van, for short. The Terror Twins, assassins for hire who held two spots on America's Most Wanted for years. They shunned any surname, preferring anonymity, and Marda indulged their need for drama.

They worked, lived, plotted, and quarreled together. Sometimes, they laughed and played; but mostly, they focused on the goal–to free their mistress, the Goddess Baalina, from her infernal prison, the chaos realm, that had confined her for hundreds of years.

After about three weeks, Marda could no longer tolerate a place that lacked a shrine to the Goddess. She cleared a space in the basement and constructed a tiny temple and personal sanctuary, a quiet place to escape to whenever their tasks overwhelmed them, whenever she grew weary pondering the injustice heaped upon her mistress.

She'd told the others she'd created it for all of them, but mostly, she'd created it for herself.

She knew everyone in the Sisterhood was loyal to Baalina, but Marda also knew her own role in the order-to-come was special. She had always suspected this to be true, and recently, Baalina herself had confirmed her suspicions. A committed student, Marda rose to the rank of high priestess, and Baalina promised that when she'd been freed of her captivity, Marda would rule at her side.

So she needed the alone time—time to commune with the Goddess.

Marda grabbed the box of matches and struck the tip against the side; the flare of brightness exposed the cool, dark, open space around her. She lit two candles, revealing the green circle surrounding the spray-painted rune of the Goddess Baalina painted on the floor in dim hues.

Across the room, light danced along the surface of a large statue. Baalina's image stood upon a pedestal and glared. Twin horns protruded from her head and curled upon themselves like the majestic ram. She stood cloaked in splendid purple robes with silver trim that befitted her stature, and her proud gaze swept over her subjects.

Marda stepped into the circle of summoning and bowed on one knee. *Proud and haughty. Of course. Why not? When one earned their place of power, one should be proud. Only the inferior would feel jealous.*

In the first month of their stay here in the college housing, Marda would dress in the proscribed priestess robes of ritual, but as her sessions continued several times daily, the rituals of honor proved too complicated and time consuming.

Today, she dressed in jeans and a loose blue sweater. "Forgive me, oh Goddess, for my humble apparel. I felt the need to seek your guidance."

She'd barely begun her meditations when she sensed the mistress touch her mind.

No forgiveness is required, my child. Your service means more to me than ancient costumes. Your loyalty will be rewarded, as surely as those who have turned against me will meet the punishment they deserve.

Eugene "Chip" Farren slumped in a pleather office chair in the basement of the home he rented with his best friend, Phil Jenson, and squinted at the code displayed on his thirty-six-inch computer monitor.

Chip and Phil had arranged three long desks in a sort of horseshoe bullpen shape. Together, the three desks supported five interlinked computers, including the committed server, running *Fantasy Free Form*, their mutual dream-child online computer game.

Although still a work in progress, Chip and Phil made *Fantasy Free Form* available to online subscribers twenty-four hours a day, free of charge. As the game continued to grow in popularity, they hoped to offset their investment by charging advertisers, and, when they reached the growth they needed, hit up their current subscribers with a small monthly fee to continue playing.

But, with only about 200 brave souls willing to put up with the bugs and environmental changes, Chip and Phil had a long way to go before that dream became a reality.

When they weren't attending classes, studying, or working, Chip and Phil spent every minute of their time in their makeshift workspace, molding *Fantasy Free Form* closer to their vision. "Time," in this case, referred to the hours of 10 PM to 3 AM. They made sure no classes started before noon the next day—at least, no classes they couldn't afford to skip.

Chip changed a few more lines of code and clicked the update button with the mouse. "There, try that."

Behind him, Phil stared at the monitor attached to computer system three and grunted. They ran all their code corrections on computer three, diagnosing problems through trial and error and game-testing fixes without affecting the live server.

Chip rotated his chair to look over Phil's shoulder.

The monitor blinked to life, showing an attractive scene of computerized forestland beauty, one of several areas they'd designed where gamers could interact through their online characters to quest, hunt, or sightsee, depending on their pleasure. Last night, an irate subscriber had fired off a note to their helpdesk email address, bringing an embarrassing glitch to their attention. Now they had to track down the problem.

In the midst of the woods, Phil's avatar, Magtog, appeared, dressed in flowing blue robes and holding a gnarled walking stick. The wizard hobbled across the forest in response to Phil hitting directional arrows on the keyboard.

Magtog's specific function was to walk to a spot in the woods where a deer would wander randomly through the forest until slain by a character. Since the program ran on the trial computer, Chip and Phil didn't need to worry about other players interfering. Only Magtog inhabited this version of the *Fantasy Free Form* world.

The two friends watched and waited. As expected, the deer galloped into view, approaching a nearby tree. To Chip's dismay, the deer walked through the tree, and, like a phantom ghost on a rampage, hopped high into the air toward a hill. The creature passed completely through the hill and continued on its way, oblivious to the minor miracles it had just performed.

Phil emitted a long sigh and wiped a hand across his forehead.

Years of friendship allowed Chip to read paragraphs in that single sigh. Bugs on background ambiance shit like this annoyed Phil to no end.

As he pivoted his large frame to face Chip, Phil's chair squeaked in protest. "Whatever you did, it didn't work."

"Damn." Chip reached up and palmed his eyes, welcoming the seconds of spotted blackness after six hours of staring at the screen. Bigger game companies could pass little bugs like this on to a staff of programmers, but here in the basement, it was just the two of them.

Lifting his bulk from the seat, Phil groaned. "And we don't have any more time, Romeo. Not if we're going to pick Blue up from the airport." Standing at full height, Phil's six-foot frame and pear-shaped mass intimidated those who didn't know him. Usually, his warm smile canceled out any uneasiness his size invoked, but at the moment, he did nothing to hide his cranky mood.

Chip craned his neck to look at his friend. "What's the matter? We'll stay on it. Blue won't keep me from doing the work."

Phil shook his head, his beefy hand swatting down toward the desk and scooping up the car keys. "It's not that. Well, maybe it is. I've got a bad feeling."

"What's wrong?"

"Look, Mary and I decided to stop being exclusive to each other almost a year ago." The words came from Phil as if forced. "And she's visited me six times since then, clearing some weekends and flying up from Florida." Phil shrugged and waved a palm at Chip. "You and Blue are supposed to be all serious, but where's she been, dude? For that matter, why haven't *you* seen *her*?"

Chip raised his shoulders in a reflexive defense. He'd heard Phil get miffed about the drive-thru guys getting his order wrong, or the daily gripe about needing to turn the air conditioning down, but this was new. "Maybe we take our schooling more seriously."

Phil waved a hand. "Bullshit. If you took your classes so seriously, you'd be cracking the books now and not messing around on Triple-F all the time."

"What's your point?"

Phil shrugged. "She's been avoiding you for over a year, and now she can't wait to see you. What changed?"

"Well, that's a good thing, right?"

Phil rubbed his palm across the two-day growth of stubble before answering. "I don't know. I hope so. Honestly, I'm worried about you." Phil folded his arms. "But then again, I can't figure it out because I don't know the whole story, do I?"

Chip flushed, even though he hadn't followed the accusation. "I don't know what you mean."

Phil's eyebrows knitted as he spoke. "The night everything changed. The night Blue's mom died. The morning I woke up to hear my best friend and his girl were in the hospital fighting for their lives." A grimace of pain and anger distorted Phil's features. "And I still don't know what happened."

Like Blue, the lie came easily to Chip after so much practice. "What do you need to know? I told you about how we chased the burglar—"

"Chased a burglar to the park. I know. Some random burglar never heard from before who left no clues, escaped the cops, and was never seen again. You sold it to the police, and you sold it to the newspapers, but what really hurts is that you thought you could sell it to me, too."

"But...Phil. That's the truth. There's nothing more to tell."

Phil only looked more hurt. "That's a partial truth, I'm sure. But come on, I wasn't born yesterday. You gonna tell me it's a coincidence that right after that incident, you lost all interest in the Ghost of Gunther? During our junior year, we should'a been a year into creating Triple-F, but I couldn't get you to focus on it. Because of your obsession with the lousy boat ride and all things Gunther."

Phil hung his head, and to Chip's astonishment, he choked back a sob. "So, the day after you almost get yourself killed, you drop both interests like the bad habits they were, and you finally get onboard with *our* game. And I'm not supposed to notice, so I don't mention it."

Phil gripped his keys in his fist, shaking them at Chip. "I'm telling you—because I'm a better friend to you than you've been to me—that if you think Blue is just coming over for a social visit, you're deluding yourself. Just like you deluded yourself that you pulled a fast one on me."

Phil's words hit like a stunning blow. An uncomfortable silence lingered for over a minute, punctuated only by Phil's wheezing.

Chip finally offered, "I don't know what to say."

Phil nodded and then shook his head. "I'd rather you leave it at that than lie to me again."

"Fair enough." Chip found the energy to lift his head and look into his best friend's face. "Phil, I know it doesn't mean much, but I'm sorry. It's for your own protection. That's all I can say."

"I figured it had to be something like that." Phil laid a hand between Chip's shoulders. He spoke with genuine concern. "How bad did it get?"

Chip swallowed back his sadness. "As much as you know, it was far worse than you can imagine." Chip's body shook with the need to tell more, and he scrunched in the chair to clamp down on the urge.

Phil patted his friend on the back a few times. "Okay, that's good enough for me."

The chirping sound-bite of the classic *Star Trek* communicator signal emitted from Chip's belt, cutting through the silence. With practiced ease, Chip slipped his cell phone from the belt holster and glanced at the text message on the screen. "That's her. Plane's running on time."

To pick Blue up, Chip and Phil needed 90 minutes to catch the shuttle north to Indianapolis International Airport. The round trip would kill the rest of their afternoon and bring them back in time for a late dinner.

Phil shook his head and stepped toward the stairs. "Let's go get your girlfriend."

WERE IT NOT WEDNESDAY NIGHT–THANKSGIVING Eve–Smittie's Pizzeria would already be packed to capacity with hungry students. The tally so far, in the midst of their six PM dinner "rush," was five pizzas served to a whopping fifteen lonely bodies.

Smittie Lagione–owner and titular inspiration of the popular student eatery–wiped his hands on his relatively clean apron. He shook his head, reflecting for the millionth time today how the restaurant was losing money by the minute.

On paper, his wife, Laverne, was head-waitress and bookkeeper, with Smittie as sole owner. Laverne had been a Colts cheerleader, years ago, in another life. And to this day, what Laverne wanted, Laverne got. Her short-cropped, dark spiked hair, disarming smile, form-fitting T-shirt and shorts that almost entered the realm of bad taste, and husky Hoosier drawl served as Smittie's secret arsenal.

Slathered on in just the right doses, Laverne's charm often secured those extra dessert orders or sides of breadsticks desperately needed for a small eatery to thrive. Smittie supported the business financially, but he counted on her targeted and harmless flirting. They understood the necessity of her sex appeal, and jealousy never entered the equation.

Hell, let the students gawk. She was still a damn, fine-looking woman. And, at the end of the day, she always went home with him.

Laverne insisted they needed to be open all holiday weekend to the students as a thank you for all the business they brought in the rest of the school year. If just one lonely, hungry kid stuck on campus during this holiday could find a friendly face and good food at Smittie's, then all the work was worth it.

So Smittie sucked it up and smiled. Even ten years later, there were worse things than watching Laverne lean against the counter making notations in her notebook, occasionally meeting his gaze and offering a wink of support. *What the hell. We'll make up the business next week.*

———

BLUE SHAEFER WALKED through the doors, escorted on either side by Chip and Phil.

From the moment she stepped off the plane and fell into Chip's welcoming embrace, old habits took over, and she thought of herself as "Blue," not "Fiona." She'd never hear the name Fiona from either of these two. But the mental change that accompanied the new environment surprised her.

It was as if the mental blocks Fiona of New York had built up for over a year were left in the luggage rack like a straightjacket, and Blue exited the plane with a cocky strut of confidence she hadn't felt since leaving. *And, oh my* God, *that first kiss!*

Well, what did I expect? She chastised herself. *Keep focused; remember what you came here to do. This is not the time to be thinking with your hormones.*

"Best pizza in town," declared Phil. "And you know I've tried them all."

Blue winked at her friend. "That's a recommendation I can get on board with." They stood near the "Please Wait to Be Seated" sign. Blue cuddled close to Chip and curled her fingers into his, basking in the positive energy his presence brought to her.

The ease with which she resumed her old role at Chip's side surprised her.

A gruff Italian voice called out, "Laverne, unpack the next crate of breadsticks. Phil's here to clean us out again."

Blue returned the grin of the plump, middle-aged man standing behind the counter, his dark apron lightly coated in flour. "Are you kidding? Phil's metabolism slowed down years ago. *I'm* the one you really have to look out for."

A curvy, thirty-ish brunette stepped forward, stopping Blue short. Laverne flashed a devastatingly radiant smile at the three of them. "Smittie, fire up the oven. This girl needs some meat on her bones." She extended a perfectly manicured hand. "Welcome to Smittie's, hon. You must be Blue. Chip just goes on and on about you."

Blue shook the offered hand, then watched, bemused, as she pulled Chip and Phil to her in a short embrace. "Always *so good* to see you two! How's the video game coming along, boys?"

Laverne's obvious act charmed Blue. *She's good! They must have maxed out two credit cards here by now.*

Chip blushed, fumbling through some explanation about a problem with a deer going through a tree.

Laverne laughed as if she understood every word and took Phil's arm, leading them to a nearby table. "I'm sure it will all work out soon, guys. Stick with it! Have a seat. Mountain Dews for the boys." She glanced at Blue. "How about you, hon?"

"Uh...root beer is fine. Better stay away from the caffeine this late."

With a final wink and smile, the waitress disappeared behind the counter.

The threesome sat for a few seconds, pretending to study their menus. Blue folded hers and leaned on the table, placing a hand to her cheek and fluttering her eyelashes in Phil's direction. She spoke in a perfect imitation of Laverne's accent. "So, tell me, *hon*, why *are* you here in Bloomington over Thanksgiving break?"

Phil laughed, but he rolled his eyes. "I'm staying away from my step-mom. After years of not getting along, I decided to hell with it and not bother anymore. Besides, I'd rather hang with Chip, anyway." He paused, then added, as if in an afterthought, "And you."

"Ah, gee, that's so *sweet*, hon!" Blue dropped the teasing accent. "But seriously, you just seem...down. You've hardly cracked a smile or said a word the entire shuttle ride back."

Phil shrugged, keeping his glare glued to a menu he must have memorized months ago. "We just put in a long day between the game and the errand, and didn't get anywhere on the bug I'm working on. I guess my mind's still on that. Don't pay it any attention."

Blue already knew Chip and his dad had gotten together the previous week to celebrate. It worked out well for both of them. A few months ago, Jim Farren had started seeing another woman—the first relationship he'd been in since his wife had died over five years ago. Mr. Farren wanted to spend Thanksgiving weekend with her family, and Chip wanted to spend it with Blue.

Laverne's voice broke in on her thoughts. "Get an order of bread-sticks for y'all?"

"Sure," said Chip. "A medium order will do."

"Oooh?" Laverne flashed a smile and wink in Chip's direction. "Are ya sure you don't want a large? We baked up a bunch extra tonight."

Blue piped in. "A medium should be fine, *hon*." She fired back her own smile.

"Tell ya what." Laverne jotted a note on her pad. "I'll charge you for the medium but bring a large. No sense in letting the bread go bad."

A flattered grin formed on Phil's face. "Oh, that's so nice, Laverne. You don't have to do that."

"Nonsense, hon. Least we can do for our favorite customers. Besides, I still say your friend needs some meat on her bones."

Blue opened her mouth for a biting retort, but Chip spoke first. "I like her bones just the way they are, but thanks for your concern, hon." Chip had collected the menus and now handed them over to the stunned waitress, who clearly wasn't used to Chip turning her banter against her. "But we'll take the large order so they don't go to waste."

Laverne smiled back, recovering and reaching for the menus. "*Touché.* I'll be right back with your order." Laverne cocked her head in Blue's direction, offering a friendly wink. "You're very lucky, hon. Chip's a keeper."

Blue flushed. A wave of guilt stole her voice.

Laverne turned toward the counter, speaking over her shoulder. "Don't let him get away."

"I won't." Still overwhelmed, Blue looked down at the red-and-white checkered tablecloth. *No, I won't let him get away. I'm going to throw him back. But now, it feels like if I follow through, it might be the worst mistake of my life.*

No! Stop it! There's no going back because you're afraid to hurt his feelings.

She took one last deep breath, shaking off her doubt. She'd known for months what she had to do. *But that's for later.* "So, what do we want on our pizza?

CHAPTER THREE_

Once again prostrate before the Goddess, Marda recalled the first time she'd heard Baalina whisper to her, following that horrible day when the girls from her new school had cornered her and surrounded her. Her so-called classmates kicked her, punched her, and called her a freak, all egged on by one jealous woman, her cries driving the group to keep striking her. "I saw you staring at Ricky Saunders, bitch! He's mine!"

Marda didn't even know who Ricky Saunders was. She tried to say so, but that didn't matter.

As beatings went, it ended faster than she expected, as if most of the participants' hearts weren't really in it. When it was over, she lay in the grass at the edge of the woods where they'd dragged her, curled up, waiting for the hurting to stop, sponging up the blood with the sleeve of her hand-me-down blouse, wondering what she would tell her parents.

Then she heard the voice for the first time.

Hear me, my child, and be joyful. You are the chosen one, special to me.

Marda sat up, her eyes searching the woods for the source of the voice, so soothing, so comforting.

I am Baalina, and I hear your cries, even though I am far away, imprisoned, just as I hear the pain of all my Sisters. They sadden me, and when I have returned to your world, I will make right these injustices you have suffered and reward you with the power that should be rightfully yours.

Life moved on, even after the embarrassing mess her father caused at the school when he saw her bloodied shirt. Several months passed before most of the girls would speak to her again.

But she was never lonely because one voice whispered to her when the world was quiet and she closed her eyes.

Be patient, my child. Be calm. Many hear my voice, many will be blessed, but you will be the most blessed of the Sisters, for yours will be the hand that ultimately frees me.

Perhaps sensing her connection with Baalina, her classmates stopped tormenting her. Even those who had participated in the beating months earlier reached out, wanting to be her friend.

Of course, my child. The weak are always drawn to the strong. Smile at them. Tell them you forgive them. But one day you will have your revenge. And when you claim the power you deserve, they will all grovel beneath your boot, begging to be spared your anger, as you had begged them, to no avail.

She never forgot Baalina's promise. She lived for that day.

In the quiet of her room, during solitary walks, and on lonely drives, Marda sought refuge in the voice more and more often. The dreary years of high school gave way to the dreary years of community college which gave way to a dead-end engineering job in which she made half the pay of her male counterparts while being overlooked during all opportunities for advancement. Baalina never failed to comfort her, sometimes with vague comments, other times more specific.

It is time for you to unite with my sisters, my child. Tomorrow, you will drive to the edge of Redraven Woods and walk toward the east. After sunset, follow the music. There, in an old, derelict cabin, you will find my worshippers gathered, communing, casting spells, and dancing in worship.

Tell them you heard my voice, and that Baalina told you to submit yourself to Mother Janice for further testing.

So ordered, Marda obeyed. That night, she discovered the Sisterhood of Baalina and received the acceptance and understanding she longed for. Over the next months, she learned the secret history of the Goddess Baalina, and of the Sisterhood itself.

Mother Janice educated her on how the Goddess had influenced humanity since ancient times, quietly, secretly, growing her power and influence on gifted women throughout the world. Baalina found those who heard her voice and answered her call over the centuries until that fateful day, over three centuries ago, she tried to break through into the physical realm.

For ages, Baalina had struggled with the Kelranian Order, self-appointed defenders of the physical world who prevented powerful beings such as Baalina from ruling over humanity, denying the Sisterhood of power it had rightfully earned.

Until one fateful night in 1797, the Kelranian tyrants had used the Divenium Crystal to defeat Madam Katka, their coven's greatest leader, and destroyed Katka's SoulStaff. She learned how they had locked Baalina off in the ether dimension where only her most loyal followers could still hear her.

Katka fell, and the portal was closed when the Kelranian Order used the crystal to cast a powerful spell that assured such a portal could never again be opened from the chaos realm into the physical realm.

But now, the time had come where a combination of technology and extraordinary action on the part of the Sisterhood could circumvent the spell.

———

Like an executioner leading the condemned, Phil opened the door to the basement and took the wooden stairway into the room with stiff solemnity. "Sorry, Blue, you brought this on yourself." He flipped the switch on the wall, triggering the hard fluorescent lights.

As Blue descended the stairs, her gaze traveled over the configuration of computers, screens, and wired rectangular doodads. She wondered if the guys noticed the oppressive hum of the overworked hard drives or the lingering pizza smell permeating the walls. She drew a deep breath and released it in a long, resigned sigh. "Okay, boys. Let's get this over with."

Chip entered behind her, his thin body standing in the doorframe as if to block any attempt to escape. "So, let me see if I understand you correctly. Our game's been live for three months, and you haven't even registered?" The tone of his voice stung.

Blue shrugged and offered a sheepish grin. "I've been busy?"

But Phil would have none of it. "Too busy to check out the first functioning video game from the supposed love of your life?"

He sounded teasing, but Blue thought she heard an accusing undertone.

"He whose countenance comes to your mind first thing every morning and whose image sends you to peaceful slumber every night?"

Blue rolled her eyes, trying to be a good sport and play along while the guilt churned in her stomach. "It's true. He completes me in every way. I'm only half a woman without him. But, boys, I don't play video games. You know that."

Chip stepped forward, gently grasping her forearm. His other arm lowered toward one of the chairs. "That's because you've never played *our* video game. Did I mention that last week's *Indy PC* called *Fantasy Free Form* 'the finest independently produced RPG freeware in years'?"

As if on cue, Phil extended a thick magazine, already folded back to the relevant page, the quoted text standing out behind yellow highlighter.

Blue nodded and reached for the pages. "Only about a dozen times." She'd already seen the copy, emailed to her as a jpeg last month from Chip. The email included a pre-created account and password, inviting her to log on and play the game. But until she could deal with the conflicts of her heart, she couldn't bring herself to do it. If she had truly felt good about her and Chip, she would've logged on weeks ago and played, enjoying the game simply because he'd created it.

And behind all the teasing and excuses, she sensed Chip's genuine hurt at her rejection of his labor of love.

She held up her hands in mock surrender and offered her sweetest smile. "Okay, I'm sorry. It's really been a crazy year. Of course, I want to see your game."

Blue dropped into the proffered seat, staring into the largest monitor she'd ever seen. With a wide screen and somewhere around thirty-five inches, the digital forest-scape obliterated any peripheral distractions. The forest, filled with lush greenery and a hint of dew and fog, dazzled her with its breathtaking beauty. Almost subconsciously, she noted the Bose speakers positioned on either side, above, and beneath the screen.

Overwhelmed by the visual spectacle, she averted her eyes, staring at the standard keyboard and mouse. The dull reality of the desk broke the alluring spell of the fantasy world.

"How do we start?"

Chip reached down and clicked the Escape button. The forest scene vanished, replaced by a list of names. She recognized the first three from their old D&D sessions.

- Daria, Warrior, Level 10
- Magtog, Wizard, Level 12
- Gallamar, Mercenary, Level 14
- Blue Angel, Hunter, Level 8
- Aloray, Mage, Level 6

Chip grabbed the mouse, pointing and clicking on the name Daria. "I tailored this character specially for you. Just one of the perks of knowing the programmer."

The name listing vanished, replaced with CGI imagery of a sword-and-sorcery warrior woman. In a split-screen, she could view a head-and-shoulders profile of the character to her left and a rotating head-to-

toe image to her right. The detailed facial features struck her as eerily familiar, and her breath caught in her throat.

"Hey, that's me. I mean, that's *really* me." The shock of her face staring back at her–the narrow shape of her eyes, the distinct curve of her chin, her thin nose, and flashing blue eyes–stunned her into silence. Even the hair, though long and wavy, parted and spiked in the front the way she wore hers. Certainly, the choice of a blue tint over the flowing locks was no accident. She continued to stare, transfixed.

Chip reached across the desk and snatched up a framed photo, waving it across her eyes. "That's the magic of scanning imagery, dearest one."

The spell of the game broken, Blue reached out and gripped the picture, recognizing it as Chip's favorite snapshot of her, taken two years ago at Perionne Park during their first date. *Two years ago–was it really that long?* The photo captured her cocky demeanor softened by the romantic mood of that particular evening.

Later, she would reflect upon that night, and the ones that followed, as the most blissfully happy time of her life.

Comparing the photo to the computer image on the screen, she could see the specific resemblance. The woman warrior of the video game wore the expression of Blue at her happiest and most confident self–certainly not the person sitting in the chair.

"That's very impressive," she said. And she meant it.

"The digital scanner allows us to take a lot of shortcuts with the artwork." Chip droned on, obviously trying to teach and impress, like a geeky peacock. "We can take the image of a tree and repeat it several times. The deer, the details of the leaves, even the houses–they all come from publicly available images, which we scan into the game."

"She gets it," Phil said, already seated at his own terminal and ready to start. "Don't overwhelm the girl with details. Let's just play."

Blue glanced over, seeing Chip close his mouth in a thin line. She could tell he wanted to say more, to brag more. On impulse, she reached out and gripped his hand. "It looks wonderful."

Chip's smile made her heart warm in response. His hand tightened over her fingers in affection, and, forgetting herself, Blue brought his hand to her lips and delicately kissed his knuckles. She released his hand and looked up at the computerized image of herself. "Phil's right, though. Let's play. What do I do?"

Chip rummaged through a nearby drawer. "Like D&D, the warrior is a fairly basic character in these games. Quite simply, you chop at things until they stop moving. Don't worry about the magic. You do have some, but it's all automatic. As you can see from your profile, you have a necklace that adds five points to your strength and a ring that adds eight points to your defense. Your sword does between 20 and 30 points of damage."

"And that's a lot?"

Chip nodded. "That's a lot, for a level-ten warrior."

"Just checking."

"Once the game starts," Chip said, "use the arrow keys to move forward, backward, or rotate left or right. The spacebar lets you jump. Click the mouse to attack, and right-click to access other options, including preprogrammed greetings and emotions that come up as you play."

The directions came at her so fast, Blue wasn't sure she absorbed them.

"It's very intuitive." Chip must have sensed her apprehension. "That's pretty much it, except this." He held a thin, wiry headset, like a delicate tiara. He reached up toward her head, and she let him slip it into place. He gently pressed an earpiece into her ear, and a microphone hovered a few inches from her mouth.

Chip's voice sounded from her earpiece with startling clarity. "Most people use an online chat window while they play, but we can use the microphones. Much more efficient." He took the seat behind her, looking at his monitor and speaking through his headset.

She turned to her screen.

The profile vanished, replaced with a view of her character as if a camera floated behind her head from above and looked over her shoulder.

She viewed a partial profile of her tall, busty, warrior woman image, clad in shapely chainmail that barely contained her heaving chest. The handle of a large sword, secured in a sheath, protruded above the shoulders, enfolded in the long waves of Daria's blue-tinted hair. Several pouches were clipped to her belt.

Blue smirked at the sight. Daria's abundant curves bore no resemblance to her own figure, with her modest B-cups. *I suppose I should be flattered she wears my face, but the similarity definitely ends there. Boys!*

Glancing at the keyboard, Blue positioned a hand over the arrow keys and gripped the mouse with the other. Looking back at the screen, she could see the room in front of her. The character stood at the doorway of a large stone structure.

She pressed the forward arrow and was rewarded with the image of the warrior taking a few steps. The click-click-click of her footsteps on the cobbled sidewalk emanated from the speakers.

Okay, cool, I can get used to this.

CHAPTER FOUR_

Marda Mercedes knelt before the statue of the Goddess Baalina. In the rooms above her, a wired network of computers had been assembled, and the Sisterhood's engineers were hard at work. The extraordinary measures–the "techno-magic," as Marda liked to call it– would be ready to be wielded shortly.

The door behind her opened and closed, pulling her from her meditation. She suppressed her irritation. She knew Cyn and Van would not interrupt her unless it was important.

Marda never found out if the so-called "Terror Twins" were truly twins or not, but the point proved moot when it came to results. They shared a love of pain and torment, and their skill to inflict both in their victims proved unmatched. Through their bond with Baalina, or perhaps through their own genetics, they shared a mental synchronicity that surprised even Marda.

"We found them," Cyn announced without preamble.

"They thought they could hide from us, but we flushed them out," continued Van.

"And they're close! Only a few blocks from here," said Cyn.

"Which makes sense. The Kelranians would want to be nearby if they plan to move against us," said Van.

Cyn leaned close, anxious to beat her partner to the punchline. "And they brought the gem with them!"

Marda rose and raised a hand. "Stop with the trade-off chatter, for Baalina's sake. Speak plainly, and just one of you!"

Cyn and Van looked at each other. Cyn nodded to Van, who faced Marda, green eyes flashing as she spoke. "We've identified the agents. Rebecca Burton and Skye MacLeod."

At the mention of the Kelranian's most successful agent, a chill ran through her. The stories and rumors circulating about Burton's deeds had not escaped even their isolated coven. *The Order has turned loose their very best to try and stop us.*

Van rubbed a hand over her shapely chin. "Once we had the names, it was easy for Natalie to track them."

Natalie Spencer, their head programmer and technology expert, had been working with little to no sleep for over three months, preparing for the first strike.

Marda reflected on Natalie's condition. She had to admit, she had been tough on Natalie over the previous weeks, blaming her lack of progress on incompetence. In the last few days, Cyn and Van had joined her in mocking the engineer. Sometimes, the teasing turned outright nasty. Marda let Cyn and Van release their cruelty upon her. She'd hoped the motivation would spur results.

But locating the great Rebecca Burton could not have been easy, and the small victory did much to validate Natalie's contributions to the Sisterhood.

A flush of guilt swept over Marda. *I was wrong to do that.*

Van began to pace the small open area before the circle of worship. "Rebecca and MacLeod have taken up residence as classmates and roommates a few blocks from here, the same as we did. Just as we plan to use the game to call forth our mistress, they also have characters in the game, presumably to stop us."

Marda drew a breath. "Have they contacted the programmers?"

Cyn spoke up, cutting off Van's response. "No. Of this, we're certain."

Marda glared at Cyn, who averted her gaze to the floor. "Sorry."

Marda smiled. "Your enthusiasm is forgiven, Sister. The fault is mine, not yours. When I'm tired, the trade-off dialog between you two can prove exhausting." Marda felt nothing of the sort, but she needed everyone on her team working together, and if that meant offering insincere compliments or taking blame for others' shortcomings, what did it matter?

Only results matter.

She smiled and opened her arms, pulling her Sisters into a three-way embrace. "But, enough. Come with me. I have a plan, and we must make everything right between us."

The group of three ascended the stairs, entered into the main part of the house, and walked into the studio living room, where a lone girl with mousy-brown hair sat before a set of computers.

The girl's head turned at the sound of movement. Behind her thick glasses, her brown eyes reflected a combination of fear and resignation. On the empty desk space nearby, a stack of Monster aluminum cans threatened to topple. "I am going as fast as I can, Marda. These things take time." Clearly frustrated, the girl pulled the glasses from her face and covered her eyes. "I'm doing the best I can. Please, just...leave me alone." A sob escaped her, and her shoulders shook.

Marda's heart broke at the display. Natalie's tears were like a dousing of cold water across Marda's face. *How could I forget? Have I truly allowed my team to fragment into the very same pecking order of bully and victim I despise in society?*

Marda reached out, her hands stroking the trembling shoulders bent before the computer screen. Another sob cut through the air. "No more teasing, Natalie. No more. You have served Baalina well and have shamed me in the process."

Natalie wept, her hands covering her face. "I didn't mean to...I'm sorry, please forgive me."

From behind her, Marda pulled Natalie's head back, which reclined beyond the top of the chair and rested against Marda's chest.

"Shhhh...relax, Sister." Her fingers snaked forward, pressing, massaging the sides of Natalie's head.

"Oh, Marda...that feels good."

Marda continued to hush the distressed programmer. "Cyn and Van told me of your discovery. Baalina is most pleased. You may rest now."

"But there's still so much to do."

"You can spare a few hours. You need the rest."

Cyn stood to the side of the chair and reached out and gripped Natalie's hand. Her gloved finger traced a trail along the inside of Natalie's wrist.

Marda felt Natalie shiver against her in response.

"Van and I are...not just experts in thresholds of pain, Sister. Until now, you have always turned us down, but...we'd love to educate you."

Natalie's body stiffened. "No, I...thank you, I'd love some time to just sleep, though."

Cyn scoffed. "I'm not asking you to marry me, Nat. It's going to be a long time before you're around men again. You may even *like* it."

"Enough," said Marda. "Don't begrudge Natalie her attraction to men. We can't help our natural impulses."

Cyn smirked. "When Baalina has conquered the city, men will be kept as slaves, breeding stock, and..." Cyn's bright green eyes took on a faraway look. "...however else they might entertain us."

"Which will still make them a viable option for a woman's pleasure, Cyn." Marda wondered at Baalina's vision of the future. Subjugating men at first struck her as impossible, but she realized most men would be slaughtered in the initial uprising, rendering the rest easier to control. They would even welcome the opportunity to serve. "Don't hate Natalie for what she can't help."

Marda bent and wrapped Natalie's arm behind her own neck, bracing to guide her to her room. "Come on, Sister. Sit up. I'll take you to bed." Natalie rose, and Marda held her tight. Already, the exhausted programmer's eyes drooped, half closed. *Cyn really does have the magic touch.*

Marda's gaze met Cyn's. "And you...if you're so anxious to try out your techniques, give me a few minutes. I'll meet you in the bedroom. We could all use a little...release."

Cyn smirked. "And which threshold would you prefer? Pleasure or pain?"

Marda met Cyn's eyes with a teasing look of her own. "Is there a difference?"

Cyn drew her ceremonial knife from its hip sheath and pointed it at Marda, waving it in a clear invitation. "Not really."

Marda's breath caught in her throat. "Save me a spot. I'll be there soon."

———

Five hours later, with everyone now much rested for a variety of reasons, the four Sisters regrouped in the front room, where a linked set of five computers sat on three folding tables alongside a dining room table serving as their round-robin meeting space.

Marda entered the room from the basement, invigorated after another short session of communing with Goddess Baalina. Natalie appeared more chipper than she had in days, the dark circles under her eyes diminished. She looked up from her usual spot at the center computer monitor and produced a meek smile before she returned her attention to the screen.

Van and Cyn slouched in their favorite seats on the other side of the table. In their black leather and with barely hidden knives strapped to their firm thighs, they looked every bit like a photo spread for *Bad Girl Assassins Monthly*.

If the Terror Twins had any Achilles' heel, it was the attention-getting theatrics that accompanied their every action. Still—the memory of their "session" a few hours earlier sent a sexual shiver through Marda—their reputation was well deserved.

Challenged not to make a sound, she'd lasted almost five minutes.

When she finally screamed her release, she had no idea if it was from pleasure or pain, and she didn't care.

She awoke, refreshed, to see Van and Cyn sleeping in each other's arms. A glance at her watch told her she'd lost four hours. But she gained a burst of clear-headed energy, and she planned to take full advantage of it.

"So," Marda said as a way to begin the meeting, "What do we know?"

Van spoke up from across the table. "We found the Kelranian bitches. We know who they are and where they live."

Cyn picked up the thread of conversation. "We know the MacLeod woman has been tailing the programmers both in and out of the game."

Van removed her stiletto from its hip sheath and motioned toward Natalie. "Nat has tagged their avatars in-game. We know MacLeod spends most of the time online playing the game and exploring the land. Her movement pattern indicates she's tracking and re-tracking over as much territory as she can with each game session."

Marda nodded. "Perhaps she's searching for something."

Cyn grinned. "Probably under Burton's orders."

Marda returned the smile. "And there's nothing for her to find...yet."

Cyn tipped her head toward Natalie. "But that's about to change."

Oh? Marda's gaze met Natalie's. "What does she mean?"

Natalie turned her chair around to face the others. She didn't have many moments of glory, and she looked ready to make the most of this one. "I told them, just before you came in. We're ready."

The three pairs of eyes all reflected amusement, all watching intently for the significance of the words to penetrate. Marda swallowed back her excitement. "You said...a couple more weeks, at least."

"I thought so, but..." Nat shrugged. "What can I say? The sleep helped."

Pleased beyond words, Marda extended her praise. "You mean you're that good, Sister. This is no time for modesty."

Natalie giggled. "As you wish, Sister. I'm that good."

"And you can track them now?"

Natalie consulted a second screen, filled with numbers Marda could not follow. "MacLeod is online now. If they proceed with their usual search routine, Burton will be on shortly."

Marda stood, excitement coursing through her. "And the programmers suspect nothing?"

Cyn spoke. "Not as far as we can tell."

"Brilliant!"

Van nodded. "The timing is perfect. The campus is on Thanksgiving break and will be in a lull. Players, students and otherwise, will have more time for recreation, even from their vacation spots."

Marda stepped up next to Natalie. "And you're saying...we can open the portal now?"

"Yes." Natalie pressed a button on a computer which showed a rotating staff with an emerald-gemmed head. "Here is the SoulStaff, recreated from photographs and descriptions of the real thing. I redrew the runes from the original scrolls. Enchanted it with the spell. Although the staff no longer really exists, we can program the image to imbue it with the power to draw our mistress into the game-world the same way we tried to use it centuries ago to bring her into the physical world."

Marda nodded. "And from there?"

Natalie shrugged. "The curse forbids us to pull Baalina from the chaos realm to the physical realm. But there's nothing to prevent us from pulling her here from the game realm."

"Wonderful...but first, we have to open the portal using the staff." Marda leaned close, watching the SoulStaff rotate on the screen. "Can you add it?"

Nat nodded. "Yes. It's a tiny change to add a single object. The programmers are not likely to notice the addition unless they're watching for it. Now...once we open the portal and create an entire area that wasn't there before...we're probably on borrowed time. They're going to notice a change that large."

"Understood. And have we tested the SoulStaff?"

"No."

"Well..." Marda considered. The plan was falling into place much better than she could possibly have hoped. "Wait until both the agents are playing the game, and then open the portal near one of them. No sense in testing it on ourselves when we have the perfect unwilling guinea pigs to dispose of."

Natalie called up a screen of programming lines. "Once we do that, and people start collapsing in front of their computer screens, it's only a matter of time before the local authorities become involved." Her voice carried a hint of warning.

Marda chose to ignore it. "Not a problem," said Marda. *The police force will be short-handed. They'll be scrambling from behind to catch us, and by the time they try to take action, it will be too late.*

"There's always that chance they'll find the file and possibly the Divenium Crystal."

Marda scoffed. "I'm not concerned. I trust in Agent Burton's ability to hide a confidential file from Bloomington's finest."

Cyn sprang up. "But not from Van and me."

Marda glared across the table at the overeager henchman. *She's hired muscle.* Every instinct told Marda that *she* should handle the search *personally.* "I appreciate your enthusiasm, but I think I'd best see to this."

Cyn glared. "Are you kidding? Breaking and entering, search and seizure, finally, some action. Van and I have been cooped up for months. This is our expertise."

Though she hated to pass along such an important job to an underling, Cyn's words made sense. "Very well. Bring back the file with the Divenium Crystal. If we get hold of that, no one can stop us!" *Before they know what's happening, we'll have absorbed the souls of every player in the game realm. And with those, we can draw Baalina, our mistress, into the physical realm.*

CHAPTER FIVE_

Control came intuitively after a few experimental clicks while Blue checked out her virtual surroundings. First, she took in the large wooden doorway of the Mountain Lion Inn. Then she strolled toward a nearby lake where several computerized characters stood on the pier, tossing and reeling in fishing line in eternal automation.

Past the pier, she turned toward the lake, and, on impulse moved toward the water, padding across the mud. As her feet struck the edge of the water, the speakers rewarded her with an accompanying splashing noise. "Cool."

"Glad you like it."

Chip's voice, so close in her ear, startled her. She realized, belatedly, that every side comment would be broadcast to all three of them.

"Don't wander out too far, though. You'll struggle not to drown, and your heavy chainmail armor will only make things worse."

"Got it." She guided Daria toward the cobbled path. As she did so, two other characters approached: one a bearded old wizard in long, flowing purple robes, and the other, a thin, boyish character whose gray, tight-fitting coveralls resembled a sort of modern storm trooper.

An alarm signaled in her ear, and a message popped up on her screen.

*Magtog and Gallamar have invited you to join their party. Accept?
{Yes}{No}*

Blue grinned, guiding the mouse to the Yes button. "You know me, boys. Daria's always up for a party."

Phil and Chip chuckled in her ear.

———

DARIA APPROACHED HER OLD QUEST-MATES, extending her arms and offering an affectionate hug to each. "Greetings, boys. It's been a long time."

"Too long, Daria," Magtog answered, his youthful voice oddly conflicting with his aged, bent appearance. "We've missed you these many months, and the forces of evil have run rampant on our simple town while you were away."

Daria folded her arms, affecting a brooding stance. "Geez, Phil, lay it on thick, why don'cha?"

Magtog blustered on, ignoring Daria's break from character. "I have received a summons from King Thunderwind. He seeks an audience with me on a most urgent matter. Gallamar, the thief, has already–"

"Mercenary," piped up Chip.

"Gallamar, the *mercenary,* has already agreed to join me, but I fear we'll need all our resources for this. Will you join us?"

Daria drew her sword, then swung it in a fanciful salute before returning the weapon into the sheath on her back. "Wow, that's cool! Friggin' impossible, but cool! Er, I mean, yes, Magtog, I'll join you. Anything for king and country."

"Follow me, then."

The wizard led Gallamar and Daria through town at a rapid pace. Soon, the cobblestone path gave way to a less-traveled dirt road, where wild bear roamed the countryside. Occasionally, other characters ran forward and attacked the beasts. Daria stopped at one point, staring in fascination as a tiny dwarf with an equally tiny bow gave chase to a large, snarling bear.

"That dwarf...he's another player in the game?"

Gallamar answered. "Yes, that's Quinton. I think he logs in from Orlando. Our membership is small enough I can still keep track of everyone. We broke over two hundred subscribers just last week. But we're growing fast."

"Is he going to be able to take that big bear?"

"Probably not. He's not a high enough level, and his weapon is pretty weak."

As if on cue, the bear swung its enormous paw, connecting with the dwarf's chest. The dwarf fell to the ground, stunned. Swirling stars circled the tiny character's head, and the bear wandered off.

WORDS FORMED in a bubble over the dwarf's head. "Come help me, guys."

She could hear Chip typing out a response on his keyboard.

A few seconds later, words formed over Gallamar's head. "Sorry, we're in the middle of something. Good luck."

DARIA SHOOK HER HEAD. "Poor little guy. Can't we at least help him to his feet?"

Gallamar nodded and laughed. "He's taking on too much, too soon. There are plenty of easier tasks to do."

"So that's 'no' on the helping thing?"

Chip chuckled. "We really can't do anything. Let negative reinforcement run its course. He's just going to have to stop being a dumbass."

The irritation in Chip's voice amused Blue. *Oh, I see. Chip does not suffer foolish game players gladly.* "So, I'm guessing he can't hear us."

Gallamar shook his head. "No, he's limited to keyboard chatting.

And even if he had a headset, he could only hear the voices of people in his party. The three of us are on a private channel."

"Hey, Magtog got ahead of us."

Gallamar nodded and stepped forward. "That's okay, I know the way. Plus, look at your mini-map in the upper right-hand corner. You can see where everyone in your party is for several yards in any direction."

"Oh, yeah, okay. This takes some getting used to."

Speaking from the air, Magtog's voice chastised them. "Come on, slowpokes. The king waits for no man."

"Or woman," Daria quipped.

Increasing to a run, the thief and warrior soon joined the wizard. As a group, they traveled up a stone ramp to a large, white-cobbled castle and entered a courtyard bordered by erect guards and populated with a variety of shops and merchants. They approached the raised iron gateway and approached the great hall.

The threesome gathered before the throne of His Regal Majesty, King Thunderwind. Purple robes draped his tiny, plump form.

"Greetings, strangers."

He addressed the party in a deep voice, his long white mustache dancing on his face as he spoke. The voice sounded suspiciously similar to Chip's.

The three figures bent at the waist in an exaggerated bow.

"I beseech you to help. Prince Goodwin, sole heir to the throne, has been abducted by an evil gang of kidnappers, led by Baron Darkdeed. My men have brought word of their secret lair—a secluded cabin deep in the woods, just north of the castle."

To Blue's surprise, Daria spoke on her own initiative. "Why not send your own men?" The woman's voice, deep and husky, read from pre-scripted dialog. *Weak.*

The king replied, "I dare not send King's soldiers to the area; if they're recognized, the villains will harm my son. Return the prince to me safely, and I will give you each forty silver, and if you should bring me the head of Darkdeed, as well, your reward shall be equal to my gratitude."

"Who wrote this crap?" Daria asked.

"Phil and I came up with it together."

"Chip, my dear, know your limitations. Ask for help from a writer."

"Is that an offer?"

Daria turned to Gallamar and winked. "We'll talk later."

———

Trudging a few yards behind the aged wizard, Daria grabbed Gallamar's hand. "Come on." She clasped his hand and pulled. "We're falling behind." They skipped through the forest, hands locked as they bounced in unison along the dirt road while heading in a northern direction on the mini-map.

Daria's off-key singing cut through the peaceful forest ambiance. "Wee-ee're OFF to see the wizard, the wonderful wizard of...um...Magtog!"

Magtog spun on his heel and turned to face them. The old man's hands raised, blue electric lightning sparking between his fingers. "Silence, warrior, or my lightning bolt attack will silence you."

Shocked at the aggressive stance, Daria stopped in mid-stride. "What is your problem, Phil?"

Behind the wizard, Daria saw a large, hulking figure wearing a black cowl pop out from behind a tree. "Oh, crap. Look out!"

Daria's warning came too late. The bandit raised a club and struck the wizard on the head.

The wizard dropped, a circle of stars spinning over his pointed hat.

Gallamar sprang forward, a dagger in each hand. "Right-click on the bandit's image, Daria. Combat is automatic."

Duly instructed, Daria jumped, the two-handed sword drawn and in her hands before she completed the leap. With a single powerful swipe, the bandit fell before her sword, even as Magtog's muttered curses continued in her ear.

Three more bandits darted out from behind the trees.

Gallamar leapt at the nearest one. With a two-handed thrust, he slid his daggers neatly into his target's ribcage and stomach. The bandit crumpled to the ground.

Running between the remaining two assailants, Daria hit the first with the flat of her blade. The attacker collapsed. The second rushed her, only to be struck by a bolt of blue lightning. Daria glanced toward the source of the energy–the wizard. Now clearly recovered, the wizard stood, arms outstretched, firing bolts of blue energy from his hands. With a final indignant cry, the third bandit fell to the ground.

Daria rushed into the forest, hoping to draw out more attackers.

As the group continued moving forward, the trees parted to reveal a small cabin in a clearing.

"Here it is, guys. Let's get him," she cried. She attacked the wooden door with a powerful swipe of her blade. The door burst into a pile of dry kindling.

"Blue, wait," Gallamar called.

"Stop," the wizard cried.

A huge, dominating presence in a black mask stepped from the shadows, swinging its own tremendous sword. A health bar hovered over the figure's head, identifying the character as Baron Darkdeed. A booming, evil laugh filled the room. With one mighty swipe of his sword, Darkdeed knocked Daria back.

Daria toppled, falling to the ground several yards beyond the cabin. The now-familiar spinning stars circled over her head. "Shit! I can't move. I'm pushing buttons, but nothing's happening."

By this time, Gallamar and Magtog stood over her. "You're stunned. The effect will wear off in a few seconds."

Magtog raised a gnarled hand, waving it in her face. "Only our combined forces will work against an adversary of his level."

"Now you tell me."

The stars over Daria's head vanished.

Gallamar extended a hand to help her up. "We tried to stop you."

Daria rose to her feet.

Baron Darkdeed stepped through the door, ready for battle.

The wizard raised his hands, preparing another bolt attack. "I'll strike first, and while he's reeling from that, you two jump in and finish him."

Daria waited, sword poised and ready to strike. "So you zap him from back here, in safety, and we do the close-in work so he can wail on us instead. That's your idea of teamwork?"

The wizard sneered. "You have the armor and the weapon, warrior. Do what you must, or we all perish."

"Yes, sir." Daria saluted with her sword. "Just remember, it's only a game."

With a guttural battle cry, twin streams of blue lightning shot from the wizard's fingers. The streaks closed together mid-stream and struck the baron firmly in the chest.

Through her headphones, the reverberation thumped her ears.

"Now!" The wizard called out.

Gallamar and Daria leapt toward the villain. The bandit swung his sword, but Daria's and Gallamar's steel combined to block it mid-swing. Daria pressed the attack. On the third strike, she penetrated his armor and found the soft flesh beneath.

She was rewarded with a graphic spurt of red.

The bandit uttered a grunt of pain but continued to fight. A second attack of lightning hit the baron in the chest, and this time, Gallamar's and Daria's blades found their mark. The baron staggered, and to Daria's amazement, turned on his heels and took off running.

"Oh, no, you don't." Daria swung her sword as she overtook the retreating bandit. The sword impaled the baron's chest, and Daria watched in glee as the baron fell.

———

BLUE THRUST both hands at the monitor, pointing with her index fingers. "Got'cha, you fat, ugly bastard. Woo-hoo!" She spun the chair around in a victory dance. Then stopped, seeing Chip and Phil hadn't joined in. Instead, they silently observed her.

Chip's expression, at least, showed approval. "So, I take it you like it?"

Blue grinned back. "Yeah, I guess it's all right." She adjusted her headset and turned back to her monitor.

———

As Daria took a step toward the remains of her defeated foe, a window opened over the prone body, labeled "Loot." Within the window was the image of a large sword. Daria pointed the mouse at the sword, revealing the text *+35 to 45 damage.*

"Hey," said Daria. "His sword is better than mine."

Gallamar explained patiently. "Just right-click, and you'll automatically arm yourself with his sword. You can sell your old one for silver pieces when we get back to town."

"Oh." Daria's sword vanished into her tiny belt-pack—an achievement possible only in video games—and she drew a larger blade with a detailed ornamental handle. She deftly dropped her new weapon into the sheath on her back. "Cool!"

Magtog walked past them.

The prince character followed, mimicking each step in brainless computerized fashion.

Magtog looked back at them. "While you were playing with your sword, warrior, I untied the prince. He'll auto-follow me until we get back to the castle. Ready?"

———

The three adventurers stood before His Majesty, who bellowed his thanks in proper ornate language. "...in return for your service to this realm, accept these 40 silver pieces and this bow of accurate strike."

Blue clicked the "accept" button and the items deposited themselves into Daria's hip-pack. "What am I going to do with a bow?" she asked.

Gallamar patted her on the shoulder. "Actually, if you sell it, you'll get another 30 silver. Or you can offer it to the dwarf in the village fighting the bear. He might not give you as much, but he'll probably be very grateful."

Daria grinned. "Poor little guy. That's a good idea. Let's go find him. Maybe we can even help him on his quest."

"No." Magtog's voice cut through their exchange.

———

BLUE TURNED in her seat to glance at Phil.

Phil dropped his headset across the keyboard, looking pale and tired. With a noticeable grunt, he rose from his seat and stepped away from the computer. "Sorry, guys. It's late, and I'm pretty wiped out. But you two can keep playing, if you want."

Blue nodded, getting to her feet and stretching her stiffened legs. "If you're tired, you should get some sleep. Especially since you've been barking at me all night."

Phil looked away, but Blue stood her ground, holding her hands open at her sides. "So, what did I do? Or didn't you think I'd notice?"

Phil took a deep breath. "Look, if you're both here and happy in the morning, then chalk it up to my lack of sleep giving me bad vibes." He shot her another angry look.

Blue's face flushed. *He knows.*

"Look, Blue. Maybe you're here to make up for lost time, and if so, I apologize. But, if *not*..." He paused, meeting Blue's eyes and letting his unspoken meaning sink in. "If not, then stop with the flirting and compliments. I expected better from you."

Blue dropped her gaze to the floor. "You're right."

Phil's snorted breathing sounded like a bull barely controlling the urge to charge. "Anyone can knock on my door if they want to." Without waiting for a reply, he stomped out of the room.

"Wow, he's surprised me twice in one night." Chip sounded cheerful and clueless. "And I thought I knew him so well."

"He's a good friend, Chip." A surge of emotion welled up in her. Her stomach cramped.

"I know, but he has a weird way of showing it sometimes."

"It's not so weird. He doesn't want to see you hurt, that's all." Blue squeezed her eyes against the tears streaming down her face.

"Who's going to hurt me? Hey, you're crying."

A shameful sniffle escaped, and she trembled at the gentle touch of his fingers wiping the moisture on her face.

The moment had come, and she was chickening out. Whatever else she'd rationalized these last few months, she had fun tonight. Simple, playful fun, for the first time since she'd boarded the plane to New York over a year ago.

But the computer game made me feel that way. Didn't it?

She took a deep, shuddering breath, reached out, and gripped his hand. She met his concerned gaze with her own. "He's right. We have to talk, and we have to talk tonight."

CHAPTER SIX_

THE MOMENT she'd dreaded had arrived, and Blue found she couldn't look Chip in the eyes before she proceeded to break his heart. Instead, she stared at the stupid computer screen showing the stupid characters still stupidly standing around the stupid receiving chamber of the stupid castle.

Stupid tears welled in her eyes, blurring the screen and streaking her face, but she couldn't cover her ears to block out the tone of naïve confusion in his voice.

"Blue . . . talk to me. What's wrong?"

She drew another breath, using her sleeve to wipe the moisture from her face. "I'm sorry, Chip. You deserve better. I can't do this anymore. I thought . . . if I gave it enough time, maybe I could get over what happened."

"You . . . said you didn't blame me for that night. You said you understood." Chip rattled off the bullet points and counted on his fingers, reviewing the facts. "You lived with me and my dad for over six months before you moved to New York. We were happy then. We *did* get past all that. You can't tell me you were pretending all that time."

"I wasn't." She glanced at Chip for the first time.

He'd crossed the room and sat in the computer chair closest to hers, swiveling it in her direction. His gaze bored into her with an intensity that made her squirm.

Still barely looking at him, she replied, "During that time, when we were together, I was happy. But I didn't process what had happened. I just pushed it aside."

God, how to explain? She flexed her tight shoulders, feeling them pop and hearing a telltale crinkle. "I really hadn't mourned. I was just numb...not thinking. Your dad made it easy for me. It was easier to go on like...like I was on some long, extended sleepover. I just put out of my mind the fact that I couldn't go home."

Uncomfortable seconds ticked away. Already emotionally drained, Blue waited for Chip to find words to his thoughts.

"So then you flew to New York with your dad, and that's when you found the time to process. Is that it?"

"I was alone!" She didn't mean to snap at him and spoke more calmly. "I missed you terribly, at first, but then I realized. I was in New York because my mother was dead. You weren't with me because my mother was dead. And my mother died because of what we...of what *you*...did that night."

"Blue, that's not—"

"It was because of your hairbrained scheme that we ended up in that park, and it was only because I agreed to join you that we dug up that money. Because...I joined you, rather than stay with Mom, like she asked me, like she *begged* me to..." Blue stopped, overwhelmed with tears and a pain that emerged like a deep, old wound torn open and freshly exposed.

"Fine. You want to hand out blame, there's plenty to go around." Chip cleared his throat, swallowing a lump. "I have to live with what happened, too. I never even met the woman, and I played a part in her death. On top of that, you had just discovered how much you loved her, and she was taken from you."

He rose to his feet. Even given his thin build, his tall frame cast a considerable shadow over her. "But I didn't kill her. Some fucked-up, supernatural creature killed your mother. I no more *pointed* him in the direction of your mother than *you* did. No one could ever have predicted or controlled that."

"That's not good enough!"

Chip flinched at the high, screeching passion of Blue's response.

"You should have known! You'd collected *so many stories* of people who'd seen him before that night. But you didn't *listen* to them."

Chip looked away, and against the glow of the computer monitor, Blue glimpsed the streak of a tear staining his cheek. "I couldn't take those ghost stories any more seriously than a six-year-old telling me about their visit from the tooth fairy."

Blue recalled her earlier experience, on the very same day they embarked on their misadventure in the amusement park, when she discovered her neighbor, Sylvia, was a ghost, but couldn't believe the evidence of her senses. Instead, she'd concocted a highly improbable but tangible explanation for what she'd seen and heard, rather than accept the idea that she'd encountered the supernatural.

"I know, Chip. And we can sit here and reason and rationalize all night, but it won't make any difference." She paused. "I've been sick."

Chip's face paled, and a look of concern swept his features. "What's wrong?"

Realizing what Chip thought, she shook her head. "No, not like that. I mean, I'm *emotionally* sick. I'm drained, I can't write, I can't focus. I'm not *me* anymore. And it's because of what happened." Blue buried her face in her hands. "We were good at one time, but we have to accept it. We're not anymore. We're poison to each other."

"Bullshit."

Blue dropped her hands into her lap, surprised at his outburst.

Chip gazed at her with an earnestness that broke her heart. "We're more than good for each other. We're *amazing* together. I keep you grounded when you go off on your tangents, and you remind me there's a real world beyond the computer screen. We complete each other." Chip paused, and Blue could almost see the new thought pop into his mind just before he gave it voice. "Is there another guy?"

On reflex, she shook her head. "No. Well, yes."

He nodded and rolled his eyes.

She kept talking to cut off the anger she knew would burst from him. "Well, he likes me, but nothing's happened. I wouldn't do that to you. I swear."

Chip bent over her, his arms snaking out and gripping each side of her chair. The intensity of his pleading stare froze her in place. "Blue...if you don't hear anything else I say, hear this. He will never love you the way I do. No one will. And you feel the same toward me, I know it. I would do *anything* for you. If you were ever in trouble, I'd lie, steal, cheat—I'd move heaven and Earth to help you, and you *know* I would."

"I know it." And she did. She remembered all-too-well his first act of love toward her. Not the silly flower bouquet, that came later, but the act of computer sabotage Chip performed to remove the presence of a hateful teacher who'd threatened to fail her for no good reason.

"And maybe you can give up on us, but I can't. And I won't."

The ache inside her chest overcame her, and tears spilled freely down her face. "Chip, no, don't do that to yourself."

Chip turned toward the hallway next to the stairs, where, presumably, his bedroom door stood beyond. He nodded toward the old cloth couch in one corner of the room, with a blanket and pillow stacked on the arm and a sheet stretched across the cushions. "We set this up for you. My bed's pretty small, and I kind of had in mind that you might need your own space, after..." He let the thought trail off unfinished.

Of course, Blue knew what he'd had in mind. The saddest aspect of this cruel joke she'd pulled on him. The months of anticipation, of longing, waiting for a night when they could both reward each other for their faithfulness through the long months apart. Denied.

Blue sobbed openly. She'd lost her voice and could only shake her head. *So stupid! I wanted this. I wanted to break up with him, and now I'm the one who's devastated!*

"You know," Chip said, "I gave Phil hell earlier for selling you short. But turns out he was right. You were pretending so well. I'm guessing you probably had a goodbye present in mind for tonight to make yourself feel better. Some sort of pity fuck to send me on my way."

"That's...not..." All she could do was cry. *How can I finish that sentence? True? Fair? It probably was true, and it's certainly fair.*

Chip took a few tentative steps toward the door, then stopped, as if he recognized the weakness he revealed even while he spoke. "If you change your mind, or want to talk, or...or whatever...you can knock on my door any time." His quiet voice mingled with her silent sobs. "I hope you stay through the weekend. I know I shouldn't try to fight for you, or convince you, but I want to, anyway." Shoulders slumped, he left.

She listened to his footsteps padding across the dim room, watched through the blur of tears as he vanished down the hallway, and was swallowed by the shadows. Moments later, she heard a door open and close, leaving her alone in the harsh glow of computer monitors.

Somehow, Blue dragged herself to her feet. Following the death of her mother, she had never thought she could feel so alone, so lost, ever again. But here she was, and she'd done it to herself.

Chilled, she grabbed a blanket and wrapped it over her shoulders. It was all she could do to keep from tipping over in the couch.

So. This was what she wanted. She remembered, hours earlier, how much she resented the hours on the plane, because it just delayed the conversation. What a release of a burden it would be, she'd thought, once it was finally over.

Instead, she felt buried alive in pain, lost and in complete darkness. Ironically, in a room full of glowing monitor screens, the most well-lit space she'd ever attempted to sleep in, she laid, strung out, emotionally drained, and only half awake.

Beyond thought, Blue stared at the monitors for the next several hours, waiting for sleep to finally overtake her.

———

"Fiona, I love you, but what the hell do you think you're doing?"

"Mom?" Blue struggled for consciousness, dimly aware that her face pressed against a couch cushion and of the accumulated wetness of her own drool under her cheek soaked into the sheet. *Oh, great, another nightmare visitation from Ghost-Mom to help pile on the guilt.*

Resigned, she pulled herself to a sitting position, half-expecting to find herself back in the old house in Perionne, and mildly surprised to see she remained in Chip's basement full of computers where she'd collapsed earlier.

She noted the nearest computer chair turned toward her, where her mother sat and looked in her direction with a decidedly unhappy expression on her face.

Blue also noticed, as her head cleared to full wakefulness, the hint of light coming through the slot of a window high above her, and the Velcro texture of her Indiglo watch still fastened around her wrist, flashing 7:23 AM. So, she'd slept through the night. *Or, at least, I'm* dreaming *I slept through the night.*

But this is wrong. This is different from last time. Although she remembered dreaming of her old living room from all those months ago, she'd also never questioned being there.

Back then, she hadn't pinched herself like she did now (*ouch!*) or tried to will herself awake, to no avail.

"I already told you I forgave Chip. I also told you he's going to need you now. And you need him! The danger is closer than ever."

"Oh, will you *stop?* Like I need this shit!" Blue slapped her hand down on the side of the couch, noting the sting of pain traveling through her arm. "Like I don't feel bad enough. I did what I had to do. I did what's best in the long run...for him and for me."

"No, you didn't, my dear. You did no such thing." The phantom frowned in her mother's usual disapproving manner, triggering a pang of painful memory. "You think you're so grown up, and now it's time to pay for your crimes. You don't blame Chip for my death—you blame yourself."

Her mother's words hit home, forcing a gasp from her.

"That's why you've felt so horrible all these months." The scowl disappeared on her mother's face and softened in sympathy. "So now you're punishing yourself and making the worst mistake possible. Rather than moving on and getting past this, you're making yourself, and him, more miserable. Not to mention what you're doing to me."

Blue shook her head. "You've been dead for over a year, but it's *still* all about you."

"Please don't mock me." The anger and sadness in her mother's voice stopped Blue's retort. "You don't know what I sacrifice each time I communicate with you from where I am. You don't know what spirits lose to return to this world, even for a short time. I can tell you that Gunther is suffering greatly, and will for a long time, for the disruptions he caused."

"I'm sorry, Mom."

"And whether I convince you or not, this is the last time I can see you, at least for a long, long time. So please, listen to me. You need to be strong *together* to deal with what's coming."

"Mom?"

"Fortunately for you, Chip's a forgiving man. But you must stop pushing him away. You're almost out of time."

"But what's going to happen, Mom?"

"There's no time, but you have to face it together if you have any chance of getting through it. Just go to him, make it right between you while you can. If he can't trust you now, when he needs you most, you'll lose each other forever."

There's no time? "Mom, wait, don't go. Please stay with me." Blue rose to her feet, stepping toward the apparition and wrapping her arms around the remarkably solid and warm form who returned her embrace.

"Mom, please stay. Just a little longer. I'm sorry, Mom."

Thin fingers lightly brushed the back of her head. "I love you, baby."

Her mother's body, so firm a moment ago, slipped through her arms and disappered.

Blue toppled across the chair her mother occupied moments earlier, calling out, "I love you, Mom. Come back. Please don't go."

The snap of a wall switch broke through her cries. She squeezed her eyes shut against harsh white light flooding the room. Rising up from where she'd tumbled, Blue blinked spots from her vision.

"Blue? Are you okay?"

Spots dissolved, and her gaze settled on Phil, his round body framed in the hallway. She scanned the room before she could stop herself, confirming what she knew—her mother had vanished. Only Phil looked on, covered in a tent-sized t-shirt and striped boxers, appearing as sheepish and uncomfortable as she felt.

Phil broke the silence. "I'm sorry. You must have had a nightmare. I'll leave you alone." He raised a hand to return the room to darkness.

"Wait!"

Rather than flip the switch off, Phil reached toward his head and scratched at the disheveled scalp with tiny strands of hair sticking out to the sides. He said nothing, just waited for her to continue.

Blue made her way to the couch, trying to rub sleep from her eyes, certain she suffered her own terrible case of bedhead. "Please come in." She indicated the computer chair already turned toward her.

Without a word, Phil padded across the cement floor and onto the throw rug in the work area, apparently used to the chill, a carefully calculated look of indifference on his face. She waited until he seated himself before speaking.

"Phil—I made a lot of mistakes last night, and I'm going to try to make it right by Chip, if he'll let me. But Chip and I made another mistake months ago. We swore we'd never tell anyone what happened... that night. What *really* happened."

Phil squirmed, a squeak of protest from the chair breaking the silence of the room. "You don't owe me any—"

"Yes, I do. Because when I made Chip promise not to tell anyone, I put myself between him and his best friend. And he loves you, but I made him promise me never to talk about it. And I'm sorry for that."

Phil blurted out, "He *does* love you. More than anything. And you don't deserve it."

Rather than argue, Blue simply nodded. "That's probably true, and I'm sorry, because I broke up with him last night. And I can't make you, or him, understand this, but it wasn't 'til I broke up with him that I realized how stupid it was, and what a huge mistake I'd made. I'm going to make it right, starting today."

Phil shook his head, his eyes flashing anger. "Nice. You're some piece of work, you know that? Does he know yet?"

Blue shook her head. "I haven't had a chance to talk with him."

Phil released a heavy sigh, rubbing his hands across his face as various emotions played out over his features. Anger, sadness, disbelief. "You two. What a soap opera. Well, let me kill the suspense for you. He'll take you back, of course."

Blue nodded. "You don't like me very much."

"No, Blue, you're wrong. I like you just fine. When you two first got together, I was your biggest cheerleader. Chip and I have grown up together. We've known each other pretty much our entire lives, and it was clear you made him extremely happy. But then we moved out here, and I watched him, day after day, make up excuses when you ignored him, in denial about the obvious. And I don't like what you've turned him into. Not one bit."

Blue reached out and tentatively placed her hand over his beefy one. "I know I have to prove myself to you."

With a minimal flick, Phil pulled his hand out from under hers. "You don't owe me anything. It's him you need to talk to."

"That's not true. I know you're upset with Chip."

Phil broke eye contact, looking down. "That's between him and me."

"No, it's not. I put him in an impossible situation with his best friend."

"Doesn't matter now, anyway." As Phil said the words, his voice broke. He squeezed his eyes shut, shook his head, and took a deep breath. Moments later, he looked up, his mask of indifference back in place, repeating his words in a calm tone. "Doesn't matter now. You're entitled to your secrets."

"And we're entitled to break them if it's in everyone's best interests. Let me tell you everything, from beginning to end, without interruption, because you're going to have a lot of questions by the time I'm finished."

Phil nodded. "Of course, I want to know the truth. Go ahead."

Blue took a deep, trembling breath. "Chip had been investigating the bank robbery of 1990 for months."

"I know. Then one day, he dropped it."

Blue said, "That's because what you don't know is that Chip deduced exactly where the money was stashed all those years ago. The thieves had buried it on the island of one of the Pirates of Perionne boat ride sets at the amusement park."

Phil's eyes grew round at the revelation, but he said nothing.

Blue took a deep breath. "That afternoon—the afternoon of that crazy night..." She paused.

Phil nodded for her to continue.

"Chip told me he wanted to find the money. His only interest was..." Blue hesitated. Should she reveal the role Chip's father played? She decided that was one secret they should continue to keep. "His only interest was recovering the loot and turning it in to the authorities. But he needed my help to dig it up, jimmy the locks, and... well, let's face it, bolster his courage."

Phil chuckled. "That sounds about right."

"I ran home to find my lock-picking pins and my switchblade. That's when Mom caught me trying to sneak out..."

At first, Phil listened in silence, his eyes growing wide as Blue recounted the entire bizarre tale of how Blue and Chip had unwittingly released the ghost of a psychotic bank robber.

As she continued to talk, Phil's expression changed from mild interest, to shocked anger, to the stone-blank stare of a man in shock, a man who has discovered that everything he thought he knew about his best friend, his town, his entire world, was a huge lie.

Blue finished the story, telling Phil how they managed to put the ghost to rest. But not before the insane phantom had slain her mother, gravely wounded Chip, and brutalized a confident, know-it-all teenager, transforming her into the meek, shallow young adult who now sat and cowered before Phil, weeping quietly.

"I lost more than my mother that night, Phil," Blue confessed. "I lost myself. And no matter how hard I try, I can't find her."

CHAPTER SEVEN_

He tossed and turned for several hours, but eventually, Chip fell asleep.

Earlier, he'd fought with his instincts to go back into the room and beg Blue to take him back, to reconsider her decision, and to tell her that he'd do anything for her...if only she'd give him a chance.

But she already knows that.

This *sure* as hell wasn't what he'd planned for the weekend.

But he knew from the shuffling sounds and the sobbing noises coming through the air vent that Blue hadn't left the house. Apparently, she planned to stay until the morning, at least. *So I still have a chance. She could be here for up to three more days. If I'm smart, she'll realize on her own that she's wrong, and we can still salvage this.*

I'll make her realize how much I love her. Failure is not an option. I can't lose her.

Sometime into the long night he'd fallen asleep, and when the knocking sound penetrated his consciousness, his mind was still reviewing his options on how to proceed. "Wha–?"

Blue's voice reached him from the other side of the door. "Please open up, Chip." The misery in her voice brought him to full wakefulness. Even as a small part of him was disappointed in himself, he couldn't fight his instincts. He still loved her, and now she needed him. He had to go to her.

He pulled on the sweats, which still lay in a puddle at the side of the bed where he'd let them drop last night. He'd slept in a plain white t-shirt. *Hardly James Bond, but it'll have to do.*

Bracing himself, he crossed the room, then gripped the doorknob. He closed his eyes. *Okay, here we go. God, please let's not start off with a fight.*

He opened the door.

Blue propelled herself into his arms.

He took one step forward, more of a stumble, really, into the main computer room.

Her arms wrapped around his waist. And there she was, her head on his chest, her tears already dampening his shirt.

His head spun, trying to catch up with the words she mumbled against him.

"I'm so sorry, Chip, I'm so sorry, please, let's forget last night, please, I don't want this, please..." She continued on, the whole time pulling him close and crying openly.

Before he could stop himself, he embraced her. His fingers stroked the back of her head while she babbled. "I'm so sorry...."

He leaned down into her disheveled hair, smelled old perfume and sweat. The heat of her body radiated against his. He shushed her. "It's okay." All he'd wanted, after all this time, was to hold her like this, and now he had to shift his stance and hope she didn't notice his body's response to her proximity. "It's okay, Blue." He kissed the top of her head.

"No, it's not. It's not okay."

Her arms tightened to the point of discomfort. Chip didn't dare mention it.

She breathed against his chest. "Damn it, I had to break up with you in order to realize that the last thing I wanted to do in this entire world was to break up with you." Her body shook with a sob. "Who *does* that? What the fuck is *wrong* with me, Chip?"

"There's nothing wrong with you. Just...let me catch up." Chip had a chance to find his bearings. He scanned the room.

Phil had the decency to look devastated. He sat in the office chair at the computer farthest from them, staring down at the floor. He couldn't imagine what Phil would say out loud if he could. Phil was not an "I told you so" sort of person, but he also had little patience for drama of this sort.

He could dismiss Phil for the moment. He patted Blue between the shoulders, trying to ignore the growing wet stain across his chest as she continued to weep openly. "Take a moment and start over. I'm trying to catch up, too. What happened?"

She mumbled one final "I'm sorry." Her body continued to tremble against him. "I don't even know...what to say. For months, I thought...if I could just do this...everything would be better. But then I did...and I knew...Oh, Chip, it was so wrong, I'm so–"

"Shhh, don't. Don't go there again. It's okay." Chip released a breath into her matted hair and kissed her again. And it was okay, he *could* kiss her, something he couldn't count on five minutes earlier. "We both made mistakes, so let's let it go now."

He ran a hand down her back one last time and pressed his palm between her shoulders. She leaned back, but when he tried to look into her face, she stared down at the floor. Fresh tears followed after the wet smudges on her cheeks.

His heart broke. He wiped a hand across each of her cheeks, but it was hopeless. Her tears continued to blemish her features. At the same time, he thought he'd never seen anything so beautiful.

She avoided his gaze. "I've been...such a mess...for such a long time."

Chip considered and said the first thing that came to mind. "How long have you been planning to break up with me?"

"Uh..." Her face flushed red. "I guess...a long time."

"Since you moved away to New York?"

Her eyebrows furrowed. "I don't know...maybe soon after."

Two years ago, and this has lain heavy on her mind all this time.

"You have to trust in us, Blue. I already know I'm better with you than without you. I knew that, years ago. You just...have to believe that, too."

Her hands reached up to her face, covering his hands. He could still feel her tremble beneath his palms. "I...don't do well with giving up the self control."

Chip smiled down at her. "Really? I hadn't noticed."

In spite of her tears, a laugh escaped her. "God...it sucks when you're right."

"Okay, let's just forget this and enjoy the weekend. It's Thanksgiving, and I want to be thankful that–"

"No."

"'No' what?"

"No." Blue shook her head against his palms. "You shouldn't just forgive me. I was *such* a bitch last night. I was horrible to you."

"I don't care about last night. You weren't a bitch. You were honest. I could see you were hurting. I'm just relieved to have you back."

"But I–"

"We're better. What more is there to discuss?"

Phil spoke from the corner. "I don't know, I'd make her grovel a bit more before I'd be so forgiving."

Blue said, "Shut up, Phil."

"Yeah, Phil, let it go, man."

"I'm kidding, people. Besides, I already knew you were a softie. But there is something important you have to know."

Chip braced himself. *Oh, God, what now? Please don't tell me she slept with that other guy. Anything but that.*

Phil continued, "A couple of things kinda happened while you were asleep last night."

Now he was confused, but he waited.

Her face somewhat drier now, Blue said, "Phil knows. He knows...everything."

Chip looked from Phil to Blue, then back again. *Everything? Does she really mean everything, or has he bought into some other lie concocted to mean 'everything'?*

Blue's eyes nearly bugged out from the intensity of her stare. Her fingers dug into his palms. "He *really* knows."

Phil's next words almost knocked Chip over. "Gunther's ghost. Blue's mom. I know."

"I..." He wanted to say "need to sit down," but the words caught in his throat. Instead, he stumbled over to the closest chair and fell into it. It was a good thing a chair was so close, or he would have dropped to the floor. "Okay, so...I guess I missed a couple of things last night."

The silence lingered.

Chip looked at his old friend and said, "I don't know what to say."

Phil shook his head. "I get it. I don't...understand it, by any means. But just to be clear...you really *do* think Gunther was a ghost when he came after you?"

Chip nodded. "There is absolutely no doubt in my mind that Gunther came after us, and that he was a ghost when everything went down. I know how it sounds, but that's how it is."

Chip could almost hear the gears turning in Phil's head. He knew Phil would reject the supernatural explanation of what happened. If Chip had not experienced it himself, he would have dismissed it, as well. Like Chip, Phil viewed the world through logic and science. It's one of the reasons they became best friends. Phil would not accept a secondhand report of a supernatural phenomenon. If anything, Phil's concern would be how Chip had allowed himself to be tricked into believing such nonsense.

But all Phil said was, "Okay. That's good enough for me. I believe...that you believe it. So, I get it."

They sat, Phil in his corner, Blue crouched on her haunches next to Chip, gripping his hand, her other hand stroking the back of his hand in a way he found difficult to ignore.

After almost a full minute, Blue asked, "So...I guess we're all good now?"

Phil laughed, and the tension in the room deflated. "Yeah, I think we are. And I don't know about you guys, but I need some breakfast."

"Oh." Chip rubbed a hand across his face, the fatigue settling in now that everything was "normal." "I can grab a quick shower, and we'll all go–"

Phil raised his hand. "No, I've got a better idea." He smiled at them. "I'll run a couple of errands, then grab some donuts and coffee down the street, and bring it all home. I'll be gone at least..." He glanced at his phone and shrugged. "Forty-five minutes?"

Without a trace of subtlety, Blue placed her hand on Chip's thigh, her fingers pressing. "You're a good man, Phil."

Chip almost yelped in surprise but somehow kept his composure.

Phil shook his head. "Please. Given where I thought this weekend was going, I'm all too happy to spring for the donuts." He looked down at himself, still in his night shirt and boxers, and flashed them a grin. "I just need to change real quick. So, keep the clothes on a couple more minutes, please." With that request, he disappeared into his room and shut the door.

Before Chip could stand, Blue dropped into his lap, her legs straddling the chair, her lips covering his hungrily, and her body grinding down against his.

His hands dropped around her waist, and he pulled her tight against him, no longer worrying about any telltale bulges.

Blue came up for air moments later, breathing urgently, eyes scanning his face. She whispered seductively, "You...are...in *such* trouble, my man!"

Chip grinned and whispered back, "Bring it on."

Her mouth covered his again. She probed and teased with her tongue. She separated from him again, her breath whispering hot in his ear. She hadn't heard Phil re-emerge from his room. "Is he gone yet?"

"Not yet."

She kissed him again. She came up for air and asked, "Is he gone yet?"

"No, but–"

"Is he gone yet?" She giggled against his mouth. "What the hell is taking him so long?"

Chip reached up and traced her cheek with his finger.

Blue closed her eyes, and a fresh tear trailed down her face.

"Blue, are you—"

"Shhh." She gripped his finger and kissed it. "I just can't believe...that I forgot. That I almost—"

"No." He reached out, placing his hand, feather-light, against her lips, as if to cut off her words. "We're done with that."

She spoke against his fingers. "Okay."

From behind her, Chip heard Phil's bedroom door re-open, but he didn't take his eyes off her. Almost eighteen months of devotion and patience, about to be rewarded. The intensity of her stare bored into his soul.

"I won't...ever...forget again."

Phil called out, a chuckle in his tone. "Okay, you two, I'm leaving! Have fun." As Phil ascended from the basement, the stairs creaked in familiar protest.

Chip found his voice. "God, I love you."

"I love you, too...so much!"

The doorbell rang.

Chip looked over at Phil, who stood, still midway up the stairs.

Blue turned her head back and forth between the two of them.

Chip asked, "What time is it?"

Phil looked at his phone. "A little after eight."

"Okay, I'll say it," said Blue. "Who the *fuck* is that dropping by this early on a holiday?"

The doorbell rang again, twice, communicating its urgency.

Blue's eyes reflected a silent plea. "Could it possibly be the morning paper?"

Chip shook his head.

"Oh, God." Her eyes betrayed her disappointment and... something else, but he couldn't tell. Some sort of insight. "Oh, God."

Phil headed up the stairs while Blue struggled out of Chip's lap. "What?"

Blue's voice took on a tone of panic. "Oh, God. Oh, God. She said, 'The danger is closer than ever.'"

"What? Who?"

As Chip got to his feet, Blue grabbed his hand, the look in her eyes making him nervous. "She said, 'You're almost out of time.'"

"Who said?"

"My mother. Last night."

It took a moment for the implication of what Blue said to sink in. "Your mother? But that's not..." Chip stopped himself.

"Go on. Say it. I dare you."

Chip shook his head and headed toward the stairs.

Blue walked at his side, fidgeting and clearly upset.

"Okay, fine," he conceded. "It *is* possible. But let's just see who's there before we jump to conclusions."

Phil waited for them in the living room, his hands on the knob of the front door. As soon as they joined him, he opened the door on a young patrolwoman officer in dark blue, with short-cropped, dark hair and clear skin the color of caramel. Reflective sunglasses hid her eyes. "Eugene Farren?"

Phil turned, looking at Chip.

A chill ran up Chip's spine and into his neck. "I'm Eugene."

"Mr. Farren, I'm Officer Selena Gonzalez. I'm afraid I need you to come down to the station to ask you questions regarding a matter of great urgency."

CHAPTER EIGHT_

"Okay, Eugene, once again, you're telling me that you're absolutely certain your video game has a fairly standard set-up, and there's no way it could cause any sort of harm to anyone? Not even accidentally?"

Chip rubbed his hands over his eyes to bring Officer Kip Kirby back into focus. He shrugged and tried to avoid looking around the small interview room. "The video game industry makes available a set of strict parameters of color schemes and flash rates that may accidentally trigger seizures. We're self-regulated, but the specs are easy to find, and Ph...I was very careful not to fall anywhere into that spectrum."

That was close. He'd almost said "Phil and I." For simplicity's sake, When Chip and Phil had registered business ownership, they'd filed under his name, Eugene Farren, with Phil as an employee.

As far as the police were concerned, Chip was solely responsible for whatever they were investigating. While that didn't bode well for him, at least he was the only one in the hot seat for the moment. As long as Chip didn't let on about their 50/50 partnership–or until the "A Squad" returned from vacation–they would leave Phil out of this.

Chip shook off the feeling that the walls were closing in on him. *For God's sakes, are we really three hours into questioning?*

Chip understood what happened, but that didn't mean he had to like it. Officer Kirby drew the short straw; he ended up stuck on duty over a holiday in a college town. Maybe he volunteered to get away from some ugly home life, and all he wanted was to coast through an uneventful four days where he could lay low, catch up on paperwork, and give his normal beat a rest until the students returned on Monday. But a hot potato had fallen into his lap, and he had no backup.

The officer shook his head. "We're not talking about seizures. I have two comatose victims on my hands."

Chip fumed. He didn't know what else he could say, and the police officer had offered nothing new for the last two-and-a-half hours of this conversation. They kept going 'round in circles.

So, Chip repeated, again, "Sir, except for carpal tunnel, eyestrain, and possibly Attention Deficit Disorder, there's little else a computer monitor can 'cause' a person in terms of medical conditions."

Chip remembered his programming class from middle school, experimenting with classic BASIC language and how lines of code could make a computer repeat itself, in theory, forever, or until the programmer interrupted the loop by giving the break command. Chip amused himself by thinking of this interrogation as a BASIC program. The code might have looked like:

Line 10: Police officer asks pointless question

line 20: Chip offers pointless answer

line 30: go to line 10.

Having executed line 20, again, Chip waited, wondering if the police officer would finally break the loop and try something else, or just go back to line 10.

Officer Kirby picked up the manila folder that had lain on the table between them through the entire conversation. He opened it, looked at something only he could see, and glared up at Chip, as if considering. *Ah, new information, maybe a line 25 that provides something new and stops the merry-go-round.*

Apparently, the police officer agreed. He grabbed up two photos from the file and slapped them down in front of Chip.

Chip picked up the one closest to him. The photo showed an

attractive woman, perhaps in her mid-thirties, with striking, bright red hair and a pale complexion. Her face projected sincerity and stoic professionalism. Chip noted the label under the photo: Burton, Rebecca, Agent, Special Investigations Unit, Base of Operations: Indiana.

The second photo showed a much younger, spunkier woman. As he continued to study the picture, Chip was fairly sure they shared a math class together. But he never spoke to her, never knew her name, until now, when he read the label on the photo: MacLeod, Skye Isobel, Contractor, Special Investigations Unit, Base of Operations: Indiana. Cute, in a geeky kind of way, with long, dishwater blonde hair, someone who gave off a nerdy vibe, perhaps a role-player, though Chip couldn't pinpoint why he thought so.

Then he remembered. Cloud McSky, a recurring name in the daily video game reports. The obvious pseudonym didn't give her away, necessarily, nor did it flag her for suspicious activity. If Chip and Phil traced down every Peter Parker, Tim Burton, and Seymour Butz that logged in on their game system, they'd have no players.

It was that her name showed up every day. Every day, without exception. Phil and Chip had flagged Mr. McSky as their first official fan. Only "he" wasn't a he. Well, that's what he got for assuming.

The officer pressed. "Something?"

Chip realized he'd been staring at the photo too long. He figured he might as well fess up. He handed the photo back to the officer. "Her. She's been playing the game, every day, for months."

"You can tell that from the photo?"

"Well, no, from the name, actually. She uses a variation of her real name when she logs in."

Officer Kirby folded his arms across the desk and leaned forward in a way Chip was certain was supposed to be intimidating. "And now she's in a coma."

"If you say so."

"If *I* say so!" Kirby slapped his palm down on the table, causing Chip to flinch. "Look, kid, you think I wanted this trouble? I have two investigators down as of last night. I'm breaking all sorts of rules showing you this, because you need to realize just how much trouble you're in. These investigators were undercover here on campus, and both their bodies were found, last night, slumped in front of their computers, and guess what was on their computer monitors in both cases?"

Chip cringed, connecting the dots. "Statistically speaking, the answer would be Facebook, but I have a feeling that's not what you're going to say."

Kirby jabbed a finger in Chip's face. "*Your* game, smartass!"

Chip closed his eyes, absorbing the information. He didn't like what he heard, but at least he knew what he was up against, and he also knew that Phil and he were innocent.

So, he'd broken the loop. That was something. At least the conversation could go forward instead of starting over for the zillionth time.

"They're both on life support and in a coma," Kirby continued, "We don't know if they're going to survive, and you're sitting here, wanting me to believe that your game had nothing to do with it."

Chip shook his head. "No, I'm not saying that. I am saying, if our game was involved, I had nothing to do with it." *Which means someone else used our game to get to them. But how?*

Out loud, Chip said, "So are you charging me with something?"

"No, kid, we're simply questioning you."

"Then if you're not charging me with something, I'm free to go, right?"

"No, that's *not* right."

"Well, which is it?" Chip raised his hands, exasperated. "It sounds like you want to charge me with something, and if that's the case, I should probably get my lawyer before I say another word."

"Look, kid, thanks to you, I have two big headaches." He held a finger out between them. "The first is that if I could get a judge to hear your case—you're right. I have nothing to charge you with. I can accuse you of suspicion of assault, which I can make stick, but what I can't make stick is assault with a magic computer monitor." He extended a second digit. "The second is–given the holiday, no one is going to even *see* my request until Monday."

He dropped his hand to his side. "Now…I trust you don't want to be in a holding cell for three days. Truthfully, I don't want to have to put you there. So it would be a lot easier if we can just leave the lawyers out of this and work with each other. But I need something."

Chip rolled his eyes. "You can't hold me in a cell for three days without charging me with something." Chip tried to glare with confidence. He really wasn't sure about what he'd just said. But he *was* sure he'd heard that on several TV shows, and he was hoping popular consensus ruled in his favor.

Not his most compelling moment, but he'd put it out there, and he had to go with it.

He leaned forward as the words flew out of his mouth, not sure where the bravado came from, except that perhaps he'd picked up a couple of pointers from his flamboyant girlfriend. "Do not mistake me for a stupid kid who can be easily intimidated. You need to either charge me with something or let me go."

The lieutenant smirked, and Chip knew he'd gambled…and crapped out. "Really? You really think that? You're not as smart as I thought. Three days? Try 90 days!"

Chip felt himself go pale.

"That's right. I can hold you three months if I wanted. Sure, the letter of the law says otherwise, but don't think I couldn't make it stick if you get on my bad side."

Chip shook his head. "You know what? Great, lock me up. But that doesn't shut down my game, does it? And there is one thing I will concede: someone out there might be using *my* game to get to *your* people. You need a court order to make me shut it down–which is not going to be easy because you can't prove anything beyond a passing coincidence. So, without a court order, you need my cooperation. How am I doing so far?"

Kirby snorted and rubbed his face in his hands.

Chip tried to keep his own expression neutral. If this was Bloomington's finest, he needed to work on his poker face.

Kirby nodded. "So, just for askin' sake, If I were to ask you, really nice, to shut down your computer game, as a sign of cooperation, would you do it?"

Chip shrugged. "Frankly, I'd want a little time to do my own investigation, sir. I might consider forty-eight hours. Long enough to perform my own diagnosis of what's going on. I'd report what I found directly to you."

"Oh, would you? Well, isn't that nice of you?" Kirby rose to his feet. "Look, kid, we can bring in men to do that diagnosis."

Chip scoffed. The noise was out there before he could stop it. "Better than Phil and I can? You really think so? We wrote that program, and I don't want to brag, but I suspect we're a couple steps ahead of any 'experts' you might assign to go through our code. Particularly over a holiday weekend."

Kirby exploded. "All right, that's it, you can stew in a cage through New Year for all I care. You're going to—"

A knock on the door interrupted the policeman in mid-rant.

Chip turned at the sound of the door opening, and the young woman who'd picked them up this morning stuck her head in. "You need to take this call, Boss."

"I'm in the middle of questioning here!"

"That's just it, Kip. It's the kid's attorney. He's insisting on talking to you immediately."

"The kid's...!" Kirby shot Chip a devastating glare.

Chip did his best to keep his face blank, though he wondered the same thing the police officer did. Who the hell was on the other side of the phone, claiming to be his attorney? And how did anyone notify that person?

But after a few seconds, Chip realized who waited impatiently for him in the front area, and he knew the answer. *Thank you, Blue!*

———

Kɪʀʙʏ sʟᴀᴍᴍᴇᴅ the door of his office and dropped down into the chair.

Every year for over a decade, he volunteered for the four-day Thanksgiving shift. Every year it was a long, boring break from the usual college kid stupidity. He had no family to entertain, so why the hell should he covet the time from his brother officers who did? Pizza was close enough to turkey, as far as he was concerned.

Besides, when he volunteered to work over Thanksgiving, he earned the clout to plan a trip to the vacation spot of his choice every St. Patrick's Day weekend—generally a nightmare for the precinct, a nightmare that he'd missed out on for twelve years.

Last year, he laughed it up in Cancun, Mexico, with Barbara, and this year he'd already booked his tickets to Myrtle Beach with Stephanie. All he wanted to do was get through this shit shift without incident. But so far, the police gods had conspired against him.

Two state investigators—comatose. Jesus! And my only lead is giving me attitude!

He sighed and snapped up the phone. "Who the hell is this?"

"Officer Kirby, my name is Ben Gerrold, attorney at law." Well, the voice *sounded* older and professional. But Kirby wasn't willing to rule out a college prank just yet.

The voice continued. "I'm informing you, as of this moment, I'm acting on behalf of Eugene Farren. I'm calling to find out what matter could be of such urgency that you need to keep a young man in your interrogation room for over three hours, so far, on Thanksgiving Day, and to see if we can't perhaps speed matters along just a bit."

Kirby decided to call this blustering man's bluff. "Bullshit. You can't be an attorney. Who holds office hours on Thanksgiving?"

"Officer Kirby, I should warn you this phone call is being recorded, so I suggest you take a deep breath and change your tone. As a matter of fact, I'm in my home office. We're entertaining relatives here at the house, so you can imagine that when I get a phone call from my ward, Fiona Shaefer, in tears, telling me how the police are ruining her visit with her boyfriend–a nice young man and a law-abiding citizen, I may add–I *make* the time to look into it."

"Fiona who?" The name sounded familiar, but–

"She's currently in your waiting room. I haven't seen her in a while, but generally, her striking hair color makes a memorable impression on strangers."

The punk girl!

The punk girl *has legal contacts?* Kirby felt himself turn red-faced. Thank God no one was with him to witness it. "Listen, Harold or Gerrold, or whatever your name is–I have two state investigators in the hospital as of this morning, and the only connection between the incidents is that both of them were logged in to your client's computer game when they were incapacitated."

"No, Officer, *you* listen. I know two things. First, that kid had nothing to do with your problems. You've hit a dead end, so you're taking it out on someone who you think has to take it. Now, I am willing to put up my personal bond money, if necessary, to guarantee his cooperation, but you've spent three hours with the young man, so I'm sure you know as well as I do, he's not a flight risk."

Kirby blew air into the receiver. That much was true. Whoever had sabotaged the kid's game and used it to do...whatever, Kirby's instincts told him that Eugene was as much a victim in this as the two agents.

The voice droned on. "Secondly, we also know that, even if you *can* come up with a court order and invent some charges that will stick– which you can't–no judge is looking at those warrants until Monday. I, on the other hand, can file charges of harassment, illegal confinement, illegal search and seizure, and whatever else I care to throw out there to embarrass your department and make sure *my* paperwork is waiting right alongside *your* paperwork come Monday morning."

"Why would you do that? What's it to you?"

"Lieutenant, Fiona Shaefer is the daughter of a colleague of mine, someone I respected very much. That colleague was murdered in cold blood a couple of years ago. Since then, I have made it my personal responsibility to take care of her as best as I can. So, when she calls me up and says her friends are being harassed for no good reason, it's...something to me. *Especially* on Thanksgiving Day."

Kirby sat in the chair, trying to control his anger. He didn't like being threatened, but the manmade sense. It's not like he'd made good use of the last three hours grilling the kid.

In the lingering silence, Gerrold spoke again. "Lieutenant, the young man you're holding had nothing to do with this crime. You have my word, he'll cooperate if you're reasonable. Right now, my word is off the record. We can go *on* the record if you'd like, but that complicates things for everyone. Now I suggest you work something out with him talk to him. Keep it off his record. And do it within the hour, or I'll start on that paperwork."

"All right, Mr. Gerrold, you've made your point. We'll try it your way. But you'd better be right about this kid. If it turns out he's hiding something, I won't hesitate to bring out my own set of charges."

"Now you're making sense, Lieutenant. I'm going back to entertain my in-laws and leave everything in your capable hands. If my holiday is interrupted a second time, I'm going to come after your station, and you, specifically." Kirby drew a breath to utter a retort when the line went dead.

CHAPTER NINE

Blue wiggled, trying to find a comfortable position on the metal bench, a simple goal, but an impossible one after three hours.

At first, she thought getting stuck in the police station foyer could have its entertainment value. They'd get a first-hand look as the patrol officers brought in the prostitutes, drunks, loiterers, and whatever other rabble needed to be cleared off the street. But between the hours of 9 a.m. and noon, on Thanksgiving morning, all they'd been "treated to" was the back of the head of the Hispanic policewoman seated at the reception desk.

Phil shifted on his side of the bench, pulling his cell phone from his holster and glancing at the screen. "What in the hell can they be asking him about for three-an- a-half hours?"

Blue shrugged.

"Did your attorney friend get back to you?" Phil grumped.

Blue sighed and rubbed sleep from her eyes. The shitty coffee the station served up no longer kept her awake. Well, that wasn't true. The frequent bathroom trips assured she couldn't doze, no matter how tired she felt. "I told you, he said he got my message and would take care of it."

"He didn't give you any idea how long before he–"

Chip walked into the foyer from around the corner.

Blue squealed. She couldn't help herself.

All complaints of fatigue fled her mind. *He's not handcuffed. He's coming toward me. That's good news, right? Please, let it be good news.* She ran forward, arms wide open, into Chip's embrace.

"Hey there." Chip patted her back as she held him.

She spoke against his chest. "You can come home, right? Tell me you can come home now, and we can get you out of here."

"I can come home now." Chip sounded deflated—beyond fatigue.

"He can go home now," the policeman standing across the room confirmed. "Cute trick with the attorney, Ms. Shaefer. That's the only reason your boyfriend isn't spending Thanksgiving in jail."

Blue glared at the man but said nothing. A couple of years ago, she'd have mouthed off and probably gotten herself thrown into the lockup, but she didn't want to risk that today.

She looked up into Chip's face, concerned at his tired, zombie-like expression. "So, what's up?"

Chip shook his head. "Nothing. Let's just go. I'll tell you about it later."

She took her place at his side, and they headed toward the door.

"Don't forget our deal, Farren!" The rude policeman called after him.

"I won't."

Holding Chip around the waist, she noticed his body trembled under her fingers. "Are you okay? Have you eaten?"

"No, but...let's just go."

"Selena, take them wherever they want to go, but get them out of here." The jerk police officer shouted to the woman behind the desk.

"Sure, Boss."

Blue reached up and stroked Chip's cheek. "Chip, are you okay? What happened?"

Chip glared at her and shook his head. "Not now. Guys, I'm starving, let's have her drop us off at Smittie's."

———

LAVERNE APPROACHED THEIR TABLE, pen and pad in hand. "Okay, what'll it be, boys? And girl!"

Blue sat between Chip and Phil. She'd just asked Chip to fill them in on what happened when Laverne broke in on them. Timing. She glared at the waitress and noted that Phil and Chip joined her in her annoyance.

Chip spoke up. "We don't know for sure yet. Give us a few minutes."

Phil raised a meaty palm. "I need a refill."

Laverne winked at him. "Just one so far? Okay, then. Chip, are you okay? You look plumb tuckered out. Blue, did you keep this guy up all night?"

Blue smiled. Laverne had no "off" button and couldn't take a hint, but she could play this verbal fencing game half-awake. "No, Laverne, I didn't keep him up all night. If I had, he'd still be deep asleep, but thanks for your concern."

"Chip," Laverne chastised, wagging a finger at him. "Don't be ignoring your girlfriend while she's in town."

"I wasn't–"

"Goodbye, Laverne." Blue shooed her away. She wasn't in the mood to get into her personal details with this way-too-nosy waitress. "I'm taking good care of him."

Rolling her eyes, Laverne picked up Phil's glass and wandered away.

Blue sighed. "Y'know, her shtick was kind of cute yesterday, but I hope she's not going to be a pain in the ass while we try to talk."

Chip shook his head. "Sure, it's an act, but she's a good friend, too."

Blue swatted Chip's arm. "Oh, come on, that whole routine is just to get more money out of you."

"Well, yes, of course, but don't sell her short. Phil and I have been coming here for months. She really *does* listen and wants the best for us. Sure, it's because we come here all the time, but that's not a terrible thing. Besides, why do you think she flirts with me so much in front of you?"

"*Clearly*, to piss me off."

"No. Exactly the opposite. She did it to draw your attention to the fact that, in her opinion, I'm a good catch and that you may want to keep me. For all I know, she was my biggest advocate last night."

Heat rushed into Blue's cheeks. "Right, Chip, because you can read people so well." Blue looked down at the menu, waiting out the uncomfortable pause.

Finally, Chip answered, "I've been doing a pretty good job with you the last couple of years."

Ouch! "Fine." Blue grabbed her straw wrapper, wadded it into a ball, flicked it off her thumb, and watched it bounce off Chip's forehead. The petty act made her feel better and ready to resume their previous conversation. "So, what's up? Two people are in the hospital, and they think you did it?"

"Well." Chip's brow furrowed. "They think someone used the game to cause it."

"But that's crazy," said Phil. "We know we came well below the frame rate and color scheme that can cause seizures."

Chip shook his head. "I don't think that's it. This seems to be something else entirely. And while I know *you* didn't do anything, and *I* didn't do anything, I *also* think someone used our game to cause it."

Phil's eyes widened, looking personally offended at the very suggestion. "You think someone hacked the game?"

Chip shrugged. "It's possible."

Phil shook his head. "Not on *my* watch. And if they did, I'll find it. Today."

"That would be good, because we only have until Monday morning."

Blue braced herself. "Until what, exactly?"

Chip looked down at his lap. "Until we have to either offer up some sort of alternate explanation, or we have to take the game down and turn it over to the police."

"We have to *what?*" Phil sounded as if he'd just been told to report for an involuntary vasectomy.

"I told him we could turn up more if we looked into it ourselves, and he accepted that. Either I agree to turn it over on Monday, or he was going to make it a condition of letting me go. I had to agree to it to buy us time."

"You agreed to turn over *our* program to police hackers?"

"No, Phil, I put off the confiscation for a few days. They would either pull the trigger now or later. What did you want me to say?"

"You say the program isn't mine to give away, and you need to talk to your partner before you commit to anything."

"I was trying to keep you out of it," said Chip. "Last thing we needed was for him to want to question both of us."

"Well, maybe *I* could have done a better job protecting *our* interests, partner!"

Wedged between the two men, Blue literally felt the heat emanating from Phil. She reached out and put a hand on each person's shoulder. "Guys, please, it is what it is. Let's just try to—"

"Phil, we'll make a backup of the program before we turn it over."

"But we'll have to take the site down during the investigation, right?"

"Well, yes, but—"

"And that could be months, right? What the hell were you thinking? We'll be ruined before we start."

Laverne called out and approached their table. "Hey, boys! I got your appetizers ready!"

Blue closed her eyes. *Oh, God, not her, not now.*

With a flourish, Laverne dropped an overloaded basket of breadsticks and multiple sauces down in front of them.

Chip piped up. "We haven't ordered yet."

Laverne frowned and looked down at her notepad. "Oh, you're right. Huh! I guess I just assumed. Well, I can't take them back, so consider them on the house. I'm so sorry 'bout that, guys. And gal!"

Blue's eyes locked with Laverne's, noting the gleam in her eyes, before the waitress turned and walked away.

Phil immediately reached out and snagged up a cheese sauce and a breadstick. The redness in his face drained away with each contented bite.

Blue released a breath. *Chalk one up for Laverne. Maybe she does know what she's doing.*

Phil spoke between bites. "I'm going home right after we eat, and I'm tracking down what's going on."

Chip shook his head. "I think we need to go to the hospital and see if we can learn anything more about the victims. He told me their names. Rebecca Burton and Skye MacLeod."

"Really? Skye MacLeod?" Blue rolled her eyes. "See, that's why parents should be required to get a license before having kids."

"Well, funny name aside, they're in serious condition at IU Bloomington Hospital."

Phil waved his hand at them. "Fine, you two go check that out. I'm going home and getting online. I'll have this shit figured out before you get back."

Blue looked at Chip, a flush going through her at the thought of a new adventure with her man. "So, what do you suggest?"

Chip shrugged. "I'll bet they're not tracking roommates. We'll just show up with that angle and see if we can get into her room as a visitor. The staff might not tell us much, but we can see what we can figure out on our own."

Blue nodded. "Worth a try, I guess."

Chip reached for a breadstick. "Oh, it'll work. Especially with my master bullshitter at my side. You'll get us in."

"Hey! I love you, too." She reached into her cup and flung ice at him.

Chip closed his eyes, letting the ice bounce harmlessly off his forehead. He leaned toward her, putting on his cutest pout. "You do, don't you?"

Blue looked down, then back up at him, *Dammit, he's so adorable!*

"Don't you?" Chip prodded.

"Yes! I guess I can't deny it now."

She leaned forward and stole a sweet kiss tinged with tomatoes and Mountain Dew.

Laverne's voice broke the mood. "Hi, guys and gal, ready for your order...or I can come back later!"

Phil begged, "No, please don't go. It's getting sickening over here."

Laverne put a hand on Phil's shoulder. "Aww, don't be that way, hon. It's true love. I think it's kind of cute."

Phil grinned. "*You* didn't have to go *home* with them last night."

Laverne chuckled. "Pretty disgusting, huh?"

"You have no idea."

"Hey!" Blue snapped, giving Phil a dirty look. "Since you're here, we're going to order the same thing as last night. I don't suppose you can get a side of turkey, gravy, and mashed potatoes with that?"

Laverne extended her arm to indicate the empty establishment. "Everyone's at the diner down the street, hon. And by 'everyone' I mean maybe four students. I'm just here to take care of my favorite customers."

Blue made a point of slurping air through the straw of her cup, causing a rude noise, then held the cup out to Laverne. "This one's done, get me another."

Laverne smirked, took the cup, and walked away.

As soon as she was out of earshot, Phil turned to the couple. "Okay, so that's the plan. I go home and check out the game, and you two go to the hospital. Sounds good. But be careful."

Blue widened her eyes and gave Chip a shocked look. "Be careful? Us? I don't know what he means. We're *always* careful."

"Always," echoed Chip.

"Just try not to raise any vicious ghosts this time."

CHAPTER TEN_

THE IU HOSPITAL campus was only a fifteen-minute walk from the pizzeria, and the sharp November breeze kept Blue and Chip moving fast, clasping hands the whole way. Blue darted through the double glass doors, cold, heart pumping fast, but with a clear head. She approached the long desk with "Information" spelled out in large, gold-painted letters overhead, pouting at the smiling greeter seated at the desk.

"Oh, hey, I just heard about my friend, Rebecca Burton! Is she here? Can we see her?" Blue returned the greeter's stare with her own, hoping to project confidence and certainty that this person should do her job and answer her perfectly legitimate request.

The woman, a sixty-ish silver-haired lady, typed on her keyboard and looked at the screen. "Burton, Rebecca, yes, room 6048. Take the elevators to the sixth floor."

"Thanks...uh, do you know if there's been any change?"

The nurse frowned at the screen. "Well, she's stable, or they wouldn't let her have visitors. So that's good, but unless you're family, we can't tell you any more than that."

Blue nodded and followed Chip toward the elevator.

The elevator doors opened to reveal a hospital bed on wheels surrounded by nurses and a doctor. Blue and Chip stepped to either side of the doors to let them pass. The teen lying on the bed flashed a brave smile as the doctors wheeled him past. The odor of ammonia and some other sanitizing chemical hit Blue's nose, and she struggled against her gag reflex.

Seconds later, alone on the elevator together, Blue spoke. "I hate this. Any time I'm in a hospital now, I think of my own stay, after Mom died." Chip extended his arm over her shoulder, and she leaned her head against him. "But the good news, I guess, is that Rebecca's stable, so she's not in danger of dying any time soon."

Chip nodded. "I'm hoping we can rouse her, see if she can talk."

"I thought the police guy said she couldn't talk."

Chip shrugged. "It's worth a try."

Moments later, still hand in hand, Chip and Blue walked down the brightly lit hallway, following the numbers along the left side consecutively counting 6040, 6042...until they stood outside the door of 6048.

At the sight of the closed door, a shiver traveled up Blue's spine. "Well...here we are."

Chip nodded but said nothing.

The seconds stretched on, and the internal twitchiness built up within her. *He'd better do something soon, or I'm darting for the elevator.* Blue finally spoke. "Well?"

Chip looked at her.

"It's your plan."

"I know, I just feel...odd, all of a sudden."

"You, too? Well, maybe we should forget about it."

"No." Chip reached for the door, gripping the curved handle. "We need to find out more. My gut tells me it's important."

The door swung inward, emitting a squeaking noise as they walked through into the dimness. From the perspective of the narrow corridor, she could only see the foot of a hospital bed, twin lumps of a pair of feet poking up from the blankets.

They pressed forward, entering the room. Natural light from the window against the far wall exposed one of the most radiant, beautiful faces Blue had ever seen.

The patient lay on the bed, her eyes closed. Her bright red hair fanned over the pillow beneath her in shocking contrast to her stone-white skin. One thin arm extended out. An I.V. tube twined from the wrist, curled into loops on a hook and back up into a bag, presumably a saline drip.

To Blue's eyes, Rebecca Burton appeared as any other patient in a hospital, her understated beauty marred by hours of lying in a bed, garbed in an unattractive gown.

But the room itself emitted a presence, a feeling that filled her with an intense sadness, sickened at what she saw.

Suddenly, it was *that night again,* when she helped Chip dig up the bones of Gunther. The nausea that overcame her as they continued with their morbid task was similar to the sickening feeling now.

They stood as witnesses to some great injustice happening before their eyes. Blue knew, if they were given an opportunity to stop this, they needed to act.

"Poor, poor dear," an unfamiliar voice whispered.

Blue noticed a nurse standing on the opposite side of the bed.

The nurse looked across the bed and met her gaze. Blue saw her body tremble, as if she'd awakened from a dream. "Oh, my, I'm so sorry." She looked at the clipboard hanging at eye level on the storage cabinet. "I came in to check her vitals and... just got distracted for some reason." She cleared her throat and removed the pen from her pocket. "So...do you know the patient?"

"Not really," started Chip.

Blue broke in. "Yes, *I* do. I had her in several classes, and...Chip is my boyfriend; he's here for moral support." She reached out and squeezed his upper arm as a warning. *Let me do the talking, you moron.* "She wrote such...wonderful poetry." She tried to project as much sadness into the lie as she could.

The nurse's eyes lit up at her words. "I'm not surprised. You can feel it, can't you? It's like she has the soul of a poet." The nurse sniffled and shook her head. "Wow, I don't get it. Working here, I've seen so many terrible things, but I don't usually fall to pieces around the patients. There just seems to be something special about this one."

Blue nodded. Given the emotions stirring within her, it was easy to follow that thought. "She is. She really is. I just hope she gets better soon." Blue shot the nurse a quick glance before looking down to the floor.

The nurse sighed, not an encouraging sign, and recorded something on the chart. "I hope so, too, but I'm just...concerned about this one."

"But..." Blue considered how to fish without looking like she was fishing. "I thought she was stable. That means she's getting better, right?"

"Well, that's what the *doctor* would tell you," the nurse said. "And the doctor knows *everything,* as he's constantly reminding us. What do *I* know? I've only been doing this for fifteen years."

Chip spoke up from beside her. "What *do* you know, Nurse?"

The nurse shook her head, her internal struggle clear in her answer. "I'm not supposed to say anything. Never mind. And I could be wrong."

"Wrong about what?" Chip pressed.

"Look...it's just me, but...these vitals. They're dropping. Slightly. Consistently. Over hours. The doctor says it means the patient is slipping into a healing coma."

The nurse made a scoffing noise. "I've seen healing comas before. You get spikes, even little ones, an overall drop until they stabilize, but not a steady plummet like this. I've never seen it, and it makes me nervous."

The nurse clasped her hands to her face. "But I don't know, and dammit, I shouldn't have said anything. I just have a bad feeling, like she's slipping away, and in a few days, she's going to be gone."

She stepped away from the bed. "I need to get out of this room."

Blue loved that idea. "We'll come with you."

Moments later, standing in the hallway, Blue took a deep breath, feeling her head clear, like a potent drug purging itself in seconds. She looked over to see the nurse, visibly shaking her head to clear it.

"I'm sorry," the woman said. "I shouldn't have said what I did. I'm usually more careful than that. But there was just something in the room."

"We felt it, too," said Chip. "But you think she's in trouble? That she's not going to last long?"

The nurse backed away. "I'm sorry, I can't say any more. You'll have to talk to the doctor. Actually, don't. He can't tell you anything since you're not related, and I told you more than I should have. I don't know what came over me."

Blue reached out for the nurse's arm. "Wait—"

"Enjoy your visit with your friend." She took off down the hall like Blue was some creature trying to claw at her.

Blue heard a noise coming from Chip's belt—something Star Trek-like, she suspected, and Chip reached for his cell phone holster. After a quick glance at the screen, he shook his head. "We have to go."

"What is it?"

"Phil says he found something in the program. He's going to check into it, and we need to get back there as quick as possible."

"Well, that's pretty mysterious. But I guess we've found out all we need here, too."

Chip nodded. "I wish we'd driven the car like we were planning to before the cop showed up at our door. Wait, we can take the university shuttle, that will save us time. Normally, there's a bit of a wait, but with so few students on campus, it's probably faster."

Minutes later, they stepped back out into the cold afternoon air. As Chip made a phone call, Blue sat at the shuttle stop, a bench, taking a moment to let her mind go blank after this long, strange morning. Her body felt jittery because she'd drunk too much coffee. Her mind raced in a thousand directions, trying to put it all together.

Who was Rebecca Burton? What was it about her that made everyone feel so strange? Who did she work for? Who attacked her, and how did they use a video game to do it? And why? Blue had no idea about any of this, but she knew she needed to see this through, at Chip's side. And for that reason, if nothing else, she felt more like her real self than she had in years.

Having finished his call, Chip addressed Blue. "Well, I was partly right. The shuttle is half-staffed, so there's a ten-minute wait. Still, it's going to be faster than trying to walk."

Blue reached out and put her hand over his, gripping his fingers tightly. "It's going to be all right."

He smiled back at her. "I know."

"Do you, now?" She felt a smirk come to her face.

Chip nodded. "Mmm-hmmm. With you by my side, this thing...whatever it is...doesn't stand a chance."

"You know it! Come here."

Chip leaned forward.

Blue gave him a kiss hot enough to send them to the public display of affection penalty box if such a thing existed. Erotic energy super-charged her body, traveled down her spine, into her legs, and settled into her stomach. For a moment, she wondered what the hell she was thinking ever giving Drew the time of day. Then she stopped thinking about Drew altogether.

Dammit, we never had any alone time.

As if he could read her mind, or her...whatever...Chip pulled back and broke their kiss. The panting she heard from him was as intense as her own. "Stop it. We don't have time." Chip smiled. "Just yet."

"I know. I couldn't help myself."

"Try harder, please."

"That's my line." She winked.

"I need to call Phil."

"Coward." She stuck her tongue out at him.

"Prudent." Chip pressed a button.

She leaned back and took a deep breath, letting the cold air calm her down. Not exactly a cold shower, but it would have to do. And, hopefully, it wouldn't have to last long.

"Hmph!"

She turned to Chip, who glared at his cell phone screen.

"What's up?"

"Phil isn't answering."

"Maybe he's grabbing a snack."

"He'd still have his phone."

At that moment, the shuttle pulled up, and the doors opened. Chip stepped in front of Blue.

The woman behind the wheel looked college age; another student who preferred to work the holiday over returning to her home situation.

He flashed a card from his billfold, then dug out a dollar and handed it over. "One guest."

Blue offered a nod of sympathy to their driver before walking past her.

They had their pick of seats on the empty shuttle. Chip grabbed the seat directly next to the door, and Blue settled in next to him. Chip stared out the window, clearly distracted or bothered.

She grabbed his hand again. "I said, it's going to be okay."

"I know."

She had no idea where they were. "How far until we get home?"

"Less than five minutes now."

"Okay, well, we'll find out. Maybe he was in the bathroom."

Chip shook his head. "That wouldn't stop him from answering."

"Oh...really? Gross. I guess that's what I get for asking."

Chip sat, eyes glued to the window, as the hospital panned away and the shuttle pulled onto the road.

Blue reached out and kneaded his shoulders. Even through his jacket, she could feel the tight knots in his muscles, the tension of his body keeping his shoulders halfway up his neck. She rubbed her thumbs over his shoulder blades, trying to get the muscles to loosen. "Relax."

"There's something wrong."

A familiar chill ran over her, it was just like...*but no. It couldn't be the same.* "We don't know anything."

Chip shook his head. "*I* know. There's something wrong."

Through her hands, his body shook as he drew a breath. She continued to rub his shoulders, the only comfort she could offer.

Like a cougar in a circus wagon waiting for a chance to pounce, Chip continued to stare out the window.

A few blocks later, Blue recognized the neighborhood. The moment the door opened, she stepped into the aisle and back, letting Chip run past her. She thanked the driver and dropped down the stairs to the curb.

"Chip, wait!" She jogged up the cement driveway, noting that Phil's Jeep still sat behind the used Chevy Chip's father had bought him for a going-away present. *So, Phil hasn't left.*

By the time she took the cement stairs to the porch, Chip had already unlocked the door and had disappeared inside the house. She could hear Chip calling out Phil's name and the lack of response.

Now it really does *feel like that night! The night that my mother...*

The thought forced her to a stop in the doorway. She couldn't walk any farther. *Oh, God, not Phil. Please, not Phil, too.*

She heard Chip open the basement door, calling down the stairs. "Phil! Answer me, now! I mean it!"

Somehow, she got her strength back and stepped across the room to the basement.

Chip was already downstairs. "Phil...Phil! Oh, God, no, speak to me!"

She stumbled down the stairs, gripping the rail and pulling herself downward. Halfway down, she saw him.

Phil, still in the computer chair, was seated in front of the screen, head craned back, eyes staring at the ceiling, lifeless.

God!

Blue dropped, her butt hitting the stair beneath her. The room started to blacken. She could hear a buzzing in her ears, and she squeezed her eyes shut, waiting for reality to return.

Chip's voice continued, panic in his tone. "Phil, Phil, snap out of it!"

She called out, her voice sounding far away in her own ears. "Is he dead?"

An eternity later, Chip answered, "No. He has a pulse."

She covered her face in her hands and wept tears of relief. *What the fuck is happening? But he's not dead, hold on to that.*

She pulled her fingers across her face as she lowered her hands.

Chip tipped Phil's head forward, stared into his eyes and called out, trying to rouse him.

Then Blue saw something on Phil's computer screen–something that froze her on the stairs. *What...the...*

She found her voice. "Chip."

"Phil, wake up! What, Blue?"

"Look at the screen."

"What?"

"Phil's screen. Look at it. Now!"

Chip stopped his ministrations to Phil's body and stood in place, as if the words took a few seconds to register. Finally, Chip pivoted and looked at the computer screen.

Chip saw what Blue saw...the wizard, Magtog the Great, proceeding down a hill toward the CGI village. With Chip no longer talking, she could hear the words from the computer speakers for the first time.

A high, tinny, mechanical voice, speaking with Phil's distinct Hoosier accent. "Blue! Chip! This is Phil! I know you'll be home any second. When you see this, get online and meet me at the Mountain Lion Inn in the courtyard. I'm heading over there now."

"What the...?" But Chip's voice failed him.

"I repeat," the wizard continued, walking under its own power with no assistance from the comatose player in the chair. "Head directly to the tavern. This is Phil! Do not wander around in the game until you speak with me! It's vitally important. I'll see you there. Chip and Blue, I know you'll be home any second..."

CHAPTER ELEVEN

Marda lay flat on the floor, prostrate before the image of Baalina. *They have returned, mistress.*

For the first time in several days, Baalina responded. *Yes, my special one, I can sense your excitement. How soon before we know?*

Marda's heart sang with joy at the direct contact. *Soon, mistress. Natalie is reviewing the folder contents and knows what to look for.* Marda considered her next thought, then offered, *Natalie was slow to make progress when we began, but since her first breakthrough hours ago, she has served you well and with distinction.*

Baalina's response reflected patience. *She will be well-rewarded, Sister. As will you all. Just as soon as I return to the physical realm.*

The Sisterhood had gained the advantage. If now, they also gained the crystal, it guaranteed they could move forward to create a brighter future. One in which the Sisterhood would no longer live in hiding, in fear, but would finally claim their place as the rightful leaders in a new hierarchy.

A hierarchy in which Marda would command, with her loyal soldiers, Van, Cyn, and Nat serving alongside her. A hierarchy in which Marda would be answerable to no one except the great Baalina herself.

The Kelranian Order had entrusted no less than the infamous Rebecca Burton to attend to the matter personally. Burton–known to the uninitiated as Agent Burton of Special Investigations.

Marda was not among the uninitiated.

She knew Burton's true purpose–her ultimate destiny.

Few people realized the threat Rebecca Burton posed to all of humanity–partly because Burton smothered her power deep within, while Marda and the Sisterhood embraced theirs.

Marda supposed she should be flattered that the Kelranian Order considered them such a threat as to send their most dangerous agent. Logically, she should be worried. But she was neither. After all, the Sisters of Baalina had struck first and gained the upper hand against the meddling Kelranian Order. With a little luck, before the rest of the Order could react, the trap would be sprung.

As soon as they returned, Cyn and Van checked in with Marda. They'd monitored the house until the police had abandoned the crime scene. Bloomington's finest had left the home supposedly secure, but, since it was a holiday and they were presumably short-handed, they didn't leave a guard behind.

Breaking in proved easy. It took only a few minutes more to determine that the bedroom mirror swung open on a hinge. Van and Cyn found the wall safe resting in a carved-out pit in the drywall behind it, sitting atop a shelf unit of some sort. The cops had already been there, so they took their time, cracked the combination and worked open the safe door, then removed the portfolio within.

They gave the bulky envelope a quick glance. Pages of notes, and a glittering red gem—perfect. They returned to their own base of operations and turned the contents over to Natalie, the true artifacts expert.

And they waited.

And so Marda waited, as well.

———

As soon as the door opened to the basement, she rose and positioned herself at the foot of the stairs.

She felt the expression of her own face change, the smile drop away when she registered the disappointment in Nat's features. The downcast faces of Cyn and Van, who both refused to meet her gaze, confirmed her fears.

As soon as they were level on the cement slab, Cyn and Van both bowed before her. Cyn delivered the news. "We have failed you."

"What happened?"

Her gaze followed Nat, who approached a discarded side table in the midst of the stored furniture and spread the contents out across the surface. Her face neutral, Nat pulled something out of her pocket—or rather, three somethings—and let them fall onto the table, as well.

Three pieces of the crystal.

Three red, broken, jagged pieces of...a nearly indestructible crystal?

"How did...you didn't..."

Nat shook her head. "No, we didn't. If it were real, we couldn't. That's the point. It's fake. Plastic. Not even a good copy. I used a hammer and screwdriver. If this were the real Divenium Crystal, with the proper imbuement, I wouldn't even be able to scratch it, but it broke with my first blow." To her credit, if Natalie felt any pleasure in the failure of her erstwhile tormentors, her face showed only disappointment.

Marda closed her eyes. As her pulse pounded in her head, she tried to control her breathing. "And the file?"

"Equally useless. With even a cursory read, it's clearly typed pages of nonsense and false information. In a section devoted to the history of the gem itself, whoever did it was quite the smartass. They list our coven leader from the 1700s as Kitka Tatanya." Natalie giggled.

The name meant nothing to Marda, though clearly it had been meant to be mistaken for Mother Katka at first glance.

Natalie stopped herself and cleared her throat, apparently realizing no one else made the connection. "That was...Catwoman's alias from the Adam West *Batman* movie. There are other, more obvious bad jokes. The supposed list of current council members of the Kelranian Order includes Peter Porker, Edward Penishands, Dick Jones–that's from *Robocop*–Henry Beamus, from an old *Twilight Zone* episode."

Marda seethed. "They mock us!"

Natalie swallowed. "The intent of the file does seem to be to send a giant 'fuck you.'"

Marda looked down at her minions, prostrate before her. In her fury, she literally saw red spots before her eyes. Her anger burst from her in spurts, between clenched teeth. "So...Cyn...this is what you're trained for?"

"I'm sorry, Marda."

"Breaking and entering...you said...search and seizure...you said." Her hand reached to her hip, fingers clasping the hilt of her ceremonial knife. Every Sister carried one, a sign of their order, each weapon hand-crafted, with an ivory grip and the Baalina sigil carved into the handle.

She drew the blade and stepped behind the bent form. She ran her thumb along the rune.

"This is what we excel at, you said."

"Marda...please."

"You, Cyn. You. You talked me out of going. You offered your personal assurances."

Her left hand reached out, gripped Cyn's wrist, and extended her arm out to her side.

"Marda..."

"But it's not really your expertise, is it? Pain is your expertise. Pain and pleasure." She drew her blade down the thin blouse, cutting away the material to reveal a white shoulder. Such beautiful ivory skin, in perfect contrast to her short red hair. So beautiful and so deadly. "Remember what you showed me in the bedroom...just yesterday?"

With practiced flicks of her wrist, the bra straps fell away, exposing her gorgeous pale shoulder blade.

To her credit, Cyn didn't shake or grovel. She did, however, call out to her partner. "Van?"

"Sorry, Cyn, I can't help you." Van reached up and clasped her hands to her ears.

Marda leaned close, positioned the blade tip flush against the shoulder blade. "What did you teach me last night? Let's see if I can remember..."

She pressed, breaking skin.

A trail of blood marred her perfect back.

"This...brings pleasure..."

Cyn's face flushed, her breathing quickened in spite of her attempts to keep quiet. "Yes...Marda..."

"Why...so it does. But with minor adjustments...in spite of any training, regardless of any attempts to block a response, it will cause the most exquisite, burning agony...that's what you said, right?"

Beneath her fingers, Marda felt Cyn brace herself. "Yes...Marda."

Still gripping the wrist, Marda forced Cyn's arm back a quarter-inch and turned the edge of the blade into a nerve cluster just under the skin.

Cyn screamed. Her body slumped forward, her face pressed against the cement, but she continued to scream, apparently oblivious to the impact against her face.

Cyn's screams filled the chamber. Marda counted to ten, slowly. "Please...stop, Marda...it's not meant to..."

She applied the slightest pressure, and Cyn's screams renewed.

She counted again from one. Toward the end, her screams had turned hoarse.

Marda withdrew the blade.

The screams immediately ceased.

She looked down at the trembling form, openly weeping and broken before her.

Van, no longer able to remain impartial, reached out and cradled her partner, holding her and rocking her.

Though the blood flowed freely down Cyn's back, Marda could see the wound would heal quickly.

Marda knelt down behind them, speaking loudly enough to be

heard over Cyn's whimpering. "The next time you two consider volunteering for something you're not entirely certain you can accomplish, don't. You wasted my time, you wasted your time, but worst of all, you wasted the mistress' time."

To Marda's astonishment, Cyn found the strength to speak. "Yes...Marda."

Marda wiped the bloodied blade on the rags of the blouse and stood. "Bandage her, then come down and clean this mess up. By the time you've finished, hopefully I'll have returned with the real crystal."

CHAPTER TWELVE_

Magtog the wizard, sitting in the tavern, continued to speak in a running monologue. The sound came through the computer speakers, clearly Phil's voice, though slightly mechanized.

Blue sat, stunned, unable to pull her gaze from the screen. "Chip, what the fuck?"

"I don't know."

"Not good enough. What the fuck, Chip?"

"I *really* don't know, Blue." Chip's breathing increased.

Blue feared he might build up to a potential panic attack. *Good to know I'm not the only one having trouble processing this!* Blue shook her head at Chip. "Oh, no. You don't get to panic. That's *my* role in this partnership. You're the logical, sensible one with the answers. So, give me some logical answers, partner!"

Chip waved a hand in the air and shrugged, his confusion clear on his face.

She reached out and gripped Chip's forearm. With her other hand, she pointed at the screen, unable to control the trembling of her pointing finger. "He's unconscious here, but he's still playing there." She dared to give quick glances at Phil. His body remained slouched, with the neck craned back and mouth hanging open slack-jawed.

Chip sat in a chair at the station next to Phil's body. "I see that. I can't explain what's going on any better than you can."

Blue held onto Chip in a death grip, balancing on wobbly legs behind Chip's chair, still avoiding long looks at Phil.

So slack, so lifeless, just like her mother. That night. After she'd been...

Her gaze shifted back and forth, taking in the blank look on Phil's face, then moving toward his computer screen, which showed an over-the-shoulder view of his wizard seated at the virtual tavern.

Is he in the game? No, he can't *be in the game. That's...* She stopped herself, realizing the next word: *impossible.*

Shit.

And yet, onscreen, Phil droned on. "...head directly to the tavern. This is Phil! Do not wander around in the game until you find me!"

Chip pulled a pair of headphones over his head. He pressed the arrow keys. On the screen, Gallamar, the mousy thief, Chip's fallback character, approached the tavern.

Panic surged through her. "Chip, what do you think you're doing?"

"What does it look like?"

"Chip...given what's happened, taking your character into the game seems like a *really* bad idea."

Chip looked away from the screen and patted the hand that still held his upper arm. "You heard him. He wants us to meet him at the tavern. My character was practically there. It should be perfectly safe."

"You did *not* just say that."

Chip shrugged. "Focus on what Phil's saying. He's telling me what *not* to do, so as long as I listen, I should be okay."

A moment later, the pats on the back of her hand turned more insistent. "Uh...that kind of hurts."

"Oh." Blue relaxed her fingers, easing back the nails that must have dug deep marks into his upper arm. "Sorry."

"That's okay. Now, in spite of what I said, I don't want you logging on until we know what's going on."

Yeah, right! A nervous laugh escaped from her. "Thanks, I'll do my best to resist."

Chip's screen showed Gallamar entering the tavern. With expert control, Chip turned the avatar's head to center the tavern's front door.

Through all of this, Phil's voice droned on from the speaker. "I'm at the tavern now. If you hear me, go directly there. Don't wander the game. I'm at the entrance of the...Chip!"

The wizard appeared on Chip's screen, looking directly at Gallamar and hobbling toward him. In her peripheral vision, Blue could see the same scene play out on Phil's computer, presenting the view from behind the wizard's shoulder.

Phil's voice continued, "Please tell me you're still playing, I mean, that you're still in the basement. You didn't—"

Chip adjusted his microphone and spoke. "Yes, we're fine. I'm here, so is Blue. Can you hear me?"

On the screen, the wizard waved an arm, and a smile appeared on the CGI character's face. Even with Blue's lack of experience with this game, the look creeped her out, borderline disturbing, like rubber forced into a shape it was never designed to go.

"Loud and clear."

The wizard's lips moved in perfect synch to the words, another detail that stood out in contrast to normal play, in which no attempt was made to emulate talking.

Gallamar returned Magtog's expressive greeting with a stone face.

The look of relief, however, was clear on the wizard's CGI facial features. "Thank God. I was scared to stop talking until I heard from you. So...uh...what sort of condition is my body in?"

Steeling her courage, Blue looked over at the body, and for the first time, focused on it.

Phil slouched in the chair, breathing deeply.

He's going to wake up with a stiff neck. Blue didn't allow herself to think he might not wake up. She glanced from the chair to the couch she'd slept on last night, perhaps ten paces across the room. But moving the dead weight—she cringed at the expression—would be an impossible task by herself.

She put a hand on Chip's shoulder. "We should probably move him."

Chip nodded. "Hold on, we're going to move you to the couch." Chip grabbed Phil's ankles and waited for her to take his shoulders.

As her boyfriend stared at her, Blue realized she didn't want to touch Phil, let alone work her hands under his arms and let his head slump across her chest. But she also knew it had to be done. It was one of those times to "man up" and take care of business, or however the clichés went.

She lifted, grunting against his weight, unable to prevent his large, denim-covered butt from dragging the floor. They finally managed to lay him across the couch, his head supported by the pillow.

Moments later, huffing and puffing, they stood over Phil. Blue gave an ironic laugh. "Look at us...strapping heroes to the rescue...evil has no chance."

Chip wiped a hand across his brow. She couldn't imagine what he might be thinking. His best friend in a coma, his girlfriend showing–she admitted it–a rare case of weakness, and he was expected to be the brave one with all the answers.

And for the moment, apparently, he had none to offer. Silently, he stepped back toward the computer.

Blue followed him and grabbed his shoulder. "Chip, what if you're the one who passes out next? What am I supposed to do then?" *Jesus, when did I become the helpless damsel in distress?*

Nevertheless, she couldn't avoid the awful truth. If Chip passed out, she'd be left standing in a room full of computers and pretty much no idea what to do. *Calling 911 would be pointless.*

Chip turned to hug her. "One problem at a time. Let's just make sure it doesn't come to that. I know it's risky, but I can't play it safe right now. He's my best friend. He needs our help."

Blue didn't know how to express the contradictions of emotions bubbling around within her. She ended up hugging him and offering a lame, "Just be careful."

"Whoever did this, they messed with the wrong programmers.

Someone's trying to take over my work, and I'm taking it back." He turned and looked into her eyes. "I know with you at my side, we're going to win."

She smiled, moved by his intensity. "All right, go get 'em, cornball. Sheesh!"

Chip sat back down in front of the computer.

Blue moved behind him, resting her hands on his shoulders.

Chip adjusted the mic. "You're on the couch, Phil. Your pulse is steady and strong. We just got back from seeing Rebecca Burton, one of the victims. Your condition looks remarkably similar."

Chip offered Blue a worried look. She was sure he recalled the same detail he refused to speak out loud to his friend at the moment–the same detail that came to her mind–that Rebecca's vital signs were weakening by the hour.

Chip continued, "I would guess the biggest concern is dehydration, so we have quite a bit of time to figure this out before we have to call anyone."

"No, *don't* call anyone." The emotion in the voice over the computer speaker came through loud and clear. "If you report another body, the police will shut us down immediately, holiday or no holiday."

That didn't seem quite so obvious to Blue. "Don't worry; if it comes to it, we can just move your body into the other room and call some-one," she said.

Phil spoke up, "Blue, I'm the lead programmer of the game. The second Officer Kirby finds out I'm in the same condition as the other hospitalized victims, no way is he going to think that it's some unrelated coincidence."

"Well...good point. But what if you get in trouble?"

"Look, we know the agent and her assistant have been stable for at least a day. Let's give it that long. Besides, if they confiscate this program and shut it down...well, my *mind is* in here. We don't know what that will do to me."

Chip considered. "Probably nothing good. Agreed. Okay, Phil, why don't you share with us what you know about–"

A new voice cut in, the words through the computer also distorted, but clearly feminine and youthful. "There he is! I told you if we kept checking back here, we'd find him."

Two additional CGI characters approached the table in the tavern. One was a tall, blonde warrior woman dressed in a knight's suit of armor, gripping a large mace. As Chip waved his mouse pointer on her body, the name Cloud McSky hovered over her head for a few seconds and dissolved.

The second, coming up behind McSky, was a striking figure, unlike any other Blue had seen in the game. She stood, garbed in white body armor, long red hair billowing around her. Her skin radiated an intense gold. A pair of tremendous wings folded back against her shoulder blades.

Beautiful! I want a character like that! Blue noted how the other avatars turned to look at her. Even Chip, using the directional arrows, tweaked his screen to center on the golden angel. His cursor revealed the name, Arby.

Chip shook his head. "Hmph. 'R.B.' indeed. Very punny, Rebecca Burton. Now I remember seeing your name on our reports. And here I just thought we had a player with a fast food fetish."

The angel figure replied in a dignified, feminine voice that matched her visual. "And you must be Eugene Farren. It's nice to finally 'meet' you. You'll pardon me if I don't shake your hand."

"That's okay," said Chip. "Now, first things first. Am I in danger just by being online right now?"

"No," said Phil.

Though the avatar's name read as McSky, Blue thought of her by her real-world name: MacLeod. "I wouldn't think so. Just stay away from the cave and you should be fine."

"So it would be safe for Blue to come online, as well?"

Oh, now wait a second...

Chip lowered his microphone. "Blue, why don't you get on your character so we can all talk at the tavern?"

Blue looked over at Phil's body. "So I should put myself in danger of going into a coma so they don't think I'm being rude?"

"They say it should be fine."

Blue folded her arms across her chest. "Oh, good, the three *geniuses* stuck in the game say it's perfectly safe."

Chip stabbed and held down a button on the keyboard–presumably a mute–and shot Blue a dirty look. "Not cool."

Blue shot back a dirtier look. "It's not smart, and you know it."

Chip released a sigh. "No, you're right. I'm not thinking straight." He un-muted and spoke into the microphone. "Blue is going to stay offline for now, in case something goes wrong."

Phil spoke up. "Safety first. I get it."

"So, okay," said Chip, "What happened, and why?"

Phil's avatar shook its head. "I think I know, sorta. To find out what might have happened to Rebecca and MacLeod, I printed off their movement report, booted up Magtog, and started shadowing them...maybe not the best plan, in retrospect."

Blue shook her head. "Clearly not."

"Chip, you can see my report there to the side of the keyboard. See the spot I highlighted?"

Chip grabbed the paper and showed the sheet to Blue. The page displayed four columns of numbers in a series list. Beyond the numbers themselves, Blue could not make heads or tails of it. She shrugged and handed the list back to Chip.

Chip glanced at the numbers as he explained, "Each player's set of coordinates is auto-recorded every fifteen minutes in case we want to go back and..."

As if physically struck, his head tipped back, taken aback by something on the list. "Hey! What the hell?"

Phil's tone spoke his approval. "You found it, I see."

"Segment 67, land 1, 245, 90, 12?"

"Yep."

Frustrated, Blue smacked Chip's arm. "Stop the geek-speak a minute. What does it mean?"

"We've only programmed 66 land segments into the game so far."

Phil piped up, "But someone else programmed a segment 67. There's also a segment 68, 69, and 70."

"Someone's added areas to our game!" Chip sounded almost as upset by the unauthorized addition of virtual real estate as the condition of his best friend.

Chip held the list out to Blue at eye level, his thumb indicating the column listing Segment 67, land 1, 245, 90, 12. "Think of the last three numbers as longitude, latitude and height–x, y, z coordinates for 3D mapping."

Blue sighed, staring at the list. "I hope I don't regret this–why the third point?"

"Land mass. This list shows where an avatar stood on the map. Plus, we have to have it to plot hills, valleys, and water depth, so there's a certain change in height charted as they move."

"Oh. That was a remarkably simple explanation."

Chip grinned. "It's not *all* magic. Just *most* of the time."

Phil continued, "I'll just cut right to it. If you head east and go up the first hill, there's the large tree—the one you based on the one in our backyard. If you look carefully, there's a small hole at the root of the tree. A dark space. You'd look past it if you weren't trying to find it. It's a cave. Any avatar clicking on it can go in there. But once you're standing at the entrance..."

MacLeod spoke up. "That's how Rebecca found it. She was tracking another player who walked to the base of the tree and then logged off."

Chip said, "And that's when she noticed the portal at the base."

Burton's eyes looked toward the tavern floor as she spoke. "And then I...well, in retrospect, my next actions were not the most prudent."

Blue cringed. *Burton noticed the opening, closed in for a better look, and fell right into the booby trap. In doing so, she created a trail that lured two more boobies.*

Burton spoke in a low, shamed voice, like a defendant forced into admitting their guilt. "I hadn't considered the possibility of a magic spell that could...do something like this. She must have known I was tailing her and brought me there on purpose."

Skye continued, "And I stumbled onto it when I went looking for Rebecca."

"Okay," said Chip. "No sense kicking yourself too hard about something that can't be changed. But what's in the cave?"

Magtog's shoulders bent in a very real shrug. "Who cares? It's just a dark space. Most likely, nothing. The hackers placed it as a lure to attract their tech-savvy adversaries. And it worked. Once you realize you've been yanked out of your body and dropped into a CGI avatar, you sort of lose your sense of adventure. I just backed away."

"That's what happened to us, too," said MacLeod. "By the way...uh, how's my body?"

Chip answered, "We didn't visit you. I'm told your condition is similar to Rebecca's."

"Oh." The disappointed tone in MacLeod's voice was plain, even through the speaker. "And what condition is that?"

Chip and Blue exchanged looks. Chip stabbed the mute button. "Do we tell them?"

Blue shook her head. "It's not like they're not already doing everything they can."

Chip nodded and released the button. "You're both in a coma, but stable. The sooner we get you back where you belong, the better."

Rebecca's avatar stepped forward, the golden glow intensifying on her body. "Now we know *what* happened. I think I can offer up some idea about *why*. And then we need to formulate a plan of action."

Chip started, "Well, actually that's what we—"

"We have three people stuck in the game that we know of, and two allies outside in the real world." Rebecca paced an open space by the table, her avatar glowing as she spoke. "Is there anyone else unaccounted for?"

Chip tried again. "Uh, no, but—"

"Okay, so we need someone to go to our residence off-campus. We've hidden some important documents that I doubt the police noticed." She paused, pondering. "However, the Sisterhood of Baalina will probably send someone as soon as they realize we're stuck in here."

Chip practically snarled into the microphone. "Hold on. The sister of what? Back up, I think you need to start over."

Rebecca continued, apparently oblivious to Chip's comments. "For that matter, as soon as the Sisterhood realizes that one of the programmers has been brought into the conflict, they may send agents over to your house."

"What?" Chip exclaimed.

The angel turned toward Gallamar. "You two, what are your capabilities? Can you defend yourselves?"

Chip looked at Blue and rolled his eyes. He stabbed the mute button. "Wow, isn't she a bit bossy?"

Blue nodded. "Sounds like she's used to being in charge."

She leaned forward, putting her face close to Chip's mic and motioned to him to take his finger off the mute. "The programmer goes by the name Chip. You can call me Blue." She flashed Chip her most smoldering look.

He responded with a flush.

She licked her lips before continuing, "I would normally debate this point, but since we're operating mostly in the computer realm, I'll concede that he's the brains, and I'm the muscle."

Burton's avatar nodded. "Okay, let me think."

Chip reached out and hit the mute button with one hand. With his other hand, he lifted the mic over his head, leaned in, and gave her a short but electrifying kiss.

She tried to return the favor.

Chip broke the kiss. "Bad! Focus. You're distracting me," he teased.

Blue shook off the afterglow. "Yeah, whatever, we both needed that."

Chip smiled, "Yeah, maybe I did."

She smiled back at him. "Think of it as another reminder of what you're fighting for."

Burton's voice reached them from the speakers. "Okay, Phil just transferred into the game, so we probably have several hours before the Sisterhood figures it out."

Blue cringed, saying aloud, "Did she ever clarify who the Sisterhood is?"

Apparently, the microphone picked her up, because the angel spoke directly to Chip's avatar as Burton continued. "The Sisterhood is an ancient cult committed to the demon Baalina, who draws power from the stealing of souls."

Blue brushed her fingers against Chip's hand, and he released the mute button. She said, "Cult...as in Satanists?"

"Yes."

"But that's not possi...fuck!" *There's that phrase again!*

"Did you break up? I don't think I caught that."

Blue cleared her throat. "Sorry, I said, Satanist cult stealing souls. Sounds dangerous. What can we do?"

"The Sisterhood managed to reproduce an ancient relic within the virtual realm. The relic was originally destroyed over two hundred years ago. It's called a SoulStaff." Rebecca hesitated. "What I'm about to propose is going to sound fantastic. But I understand you two have had previous experience with the supernatural."

Chip and Blue traded expressions of shock and surprise.

Chip stabbed the mute button. "You want to field that, or should I?"

"Maybe Phil told her?"

"Phil wouldn't do that," Chip insisted.

"Okay...sorry. Let me talk." After Chip released the mute, Blue said, "Some, yes. Can I ask how you know that?"

"I'm a paranormal investigator. Few events of a supernatural nature can occur without my being aware of them sooner or later. My point is, your past experience might prepare you for what I'm about to say, but it might not."

"Try us."

"The SoulStaff was designed for one thing and one thing only. It drains souls from the people around it and uses those souls as magical energy to create a portal to summon Baalina, a bound demoness banished to the chaos realm. Let loose, Baalina is powerful enough that she could potentially subjugate the city, maybe a big chunk of the Midwest. A group of her followers hacked this game platform to test their powers before applying them to the physical world."

Chip spoke up. "Wait, you're saying they plan to raise a demon in our game?"

"A virtual version of the demon, yes."

Blue and Chip exchanged baffled looks.

Well that's...this time, Blue's mind did not conjure up impossible. *Ludicrous.* Blue shrugged. "I don't get it."

From Chip's tone, she guessed *he* didn't get it, either. "Yeah, seriously, why? To what purpose?"

Burton paused. "My best guess is that a virtual fantasy game is one of the few places where a giant demon can be conjured before dozens of spectators and be dismissed by the witnesses as ambiance."

Chip's brows crinkled. "Well, that sort of makes sense, I suppose. But what's the point?"

The angel nodded. "Before anyone would know what has happened, the demon would draw off all the souls of the players in the game and use those souls to open a gateway into the real world."

The words hit Blue like a sack of bricks to the gut. *Are you shitting me?* She moved away from the computer screen. The layers of impossibilities left her numb. *Demons. Soul stealing. End of the world stuff, and Chip has created the perfect laboratory for them to experiment in.*

The silence lingered.

Finally, Phil cut in. "Great! And you didn't come to us and tell us...why?"

Skye looked down, almost shame-faced at being called out. "We weren't actually sure *what* was going on. We just knew key members of the Sisterhood had gathered in Bloomington and had taken an interest in your game. That's why I've been on campus all these weeks, to explore the game and search the area. We didn't really know what they had planned...well, until this happened." Her tone projected pure misery.

"It's okay," said Phil, the anger leaving his voice. "I'm sure you did all you can."

"Doesn't feel like it, now," moaned Skye.

"It's okay," said Phil. "We're all going to get out of this, and then laugh about it later."

The exchange touched Blue. *Phil has someone to worry about. I guess that could be a good thing. I just hope he's right, and we really do have a later to laugh about it.* "So, what do we do now?"

The golden angel figure continued to pace her area, her wings occasionally fluttering. "There's a dossier hidden in our headquarters," Burton offered.

"We rented an off-campus residence," added MacLeod.

Rebecca picked up the story. "Someone from the Sisterhood will undoubtedly try to find our file once they figure out that both Skye and I are no longer there. It contains a history of the Sisterhood, as well as the Divenium Crystal."

Blue braced herself. "And that is?"

"A crystal of white magic imbued by the Kelranian Order and used to defeat them over three hundred years ago."

"Of course. We girls have to accessorize."

As Rebecca rattled off the street address, Blue jotted it down.

Chip nodded his head. "That's just a few blocks from here. Ten-minute walk, tops."

Burton continued, "In the bedroom, you'll see a mirrored vanity. The mirror swings out to reveal a hollowed-out wall with a safe."

Blue considered. "Really? Is that going to work if they send someone over to do a serious search?"

"No, but a fake file in the safe, plus the fact that the dossier is taped in the hollow of the drywall above the safe, might."

"Hmmm...maybe. In any case, you need me to get the file?"

"The sooner, the better."

"Okay," said Blue. "That's something I understand. I'm on it."

"Be careful," advised Burton. "We've identified the leader of the group here in IU as Marda Mercedes, and from what we can tell, she's quite dangerous."

Blue shrugged. "Yeah, well, so am I."

Chip whipped off the headset, concern in his eyes. "Are you sure?"

Blue nodded. "Yep. You said it was a few blocks away, right? Just point me in the right direction. I'll be back in no time."

Chip hesitated. "Are you...do you want me to come with you?"

Blue smiled. "No, offense, great hunter, but you'll only slow me down. Besides, you'll do a lot more good in this pow-wow huddle." *I, on the other hand, need to get out of here before I go crazy.*

"But you don't know what you're walking into."

"Look, Chip, if I stop now to think about all the elements and ramifications of what we're dealing with—demons, souls, covens, Phil's life—I'm going to freak out, and I'll be useless to you."

Chip leaned back from the force of her outburst.

"You wanna know how I got through that night with Gunther's ghost? I didn't think about my mom having just died or what that would mean." Blue clenched her hands into fists. "I just focused on what had to happen next. Right now, I need to get a folder and bring it back to this house. That's what needs to happen. And I can do that." She drew a breath. "Just let me do that."

Chip looked away, clearly not happy. "All right. Be careful. Take your phone, and be back soon."

Blue offered a smile, hoping it reassured. "Sure. Show me where your tool kit is. I don't have my lockpicks with me–hell, I'm not even sure where they are these days. Packed away in New York, I guess. But I can make a couple of mini-screwdrivers work."

Chip nodded. "Right. Okay, follow me."

Moments later, in the garage, Chip handed Blue two mini screwdrivers from the toolbox. "Be careful, and call me if anything happens. This could be incredibly dangerous."

"I will, but you be careful, too." She leaned in and gave him a kiss she hoped he wouldn't forget for a long time.

CHAPTER THIRTEEN_

WHERE IS IT, you Kelranian bitch! Marda scanned the trashed great room. She'd torn open the couch, knocked over the bookshelves, gutted each thick book, amd punctured the walls.

With a swift kick of her combat boot, she sent the office chair tumbling across the room. She looked around the rented duplex.

The quaint, dark-wood cabinets and furnishings clashed with the modern track lighting and movie posters that once hung on the walls—before Marda had knocked them down. The sturdy wood front door opened into a modest sitting room with multiple bookshelves and chairs, retreating directly back to a dining room, with a swinging door to the kitchen beyond.

A hallway from the dining room breaking to the side and running parallel to the kitchen led to the only bathroom and two bedrooms. Efficient for two roommates without the extras. Small enough to search in about ten minutes.

Marda had been trashing it for over half an hour.

Given the stillness when she first entered, Marda was certain the connected neighbors had to be vacationing for the holidays. Now she knew it, because they would have called the police for certain, given the ruckus she'd made as her frustration built up.

Tricked! Even now, trapped in the game realm, Burton had found a way to trick them.

Somewhere here in the house, Rebecca and her right-hand woman, MacLeod, had stashed the damned Divenium Crystal. *So, where the hell is it!*

She returned to the larger of the two bedrooms, her eyes scanning the space, falling upon an antique ivory desk set against the far wall. She took in the art deco vanity next to it.

In the mirror, her angry face reflected back at her, including the distortion caused by her crinkled eyebrows. She knew about the safe behind the mirror, the red herring that had tricked Cyn and Van. She wouldn't waste time pursuing the same false lead.

She noted a conspicuous rectangular space of emptiness and the shifted dust outline on the desk's wooden surface, indicating a PC or laptop computer that likely filled the spot a few hours earlier, a computer now confiscated by the local police.

A computer that almost certainly had no information of any real use.

No, the file is still here. Someplace hidden. Someplace tricky.

A rattling of wood–the door from the back of the house–froze her in place. *What the...*

More noises. Metal against metal, and a doorknob being shaken, the frame straining to resist an intruder pressing from the other side. *The police!*

No, more likely, back-up agents sent by Burton to retrieve the folder before we obtain it. Burton had plenty of time to get a message out, something she could have set up before getting trapped in the virtual world.

Now that mechanism had been triggered, and Burton's backup had arrived.

Thank you, Goddess!

She reached to the sheath at her waist and gripped the hilt of her knife. She spied the bedroom closet.

She opened the door, pleased at the sparseness of clothes and personal items within, offering plenty of room to slip inside and wait.

All she needed to do was to bide her time until the newcomers retrieved the folder, then eliminate them.

———

Down on one knee, Blue wiggled the screwdriver tip under what she hoped was the final pin. She lifted it up flat and out of the way, pressing it flush with the others, then probed farther into the keyhole shaft. She tried to calm herself, control her anxious panting, and ignore the shakes in her hands.

Resistance, and nothing to pry. She'd reached the end, which should mean...

She extended the second tip into the keyhole and gave a simple twist.

The doorknob turned easily.

She gripped the doorknob and pulled the door open.

She waited, listening.

Nothing.

Her noisy lock-picking ruined any hope of surprise, but if the house was empty, as she hoped, it shouldn't matter.

Still, she couldn't ignore the possibility that someone had beaten her here and now waited inside to ambush her.

She reached down and retrieved the screwdrivers. She grinned. *I've still got it!*

She pocketed the tools and ran a sleeve across her forehead. *I haven't done that since...*

It always comes back to that *night, doesn't it?*

The door opened into a small kitchen with painted cabinets and an oven with four stovetop gas burners. The wood looked from an older home, while the spotty psychedelic patterned paint job, modern microwave, and espresso machine told the story of college-age renters going back decades.

All the cabinet doors had been flung open, and the pots and pans and cans tipped over or re-stacked haphazardly. Blue figured the police had gone through the cabinets and found nothing.

She pushed open the swinging door next to the oven, which opened out onto...*holy shit!*

A dining table, and beyond it, a ransacked front room. Destroyed. Furniture flipped, two bookcases toppled, office supplies, clothes, and doodads all vomited onto the floor, with coats dumped out before an open front closet.

She didn't know from firsthand experience, but she didn't think the police would leave chairs and closets turned out. *The desk chair, on the floor, sideways. Why not at least pick that up and put it back? Surely, it would potentially trip any sort of evidence team.*

And tearing books in half at their spine? That didn't strike her as a preferred method of a team search who had the space to themselves.

That's the act of someone in a hurry. Someone who doesn't care about inflicting damage.

She noted the hallway that presumably led to the bedrooms beyond. She closed her eyes and listened.

Just the rustling of grass, the heater powering up to blow dry air through old vents. *Creaky wood. What caused the creaking? Footsteps in the other room? Neighbors next door?*

Maybe, or maybe just the house settling.

Of course, that didn't mean anything. If the Sisterhood had taken the bait, they'd eventually figure out the switch and come back. *Either I beat them to it, or I didn't. If I didn't, it doesn't matter. If I did, I'm wasting precious time.*

Or...someone may be waiting here for me.

Still, standing here frozen, trying to calm her nerves, would not accomplish anything.

She looked down at her trembling hands like some sort of alien body part springing from her wrists. *Jesus, Blue, what's wrong with you? Why are you so rattled?*

The thought dawned on her that, screwdrivers aside, she'd come into the situation unarmed. She could hardly have brought her switchblade with her. There was just no getting around airport security with something like that.

Plus, why *would* she bring it? *This wasn't supposed to be* that *sort of a trip.*

She needed a weapon.

She didn't see the usual wooden block of steak knives, and opening a drawer revealed some silver butter knives and a couple smallish, serrated steak knives all the rage, she would have guessed, back in the 1960s.

I guess college kids don't leave steak knife sets behind. And just my luck, looks like Burton and MacLeod didn't eat in much.

She wrapped her fingers around the handle of one of the serrated blades. It would have to do.

She approached the bedroom door, scanning the hallway, and straining to listen for any unnatural sound.

Is someone there? She waited for telling creaks of wood, or other noises. Outside, a car passed by, and, a few houses away, slowed. The engine cut off. The age of the house pressed on her. *Better to just go and try to get the hell out.*

She threw open the door and looked along the wall. Her gaze traveled over the closed door of a closet. *Why is that door closed? Or am I second-guessing myself?*

If I check the closet, and someone's there, I might not be able to see what's coming toward me before it's too late. If I go across the room and let them think they can spring a trap, they'll have to come to get me. Do I trust my ability to fight my way out that much?

She did.

Besides, it may be nothing.

A queen-sized bed stretched out to her right, headboard against the far wall. The covers had been turned over to one side. She didn't see any pillows from where she stood.

Cautiously, dividing her attention between her goal and the closet behind her, she approached the vanity mirror over the ivory desk.

She gripped the left side of the mirror and pulled. It stuck tight.

Panic rushed through her. In the mirror, she saw her face flush. *What's up? Why won't it...*

She took a deep breath, reached to the right side of the mirror, and pulled.

The mirror gave easily, swinging on hinges.

Behind the mirror, she saw a literal hole in the wall. A fireproof combination lock safe sat upon the shelved alcove. The wall looked punched through with a hammer, maybe several blows of a hammer, jagged edges surrounding an opening just large enough to build a shelf and fit the safe.

She reached up and slipped her hand into the gap above the safe and encountered an open space in the drywall above it.

She extended her arm to the back wall, probing with her fingers. *Nothing there, but...*She turned her hand, reached and reached forward, pressing her palm to explore the back side of the nearer wall.

Aha! Something was taped against the inner wall, a package of some sort, exactly the size of a bulging folder. She could feel the masking tape straining over the bulk.

She gripped the bottom of the package and pulled.

The package tore away from the wall, and she lowered a red portfolio folder, bulging, with accordion sides, strips of tape still marring its surface. *Gotcha!*

She held the packet in one hand, patting at it with the other. Pieces of drywall dumped into the room, kicking up a cloud of white dust that made her eyes water.

She coughed and waved the envelope to clear the air.

"So!"

At the sound of the crazed voice, Blue startled. She turned.

Framed in the closet door stood a tall, long-haired brunette. She raised her arm, and the sunlight from the window glinted off a large, ornate blade.

Fuck...figures!

She gripped the handle of her own inadequate weapon, waiting for her opponent to make the first move.

To Blue's surprise, her inner panic subsided. She'd half-expected an ambush, but what she really feared was an ambush of superior numbers or greater skill.

Blue sized the stranger up. Whoever this woman was, she knew nothing about how to fight. She stood before Blue in an awkward stance, gripping the knife to come down overhand like a movie slasher instead of underhand for greatest effect.

A dumbass attack like that would be easy to avoid. Crazy, perhaps, but, she was certain, not skilled.

Still, she reminded herself, *overconfidence can also kill.*

The crazed look in the woman's eyes matched her zealous tone. "My Sisters were closer than they knew! Now I'll return with the real package, triumphant."

Blue placed the folder down on the desk and turned to face her opponent. "Marda, I've handled worse than you while hungover, 'Sister.' You'd better put that knife away before you get hurt."

Her opponent's eyes widened at the use of the name. "How did you..." Then she stopped short.

"Terrible poker face, Marda." Blue pressed forward, putting her body between the nut job and the folder. She'd faced down Gunther and the horrors of that night. This bitch wasn't even in the same league.

The woman extended her arm, palm out. "Hand over the folder, and maybe I'll let you live."

Blue kept her gaze on Marda's other hand, the one still gripping her knife. "Put the knife down. Maybe I won't take it before I break your nose."

With a guttural growl, the woman lunged, swiping the knife.

Blue stepped aside, let her own useless weapon fall to the floor, gripped the woman's arm with both of her hands, and pulled her close.

Blue twisted, propelled herself, using the full weight of her body to throw her adversary off balance.

They toppled. Blue's opponent slammed to the floor, only to have Blue's body come down on top of her.

The woman went slack.

Blue's hands gripped the wrist with the knife. She dropped into the crook of the woman's arm with her shoulder, pinning it under her.

Her opponent gasped, and Blue twisted.

They glared at each other, face-to-face.

Blue pinched her attacker's arm in a v-lock. In a quick move, Blue released her opponent's right hand and thrust her arm forward, palm-first, striking the woman's face.

Blue's blow struck the nose with a satisfying crunch.

Her opponent's yelp cut off short; her face jerked back. Blood gushed, and the woman's eyes watered.

Renewing her grip on the wrist, Blue shifted, bringing her weight full against the crook of the woman's arm. As the bone extended to the verge of fracture, the woman drew a sharp breath.

The woman's wrist twisted, waving the knife through the air.

Blue shook her head. The sound of her intense panting filled the room. *She's a feisty bitch, for all the good it'll do her.* "No, you don't!"

The woman fought, and Blue struggled to re-secure her grip, her breath coming in gasps from the exertion. But it wasn't much of a fight.

Blue gripped the wrist again and bent the arm one last time at the breaking point. "Enough. Drop...the...knife." She pressed.

The woman drew in a sharp breath.

"I'm not kidding you, bitch!"

With a cry of frustration, the woman let the knife fall to the ground. "Thank you."

Blue pivoted and thrust her elbow into the woman's face, connecting with her chin.

The woman coughed, then went slack.

Blue grabbed up the knife and rose to a crouch, holding the blade in one hand while she caught her breath.

But her caution wasn't necessary. The woman lay on the floor, blood sprayed against her nose, her arms and legs slack.

Blue stood, drawing air in deep gulps, waiting for her hammering heart to quiet.

The tussle had winded her more than it should have. *Good God, am I getting old?*

Her breathing steadied, so she stumbled to the desk, grabbed up the packet, and held it under her arm.

What to do? She couldn't carry the woman back to Chip's house. She didn't have time to interrogate her. *Like I even know what to ask.*

The woman moaned, and her eyes fluttered open.

Blue crouched, reached out with the knife, and pressed the edge under her neck.

They locked gazes, and Blue's inner voice spoke to her in a tempting whisper. *Just slice her throat. Leave her here. It would solve a lot of problems. Just do it.*

The thought repulsed her. *No!*

Blue flashed back to when she'd threatened Clinty, the school bully who harassed her and Chip back in Perionne, in a similar manner. The anger coursed through her that night, tangible, fierce. Clinty's fate rested in her hands. She'd wondered if she might not kill him, and she drank that power in like a drug.

Marda started to move.

Blue pressed the knife. "Don't try it."

Marda submitted, her body going slack.

This time, Blue felt no thrill, no power, only a profound sadness at seeing this lost woman.

A smile formed on Marda's face. "You're not...going to kill me. That's not what you do." Marda laughed. "You're too good, too...*merciful.*" Blood, which had leaked to her mouth from her nose, sprayed with her next words. "Too *weak.*"

Are you kidding me? Blue shook her head. "I am not *that* girl, I promise you."

"Then prove it. Kill me, if you're so strong."

Disgusted, Blue stood, drew her foot back and kicked the woman in the side.

She rolled over and curled up. The woman lay and struggled for air, too stunned to move.

It will have to do. Blue extended the envelope down, just within the woman's vision, shaking it like a cat owner teasing their pet. "Tell your people you failed. Tell them to forget whatever you have in mind and just get the hell out of here. We now have what you needed. You're not getting it back. Next time, I won't be so gentle."

Blue turned her back and stepped toward the door. As she exited the room, a mocking cry followed after her. "Coward."

CHAPTER FOURTEEN_

MADE IT! Blue burst into Chip's house, paused long enough to shut the front door, and made a beeline for the basement.

As she approached, the door opened.

Chip held his arms out in a hug, relief apparent on his face. "Thank God."

She all but dove into his arms, nuzzling her cheek against his chest and holding tight. Finally, she could allow her body to tremble. *Figures, now the shakes hit.*

"Hey...hey! Whoa, what happened?"

His hands gripped her shoulders and gently pushed her back.

She obliged, letting herself relax to his guidance so he could take a good look.

His eyes widened. "Oh, my God, are you hurt?"

She looked down at herself, startled to see red streaks across her denim jacket and t-shirt. *Blood.* "No, it's okay; it's her blood, not mine."

"Hers?"

Blue shrugged, hoping she projected unconcern. "One of the Baalin-istas or whatever. She tried to ambush me. Just let me clean up."

Chip continued to hover. "Are you sure?"

"Trust me, it might have been one of the most pathetic attempts at an assault in the history of assaults. And lookie," she pulled the dagger from the loop of her denim jeans, speckled with blood. "A souvenir." She extended the knife toward him.

"Oh, my God." His eyes widened. "You didn't..."

She realized how it looked and chuckled. "No, but it took all the reserve I had *not* to. She had no idea how outmatched she was. Even when I gave her a busted nose to remember me by. She bled all over the place, but I left her alive and probably very pissed off."

"She's going to be even more pissed off when she checks in with her coven."

The sheepish grin on Chip's face caught Blue's attention. *Oh-oh.* "What did you do?"

"The bitches hacked my game. *My* game." Chip jabbed his index finger back at himself.

She knew he had another revelation for her. "They dropped an unauthorized object into the code and used it before we knew about it."

"The SoulStaff, right?"

"So I found their hack and deleted the SoulStaff." He slapped his hands together and rubbed his fingers, a mimic of sprinkling magic dust. "Added a block to keep them from trying the same trick again."

"Oh." She raised a hand. "High five on that. So, is this over?"

He brushed his fingers against hers, causing an answering tingle down her spine she knew she should ignore.

Chip looked at the floor. "I'm afraid not."

"Why not?" She handed the folder to Chip.

"Because...no matter how awesome I think I am, I'm sure there are several more ways for them to hack the game that I'm not aware of. But, they have to re-render the SoulStaff, just as we have to render the crystal. Rather than them attacking us before we're ready, it's a dead heat as to who gets finished first."

Instead of heading directly downstairs, she decided to detour across the hall into the bathroom. She supposed that was good news, but she hoped to hear about a knockout punch that would end this craziness. "What's going on in the game now?"

She snapped on the light switch. The row of light globes over the bathroom mirror illuminated a pea-green sink, matching walls, toilet lid cover, and the clear plastic curtain cupping the shower.

"We've kind of camped out by the large oak tree. If the Sisterhood wants to come in and get to Baalina, they have to come through us. In the meantime, the group has been dueling like crazy."

At Blue's confused look, Chip clarified, "It's formalized practice, built into the game so players practice fighting in the game. In this case, they're using it to get used to their virtual bodies." Chip opened a linen closet and handed her a washcloth. "It's...well, it's quite impressive, actually."

"How so?" She turned on the cold water, dropped the washcloth into the basin, and pulled the drain stop to let it fill.

She looked at herself in the mirror. A distinct splatter of blood had sprayed her across the face and neck. Possibly her hair, as well. She squinted at her blue locks...*well, three-quarters blue with dark roots.*

She saw no obvious signs of blood splatters in her hair and figured daily shampooing would clean what she couldn't see. She assessed her clothes.

Ick. Streaks marred the chest of her Paramore t-shirt. It looked badass, but she sure didn't want to wear it much longer.

Chip extended the dagger, handle-first, at her. "Well...it's clear that Rebecca, Phil, and MacLeod have a huge advantage by virtue of having bonded with their avatar, at least in terms of combat. Phil could never beat me when we'd battle in 'mock-duel mode' the standard way, with both of us using the keyboard."

She gripped the blade just long enough to drop it back into the water, using the washcloth to scrub it clean. "And?"

"And, he's wiped the floor with me in over thirty fights now. I don't mean by a little bit, either. We have no way to be sure, but I'd say Phil's character's reflexes have improved forty to sixty percent, maybe more."

She held the blade up, now clean and ready to drip-dry. *Gorgeous.* The ornate, hand-carved handle fit her palm comfortably.

She examined the ivory hilt and traced her thumb along a hand-carved symbol, like an ornate X. A sigil, she guessed. *Baalina, I presume? These ladies may be warped psychos, but they make an incredible weapon.*

The business end extended about six inches, fine metal, thin, razor sharp...She held it up, vertical and eye level. Perfectly straight. It didn't look manufactured. Custom-made by an expert craftsman, she was sure of it.

*Most likely a crafts*woman, she realized. Between what Agent Burton had said and hearing the woman's rants for herself, she suspected the Baalina-ettes followed a strict, no-testosterone policy.

Too bad I didn't think to take the sheath, as well.

Her mind returned to the conversation. Chip was still moaning about Phil kicking his ass. "Maybe you're just tired."

Chip shook his head. "Don't get me wrong. Yes, I'm tired, but truthfully, Phil likes programming the games a lot more than he enjoys playing them. He just isn't very good."

"You might still be having a bad day."

Chip sighed. "Rebecca, who told me she logs on only when she has to, was also experimenting with combat. She trounced my ass a few times, too."

"Oh." She cut off the cold water and looked at her reflection in the mirror. She really had no choice but to ditch the shirt and soak it. She thought she might be able to spot-clean the jacket, though. "Well...that could be good for our side when it comes down to it."

The look on Chip's face, reflected in the mirror, drew her attention to him. "What?"

Chip looked away. "Nothing."

Nothing, my ass. She knew the look of someone who wanted to approach a subject but didn't know how to start. "Hey, I need to change this shirt." She let the denim jacket fall past her shoulders, offering her best come-on smile. "Be a dear, go downstairs and fetch me a new one from my backpack, and I'll let you watch."

Chip was already on his way at the words "I'll let you."

The thump-thump-thump of descending feet racing down the basement stairs reached her, and she let out a stress-relieving giggle. *And I almost let this dear, dear guy go. What the hell was I thinking?*

———

Marda Mercedes braced herself in the chair. Her hand gripped Van's, and her legs pressed into the cement floor. Behind her, Van's other hand stroked her hair.

Cyn looked down on her with a stone-cold, unreadable expression. "It's going to hurt like hell."

Marda gulped, trying to control the trembling in her voice. "I know that. You already told me. Just do it."

"I mean, it's *really* going to hurt like hell." If Cyn felt any satisfaction at the cruel trick fate had played upon them, she gave no indication.

Deep down, Marda had no doubt Cyn would enjoy every second of what would follow. Marda wiped the back of her hand across her forehead, swiping cold, clammy perspiration. "You just told me the cartilage shifted out of alignment, and there's no chance it will heal properly without shifting it back." She tried to ignore the nasal quality of her own voice in her head. "I intend to rule, regal and unscarred, beside the mistress. As will we all. Do it. Besides, you owe me a little pain. Don't tell me you can't appreciate what's happened."

Cyn nodded and lowered both hands toward Marda's face. She allowed a half-smile to creep over her features.

Marda tried and failed to keep a shiver out of her voice with her next words. "Just promise me you and Van will use your expertise to deliver a payback in full for all that we've suffered."

"She shall suffer as no one has."

The cracking noise was lost to a blast of blinding pain. Her world exploded in white stars.

Marda screamed, a shriek of agony that did nothing to help her. Her body spasmed.

A moment later, she opened her eyes. Her breathing forced from her in pants. She realized she'd have fallen out of the chair if Van hadn't held her up, both hands on her shoulders, steadying her. "Goddess!"

Cyn extended a bottled water. "Easy, it's over. It's still going to hurt, but you got through the worst of it." She knelt down.

Marda noted how Cyn's gaze scanned her face like she controlled some personal, built-in targeting.

"It looks straight now. I think that did it. I hope so. I can't imagine you want to do that again."

"No!" She spat the next words at Cyn. "And you'd better have not done it wrong on purpose just to..." She stopped herself.

Van's hands squeezed a warning against Marda's shoulders.

For the first time, Van spoke, her breath hissing in Marda's ear. "My partner and I have been gracious and loyal to your every whim, Priestess. If our service has been less than perfect, we have always acted with the best intentions and without subterfuge."

Cyn punctuated her partner's thought. "Your words could be interpreted as...disingenuous." She let the veiled threat hover.

Marda looked at the floor. She wanted to rise from the chair, strike these two down, and punish them because she couldn't punish the blue-haired bitch who'd humiliated her and put her in this position. That they'd refrained from treatong her the way she'd treated them only added to her shame.

But she needed these two. She waited and took time to swallow back her anger before she spoke again. "Forgive me. Forget my words." She drew a deep, calming breath. "It was the pain talking."

———

Blue descended the stairs into the basement, dressed in a new t-shirt after having left her denim jacket upstairs to dry.

Her body still tingled from the recent manhandling. They'd only had time for a couple minutes of petting, but it was *very friendly* petting, and she made sure to include a promise of much more to come in every kiss she returned. *Damn the crisis.*

Ultimately, Chip had to be the voice of reason–*who knew?* Blue was willing to risk it, but he reminded her it was his best friend in jeopardy. They were racing the clock, and they had so much to do. *And he's right. Damn it all.*

They ended in a hug. He trembled against her, and the evidence of his arousal did not escape her notice, even as she quivered against him.

She spoke against his chest. "You're going to be in *such* trouble."

"Bring it on," he said into her hair. "Just...not yet."

She pushed him away and grabbed for her shirt. "We need to stop now, or I won't."

"I know." Chip held the red portfolio up. "I'll be downstairs speed reading this."

She grabbed up her new shirt. Lady Gaga stared back at her, a dagger shoved into her abdomen, a black-and-white screen image oozing gray blood against a black shirt. *Glad to see this crisis has not deterred Chip's sense of irony.*

In the basement, across the room, Chip sat on the cloth recliner. He'd already removed a stack of papers. Next to him, Phil's body lay on the couch, his annoying and regular snores making it unnecessary to check if he was still breathing. Blue's gaze locked onto the fist-sized, brilliant red transparent gem. The center glowed angry crimson, seemed to pull all light from the surrounding space, and cast a blood-red tinge throughout the room.

In spite of herself, Blue walked over to the chair. She reached down and wrapped her fingers around the gem. Despite its appearance, the crystal lay in her hand comfortably, lightweight and cold to the touch. "It's incredible."

She shifted the stone, letting it lay in her palm. She sensed, intuitively, that the ruby could do serious damage if she lost her mind and struck someone with it.

Her fingers traced a set of runes carved into the face, sharp, laser-accurate lines that she was certain were etched hundreds of years before laser technology. The runes followed the circumference of the gem while encircling a larger symbol in the center of the ruby face. The etching felt new and deep under her thumb.

Chip nodded. "You don't know the half of it. Apparently, Brother Andrew Kelran himself of the Kelranian Order engraved the symbols onto the gem face using white magic."

"I can believe it." She ran her finger across the surface. "Wait, Kelranian, what's that?" She recalled the psycho woman had called her a Kelranian bitch. *Might as well find out if I need a special jersey or something.*

Chip shrugged. "The simple answer? They're team Burton."

"Well, I guess that's the team that drafted us, then, so the woman who attacked me got that much right. So, what are they again? I mean, what does our side represent? Truth, justice, and the American way, right?"

Chip's eyebrows rose on his head, and if he had any further questions, he kept them to himself. "The Kelranian Order is an ancient secret network of white sorcerers." He looked up and smirked, waiting.

Blue met his gaze. "Go on."

"Okay. So...you don't need time to absorb that?"

Blue shrugged. "You're talking to Ms. Fought a Ghost on a Roller Coaster here. It's taking a lot to faze me these days."

His eyes returned to the paper. "So, the Kelranian Order traces itself back to the sixth century, formed by Merlin during the reign of King Arthur."

Blue raised a hand. "Okay, wait. Just to be clear. *The* Merlin."

"Yes."

"*The* King Arthur."

The twinkle in Chip's eyes betrayed his amusement. "That's what it says."

"Just checking. Go on."

Chip looked back down at the file. "Anyway, according to legend, the original group began as an alliance between Christian monks and

Avalon druids, intent on finding a balance between the white magic of the ancient practices and growing Christianity."

Blue raised her hand. "Sorry, I'm behind on my Dungeons & Dragons speak. Druids are…?"

"In this context, the druids are the women sorcerers who lived on the isle of Avalon. Among their feats, they trained Merlin and practiced white magic in the service of Arthur. The Lady of the Lake was an Avalon druid. She was the guardian of Excalibur, Arthur's enchanted sword."

"Right," said Blue, remembering the old Disney cartoon and several classic paintings. "The girl's arm rising out of the water."

Chip shrugged. "Not likely a literal arm in the water, but yes. Anyway, as Christianity spread, one interpretation of the legend says the magic of Avalon dwindled and the druids vanished from existence along with the island itself."

"Wow, that's gratitude for you." Blue motioned toward the report. "But the file says?"

"Oh, the file has no comment on the legend. Only that a handful of druids allied themselves with the monks to help form the Kelranian Order." Chip turned a page. "Those must have been some interesting board meetings," he quipped. "The druids drew power from nature and from themselves, which would have clashed with a monotheistic belief system. But through cooperation and experimentation, they generated a potent form of white magic."

Blue scoffed. "Yeah, whatever. Isn't that the way it always works for the girl? Eve ate the apple, and everyone gets kicked out of paradise. Lot's wife takes a peek and gets turned to salt. Mary Magdalene is the only woman disciple of the Jesus gang, and everyone thinks she's a prostitute. Oh, except there's nothing in writing that supports this, but it sure makes for a great story." Blue rolled her eyes. She knew she was venting on her soapbox, but she couldn't help herself.

Chip bristled. "Well, okay, maybe. Can I finish now?"

"Sorry."

"The Kelranians continued to operate, always in secret. They created a tight network of white wizards throughout Europe, and eventually, the entire world. A few rode over on the Mayflower. A few more after that. It's probably no surprise to know that the Kelranians helped spearhead the witch trial paranoia in Salem."

"Oh, another black mark in history where innocent women were killed for no good reason."

Chip glanced at a page, hesitating. "Well..."

Blue waited. "What?"

"Maybe not so much. I mean...maybe not in *every* case."

Blue tossed the crystal up and down in a mock threat. "Really? Salem was infiltrated with Satanists? Bullshit. Wiccans, maybe." Blue knew a couple of Wiccans in her poetry classes who lamented about how, throughout history, their kind were frequently mistaken for devil worshippers and executed. "Wiccans are generally harmless, and Wiccans aren't Satanists."

"Hey, you're the one who said you could handle anything I threw at you. The Kelranian Order, *today*, is made up of white sorceresses...modern druids who trace their lineage back to Avalon."

"Really?" Blue considered. "Well...good, then. Maybe that's kind of cool."

"In fact..." Chip hesitated. "According to this file, Ms. Burton falls right in line with that lineage. It says in here she's the final product of some sort of combination white magic spell and genetic manipulation called the...*Tesh Ka Ra*."

"And that's what?"

Chip flipped through a few pages, forward, backward, then finally shrugged. "Doesn't say. It seems intra-organizational, like they expected anyone who might read it to know. From the context, though, I'd say it was some sort of multi-generational breeding program or something within the Order. And it appears Rebecca is either the most current prodigy in the line, or...the end result of it."

"So, Rebecca is...some sort of super-sorceress?"

Chip smiled. "That's how I read it."

Blue shook her head. "Ms. I-blundered-into-a-trap-and-got-my-ass-turned-into-a-video-game-character...is some sort of super-sorceress?"

"Well, now that you put it that way..."

Blue rubbed her eyes. The adrenaline rush had left her drained but otherwise accepting most of the craziness Chip was dumping on her. "I still say that most of the women condemned for witchcraft in Salem were innocent nannies burned at the stake because some Puritan patriarch was covering up his adulterous affair." She jabbed a finger at him.

Chip looked back, stone-faced. "Probably, doesn't matter."

"Humph. Anything else?"

From the expression on Chip's face, she knew what he would say. "Oh, yes. A whole lot more. But rather than repeat myself, how about you get online while I finish reading, and I'll update everyone at once?"

With some reluctance, Blue put the jewel back on the couch and turned her back to it.

She seated herself at the left side linked console, next to the offline computer. She thought of the console as "her" spot, even though she'd only played one game session on it.

She logged in to the game and adjusted the headset and mouthpiece while she waited for the screen to boot up to show the over-the-shoulder view of Daria, still standing outside the tavern where she'd left the avatar over twenty-four hours ago. She noted, peripherally, that Chip logged on to his computer.

She guided Daria into the tavern and found herself the only CGI character in the building except a non-playing character bartender. *Wow, holiday break, just like real life.*

Chip leaned over from his chair. "Exit and go due north according to your mini-map. You'll find everybody else clustered together by the tree." He pressed a button and spoke into his mic. "She's on her way."

She walked Daria out of the bar, across the cobblestone path out of town, and into the woods. She noted the lack of any other player characters. *Well, of course. Everyone else is eating turkey and spending time with family like any other normal person.*

After a couple-minute walk through the woods, a cluster of CGI fantasy characters came into view near an oversized tree. On her screen, she recognized Phil's familiar wizard Magtog, the angel warrior Burton, the lady knight Skye, and Chip's thief, looking decidedly lacking in armor compared to this motley crew.

Blue looked away from the screen to see the real Chip. "Don't you have any, I don't know, barbarian characters for backup?"

Chip shrugged. "I wouldn't underestimate the ability to slip a knife into the joints of a suit of armor. I can hold my own in this game pretty well."

At the same time, wizard Phil extended a hand while his voice spoke through the speakers. "Glad you made it back, Blue."

Skye added, "It's been a little while since you'd left; we were starting to get concerned."

Rebecca's voice rode over the others. "Did you get the file and the gem?"

All business, Blue mused.

Chip spoke into his mic, his voice now coming through her headphones. "Yes, she got it. I've been reading the file."

Rebecca didn't respond right away, and all heads, one by one, turned toward her.

Finally, she said, "I'd have rather I guided you through some key points."

In her peripheral vision, Chip shook his head, an action that did not translate to his avatar, though the tone of his voice made his meaning plain. "If you want my help, we're going to do things my way."

Blue turned to take in Chip directly. *Well, look at Chip! You go, my man!* Her gaze drifted down to where she imagined a pair of huge cartoon testicles visibly enlarged his pants. She stabbed her mute button so no one in the game heard her stifled giggle.

Rebecca considered, the white wings protruding from her back twitching in apparent consternation. "Fair enough, but there are some confidential matters I may not be able to answer."

Chip adjusted his microphone. "You mean, like the references to *Tesh Ka Ra*?"

Could a CGI character blush? Because Blue was certain Burton's did exactly that.

No doubt about it, the angel-warrior started pacing back and forth, and as she spoke, her voice cracked. "Mr. Farren, you have me at a disadvantage, but that is a topic I'm not..." She stopped, and her eyes stared at the ground.

Blue pressed mute. "Shit, you hit a nerve!"

Chip raised his hand for silence. Perhaps he was afraid Blue's voice might carry over to his mic.

Rebecca tried again. "The details regarding the Tesh Ka Ra are...on a need-to-know basis. I'm asking you to respect that."

Skye cut in. "For what it's worth, I've been working alongside Rebecca all semester and I have no idea what you're talking about."

From where Blue sat, Chip looked like some sort of TV prosecutor chasing a lead, his face reflecting a mixture of professionalism and barely contained excitement. All wasted on the avatars. "I just have to wonder. If you're one of the good guys, like you say, why are you being so secretive?"

The angel looked decidedly flustered. "Listen, Mr. Farren, even if I told you exactly what you wanted to know, it won't do you any good, here and now, in this situation. But I have never pretended to be anything other than what I am, a government agent with security clearances that give me access to certain privileged information, and if–"

"Bullshit you're just a government agent."

Chip's bold, open call-out left Blue's head spinning. *Oh, my God, Chip, what kind of strategy is this?*

"And if..." Burton continued, raising her voice, "I know anything relevant to help us, you have my word I'll share it immediately. I want to get out of this as much as you do, Mr. Farren, but inquiries about the Tesh Ka Ra are simply a waste of everyone's time."

Chip sighed, his face betraying frustration. He stabbed the mute and shot Blue a look. "She's full of shit. There's something *huge* she's not telling us."

Blue placed a hand on his shoulder. "I know, but...what I do believe is...she's trapped, and she's scared, and she doesn't like not being in control. I don't think she'll respond well to threats."

Chip blew off a long sigh. "She's probably right. It's not relevant right now, but I'd sure like to know what she was genetically bred for."

Blue grinned at him. "Relax. A multi-generational breeding program to be the best video game player doesn't seem likely."

Chip chuckled and stabbed a button. "Okay, for now, Ms. Burton. But there is a story in the file I think everyone needs to hear. The story of what exactly happened in 1797. I'd like to share that."

The tension between the virtual world and the outside hung, palpable, as the group waited for Burton's answer.

Burton's avatar held her palms out and open in a shrug. "You may proceed."

Chip gently laid a couple of pages across his keyboard and squinted at the type. "According to this, the Kelranian Order barely stopped the coven from opening a doorway from the chaos realm to the physical realm, which would have allowed the demoness Baalina to enter our world at a time when humans could not have possibly fought against her. The Kelranians barely managed to stop her, but not without a terrible sacrifice..."

CHAPTER FIFTEEN_

Louisville, Kentucky, 1797

Brother James Krane of the Kelranian Order rubbed his hands over the fire in the makeshift pit created to stave off the bitter cold. He squatted near the warmth, waiting with growing impatience for his allies to arrive. Darkness closed around him like a stifling shroud, and he couldn't shake the feeling of exposure, of being an easy target to be swept aside if the Sisterhood approached before they were ready.

He rubbed his hands over his tiny, inadequate flames, noting how his skin poked through his thread-bare gloves, coverings long overdue to be replaced. Just one more menial task forever on his errand list that he'd never gotten around to against the greater goals of his mission. He thanked the Lord that the chase had moved him out of Salem and a bit south. Just a bit. Though the cold made his fingers ache, 'twas nothing compared to the bitter chill of a Massachusetts November.

He'd received the message from his contact three nights ago. Sister Minerva Crystin, a Kelranian agent operating deep undercover within the Baalina cult, planned to break her cover and meet him here. She'd specified this tree, a large, pock-holed monster of an oak that dwarfed the rest of the forest for its height and girth. If all proceeded as planned, she'd rendezvous with him shortly before the Sisters made their move, presumably with adequate time for James and Minerva to mount their defense.

Two against—who knew how many? Rumor speculated as few as five and as many as dozens. In spite of their success in planting Minerva among their number, their intimacy...or perhaps the tightness of their surveillance measures...meant that even one of his most trusted agents could send only small bits of intelligence.

But their plan rested on one other contingency, spelled out in the decoded message. Brother Krane had retrieved it personally and brought the item with him. Now brought to mind, Krane reached into the pocket of his layered garment and removed the lump that lay within. As he held it in his palm, the stone radiated its own heat, right through the cloth rags he'd wrapped it in.

He unwrapped the stone, and, moments later, the Divenium Crystal lay, exposed and glowing, where it caught the light from the fire, the woods, even the stars, and bathed the area in a hue the color of blood.

Movement! Krane turned toward the shifting branches at the edge of the woods. A cloaked, shadowy figure stepped out and stopped at the perimeter of the fire.

Too late, Krane threw the rag over the crystal and reached for his staff. *Stupid! If this is a Baalina witch seeking to steal the crystal...*

"Put your staff down, Krane."

Krane released his held breath, and he swallowed, waiting for the pounding of his heart to subside. *Minerva!* He'd recognize his erstwhile partner's sarcastic tone anywhere.

The woman lowered her cloak to reveal a head capped by close-cropped, bright red hair that surrounded severe lines etching a serious face. The amused twinkle in her eyes softened her features. "I broke ranks and beat the Sisterhood by several minutes. Fortunate for you!" She motioned to the bundle in his hand. "What sort of lapse of senses would possess you to expose the Divenium Crystal like that?"

Even the druid's chastising sounded as music to his ears. *Thank the*

Lord she slipped away! She is safe! He held his arms out, and she stepped forward, inviting his embrace. As he shivered here in the cold, he welcomed her warm, returning hug. Moments later, he kissed her forehead and muttered a blessing before they separated. As he held her face in his gaze a moment longer, he noted strands of gray about her temples he'd not noticed before but knew better than to mention them.

Her flashing eyes, normally bright green, appeared as a pink haze in this light. Nevertheless, he recognized a similar relief in her look. "It's good to see you again, James."

Krane nodded in her direction. "I won't lie. Months ago, when I heard the Order chose to send you to the Sisters, I feared I might never see you again."

"Really?" A suspicious expression passed over her face in the fire-light. "I'd heard you co-signed the order to approve the choice."

His eyes focused on the fire before him. He dared not look at her while she spoke her words, part question, part accusation. He hoped the amber aura hid the flush he knew had come to his face.

He had never lied to her before, and he would not start now. "It's true. Although I wanted you safe, I couldn't let my personal feelings get in the way when I knew you were the best person to send."

He dared to sneak a glimpse at her. She'd also given her attention to the fire. Apparently, she found this conversation as distasteful as he. Her hair, bright red even in normal daylight, now glowed with an inner intensity. He cleared his throat. "Forgive me?"

"Of course. I am the most gifted of the Order, man or woman. It's nice to hear an acknowledgement of that fact, even in private."

"That's not fair, Minerva. I speak highly of your gifts to the High Council."

"You mean the Brothers-Only meetings to which your Avalon, druid-descended allies are not privy."

He opened his mouth to object.

She extended her palm and shook her head. "Never mind. I must ask you to forgive me, James. The months I've spent amongst the Sister-hood have proven...trying. Their extreme views can wear a woman down, especially a woman of independence trying to find her full potential in a patriarch's government."

James cringed. In the years they'd worked together, she'd never addressed her heritage as a direct descendant of the Avalon druids so directly. "You know I hold you in the highest regard, Sister Minerva."

Minerva returned a smile of pink teeth that would have gleamed deadly white in normal light. "As you should, Brother Krane. As you well know you should." She held out her hand. "The crystal. Give it to me. Time grows short, and we must set up our defenses here."

Krane deposited the crystal in her hand, happy to be rid of the burden. Between the two of them, he had no illusions as to who better manipulated the white magiks, and he was glad to pass on the responsibility to his trusted ally.

Minerva stepped before the oak tree and placed the crystal on the ground before it. She twisted the crystal against the soil, securing the base in the damp dirt. Her head tilted back, taking in the magnificence of the naturally grown structure before them. "The Baalina Sisterhood chose a good tree, one ancient and full of Earth magiks."

Krane swallowed back a reply. Unlike the druids, who attributed the source of white magiks to the gifts of the Earth, the monks credited the One True God as the source of all power, including any gifts yielded by the Earth which the god had made. The Kelranian Order had ended that division of "old thinking" and "new thinking" by embracing their differences as a matter of semantics.

Brother Krane was quite comfortable with this compromise, especially whenever he witnessed Minerva's superior handling of the white magiks.

Minerva waved her hand, palm down, at the crystal. As she chanted in an ancient language known well to her people and the few descendants of her generation, the inner light intensified. "Fortunately, the tree has more than plenty of power for everyone."

"Oh, I don't know," said Krane. "It might have been nice to drain the tree ahead of time so its power would be useless by the time the Sisterhood arrived."

Minerva cringed and glared. "Your kind claim to treasure the world the Creator gave you, yet your every statement speaks otherwise. To drain the tree and leave it an empty shell would be a colossal waste and a tragedy."

Embarrassed, Krane said nothing. He feared to provoke her, knowing her powers could be the difference between their mutual destruction and actually surviving this night. Minerva's attitude confused him. As a rule, Avalon druids didn't express their frustrations so openly.

If they both survived this night, he would have to discuss this with her further.

Minerva continued to chant. The lilting progression soared and swirled around the campfire. The sounds soothed and emboldened Krane in the certainty of their victory, pushing aside all doubts of the righteousness of their stance. As she sang, the crystal's inner light grew, engulfing the tree, the fire, and the two figures beneath it. The shadows of the surrounding forest fled, exposing bare the branches and hiding places of the area around them.

Krane noted that the advantage of stealth was now lost on both sides. Not that it mattered. They knew the Sisters of Baalina approached, just as they were equally certain that the Kelranians waited to block them.

Her eyes now aflame, her hair and robes fluttering beneath the power of her spell, Minerva paused in her chanting to address him directly in a commanding tone. "Prepare yourself, as I have prepared myself, Brother Krane. We haven't much time."

She stepped forward and lowered her voice to a more conversational level. Apparently, whatever spells had been cast could attend to themselves. "Listen to me and obey. The protection spell I've cast will not likely hold. If the Baalina Sisterhood succeeds in creating their portal into Chaos to draw out the demoness, our only chance to defeat them is to destroy their SoulStaff and then use the crystal to close the portal. One of them, the elder, Mother Katka, most likely, will wield an ornate redwood staff covered in runes. On my word, use the fire spell I taught you and burn the staff. Don't worry about the woman holding the staff, and don't worry about her companions. You must assure your shot is true, and that you incinerate that staff. Do you understand?"

Krane nodded. "Gladly, Minerva. I am honored to assist you." He paused to recall the chant Minerva taught him over a decade ago, back when he was newly indoctrinated into the Kelranians and submitted himself as her student to learn the intricate art of white magik.

The words came to him, and he began to chant. As the words flowed from him, the power of his defenses grew, even as sparks of white magik lit up his fingertips.

Minerva held her hands out before her. A panel of magik energy, its border glowing purple, flickered in the space before her. "If they open the portal...closing the portal will require a sacrifice. James...if my words seem...bitter, and out of character, it's because I'm preparing myself for what must be done."

Growing alarm overrode the coaxing peace of the magik. "No. You can't."

"It's not your decision to make, old friend. Do not interfere."

Off in the distance, Brother Krane could barely make out the silhouettes of three indistinct figures closing in. The crystal's light caused distended, distorted shadows to streak away and behind their forms.

Minerva's gaze met Krane's. "Brace yourself, James." In spite of her grim words, her fiery eyes flickered with confidence.

Before them, three cloaked women approached. The center figure, stooped and trailing behind her two escorts, held before her a large staff. Brother Krane presumed the gender of these foes, even though he had no visual evidence to support it.

As if the witch in the middle could read his mind, it extended a gnarled hand, reached up, and pulled her cloak back from her head to reveal the weathered face of a gray-haired woman. Still, her voice bridged the distance in a confident tone. "So...'Sister' Minerva! You now reveal your true allegiance. That betrayal comes with a severe price, bitch! Tonight, you will bask in the bitter wine of your own destruction."

If the demon worshipper's threat had affected Minerva, Krane could hear no trace of it in her reply.

"Whereas, I will offer what mercy I can for you and your poor, wretched followers." Minerva raised her arms, and her voice traveled upon the wind, amplified and chilling. "Deluded fools, lower your weapons, do not let the trickster Baalina continue to veil your eyes. Leave her to the Chaos realm she placed herself in centuries ago when she first defied the greatest power."

Brother Krane, moved by his comrade's words, called out, "She has no power over you except that which you willingly give to her in exchange for her empty promises."

"How dare you!" The woman to Mother Katka's right lowered her cloak to reveal a head covered by dark hair and holding equally cold, dark eyes. "The man next to the traitor now speaks of empty promises!"

A high, lilting laugh pierced the air. To Krane's left, the other escort raised a delicate hand to uncover a blonde head of hair, pale, almost luminescent skin, and glowing blue eyes. "What did you expect, Sister? Men through the centuries know how to speak empty promises so well."

In spite of himself, Krane found his gaze traveling up and down the form of the light-skinned woman, appalled by her transparent fury and utter contempt.

The woman reached down and placed a hand upon her hip, letting the cloak nip in upon her shape. She met his gaze with a cruel smile. "Tell us, 'Brother.' Tell us how men speak meaningless oaths words to gullible girls to get what they want. Demonstrate your talents, sir. Entertain us with your meaningless words."

Krane felt his face flame at her accusation. "Damn you, witch, I have never...I don't–"

Minerva cut in, her voice still overpowering the others. "Do not let these girls trouble you, Brother Krane. They have spent their lives assaulted by tricks and lies. Tonight, they lie to themselves. You don't owe them an answer, just pity them for the lost souls they are."

By now, they'd closed the distance to a few dozen feet. The group of three stopped, staring across the open plain to the two guardians waiting on the other side of the firepit, prepared and ready to defend the great tree.

The silence elongated as neither side dared move or speak.

Krane knew he should be terrified, scared and on the verge of wanting to flee. And yet, he waited, calm, ready, and willing to die this day if that was what his Lord demanded of him.

The old lady broke the silence, her voice a dry cackle. "It is you who will need pity soon, Sister Minerva Crystin. Pity for choosing your impotent ally, and pity for what we shall do to you when you lie helpless before us, unable to defend against our whims. You have no idea how much our order delights in the suffering of our enemies. I look forward to showing you tonight."

Katka and Minerva glared at each other across the distance. It was Katka who broke off, shifting her gaze to meet the eyes of the only man in this contest.

Krane felt his blood chill under the weight of her stare.

"What do you say, 'Brother?' My Sisters can introduce you to the pleasures of our company. I noticed you appreciating the charms of Sister Gwendolyn. She would reward your cooperation, and perhaps we would let you live long enough to witness the birth of your daughter."

Brother Krane grimaced, trying to cover his shock and his morbid fascination with their antics. If this was where he would make his last stand, then he had made his peace.

He would not dignify Katka's mockery of an offer with a reply. Instead, he leaned toward Minerva. "Do they plan to talk us to death?"

"They hope to distract us while Mother Katka sets up her spell. Prepare yourself. Our spell will protect our souls from being drained, but I can't help everyone. The entire village to the west, for instance. Their souls will be pulled from their bodies and claimed by the staff.

But if you can enflame it on my mark, the souls should be released back to the bodies just as quickly."

"Should? Are you certain?"

Minerva shrugged. "As well as I reasonably can be, James. How does one put such ideas to a test?"

As Krane pondered his answer, the old witch screeched, her command to attack riding upon the wind.

The women on either side of Mother Katka both motioned with their hands. Dark blue streaks of energy lit up the night, closing the distance like bolts of lightning toward Minerva and Krane.

Both bolts struck a panel of white energy, which lit up into a visible glow on impact and vanished a moment later.

Krane blinked spots from his eyes. The flashes of light from their opponents' hands had nearly blinded him. He uttered a swift prayer of thanks. *Thank God Minerva raised those ahead of time. I would never have seen that coming.*

The women shifted their stance in a coordinated motion, letting loose a second barrage of dark magik bolts, then a third. The barriers lit up as each wave struck in their turn, but they held.

Out of reflex more than fear, Brother Krane took a few steps back while he chanted his own offensive energy spell. Growling on the last syllable, he thrust his fist toward the grimacing brunette.

The projectile blast of energy shot from his hand and traveled in a slow, unsteady arc at his intended target.

She stepped to one side, dodging easily.

Frustrated, Brother Krane pumped both fists, sending one energy blast, then the other, toward her.

She stood her ground, watching his energy slap the ground without useful effect.

Before she could react, he punched the air a third time, sending a bolt traveling at twice the speed directly at her.

For just a moment, Krane glimpsed the look of shock on his opponent's face before his blast knocked into her.

The bolt struck with a stunning force, and her body collapsed to the ground.

In the meantime, the blonde had broken into an intricate attack dance, combining lunges and attacks. As she cut the air with a series of grunts, bolt after deadly bolt came at him.

Each bolt, in their turn, impacted against the shield.

Krane turned his attention to the old woman.

She'd planted the staff into the ground, and the sound of her crackling chant broke in on the tranquility of the forest, as if some great force sought to gut the forest itself.

The woman croaked in an ancient language Brother Krane did not recognize, and, as of this moment, vowed to never learn. The staff glowed, its carved runes along the sides illuminating the night a putrid green color.

The attractive woman had stopped her elaborate attacks and stood, a look of frustration marring her face. The old witch broke her chant and called out to her companion, the blonde. "Charge at the man directly, Gwen! The Kelranian witch's shield will block your energy attacks for hours, but it won't block your physical body! Kill him!"

Krane watched, panic welling up within him, as the blonde woman reached to her side and withdrew a small, nasty-looking object. Even in the near-darkness, he recognized the reflective silver edge of a dagger extending from a pale handle that fit comfortably in her grip. *She's coming for me!*

Sure enough, Gwen ran at him, closing the distance rapidly.

Krane fought back growing panic and called out, "Minerva? Is she right?"

"I'm afraid so! Prepare to defend yourself."

"But I have no weapon!"

"Then, as a man, use your natural superiority to overcome her. Or perhaps the defensive techniques I taught you."

Sarcasm? Now? Really? Krane bent his knees and raised his arms, hoping to throw her when she closed in.

Gwen, a dark-cloaked projectile picking up speed, cleared the energy shield without so much as a stagger.

Brother Krane braced himself for the attack. "That's not very damn funny!"

He had no time for further banter. He watched the hand with the knife raise and prepared to grab at it. At the same time, he pumped his feet backward a few steps to lessen the impending tackle.

As her body slammed into him, he reached up, his hand gripping the hand with the knife. At the same time, he kicked back. They fell together beyond the large tree into the brush beyond.

Krane twisted and rolled and pushed her past him. Her own momentum propelled her far beyond her target.

Screaming like a wildcat, she tumbled in the grass and settled several yards past. She came up onto her knees, and a growl–Lord help him, a literal growl!–escaped her throat.

She darted back at him in a full running charge.

"I don't want to hurt..."

Rather than running past, she jumped, and the knife's edge glinted in the light as she thrust the blade down.

He grappled her wrist and blocked her blow...partially. He toppled backward into the grass.

Her body fell over his. As the blade sliced through his robes and into his upper arm, his shoulder burned.

She pressed her weight down on him. Her eyes reflected primitive fury, glaring their hatred.

Instinct–and some of Minerva's training–took over. Brother Krane turned the fall into a back flip.

The momentum of her tackle pitched her over and out of control. This time, however, Krane gripped her wrist.

The woman tried to spring beyond his reach, but his hand held tight and caught her short, jerking her back and dropping her into the grass.

The woman lay, perhaps stunned or disoriented.

Krane knew exactly where he was and pressed his advantage. He rose to a crouch, then propelled himself forward to bring his weight down upon her prostrate body.

The advantage now his, he pinned her wrist, the one with the knife, down flat against the ground while his other hand pressed against her throat.

Seeing red, he closed his fingers. Vision and clarity returned, and he saw his own hand grasping her throat, her eyes bugging out beneath the strength of his fingers. *Christ! No, that's not–*

Appalled, he released her.

She struck at his shoulder with a targeted thrust of her fist.

The blow sent sharp, burning agony through his arm. *Damn you, woman!*

He balled his own fingers into a fist and pounded down on her head.

Once, twice.

Her arm fell, and the knife dropped into the grass.

He collapsed, struggling for breath. *Lord! I didn't mean to...but she tried to kill me...But still...*

Distantly, he heard Minerva call out to him, her tone growing more urgent, finally penetrating his thoughts.

"James! I need your help! Now, James, hurry!"

"What?" He struggled to pull himself up, using his one good arm to prop up and take in his surroundings.

Across the field, the old woman continued to chant, and the Soul-Staff glowed brighter than moments before. Her features contorted with effort, and the woods surrounding her lay exposed in the expanding, eerie glow.

Minerva's pleas continued to reach him. "She's found a way around my defenses, James. She's tapping the tree. Hurry! Destroy it! She's drawing on all the souls from the nearby village to form the portal."

Alarmed, Krane turned. Behind him, a circular gateway of energy hovered in the air between the great oak and himself. Within, as if looking through the window of a cabin set afire, flames flickered and spewed around the silhouette of a hideous creature. A regal, gray-skinned woman, with glowing green eyes and a pair of curved horns protruding from her head, looked out haughtily from the top of a cliff face.

As he watched, open mouthed, the portal wavered with energy, continuing to open and expand, though too small for anyone to step through just yet.

He didn't have much time. *Christ!*

He turned to face down the cackling hag, her face lit in rapturous delight, her eyes drinking in the vision of her mistress.

In his panic, he struggled to recall the spell of fire purification, but his arm remembered the finger motions and traced the pattern through the air, even as his flesh burned in protest from its injury. He didn't so much block the agony as ignore it, focusing on the staff and the incantation. Once he began, the motions and words came of their own power, as if from outside himself.

As he chanted, the staff changed hue, from a bright green to a dull, yellowish tinge, then ivory, and finally, an overwhelming bright white.

The old woman stopped her words, then, as if repelled, threw her arms over her head and leaped back. With a screech, she released the staff just as it burst into pure white flame.

Mother Katka fell sideways, her robe catching fire and exploded into bright light.

At the same time, Minerva crouched and grabbed the Divenium Crystal, still glowing red, its illumination diminished before the white light onslaught. She raised it over her head, holding it out toward the portal, which now hovered as a tight, puckered opening of energy, perhaps, James estimated, four handspans all around. The opening no longer increased, but stood stable, a small but accessible doorway from one realm to the other.

Minerva advanced, holding the crystal out. The edges of the energy barrier turned a reddish tinge. "Use me," she called. "Use me, great power, to close this unholy portal and seal the demoness—"

A blur of blackness tackled her from behind.

Minerva shrieked.Krane recognized the blonde tresses of Gwen, the witch that Krane thought indisposed. *Damn her! The witch must have lain, biding her time for the perfect moment to strike.*

As Krane rushed forward, the Divenium Crystal arced through the air and landed near his feet. He bent and retrieved the crystal. He tightened his fingers in a death grip and approached the struggling women writhing in the grass.

The witch, Gwen, pulled herself up atop Minerva, blood still streaking over her face, and her eyes flashed insanity. She raised the dagger to strike.

Krane struck first. He slammed the crystal down, hearing a disturbing crunch through his arm as his weapon hit the back of her head.

The witch's body went slack, and she crumpled over Minerva. His old friend struggled against the dead weight, trying to untangle herself from robes and limp limbs.

Certain that his friend could free herself in moments, Krane stood before the opening, watching the demoness' hand reach out and extend through the portal.

The demoness shoved her head through. Her glowing eyes met his, and she shrieked with inhuman fury.

Krane braced himself and raised the Divenium Crystal, repeating the words Minerva used. "Use me, great power, to close this portal and seal the demoness within!"

A surge of energy coursed through his body. "Amen!" he called after.

His body rose from the ground, and he felt himself lifted and pulled bodily toward the portal.

"James, no!" Minerva cried behind him. "No, it should have been me! You don't know what you're doing!"

He floated toward the opening. Even as the glare of the evil Baalina greeted him, his body flushed in a euphoric calm. His body crossed through the portal opening. First his head, then his torso.

The demoness hissed, and a barrier of white magik energy seemed to shove her aside. She resisted, but the magik held her at bay.

"No! Damn you, Reverend." As he pressed forward into the flames, she laughed.

His arms crossed through the barrier, and the crystal pried itself from his grip, pulled back toward the Earth realm by a power he had no strength to fight. *It doesn't matter anymore. It is finished.* A moment of panic welled up in him, but his body pushed through to the other side.

He settled on the edge of the same cliff and the flames licked at his layers of cloaks; in seconds, the flames met skin. He turned, contemplating a retreat, but the portal closed behind him.

The demoness uttered a scream of anguish.

They stood, scrutinizing each other. Reverend James Krane raised a hand. "I banish you in the name of our Lord and Savior. You cannot hurt me."

The demoness tilted her head and laughed. "You banish me? You...banish me?" Her eyes lit up in green fury. "You cannot banish me to Hell, Reverend. We're already *in* Hell!"

An arc of flame spewed from under him and covered his body.

Brother James Krane raised his arms, a futile gesture to stave off an agony he could not defend against and could not stop. As he swung his arms and kicked his legs at the flames, they covered him; the voice of the demoness reached him over his own screams.

"Congratulations, Reverend. You have defeated a demoness this day. Receive your eternal reward."

He screamed. His body engulfed in flames, and he burned. He screamed again. And when the flames died down, he realized he lay, in his robes and intact flesh, surrounded by flame. *God, no...it won't stop...it won't...ever...*

The demoness granted him a moment's respite before the flames licked out to burn him again. Vengeful laughter echoed in his ears.

CHAPTER SIXTEEN_

IN A ROOM full of stunned listeners, both in the room and those listening virtually, Chip's voice continued on, finishing the official report of the bittersweet victory. "'...In the days that have since fallen, I am often awakened in the dead of night, when the dark magiks are at their strongest, soaked in a cold sweat. On those nights, I hear cries on the wind. Are they the tormented screams of my fallen comrade, or the imaginings of a sleep-deprived mind?

"In the end, I suppose it matters not, as long as our order never forgets the sacrifice Brother James Krane, my dear friend, made for all of us on that terrible night, a night for which he suffers for all eternity, long after the rest of us are no more. Lord Help Us All. So sworn this day, the third day of February, the Year of Our Lord, 1798.'"

Chip's voice broke as he read the last line into the microphone. "And she signed it, Sister Minerva Crystin, Kelranian Order."

Blue watched as Chip gently closed the file. No one dared speak. Then, after several seconds, a noise like momentary static sounded over the speakers.

A second time, and a third, then a woman's voice, whispering. "Damn. Just...damn."

Blue identified the "static" as an avatar weeping. Shifting her gaze to the screen, Blue picked out Agent MacLeod–the one the other agents called Skye. Twin streams of animated tears trickled down the warrior girl's face, which brought all sorts of annoying questions to Blue's mind. *How does that work? She's not real; she's a computer-generated image. I get that she has emotion, but why would the image express it?*

What electronic tears do avatars weep?

Whatever the actual substance, weep the avatar did, and as she wept, her shoulders shook. And when she spoke, her voice carried the sadness of her words. "I know...to some of you guys...this is legend. Myth. But...I've fought demons. I've fought ghosts, and they're real. Somewhere, for over two hundred years, the demoness Baalina has been torturing a good man. I can't even imagine..."

As Blue watched, another avatar, the wizard–*Phil*–stepped up to Skye and patted her shoulder. *Can she feel his hand on her? Can she feel he is trying to comfort her?*

What do avatars feel with virtual nerves?

But sure enough, as she watched on the screen, Skye leaned her head into his shoulder and continued to weep.

The vision caused a lump to grow in her throat. Phil, whose physical body continued to vegetate in the couch, had someone to focus on, someone to protect, at least for the duration of the crisis. Perhaps that would help take his mind off his own crazy situation. She hoped it would help in some small way.

After what he must have thought was the proper pause of respect, Chip spoke into the microphone. "There're a few things we know. First of all, since the Sisterhood plans to recast the spell and bring that demon bitch into our game, we need to recreate this Divenium Crystal and upload it into the game as fast as possible. If I can digitize it as an item, imbue it with some sort of power within the game engine...well, maybe the runes can help counter the spell they intend to cast with their digital SoulStaff. Exactly the way it worked years ago."

"Exactly?" asked Phil.

Chip nodded, caught himself, and spoke into the microphone. "Yes."

As Phil's voice continued through the speaker, Blue heard the hint of a tremble. "Let's not kid ourselves about what that means, then. Someone here will have to sacrifice themselves to lock Baalina back into the chaos realm."

Rebecca Burton stood, her golden wings fluttering momentarily along her back before vanishing again. "Leave that to me."

"No way, Obi-Wan!" cut in Skye.

Rebecca raised her hands in a calming gesture. "I assure you, I have no intention of sacrificing myself the way the Jedi did, nor the way Brother Krane did." The angel avatar smirked. "As Han Solo said in the same movie, 'I still have a few tricks up my sleeve.'"

Skye rose and confronted Rebecca. "Of course, you'd say that, to keep me from stopping you. But it won't work."

"Skye." Rebecca placed a hand on her shoulder. "There's a lot you don't know about me. It's true, there's a certain...expectation...that I will do great things in the future. But that doesn't change the present. I'm the best person to do this, because of what I'm preparing to do. It's a long time from now, and I've trained my entire life to do it. If Baalina tries to attack me, she's in for an unpleasant surprise."

"Bullshit," snapped Skye. "She's a demon. You're a human. You can't argue with those two basic facts."

Rebecca sighed. "Essentially true." She paused, considering something. "Well, as the saying goes, we'll cross that bridge when we get to it. In the meantime, Chip, you need to program the crystal, and...have you talked to Blue yet?"

Blue blinked and looked at Chip. All this time, she'd been glued to the screen, watching the drama unfold like some movie. The illusion shattered when the characters mentioned her by name. "What does she mean?"

Chip sighed and spoke into the microphone. "No...I had been trying to figure out how to approach it."

A chill ran up Blue's spine. *Oh, boy. I don't like the sound of this.* "Approach what? What is she talking about?"

"Blue...we're sixty percent less effective on this side of the screen. That's an inarguable fact."

"Oh. This side? What are you–" Then the meaning of his words hit. "Now, just a damn second!"

"Once the fight starts, we can't do any good from out here. We might as well just watch the fight on the screen for all the help we'll be."

Blue opened her mouth to protest, not sure which of the many arguments in her head would come out first.

But Chip cut her off. "Or, we can get in there and possibly actively affect the outcome for the better. If it goes the way we hope, we won't be in there any longer than a few minutes."

Blue began, "You don't know–"

"We *all* come back out," Chip emphasized, "with Baalina either locked away in whatever virtual space they've created for her or her ass booted back to the real chaos realm."

"You don't know that. We could *all* end up trapped in there."

Chip conceded, "That's right, and we might die. But that can only happen if the Sisterhood succeeds. And if they succeed, we'll have no real world we'll want to come back to, anyway."

Blue still didn't like it. "You can't honestly be saying we're better off in there than out here."

"Once that battle starts, the virtual realm is the only place we're going to make a difference. And if our friends lose because we refused to act...well, I know where I'm going. I just hope you come with me."

"Don't you do that!" The words forced their way from her, from deep inside. "Don't you make it about *me*. This is just like last time, you son of a bitch! Do you remember? Because I haven't forgotten! 'I'm going, Blue, you can choose to come with me if you want, but I'm going.' And I followed you like a fucking idiot, right into the lion's mouth, and we both know how well that turned out, don't we?"

Chip hesitated. The words hung between them, unchallenged.

"Don't we!"

Chip flinched. "That's not fair. And...it's not the same thing."

Rebecca cut in, the mechanical nature of the computer speaker garbling her words. "It certainly is not. Chip isn't asking you for a personal favor to help his father. And there's your mutual friend to consider. Not to mention the hundreds of players in the game that could be the first victims of an attempt to accomplish nothing less than worldwide domination."

Still raging, Blue turned toward the computer. *Who does she think she is?* Out loud, she said, "What do *you* know about it?"

"That your mother died tragically during your encounter with a ghost. That through great personal sacrifice, you managed to defeat it and set matters right. That you still hold, to this day, a great anger toward your boyfriend over what happened."

Blue glared at Chip, seeing red. "You talked?! To a stranger? You son of a–"

"I didn't say a word, honest! Why would I? Blue, I promised you–"

Rebecca interrupted. "Chip didn't have to, Fiona. There are very few things that happen of a paranormal nature that I am not informed of, even if it's only after the fact."

Blue rejected that comment. "But...there's no way. Nobody could have found out."

Rebecca replied in a calm voice. "That's correct, Fiona. No one could possibly have found out...through normal channels. You covered your tracks well."

Blue glared at the screen. "Then how did *you* find out?"

Rebecca hesitated. "Let's...just call it magic, for now."

"But you had to have found out from someone. And it wasn't me. Did Chip's father–"

The angel figure on the screen shook her head. "No. I have other sources not available to most people."

"No sources recorded that! Nothing short of a crystal ball that shows you everything you need to know about ghosts."

Burton spoke carefully. "That's...possibly closer to the truth than you might ever know. And for whatever it's worth, Fiona...Blue...you did a fantastic job taking care of the problem and hiding what happened afterwards. I couldn't have done better, and believe me, that's saying something."

Blue considered. "As long as it didn't come to you through Chip."

"It did not. Now, please, at the risk of sounding melodramatic, hundreds of lives may be at stake, maybe more, if we delay. That includes Phil's, and, to be blunt, my own. Possibly many more, though I'll admit, I'm still at a loss as to how they mean to accomplish the transport of a demon from here into the physical realm."

Skye added, "But if we stop them here, it won't really matter."

"And for us to have the best chance, we need every advantage at our disposal."

Phil emphasized, "And we've been sparring with Chip for quite some time. Trust me, you won't make much of a difference trying to control your avatars from out there."

Blue raised her hand, mainly for Chip's benefit. "Wait a second, just slow down. If Chip and I both go in, we have no way of getting out."

"Not to put too fine a point on it," said Skye, "but we have no way of getting out with you two out there, either."

Burton nodded. "The SoulStaff and Divenium Crystal are the key. The Sisters used their avatars to manipulate the staff and open this portal in the game that pulled us in. Once they pull enough people into the game, they'll attempt to bring Baalina through. But the crystal can also close the portal, and in theory, destroying the SoulStaff will bring us all back."

"In theory?" asked Blue.

Rebecca paused before replying. "The theory is a sound one."

Swell.

Chip held out a small digital camera for Blue to see. "I'll get the crystal photographed, scanned, and programmed into the game in just a couple of hours."

"Says you," quipped Phil. "I've seen your 3D rendering. There's a reason I'm lead graphics programmer."

In spite of the circumstances, Chip chuckled. "It will work."

Blue ran her hand through her hair. Anxiety had settled in, almost like some sort of claustrophobia, a need to run and get away, even though she stood in the basement, safe and sound, for the moment. "Okay, even if I'm willing to do this, someone *still* has to sacrifice themselves so everyone else will be freed."

Rebecca cut in. "I already said, I'll take care of that."

Chip reached out and hit the mute button, his eyes locking on Blue's. "So...what do you think?"

Blue was terrified, and she couldn't shake the feeling she now gave voice to. "Something is going to go terribly wrong."

"I agree that it's a risk."

That's not what I said. Blue met Chip's gaze. "I don't care what Burton says, this is just like last time. You get that, don't you?"

"I won't let anything happen to you."

"You can't promise that."

Chip's eyes shifted, then returned to meeting hers. "I promise I won't let anything happen to you."

She took his hand. "Those are amazing words, Romeo, but you still don't know how this is going to turn out."

Chip pressed. "I won't let anything happen to you. This is *my* game. They've come into *my* world this time. Look, everything that happened last time, even after your mother died, you did to protect me. We were fighting, on the streets, with knives–fists! You couldn't give up, because you knew I'd be helpless in that environment if you did. And I was helpless! As it was, I almost died, but I'm here today because of you."

Blue felt her face flush. She looked at the floor. She hadn't thought of it that way. "So, what makes this different?"

Chip released her hand and motioned toward the computer screen. "This is my world. They can't kill you. They might be able to hurt you, but even if they do, I'll come for you. They can't hide you from me.

And if Phil is with me, they don't stand a chance, but even without Phil, if you get into any trouble, I *will* come for you. They can't possibly know more about this game than I do."

Once again, his naïve sincerity brought tears to her eyes. "You'd better."

"What was it you said that night? 'They don't know who they're fucking with.' Well, it's true *now*, too. Only here, *I'm* the more dangerous one, and they have no idea what's going to hit them. I told you, we make an invincible team."

Blue swallowed. She nodded her acceptance, but the thought wouldn't go away. *I just hope I don't regret this.*

Chip released the mute button. "Okay, she's in. I'm going to start photographing this gem, and we'll join you as soon as we can."

CHAPTER SEVENTEEN

Blue assisted Chip as he draped a white sheet over the back of the chair, creating literal white space to photograph the Divenium Crystal against. He took a couple of photos in the dim lighting of the basement and those proved too dark. Then he tried the flash. Not surprising to Blue, the flash created harsh red spotlights against the sheet and flares along the surface, resulting in useless images.

He didn't want to take the time to do it, but Chip finally dug around in the garage to find portable work lamps.

After a few minutes of struggling to clamp them against the side of the desk, he succeeded in illuminating the surface of the chair in a soft white light bright enough for the crystal to show clearly without a flash.

Next, he photographed the crystal from every conceivable angle: sides, bottom, top, 60- and 120-degree side shots. After an hour of patient workmanship, he'd downloaded a usable set onto the mostly-unused third computer. As he arrowed through them, the crystal appeared to spin in place in a crude animation effect.

Blue sighed, relieved. "Glad that's done!"

Chip's eyes met hers, amusement reflecting in his face. "That was the easy part."

"Excuse me?"

Chip stabbed a few buttons. "Now we have to render the images and assemble them as a 3-D model–"

"Oh...how long will that take?"

"–then I need to crop away their background, assemble the images together, and let the computer extrapolate the 'in between' views from the ones it has. And that's not counting manually recreating the runes on each crystal face. Otherwise, they won't be a part of the virtual version of the crystal, and I'm sure they're vital for this to work. Fortunately, our extrapolation program is pretty sophisticated; it's just a matter of waiting." Chip sighed. "Looks like Phil was right. This is going to take a bit longer than I thought."

Blue's mood sank with each word. "And then?"

"Then I can drop the completed image into the game and set it to appear by the tree."

"So...how long?"

"Well...longer than two hours, that's for sure! More like four."

"Ugh."

"And that's assuming I don't make any mistakes."

"Double ugh!" Blue sighed. "I can't believe I'm going to say this, but can I just get zapped into the game now? Or is there something else I can do to help speed this along?"

Chip considered. "No, not really. And I won't be much longer after you. Once I get the program automations in place, it takes care of itself. I can join you in maybe another hour."

———

Marda awakened with a jarring jolt. Hands shook her shoulders. She snapped open her eyes, only to close them again as pain from her injury made her nose throb. Natalie's face fell into focus before her, reflecting sympathy.

"What's the matter, Nat?"

"We've...had a complication."

The words brought her to full alertness. "What happened?" She sat up in the bed.

"We wanted to give you some time to rest. But after you fell asleep, I logged back on to check on the SoulStaff, and..." Nat averted her eyes, and Marda could see fresh tears streak her cheeks. "I'm afraid it's my fault." Marda braced herself. "Tell me."

"We hacked their system, inserted the SoulStaff, and tested it. I should have known what would happen next, but–"

Marda rubbed her temples, mentally counting to ten. She'd vowed not to yell at Nat anymore. She'd promised to appreciate her contributions and genius, giving her the recognition she deserved. But the girl could be so *trying* sometimes. "*Tell* me. And put it simply, please. I have a terrible headache."

"Put simply, they hacked my hack. The programmers–probably Eugene, since we know Phillip is captured in the game–deleted the SoulStaff from the game matrix. It's...just not there."

Marda rose, fury building up past her injuries. "You're saying that, for all our plans, we're defeated!"

Natalie held her hands out in a defensive gesture, as if afraid of what she might do next. "No, Marda, we're not. We've simply lost our advantage."

"But you said they *destroyed* the SoulStaff."

"Yes...I placed the object into the game. Now they've turned around and removed it from the game again. But they didn't remove the work I've put into it here on my system, creating the SoulStaff and animating it. That's still saved on my computer. I just have to re-upload and re-render it into the game. And I'll take steps to ensure it won't be as easy to hack us next time. We've lost maybe hours, not days. We can still go forward. Still–I should have anticipated this. Cyn still thinks we should–"

"Sister, when we are alone, do not mention her to me." Marda reached out and placed a hand on her shoulder.

She felt Natalie flinch in response.

This is no good, I need Natalie on my side. She's a simpering coward, but she's truthful. After what happened, Nat is the only one on my team I can trust. "You can't be expected to second-guess every technology contingency, and I know you'll make it right. Between you and me." She pulled Natalie into an embrace.

She resisted at first, then returned the hug.

Marda whispered in Nat's ear, "At this point, I wouldn't trust Cyn to tell me where the bathroom is."

Natalie squirmed against her, and when they separated, Nat's gaze darted to the floor. Marda had to strain to hear her words.

"Cyn...has great skills that have served us well in the past."

"She's a fighter; she's persuasive. She is not a great strategic thinker. I need *you* for that."

Natalie sighed. "Yes, Priestess."

"Marda."

"Yes...Marda. It's going to take a little extra time to do it. A couple of hours. It's unfortunate—we had the advantage, now it's going to come down to a dead heat."

"Nonsense." Marda tipped Nat's chin up to face her, then bent and kissed Natalie on the forehead. She noted, with some satisfaction, that Natalie flushed pink in response. "We are four Sisters. They have two *men* on their side."

Natalie chuckled but said nothing more.

"In a 'dead heat,' as you call it, I'd bet on our side. Every time. Come, Sister, let's prepare."

———

BLUE SAT and stared at the monitor. The huge CGI tree loomed, dominating her vision. "Okay, then." A shudder caused her voice to tremble.

Chip spoke from behind her. "All right, Blue, I'm right here. And I'll join you in a few minutes."

"Yeah..." Her finger hovered over the forward-arrow key, but she couldn't bring herself to apply pressure to move the avatar forward. "Um...so...I'm going to go now."

"Now is good."

"Okay...uh," She swallowed back bile. Suddenly, she thought she might be sick. "I *really* don't want to." She wondered if she'd still have this upset stomach when she transferred into a CGI body. *Can avatars vomit? Who the fuck gets to find these things out?*

Chip's hand fell on her shoulder.

She closed her eyes, listening to Chip's tone, willing herself to let his words reassure her. "I've got you. I'll take good care of your real body."

"Uh, huh. Perv." She meant to sound teasing and flippant, but she couldn't keep the quiver from her voice. "I know how you are. Send me away, and have your way with my poor, unconscious body. You forget, I know all about you lonely nerd types and your secret, lascivious desires."

"I won't do anything to it without buying it dinner first."

She laughed at the bad joke, then reached up and gripped the hand that lay on her shoulder. "I *really* don't want to do this."

"I know. I love you."

"I love you, too." Still, she hesitated. "Damn, I hate peer pressure."

"Do you want me to count to three?"

"No, I'll do it." She pressed the forward key. "Three!"

She thought she'd close her eyes as the animated character stepped forward, but instead her eyes locked open as the tree came fully into view.

And then her vision faded away into a bizarre, pixilated dissolve.

———

BECAUSE OF THE nature of her then-new-boyfriend, she couldn't escape seeing certain nerd movie standards from his DVD collection during the last half of her senior year.

One of those standards was *Tron*, the 80s Disney experimental cult classic in which a computer programmer gets "zapped" into the video game he'd programmed years earlier.

Though she couldn't honestly say she *liked* the movie, one sequence struck her at the time, a sequence she still remembered in the years since, and which had been replaying in her mind nonstop since knowing she'd be transporting herself into a computer game.

The programmer–whose name was Flynn, she thought, Jeff Bridges at his most hunky, for sure–gets zapped from behind by a conveniently placed matter breakdown gun thingie, and his body transports block by neat digital block into the video game, where he is then just as systematically re-assembled on the other side.

In the meantime, Flynn gets treated to the best LSD-inspired cinematic hallucination sequence since 2001: *a Space Odyssey* (another movie she saw that same year, and enjoyed more, somewhat) courtesy of the finest computer graphics of 1982.

Her actual transport into this actual virtual world was nothing at all like that.

Instead, one moment, she stared at the computer screen with her own eyes. Then everything faded away, like those times she'd stood too fast and got a momentary dizzy spell.

But when the black spots faded back to normal, everything changed.

The texture of the world had changed.

The tree still loomed in front of her, only now she was standing in front of it. And she could step away.

But it didn't *feel* right, it was like standing in thick rubber boots up to her thighs.

She reached down and ran her hands over her legs–her now perfectly shaped, gorgeous legs. But her hands lacked sensation as she rubbed along her leg muscles.

She held her thumb and index finger in front of her eyes and rubbed the digits against each other. Still a partial numbness, but also a tingling sensation.

She turned her head, or rather, thought of turning her head. The view shifted before she registered her neck muscles moving.

Before her, the gargantuan tree rose as far as she could see, tangled, gnarled branches reaching up and out from the base and extended in a cluster of twigs, towering over the entire group as if all of nature wanted to embrace them in a hug of support.

And yet, though the tree stood dark, oppressive, and majestic, she could distinctly make out the neon electric texture that caused even the blackness to glow with an artificiality, the same CGI texture as her skin, the leaves, the forest around her, and the bodies of her friends who surrounded her now.

"Wow..." Hands reached out to support her, though she didn't feel like she'd fall over. Nevertheless, trying to take in the bizarre new stimulus froze her in place.

"I know." She recognized the voice as Phil's, though it came to her filtered through layers of electronic static. It took her several seconds to sort out the noise from the voice.

One of the new women, Skye, stood in front of her, dressed in a silver knight's armor with oversized shoulders. Blue registered, belatedly, that she'd reached out and entwined Blue's fingers in her gloved gauntlets.

"It's going to take some time," she explained. "It's like, your mind has to re-configure how to interpret the stimuli."

In spite of the circumstances, Blue laughed. "What mind? My brain is back..." She waved her hand out vaguely. "Out there. How can I even..."

This time, her legs really did try to give out, but she fell against Skye, who seemed to have no trouble holding her up.

"Easy. I know, it's confusing as hell. As much as you want to think it, though, your mind—that which makes you...well...you...is no longer in your head." A gloved index finger pointed at Blue's forehead. "It's in here now."

"But that's not..." *Fuck, how many times in one day?*

Then she thought of the bodies left behind. Slack. Not just slack, not just comatose, but slowly, inevitably, dying, a process taking days rather than years, if left unchanged. As if something vital had left the physical body and had been transplanted elsewhere.

A vital something that could transfer into the digital world and take up residence in a body that, by standard definition, had no substance whatsoever.

If I weren't living it, I'd find the very idea ludicrous, like a demon cult out to take over the world or a maniac ghost set loose and looking for revenge.

Or a couple of college students joining forces with government agents in league with a secret society of white magic druids trying to protect the world from the evils that normal people don't even know about.

Just us special, lucky ones. Like me.

Blue sighed. *Yay, me.*

At least, the world had normalized during her stream-of-consciousness moment. She looked at the people gathered around her. Though her eyes saw a wizard, a lady knight, and a golden angel, she thought of them as her friend, Phil, the concerned assistant agent, Skye, and the self-appointed leader and apparent V.I.P. of the group, Rebecca Burton.

The dizziness, the disorientation, had lessened. She rubbed her fingers together. She could feel more, and sensation seemed to heighten through her body by the moment.

The ground now lay solid beneath her feet. The people, flamboyant though they appeared with their fanciful weapons, idealized physiques, and oddly clear complexions, now looked more natural to her own artificial eyes. The sharp contrasts of the flowing grass and billowing trees also lessened. It still looked artificial, highly unnatural to what she remembered of the real world (not that she'd taken many strolls through the forest in her day—a thought that hit her with a twinge of regret) but neither was it as overwhelming.

Now that Blue could sense her hands properly, she wasted no time untangling her fingers from Skye and taking a step back. Blue liked her personal space, and this girl was hovering a bit close for comfort.

Phil the Wizard stood close by. His gaze fell upon Skye and locked, then drifted toward Blue like an afterthought. "How are you doing?"

Blue looked between one and the other, amused. "I'm fine, Phil, thanks for asking." *Somebody's crushing.*

Skye, on the other hand, spared Phil only a brief look and then returned her attention to Blue.

Poor Phil. Either she doesn't notice or doesn't care.

Phil waved his hand in some vague motion that indicated "the real world." "So...uh...how am *I* doing...out there?"

"You seem comfortable enough. We moved your body to the couch. You still snore."

"Oh. Sorry about that."

Blue giggled. "No worries. It's how we know you're still breathing."

The wizard stood before her, tall and strong, a stance contradicting the CGI character when it was "uninhabited" by someone. "I suppose it's hard to point out the positives in a bizarre situation like this."

"Little bit." Blue stepped into the open space the group had created for them. "So, what now?"

Skye sounded like an overexcited sensei. "You'll find that you can move at the speed of thought. It's pretty shocking at first. For instance, think of drawing your weapon from your shoulder and you...yes, exactly!"

As Skye had given the command, Blue had done exactly that, and her hands moved of their own volition. In a blur of motion, she stood, in a ready stance, the sword drawn out before her, a moment later. "Wow, neat!"

With another thought, she drew back her sword then whipped the weapon through the wind with a series of swooshing swipes. She suspected the noise was an audio effect added by Chip or Phil, but here, it was the reality of their world.

The sword's hilt dwarfed her wrist and extended out from her hand looking as much a granite block as a blade. Exaggerated and grotesque, a real-world equivalent of the weapon would have weighed over 100 pounds, but she hefted it as easily as she would swing a loaf of bread—not that she'd be inclined to swing a loaf of bread at someone as a weapon. The attack took almost no physical strength on her part, nor the one after that, nor the one after that. She swiped her sword a few more times, adjusting to the new effort...or lack of effort.

Skye took a few steps back from her. "Okay, now try jumping at me."

Blue attempted an experimental jump. She flexed easily at the knees, and even with a tentative try, she sprang through the air several feet, straight up, then back down. She jumped in place a couple more times. "Wow! I'm like Wonder Woman or something."

The wizard stood in place, his staff pointed at her as he nodded. "Kind of feels that way," Phil said. "Now, be careful when you jump at me. It doesn't take as much as you...whoa!"

Blue sprang forward. Even with what she thought would be an easy skip, she propelled up and flew toward him. As she passed, she swung her sword, and, to her shock, connected.

"Hey!" shouted Phil.

"Sorry, I thought you were ready for me." Several yards away, Blue settled to the ground, light as you please on her new, hyper-accelerated feet. She spun on her ankles to face him again.

"Actually, it's okay. You can't kill me. At least...well..." The wizard rubbed his beard, contemplating. "Did you ever die in the game?" A gleam flashed in the wizard's eyes. "You probably need to experience that–"

Like a cannonball, the wizard's body shot toward her.

Instinctively, she held her arm up. The blunt edge of the staff came at her head, and she held her sword out to block.

At the last moment, the staff dropped, striking her in her gut.

The impact forced the air from her...or whatever passed for air.

The wizard landed behind her, and as she tried to turn, three more blows fell.

In quick succession, pain erupted at her shoulder, knee, and a resounding crack to the head.

She found herself looking up at the sky. She hurt like hell, no question, but she also suspected the pain was not nearly what she might experience had she endured a similar attack in the real world.

Yet another blow struck her in the head, the pain penetrating like lightning. "Damn you, Phil!"

Everything faded to blue, and she found herself hovering...somewhere...in some other place...some...*clouds? Those are clouds? I'm...am I in the sky?*

And she could speak. "What did you do to me?"

"Uh..." Phil's voice, sheepish. "I guess you could say I 'killed' you. We had a duel, and you lost all your health."

"Thanks a lot! Now what do I do?" Even as she asked, she regained her sense of direction, could feel she was dropping down, down...the view shifted, and she could see, still far below, the ground.

She descended down toward it.

"Now? Well, nothing much. You're in a sort of penalty box. In our game, when you die, you get removed from the action for about two minutes while you wait to resurrect and your body to reform. You re-enter the game at about half strength and quickly return to normal."

"Wow, the colors, this is better than an LSD trip." She realized what that sounded like and added, "I mean, the LSD trips I've seen in movies, of course."

"Yeah, yeah, I like *The Wall*, too."

Blue giggled. "But damn, that still hurt!"

"I know, sorry, it can't be helped. You need to get over this shock now and experience it before we go to battle."

"You could have warned me." Blue watched the ground draw closer, then conceded, "Still, I suppose you owed me a lump or two."

"I just..." Phil floundered.

She wondered if he'd deny it.

Finally, he said, "Yeah, okay, I was kind of pissed at you for how you treated Chip...you know, like shit and all."

She really couldn't disagree. "That's fair."

"So, I figure, this is a safe place to vent some of that." She could almost hear the shrug in his voice.

As he spoke, Blue's perception dropped to ground level, and she felt her body shape itself around her form, or behind the eyes of her body, or avatar, or...*fuck it, I might as well think of it as my body for the foreseeable future.* She gave her fingers an experimental wiggle and turned.

The pseudo-death experience actually left her weak and winded. "All right, you took me down once, but you'll have to earn the rest."

The wizard's shoulders slumped where he stood, and his eyes looked toward the ground. "No, I'm done, Blue. My heart's not in it. I thought I wanted to hurt you, or at least, make your life inconvenient for a few minutes, but..." He looked up, his gaze meeting hers. "I love you, girl, you know that. I don't want to see you two fight. Chip's my best friend, and..."

An odd noise erupted from him. Maybe a sob? "I'm just glad we're past that."

Blue didn't know how to answer.

In the silence that followed, Phil pressed, "We *are* past all that now...right?"

Okay. Phil deserves an answer. She tried to control her frustration and keep her voice level. "Look, I can be a confused mess in the best of circumstances. And the last couple of years haven't been the best circumstances. I had to process what happened in my own time and my own way. I was in pain, and I thought Chip was a part of it. I thought breaking up with him would end the pain. In the end, it had nothing to do with him. I know that now."

"He trusted you."

Blue flinched at the accusation. "I know that, I just..."

"No, you don't get it." The wizard stabbed with his staff from across the meadow. "He trusted you. His faith *never* wavered in you, all these months. First over a year, then it stretched out to eighteen months, and you'd barely spoken to him. *I* had to sit and listen to him justify your indifference." Phil's voice shook with emotion. "But *I* knew, Blue. *I* knew you were done with him, do you get that? Do you know how many times I tried to tell him he needed to move on?"

"Phil, I–"

He cut her off. "But *he* had faith. He had absolute faith. In you."

She closed her eyes, ferling her tears fall over her cheeks. *I don't want to hear this.*

"It never wavered, not once. Not even after you dumped him, and you need to realize that."

The environmental trappings fell away. It was as if Phil and Blue were back in the dorm room. She wondered if the others could hear them, then decided it didn't matter. Phil and she needed to have this out. She shrugged, exasperated. "What do you want from me? What do you want me to say?"

"I want to *know* that you're committed to him the way he is to you. That this isn't some tentative trial continuation and that you're not just waiting for the next excuse to bail out."

"Do you see me here?" She growled and shifted her weight, giving her hips a sultry wiggle. "Do you think it was *my* idea to transport into this CGI body? Do I have any fucking idea how we're going to get out of this? No. But Chip told me *he* does. He told me to trust him, and I do! Does this–" She sprang into an easy, controlled leap which put her to exactly where she wanted to be, in front of Phil.

She swung at him with the flat of her sword...not hard enough to damage him, just hard enough to knock the cocky wizard back on his ass.

He dropped but glared at her from the ground.

"Do you think I'd be here if I considered our relationship a 'tentative trial continuation' whatever the fuck that even is?"

"I just want to make sure...you know where he's coming from." The wizard struggled to his feet. "Because if you break his heart again, I'm the one who has to repair the pieces you leave behind, and it's going to be nasty. So, if you're going to do *that*..." He let the words hang, the thought unfinished.

"That's not going to happen, Phil. I couldn't do that to him again. I couldn't do that to me again!"

"But you can wake up tomorrow and change your mind. You could go home, and, after a few weeks, rationalize–"

"I could go home and get hit by a bus, Phil! We might all die here today. I don't know what you want me to say. I love Chip, and today, right now, I intend for that to be forever. Today, right now, it's the best I can offer you."

Phil sighed, clearly still frustrated. "Someday, maybe you'll understand. I just don't want to fight anymore."

"I'm not the one picking a fight, Phil."

With ironic timing, a new CGI character phased in amongst them, and Blue saw the small, lithe form of Chip's thief character. *Can their conversation be picked up through his speakers? Hell of a time to think of that!*

She felt herself flush and wondered if her new facial pores showed an outward blush.

"Hey, guys, I just wanted to give you all an update. I traced a few of the runes on the crystal so they're dark enough to see on the CGI image. The work's going pretty quick, so I'm guessing I'll have the final object scanned, rendered, and dropped into the game within the hour."

"Which reminds me," said Phil. "Why do you suppose we don't have any company yet? Didn't we determine they needed to come here to set up their soul spell?"

Chip answered, "I threw a monkey wrench into that. I found their version of the SoulStaff they'd hacked into our game and deleted it from the inventory database."

"Very nice!" Phil sounded impressed.

The thief flashed a sheepish grin. "I don't think it will stop them, but it had to slow them up. We know the staff was destroyed. Assuming they only have access to the notes and drawings in the file, they had to recreate it...in other words, redraw the whole thing from scratch...in order to render the object. On the other hand, we had a physical object to scan, which gives us a huge advantage."

Blue nodded. "But they're still going to come, aren't they?"

"Yes," Chip said. "They'll come. And we'll just have to hope like hell we'll be ready for them."

CHAPTER EIGHTEEN_

Despite his optimistic prediction, ninety minutes passed before Chip returned to the game as his thief character. By that time, Blue had had plenty of time to practice and adjust to the nuances of her new body by sparring with Skye, Phil, and sometimes even Burton the Angel.

She learned how to strike with the sword without hurting...much. The others had already figured it out. As a result, when someone struck her, it would sting at the place they connected...usually the shoulder or arm, sometimes the leg, and more painfully, across the stomach, and then through the magic of video game character health restoration, she'd fully recover in seconds.

Striking an opponent full force was easy–almost too easy–so they didn't spend a lot of time practicing fatal attacks. Getting hit with a "fatal" wound took you out of the action for over two minutes, and that didn't serve any useful purpose, so it was better to deliver the light taps when practicing.

After a while, while sparring with Skye, Blue started opening herself up to other options, getting creative with it, bringing her real-life street fighting skills to the party. During one round, they leapt at each other, and in one motion, Blue slid her sword into her back-sheath, shifted in midair around Skye's weapon, grabbed Skye's arm, and twisted in a full roundhouse kick. As Blue landed, she used Skye's own momentum to flip her over Blue's back, dropping her to the ground, stunned.

Skye lay, blinking up at her for several seconds. Then she looked around as if just shaking off the move to take in that Blue now held her sword in her hand and tapped Sky's stomach. "And while you were still lying there, I'd have already killed you," Blue said.

Skye worked her way up onto her elbows. "Nicely done! I didn't even see that coming. I'll bet they won't, either. They'll still be thinking about video game moves."

Blue sheathed her sword and extended her hand. "Exactly."

Skye gripped the offered hand and pulled herself up. "Show me."

She did, and then she showed the rest, one by one. Before Chip reappeared, they'd all attempted to add flips, dives, grapples, and other inventive actions that took their options beyond the basic, stab-and-block motions of the video game, with various levels of success.

Skye and Burton picked up on the new moves with ease, while Phil fumbled along at a more remedial skill level, successfully pulling off most of the actions half of the time, and ending up with a face full of grass the other half. The more they worked out, the more the exertion seemed to take its toll.

Phil joked that he shouldn't have picked an old man wizard body as his avatar. Though Blue didn't say anything out loud, she suspected the talk was just an excuse. In the real world, Rebecca and Skye were law enforcement agents of some sort. It stood to reason they were in reasonably decent shape. And although she'd been somewhat sedentary the last couple of years, Blue hadn't let herself "go" by any means, either. The campus provided ample opportunities to walk and jog, and her father's apartment complex offered a basic gym setup she took advantage of a couple times a week.

Phil, on the other hand...she loved the man as Chip's best friend, but if anyone she knew fit the definition of "couch potato", that was

Phil. He was a hefty pear shape when they'd first met, and she estimated he'd put on another thirty to fifty pounds since graduation.

———

After about an hour, Burton got into the act, and the agent lined the group up and taught them some basic boxing and karate strikes, how to target vulnerable spots on the shoulder, stomach, jaw, nose, groin, and other areas. When tested on each other, the strikes stunned and slowed the movement on their CGI bodies the same way they would affect flesh and blood. Plus, it hurt like hell to get hit.

Blue worked with Phil, getting in a few extra throws. To his credit, he cooperated, bringing his best effort. Eventually, he learned to flip opponents pretty well, could pull off some of the karate blows, but as much as he tried the dive tackles, more often than not, his body hit the dirt after a total miss.

After a while, they'd broken out into two pairs, Rebecca and Phil, and Blue and Skye, then they shifted partners every few rounds, trying to pass on a few new but simple tricks as fast as they could, not knowing how much time they had.

By the time Chip had reappeared, they were well into their routine, but they gathered around to hear his news.

"Okay, so I completed the image generation and dumped the information into the game. The Divenium Crystal will appear right here, at the base of the tree, in about five minutes. I tested it on our backup server, and we'll be able to handle it like any other object."

Skye broke in, "Does it work? Will it do what we need it to do?"

Chip shrugged. "Well...it's the crystal...it has the runes. I can't program it to do a damn thing. This isn't about video game magic; this is about trying to conjure the real thing. You guys just need to cast the spell, say the magic incantation, do whatever you need to do, and we'll see. I can't program the image any more than the original crafter could 'program' the real thing."

"Then it should work," said Burton. "I'll cast the spell when the time comes."

"Okay," said Chip. "Good enough, now we just need to...ah-ha!" He pointed toward the tree.

A transparent pink object solidified in the grass beneath the tree. From where Blue stood, it appeared identical to the real crystal as best as she remembered it, with an additional neon quality created by the video pixels that added to its overall allure.

Blue stepped forward, crouched, and picked up the crystal. It felt solid enough in her hand and fit in her palm easily, the same way she recalled the original stone.

Chip stood at her side, a look of expectancy on his avatar's child-like face. She'd already grown accustomed to reading the animated facial expressions.

"So?" Chip tipped his head to indicate the crystal. "How did I do?"

Blue held it up between them. "It lacks the heft of the real thing, but I think the important stuff made it through. And it feels like the right size." She inspected it more closely. While the original runes had been carved directly into each crystal face, this one held white, drawn images along its faces. As Blue rotated it in her palm, it struck her as similar to someone having applied stickers to the surfaces.

Chip must have noticed her scrutinizing the runes. "That's what took so long. I had to manually re-draw each design."

"Feel pretty good about it?"

"Yeah." He moved in close and lowered his voice. "In a way, I'd almost rather it didn't work."

Blue returned a questioning look.

Chip continued, "If ours doesn't work, chances are, theirs won't work, either. Our spells won't hold and we all just go home."

"We're already in the game, Chip. Their SoulStaff accomplishes at least that much."

Chip shrugged. "Yeah, but if they ultimately can't open a portal to free their demoness, what difference does it really make?"

Blue considered. "I don't think we're going to get that lucky."

"I don't, either." Chip extended his hand out toward Burton. "But we should ask an expert."

Burton noticed Chip motion toward her. She stepped away from the group, still intimidating in her golden demeanor and slashing angel wings. "I'm hardly an expert, but let me see, anyway."

Blue dropped the crystal into Burton's extended palm. The angel–Blue couldn't think of her any other way–turned the object around in her hand.

"I agree it lacks the heft. I also agree it probably doesn't matter." Burton closed her eyes and muttered a chant–a singing, lyrical sound.

From within its center, the crystal lit up red, filling the area with a pink glow.

Blue folded her hands and gripped her elbows, warding off an imaginary chill. "Must have triggered the 'on' switch," she quipped.

As soon as she said it, she wondered if the comment was out of line.

Rebecca smiled. "More or less. You could also say I checked its batteries. The point is, this crystal works, and I suspect will function in this environment the same way the real one would work in our world."

Blue sighed and turned to Chip. "And once they clear the problems you threw at them, their SoulStaff will work, again, as well."

"Very likely."

Blue remembered that, for all their communication with his avatar, Chip hadn't yet abandoned his spot, watching everything from the real world on his computer monitor. "Maybe you should rethink this and stay out there to keep deleting her hacks."

"I could do that, but chances are, they're going to be ready for me this time. While I'm messing around trying to block their code, they're going to attack, and you'll be one person short."

"But if you can hold them off–"

"It might not matter if we can reverse the spell that has everyone trapped in here right now and close the portal." He turned toward the angel avatar. "Right, Rebecca?"

"Agreed." She called out to the others. "Everyone, gather around, it's time."

"One second," said Chip. "I'm going to join you."

"Why?" asked Blue. "What's the point?"

Even as he spoke, the avatar stepped toward the tree, purposefully heading toward the spot that would trigger the spell. "Because we can be attacked any moment, and I don't want to be on this side of it."

Chip stopped before the tree. Blue had kept pace with him and knew exactly where he would need to go to trigger the spell. As soon as he hit it, the figure stopped walking.

Blue stood close, watching the figure's face for a change of any sort.

After a moment, his blank, stone-faced expression took on new, malleable features. He blinked rapidly, his mouth hung half-open. When he stumbled, it was a natural stumble, not the stiff movement of a directed puppet from the outside world. "Whoa. Wow."

Blue reached out with her arms and cupped his shoulders with her hands. "Easy." It was fascinating to watch the same process she'd just been through, knowing exactly the disorientation Chip experienced. "It takes a few minutes. Give yourself some time to get your bearings and–"

"Guys!" said Phil. He stared out across the gentle hills of the forest.

Blue cringed, already knowing what he was about to say. *Crap, that just figures.*

"We've got company!"

Sure enough, at the top of a distant hill, four additional figures had gathered. Even at this range and disguised in her character form, Blue recognized the leader, waving a large totem staff, but with the same mad look in her eyes, a mixture of insanity and hatred, now fixated on Blue, even from across the plain.

"Gather close," called Burton. "Don't leave the portal unguarded. They want us to charge."

Marda, acting as leader of this group, planted the staff into the ground. Moments later, the four figures held hands, forming a circle around the object.

They started to dance. Two identical avatars, red-and-black costumed harlequins with matching demented grins on their matching demented features, skipped as they circled. A third, the only one dressed in what equated to moderate armor, held to a simple circling. Marda, also wearing minimal padding, swooned as much as danced, letting the others pull her around the SoulStaff.

In real-world distance, the groups were separated by perhaps a couple hundred yards of ankle-high grassy plains, yet Blue could hear Marda's chants clearly.

Chip took a couple of tentative steps in their direction. "What are they doing?"

"Calm, be still," commanded Burton.

Chip turned, his gaze leveling at Burton. "I said, 'What are they doing?'"

"They are most likely calling in all the human souls in the area."

Alarm lit up Chip's face. "'All the souls in the area,' what does that mean? We're the only souls literally nearby, and we've already been absorbed."

"Locally would refer to the persons in this land. How many players...human players...subscribe to your game?"

Did Chip's face flare red? Could a CGI face do that? Blue also recognized his familiar grinding jaw whenever he was confronted with something baffling.

"Last I recall, over 200. Maybe 220."

Burton nodded.

Chip's eyes grew wide. "You don't mean–"

"Perhaps not, Mr. Farren. How many people are generally logged in at any given time?"

"This time of day, about thirty or thirty-five, but–"

"Perhaps less over a holiday?"

Chip opened his mouth to speak.

But Phil beat him to it. "No, probably more. It's a student holiday, and this is an online game. There were several gaming parties planned for the long weekend."

Chip stepped forward. "But will the staff pull only the active online people, or everyone?"

Burton opened her mouth, then shut it. The angel's head tipped, her look of confusion easy to read on her golden features. "It's impossible to know. There's no precedence."

"My God," said Skye. "If it pulls people out of their bodies, people driving, people walking, people on stairs, and suddenly they enter into a coma—"

"We don't *know* that," insisted Rebecca.

"Assuming only active players online, how many?" Blue could hear the tremble in her own voice.

Phil offered a guess. "Forty, maybe seventy."

The angel avatar closed her eyes, then slowly opened them. "That's more than enough for their purpose," Burton said.

Chip took a couple more steps across the field. "We have to stop them!"

"We can't, Mr. Farren." Burton's commanding voice apparently caused Chip to stop in mid-step. "The incantation is almost complete, and Baalina will be transported into the new virtual chaos realm they've created for her. If we leave this vicinity, the Sisterhood of Baalina will have easy access to get in front of the portal and cast the spell to send her into the real—"

Behind them, the air erupted from a loud explosion. The force knocked Blue to her knees. *My God!* She struggled back to her feet and turned.

The portal, still hovering in the air behind them, now swirled in a cacophony of orange light.

Blue shielded her eyes with her arms, squinting into its center, where a single dark silhouette waited and seemed to stare back out at them.

A pair of green eyes found her across the distance, and as those eyes gazed upon her, Blue knew terror. *They did it. Holy shit, that's a demon on the other side, and it wants out.*

She turned to Chip. She struggled to get the words out, her voice cracking with the effort. "Chip...what are we going to do?"

Chip still argued with Burton. "But...people travel for the holidays.

People all over the country may have been pulled in, and if that's the case, we don't–"

Rebecca cut him off. "It's a bloody nose compared to allowing a demon to wreak uncontrolled havoc across the face of the Earth, Mr. Farren."

"Heads up, people!" Phil called. "The dance is over. Here they come."

Blue looked across the plain, her body lit up, ready for battle.

The group of four now charged toward them, but Blue's gaze had locked on the leader.

She recognized the crazed woman who waved the SoulStaff like a war banner. Fury reflected in her eyes and a war cry tore from her throat as she ran, charging straight for Blue.

CHAPTER NINETEEN

Blue drew her sword and stepped forward. The charging group before them continued on, closing the distance rapidly.

She fell into a ready stance, waiting for the foolish leader to break from her group running at full speed and make a stupid mistake. Based on their previous encounter, Blue figured pretty good odds on that. She just had to keep her head. "Stay behind me," she said.

Chip's hand patted her shoulder in what he must have thought was reassuring. "I'm okay, go."

"Says you!" Her gaze swept over his figure head to toe, taking in his thief—what she'd laughingly call—"armor." Black leather head to toe. "You're still disoriented, and you're a little underdressed for this party, sweetheart."

"Trust me. Just keep the battle around this tree; I'll do my part."

"Close in!" commanded Burton, her skin now glowing with a golden aura that the group naturally drew toward. "I need to concentrate to cast the spell to close this portal, so I'll fall back by the tree. The rest of you focus on destroying the staff."

Blue offered, "Chip says he's most effective behind the tree."

"Great, then he can be my backup."

Blue proceeded to the front, past Phil the Wizard, to join Skye, their only other heavily armored figure, at the front line.

If their battle-readiness had concerned Blue, one look at the group charging them alleviated her fears–somewhat. Two clowns–literally, identical harlequins, each armed with stilettos–led the charge, their screams...no, maniacal laughter...preceded them, ensuring the group would take no one by surprise.

Marda Crazybitch continued her mad charge, garbed in warrior armor similar to Blue's, but she also carried the staff, which meant she had to focus on casting spells, and they had to focus on stopping her.

Next to her was a cloaked wizard. She looked again. Not a wizard, the cloak covered a smaller, shapelier form. The cloaked *druid* kept pace with the leader, holding her arms out, palms up, the sparks of red energy already flaring up in her hands, her obvious intent being to pitch them like the first throw of a lethal game of hacky sack.

Burton's command reached her. "Steady, hold here. They're so determined to come to us, let them. They're being stupid and reckless; we can win this by playing it smart and strategic."

Now she felt it–the adrenaline. Or...whatever counted as adrenaline in her new body. A clear-headedness, a giddy excitement, a...

Feeling of being exactly where she was needed and wanted.

And there it was.

For the first time in over two years, locked in a life-or-death struggle in a scenario that bordered on the ludicrous, she felt *herself* again.

Okay, then. Fuck being normal; fuck laying low, trying to blend in.

Blue drew her sword back, waiting for her first target to blunder into range. Nothing else mattered but this. Saving lives, stopping the bad guy, protecting Chip. Not necessarily in that order, but she'd get it done, just like she got it done last time. *Time to tear some shit up.*

And then she had no more time to think.

———

With a wide wave of her sword, Blue diverted the charge of the two giggling ass-clowns to either side. She heard the crackle of their wizard's lightning bolts strike something. The giggles of the harlequins turned to screams of pain. Blue smirked. *Atta boy, Phil!*

The druid decided to fling her own fireballs to each side, probably aiming for Burton and Skye.

Marda charged. As she swung the SoulStaff like a war club, she let loose a blood-curdling scream and ran at Blue. She closed the distance and jumped, swiping the SoulStaff for Blue's head.

Rather than jump to meet her, Blue kick-stepped into a backward hop, diffusing much of Marda's speed. She held her sword up to protect her head.

She felt the impact in her wrist, but the blow otherwise deflected without harm.

Blue twisted in mid-air, landing gently on her feet. She watched, bemused, as Marda kicked and bounced out of control, trying to change direction in mid-charge.

Clearly, the Baalinistas didn't take the time to practice the way we have.

Marda bounced one last time before slamming into the large oak tree. She slumped down the trunk and landed on her ass. "Damn you, Blue-hair. I recognize you. I owe you for what you did to me."

Blue offered her a mock salute with her sword. "I recognize you, too. Your lack of basic fighting skills has accurately translated into the game."

Marda bared her teeth and pressed against the tree with the staff to help raise herself. "I'll show *you* who has a lack of fighting skills!"

Even as Blue pondered the irony of that declaration, Chip's thief character peeked out from behind the tree. Using the grip of his dagger, he thrust down, striking Marda on the back of the head.

Marda yelped in surprise and dropped the SoulStaff. Apparently reeling from the pain, she fell to her knees.

Chip turned the dagger in his hand, then wrapped the fingers of his left hand over his right. With a cry of fury, he thrust the dagger into Marda's back.

Marda's face froze in a dumbfounded stare, then her body

vanished.

Chip's eyes met Blue's. He winked and offered a quick salute before he disappeared behind the tree.

Blue relaxed and approached the SoulStaff. *Wow. She showed me her lack of fighting skills, all right.*

Having experienced "death" in the game, Blue knew she had a couple minutes' reprieve from Marda's madness. She scooped up the SoulStaff and scanned the meadow.

Phil and Skye were each tussling with a harlequin. The druid and Burton were facing off, the druid girl flinging more fireballs, which Burton dodged with minimal effort.

Blue charged the druid but detoured past Phil and the dagger-wielding maniac he was trying to fend off. She paused long enough to swing her sword down.

The harlequin's head dropped off from the body, still chortling as the head bounced and settled into the field.

A moment later, the body vanished.

Blue extended a hand that Phil gripped firmly.

"Thanks, Blue! What a hellion!"

Off in the distance, the other harlequin slipped her knife between Skye's ribs.

Skye uttered a cry of shock, and, a moment later, vanished.

Blue pointed toward the little assassin already charging Burton. "Stop her, Phil!"

"On it!" Streaks of lightning shot from Phil's staff, knocking the approaching nymph off her feet.

Blue leapt toward the cloaked druid woman, hoping to blindside the attacker while she focused on flinging fireballs at Burton.

Blue closed the distance just as one of those fireballs struck Burton's thigh. Blue ducked and leapt low. She swiped with her sword, even as her tackle knocked the cloaked druid off her feet.

Both the druid and Rebecca let out yelps of surprise and pain.

The druid tumbled sideways, and as they parted, Blue's sword penetrated skin and sliced through the druid's back.

The druid's gasp changed to a scream, and she collapsed in a heap.

Yikes! Blue landed to stand before the woman's crumpled form. Blue raised her sword and...hesitated.

The woman struggled to pull herself along the meadow. "Get away from me!"

Blue watched the wound close moment by moment. *Do I kill her? It's not like I'd really kill her, but...*

"Get back!" the druid cried.

"Look, I don't want to..." *What should I even say? The woman...change that, girl...can't and won't stop me, either way. Whoever she is, it's not in her.*

Instead, Blue ran a beeline past the girl, straight for Burton.

Burton had struggled to her feet, where she appeared to be distracted by the visible healing taking place on her own leg.

Blue extended the wooden rod. "Here's the SoulStaff."

"Very good. Phil should be able to destroy it with a lightning strike. In the meantime, I need protection to cast the spell to close this portal. Oh...watch out."

Blue turned.

Still on her elbows, the druid girl held her palm out, orange energy recharging in her hands.

"Really?" *That's what I get for not hurting you when I had the chance?*

"I need to stop you!" the druid shouted, as if that explained everything.

Blue rolled her eyes and re-drew her sword. "Seriously, go home, little girl. You have no business fighting in this battle."

The druid responded by flinging twin fireballs at Blue. Irritated more than threatened, Blue struck both fireballs with her sword, deflecting them to either side.

"I have to stop you."

"Have it your way." Blue leapt forward and feigned a sword-swipe at the druid's head.

As the druid ducked a blow from the wrong direction, Blue struck low, chopping deep into the girl's torso and causing a scream to pierce the air before the figure vanished.

Blue landed and immediately leapt back the way she came, to land next to Rebecca in a fluid motion.

"You're a natural," Rebecca observed.

"Thanks." She shook off a chill. "I can't help but feel like I just killed someone's kid sister."

"Neither. You just put one of our enemies into a penalty box."

It wasn't that simple, and Blue knew it. "Still...getting stabbed like that hurt like hell, I'll bet."

Burton nodded. "I sincerely hope neither of us ever find out."

As Burton faced the large tree, Blue scanned the battlefield. The skirmish had gotten off to a good start.

Phil threw the remaining nimble harlequin off of him, following up with a lightning bolt that took the character out of the game.

For the moment, the battleground had cleared. "Phil! Over here."

Phil nodded and ran to close the distance.

From the opposite side, Skye also closed in.

Blue craned her neck back and then turned her attention to the front, divided between watching Burton–too damn slow for Blue's taste–lower the crystal to the ground at the base of the tree and then stand over it, a hand outstretched. Burton closed her eyes and emitted a lyrical chant, the foreign words almost songlike even through the CGI vocal cords.

Phil arrived first.

Blue threw the SoulStaff at his feet. "Get rid of that."

"With what? I don't know the spell."

"The spell is...shoot the bejesus out of it."

"Oh." Phil pointed his wizard staff, and a streak of blue sparks engulfed the opponent's staff. After a few moments, the SoulStaff lay before them, smoking and blackened but otherwise intact.

"Shoot it again, Phil. Just keep shooting until it goes away."

"It might just come right back again."

"We'll worry about that if–" Movement several yards away caught her attention. "Heads up!"

The pair of harlequins scuttled out of the woods that surrounded the meadow, both figures wielding daggers.

Blue charged, swinging her sword at one of the screaming harpies and delivering a fatal blow to her chest.

The harlequin's cry cut short, and the body crumpled, folded over backward, then vanished in mid-fall.

Blue landed in front of the second harlequin, who danced madly from foot to foot, screaming her anger. "Damn you, that's the second time you've killed my sister."

There's something you can only say in a ludicrous situation like this, mused Blue. "Hope it's not the last, you crazy bitch."

The harlequin pirouetted to the left, then the right. "We owe you, Blue-hair! We owe you for the pain you caused Marda, and now the pain you've caused Cyn. I'll pay you back, and more!"

Gunther's prolific words from that terrible night returned to her, unbidden. *You'll pay in blood.*

She put the memory away and focused. "Tough talk for someone trying to conquer the world by raising Ms. Pac Man." Blue didn't even know what that meant, but it sounded mocking, so there it was.

The harlequin girl stepped left, waving her knives.

But Blue knew a feint when she saw one and didn't go for it.

The girl returned to her starting point and swiped her daggers.

Blue swung her two-handed blade across, knocking both knives from the harlequin's hands.

She heard a sharp cry from behind her.

Then Phil's voice cut through the air. "Oh, my God!"

Blue turned to see Burton, now with a dagger sticking out of her back. Behind her, the druid stood, and as Blue watched, the cloaked figure shoved a second dagger between Burton's ribs.

You've got to be kidding me. After cutting the girl a break, this happened. And that act of mercy may have jeopardized their success.

Even impaled, Burton closed her eyes and held her hand toward the portal, still chanting the words of the incantation. She trailed to a stop several seconds later. She opened her eyes and held the crystal out toward Chip. "Quickly, someone needs to–" Then her body disappeared.

The crystal, now glowing a fierce, fiery red, bounced off the ground and landed at Chip's feet.

Chip bent to pick up the crystal.

The druid jumped upon him.

"Chip, no!" Blue leapt toward the struggling pair. But she barely launched before a loud crack sounded, and her ankles were wrapped against themselves by an unseen binding. Her legs seared and flared with white hot agony.

Blue's leap stopped short, and her body was slammed into the grass. Her face hit the ground with stunning force.

*What the...*She kicked out, but someone fell over her. As she tried to move her legs, she detected a coil or cord wrapped around both of them, holding them together.

A bola? A whip? She tripped me with a whip!

A giggle of maniacal glee sounded in her ear from the body pressed against her back. *Fuck this!*

Mustering her strength and using the superior armor and weight advantage of her warrior body, Blue forced herself to her elbows and rolled over the ground.

Teeth bit into the back of her neck, fresh pain emanating from the spot. *She bit me? Seriously?*

Gripping her sword with both gloved hands, she twisted the point back toward herself, then held the sword out to her right.

She thrust it back and behind her, hoping to jab her mad-dog opponent. Anywhere would do.

The giggle turned into a howl of surprise and shock.

"Get...off...me!"

She gripped the handle and shoved in a second effort, this time feeling the sword sink into flesh, impaling her opponent.

She threw the sword aside, flinging the injured crazy woman along with it, and rolled onto her back.

She looked at her legs. Sure enough, they'd been bound by the coils of a whip, a weapon currently lying slack without an owner.

With a strangled cry, the body impaled on her sword vanished, and Blue retrieved her weapon. A couple swipes later, she freed her legs and stood.

She looked over, hoping to help, only to see Chip remove his dagger from the throat of the druid girl.

She stared back at him, her mouth open in an "O" of surprise even as her body vanished.

Chip reached down and held the crystal up toward the portal.

The crystal flared a fresh, intense red.

As the crystal flashed to life, disturbing thoughts also flashed through Blue's head. *Chip, taking the place of Brother Krane. Chip, engulfed in flames. Chip, his never-ending screams of agony wasted on the demoness. Chip, tormented for all eternity.*

That could not happen.

Before she could think it through any further, she drew back her heavy two-handed sword, stepped behind Chip, and thrust her weapon through his gut.

"What—?"

She heard his cry of surprise. She closed her eyes and pulled the sword out of the writhing body, hearing a second cry of pain and shock.

She blinked away a scrim of tears in time to see the red fireball hit the grass once again.

At the same time, Chip turned, ready to face the enemy who'd blindsided him. His look of pain turning to shock and surprise.

"Blue?" He fell to his knees.

But she stepped forward, cradled the slack body, and lowered it gently to the ground.

Chip shook his head, as if unwilling to accept the evidence of his eyes. "No. Blue...you can't..."

"Yes, I can. It's not your fault. I won't let you."

"But—" His body vanished, the look of pain and betrayal still distorting his features as he faded from her vision.

She knew she didn't have any time. She steeled her courage, gripped the fiery-red stone in her gauntlet, and stood before the portal, holding her palm out to the doorway.

Nothing happened.

Come on, bitch! Come and get me, I'm waiting! She waved the talisman as if sheer force of will would compel it to complete its purpose.

"Here I am, Baalina! I hope you like your new virtual prison, you hellspawn bitch! You need a sacrifice, take me! I'll give you an eternity of good sport. But I'm all you're getting today, you and your pathetic, deluded band of followers. Bring it. I'll make sure you choke on it for all eternity."

The edges of the portal lit up a brilliant green, and in her hand, she felt an intense burning start in her palm and build up into her arm. The world turned flaming red, and the cackling silhouette of the angry demoness drew closer and closer.

No, she looked around. The demoness wasn't coming to Blue, but Blue was being pulled toward Baalina. She floated bodily through the air, toward the portal, beginning her one-way trip through the gate of chaos.

Goodbye, Chip, please don't think poorly of me. I love you.

And then the flames consumed her, and Blue's world turned to burning agony.

CHAPTER TWENTY_

CHIP OPENED HIS EYES. Before him, the computer screen displayed his avatar's spirit floating in the pre-programmed timeout, drifting down, returning to its body, where it would soon try to rejoin a fight that had concluded moments earlier.

His real body still reclined in the chair where he'd sat several minutes ago. He reached up and rubbed his eyes, trying to recall what had happened. Across the room, from the direction of the couch, he heard Phil utter a similar groan.

He was back in his body. Phil was back. That meant everyone in the game was coming back. They'd won.

But how?

I'd grabbed the crystal, then...

Oh, no!

Blue!

He stood bolt upright. "Blue!"

Looking to his right, he saw Blue, her head bent backwards, her body slack, eyes staring open and lifeless.

"Blue!" He grabbed her chair and wheeled it away from the desk. Her body slumped forward.

He gripped her shoulders, delicately turned her, and lowered her to the rug.

Exactly the same way she'd handled me when—

No, she didn't betray me.

She's taken my place. Which means...

"No! Blue, wake up. Come on, sweetie, wake up." He shook her, panic building within him. "Blue...honey, come on, wake up. Please, honey, please. Don't do this. Don't tell me you did this."

He reached for her wrist, his heart pounding, even after he found the thin, thready throb that indicated a minimal sign of life.

"Fuck!" In his anger, he struck out at the chair and sent it tumbling across the floor behind him.

What to do, what to do? I can't think. I need to think.

As if from a great distance, Chip heard Phil's voice. "Oh, no, what happened, Chip?"

"She did it, she...what Rebecca was supposed to do. What I tried to do. She..." He couldn't get the words out, and he quit trying.

Phil got it. "She used the crystal? Like Brother Krane? She's the one who closed the portal?"

Chip found his voice again. "Yes. I was going to, but she stopped me." His head still spun, searching for options when he didn't have any. His mind reeled, looking for someplace to connect to and finding nothing.

Phil's voice again reached him. "How?"

"She ran a sword through me."

"Oh." Then: "God."

Chip rose, then turned to see her computer screen.

Phil stood nearby, his eyes already looking at it.

It showed only blackness.

Chip started talking out loud, hoping Phil could grab on to something he didn't see. "She's somewhere we've not properly mapped for the game. She's beyond what this can show us, but we know where she is, Phil, she's back in that extra room, that simulated chaos with Baalina's virtual self. She's still in the game."

"Yes, and we're not. And that means no one else is, either. So, take a second, think this through."

A thick hand landed between Chip's shoulders. He looked into the face of his best friend, though Chip still saw everything through a tunnel.

Fresh circles darkened Phil's eyes, his shirt fit rumpled over his plump body, the neck defaced by a fresh line of drool. But overall, Phil looked otherwise unharmed.

At the moment, Chip couldn't begin to appreciate the victory.

Phil's voice still sounded from a distance. "I know it's not where your head is, but she broke us out of there. She broke everyone else out of there. She did good, Chip."

Chip shook his head. "No, you're goddamn right, I don't want to hear that." Anger flared up at Phil for wanting to find any sort of "bright side." "It doesn't mean anything. If we can't get her back, it doesn't mean a damn thing, Phil, please. Help me get her back, or shut the hell up."

The words hung between them, two best friends facing each other —one clearly in shock, the other dealing with the aftermath of his own medically uncharted trauma. Their mutual heavy breathing from the intensity of the experience filled the room.

Chip froze, overwhelmed to the point of inaction. All he could think about was, as they sat here, recovering, taking inventory, Blue was going through God knew what, trapped in an inescapable prison with a vindictive master of torture.

He had to get her out of there. Somehow. And soon.

Phil nodded. "All right, first things first. Let's move her to the couch and out of the way. Then we can evaluate with the computers and see what we can do from this side."

Chip wormed his hands behind her shoulders and waited while Phil positioned himself on the other side to grab her legs. A few moments later–Chip couldn't help but notice that Blue's more reasonably proportioned weight made the task of moving her far easier than moving Phil–they left her lying across the same couch Phil had occupied moments before.

He grabbed a blanket and, ever so gently, covered her to her neck. He bent down, intending to kiss her forehead, when the body trembled, and Blue called out, "No...no, stop..."

"Blue?"

He could see her eyes moving behind the lids, some sort of REM sleep. *But her mind shouldn't be active. She doesn't really occupy it anymore. Unless...the old body still holds some sort of tentative psychic connection with its mind, and whatever is happening was so powerful...*

"Blue, wake up."

"Chip." Phil had come up behind Chip and now laid his large, beefy hand on his shoulder. "Come on. I know it sucks to see this, but she's not in there. We can't help her that way."

"God...what's she going through? It should be me, not her."

"You don't need me to tell you that Blue is spontaneous, but not this time, buddy. I'm sure a part of you is still pissed as hell that she betrayed you in there. But whether by accident or by design, she probably made the smartest choice possible by taking your place."

Chip bit back his angry response. "How do you figure?"

"Because it's you and me out here now, and those fuckers tampered with our game, Chip. If you had followed through with your plan, let's face facts, it would just be me working the computers, and she'd be pacing the room, useless to everyone."

"Well..." He didn't want to say it, but that made perfect sense. *And yes, it's just possible Blue had seen it, as well. And that means she's counting on us to do our part.*

"Now," Phil continued, "The last thing *you* need to be doing is pacing the room, useless to anyone."

"You're right." Chip stood, only to settle in front of his computer console a few steps across the room.

Phil called up a game report on his screen. "There were about 60 players online up until the very moment we were all pushed out and our souls returned to our bodies. We can assume that everyone who had been playing when the spell triggered were all zapped into the game. By my approximation, it looks like the electricity level spiked less than ten minutes ago. No explanation, but I'm sure that's when it happened. Then, everyone except Blue all logged out about six minutes ago. Every one, and all at the same time."

"So, these people, whoever they were and wherever they were, all collapsed at the same time? In their dorms? In their homes? Back in their parents' house waiting on Thanksgiving dinner? That's going to–"

"Be noticed. You bet. That's a lot of panicking parents, a lot of 911 calls, and a lot of people putting two and two together."

Phil continued. "As soon as I sat down, I locked out all users. No one can get in. No affected players, and no players who are clueless about what they missed. That includes our Baalina psychopaths. So that's that."

"Good idea, but it doesn't matter. They're going to come for us," said Chip. *God, can this get any worse?* "There will be a public outcry, and the authorities will insist we shut down the game. Not in forty-eight hours, but immediately."

"We don't know how long it will take them to connect the dots," said Phil.

"A couple hours at most, Phil."

Phil seemed to consider. "Okay, well, let's look at that option. What if we shut the game down?"

As if on cue, Blue moaned from the corner again. "Please...no..."

Chip stole a look in her direction, then shook his head. "We can't risk it! I didn't shut it down when you were in there for the same reason."

"Look...we don't know what might happen if we shut the system down. Maybe nothing at all. Maybe...it might fix this."

The very thought of shutting down the game terrified him. "No. We can't. The chances are far more likely that the electrical current going through the game is the only thing keeping her mind...her soul...locked here in the vicinity and not...cut loose. We kill the power, and we might kill her. We can't risk it."

The doorbell rang, then twice, three times, with urgency that would not be ignored.

To Chip, the sound signaled fate arriving to take the decision away from them. "Oh, my God."

Even from in the basement, they could hear the pounding at the door, followed by two more presses of the doorbell.

And then the sound of a voice blasting through a bullhorn. *"This is Officer Kip Kirby of the Bloomington Police! Come out now, or we're coming in!"*

Chip started to ascend the stairs.

Phil gripped his arm. "We need to stay here."

"They're going to beat the door down. Like we're some sort of armed robbers or drug lords. It's a goddamned raid!"

The amplified voice continued to scream its irritation. "We're giving you five seconds, and then we're coming in!"

"We step away from these machines, they will pull the plug before we can get a word out."

"One!"

"Phil, you're only buying us a couple of minutes."

"We need to talk them down, is all."

But he could read Phil's face. "We can't. You know that."

"Two!"

"We'd better think of something. Because it's our only play."

"Three!"

Phil folded his hands behind his back, nodding toward Chip to do the same.

"Four!"

"Let's stand in front of the servers," said Phil, doing just that. "Maybe we can distract them with having to arrest us, and we can talk them out of pulling the plug."

"Five!"

"That's your plan?" Nevertheless, Chip joined Phil in front of the servers, matching his pose and waiting for the police to force the door.

———

For a moment, darkness.

Then fire flamed up, discomfort flared to blistering pain.

The pain roused Blue, and she sat up.

She found herself huddled on hard, unforgiving ground. No, not ground, a stone slab that extended out in all directions. Yet somehow, the stone ground could burn, as flares of flame shot and flickered in areas around her. It radiated heat, burning her palms and forcing her to her feet.

I won't cower. I won't cower. Still, she couldn't control the inner shaking of her legs as she tried to stay on her feet.

Before her, some distance away, a cloaked, horned silhouette watched, eyes glowing green. Her voice spoke cold malevolence. "So. Here stands the insolent worm who dared to defy my followers."

Blue reached to her scabbard and, to her surprise, gripped her sword. She still possessed her armor and weapon. The knowledge roused her courage. "This 'insolent worm' stopped your demon ass cold."

"Temporarily. No more than that."

Blue stared across at the distance, calculating the needed leaps. Even as she had to hop from boot to boot as the stone heated beneath her, she thought she could make it in two or three leaps.

The demoness continued. "My defeat is only temporary. Yours, wretched one, shall be eternal."

"We'll see about that!" Blue leapt, sword pointed toward the erect figure. But she'd barely left the ground before a pillar of fire engulfed her body in searing, exquisite agony.

Rational thought left her. All she could do was follow the instinct to try to escape the inescapable flames.

She hit the ground, unable to keep her feet, and collapsed against the searing stone.

The fresh pain to her arms, knees, and hands was a distant footnote to the torment of the flames that enfolded her.

She rolled, and she twisted. The handle of her sword grew too hot to hold.

She couldn't see.

She wasn't even sure she had eyes anymore.

Or skin.

She opened her mouth to utter a scream, but no sound came out.

"Feel my power. Feel the agony and know your worthlessness before me. Know that this is just the beginning of your torment, which will continue now until your end! Your body may not break, but your mind, that is another matter, isn't it?"

Chip, someone, help me!

And then she died.

———

Blessed relief.

She hovered over her charred body, untouchable to the whims of her tormentor.

And yet, the wounds could not heal fast enough. And already, even as coherent thought returned to her, she drifted back. Back to a renewed, rejuvenated, healthy body.

Ready to be burned and tormented again.

No! Please, no, not again! Please...

CHAPTER TWENTY-ONE_

"Freeze!"

"We're not resisting, Officer!" Phil called.

His voice loud but shaking, Chip guessed, in an effort to meet the fine line that's loud enough to be heard and yet not forceful enough to be considered a threat by their gun-wielding guests.

From his vantage point, Chip could see the door at the top of the stairs, shrouded in darkness. The door was thrown open.

In the white-lit rectangular opening, Officer Kirby leaned forward to take in the computer bullpen area beyond the darkened stairway. He held his gun up toward the ceiling and settled his gaze on the two unarmed, waiting nerds doing their best to project harmlessness.

Chip bit back his terror enough to speak. "You promised me two days, Kirby, it's barely been six hours."

"That was before everyone playing your game started collapsing into comas, Farren!"

Kirby practically fell into the room, along with four other troopers who piled into the room after him.

Phil called out, "It's not like that, Officer. We fixed the problem."

Kirby glared, his eyes sweeping from one to the other. He raised a finger in warning. "You'd best not say a damn thing right now."

One of the troopers bent over Blue. "Sir, you need to see this."

Kirby approached the trooper.

Chip caught pieces of their brief conversation, which concluded with, "Just like the others."

Chip closed his eyes and swallowed back bile. *Oh, hell, no. Not like the others at all.*

The other troopers, guns drawn, scurried across the room like beetles. Two of them glanced at the screens, then looked at each other. From what Chip could see, they had no idea what they were looking at.

"Officer," Phil called again, "you really need to listen to–"

Kirby glared. "I told you *not* to say anything."

"Fine," said Chip, unsure where his nerve had come from. "I'll say something."

Kirby focused on Chip, his face distorted in fury. "Oh, good, because I can't wait to hear what the pompous nerd-boy has to say. Do you think I've forgotten the tricks you pulled? Do you think I don't remember that I wanted to shut down your operation hours ago, but you talked me into giving you more time?"

"We still need more time to–"

"To what? You sent half of your players into comas. Did you think no one would call the police? Did you think we wouldn't make the connection? We're shutting it down. Now."

"You can't. Blue's life may be at stake."

"That's right, pal, because of your game. Because of what you've done."

"No, you need to listen. If you shut down the game, it might kill her."

Kirby stood by the couch, his gaze lingering on Blue's unconscious form. "I'll say this for you, Farren, you got a hell of a way of showing gratitude to the people who helped you." His eyes widened. "Ms. Shaefer, right? She's the one who sicced the attorney on me. And this is how you repay her?"

"I didn't do this!" Chip snarled, then stopped. He tried again, struggling to keep his tone calm. "We didn't do any of it. We're trying to reverse what happened. If you'll check around, you'll find most of the people have recovered. That's *because* of our efforts. But we still have to get her back."

"What is it, some sort of computer narcotic? You get them hooked in, and you blitz their mind?"

"What? Why the hell would you think–"

"You think I worked this long in the city with one of the largest colleges in the state and haven't picked up on the drug scene? Far as I can tell, you kids want two things—your technology and your vices. Looks like you found a way to combine both, a brand-new type of crime, right here under my nose. It stops now."

"No!" Even as he cried his frustration, he understood Kirby's conclusion. What else could he think? The truth was too far outside the evidence to stumble upon.

The two troopers had followed the cables back to where they plugged into one of the main surge protectors.

One of the troopers looked to Kirby. "Should we try to shut it down or just pull the plug?"

Kirby snapped back, "Just pull the damn plug."

"You can't!" yelled Chip. He moved forward, but two troopers gripped his arms.

Phil started talking, "You pull that plug, you might very well commit murder, Kirby. If you've never heard anything we've said until now, hear this–Blue is somehow connected to that machine. We don't know what will happen if you cut off the power, but chances are, nothing good. Do you really want to take that chance?"

Kirby and the two troopers who hovered by the plug all turned toward Phil.

Clearly his words gave the two troopers pause. *Good going, Phil. Now, if we can think of something more to say.*

But Kirby scoffed. "Really? You got a hell of a lot of nerve, buddy! This machine put half of our students into comas, and you want to talk to me about committing murder?"

Chip cut in, "It's hardly half the–"

"And you shut the hell up, nerd-boy!" Kirby stabbed a finger at Chip, shooting him a look deadly enough to scare Chip into silencing himself. "I've had it with you and your partner in crime here. We tried it your way, and this is where it got us."

Kirby nodded at the troopers. "Do as I say. Pull the damn plug!"

"Belay that!" A woman's voice called from the top of the stairs.

A female figure appeared, tall, red-haired, dressed in a black leather coat, her boots banging down the stairs as she descended as fast as she could. Behind her, a second, tall, mousy-looking girl with dirty blonde hair eased her way after.

Chip knew the tone and the voice. *Rebecca Burton!*

Burton held out a badge, her authoritative voice barking at the two troopers. "Touch those machines and you will face immediate prosecution from the federal government for obstructing a high-priority investigation."

Kirby snarled, "Agent Burton, what the hell are you even doing here?"

"Keeping you from ruining your career, Kirby. And you'd better listen to these young men. Shutting down those machines could very well mean ending the life of Ms. Fiona Shaefer there on the couch."

At Burton's words, the two troopers backed away from the surge protector.

Chip released a breath he hadn't realized he'd been holding with a whoosh of relief and gratitude.

Kirby exploded. "You're as cracked as they are!"

"Maybe, maybe not. But it's officially not your problem anymore."

Rather than back down, Kirby stepped up, eyes blazing, finger shaking in the face of the federal agent. "They're putting students into comas, and you're telling me it's not my problem!"

Burton met his emotional tirade with a stoic, stony look.

Chip cringed at the display of useless machismo. It was like a scene from a bad cop show.

Kirby's rant continued. "This may be the strangest bust in my entire career on the force, but whatever is going on, these people have got to be stopped."

Apparently unruffled, Burton replied, "I agree. But these boys have been telling you the truth. Their game was hacked by technology terrorists and used for malicious purposes outside of their control. And the fact that the mass coma crisis reversed itself within minutes of being triggered is a credit to their skills."

"Minutes my ass, Burton! You were hospitalized for two days!"

"And yet I'm not the one yelling, Officer. Think about it."

If possible, Kirby turned even redder in the face, but to Chip's relief, finally shut up.

Burton surveyed the room. "Officer Kirby, I'd like to offer a proposal. I will need assistance nabbing the real perpetrators of this crime. You and your men can be a part of it, if you're willing. If not, I'll find someone else. But either way, your men are going to clear out of this house and leave the equipment untouched, and free these kids, and forget whatever charges you think you have on them, immediately."

This time, Burton allowed some anger to show through, and to Chip's surprise, Kirby backed down.

"That's my direct order as your superior. You let me know about the rest."

Chip waited, not sure whether he dared move.

Finally, Kirby made a scoffing noise and turned his back.

Burton grabbed his arm, turning him to face her.

He glared, his eyes darting to where she still held his arm. He opened his mouth, then shut it as if he'd reconsidered.

Chip imagined it was a rare thing for anyone to handle him like that, especially a superior.

His voice trembled. "What?"

Burton said, "There are actual bad guys out there. Their plans are falling apart, and pretty soon, they're going to try to make a break for it. It's not these kids, but I can point you to the real criminals. I could use your help."

Kirby glowered a bit more, and then his features settled into a businesslike expression. "You going to come clean and tell me the truth about what is going on?"

The famous movie line traveled through Chip's head. *You couldn't handle the truth.*

Apparently, Burton chose not to rise to the bait, but answered, "Most of it. Whatever isn't classified."

"Classified?"

Burton nodded. "This is much bigger than you know. I wasn't exaggerating when I used the term technology terrorists. Right here in Bloomington. Want to be a part of the bust?"

"Of course."

"Okay." Burton released his arm. "Get your men ready. Stand by. We'll be moving soon. Oh, I hope you didn't break open these kids' door."

Kirby shook his head. Did Chip see a twinkle in his eyes? "It was unlocked."

Burton nodded. "Good. Please leave in an orderly fashion. We have work to do here."

Moments later, they were gone, save Burton and the other girl–Skye, he presumed–and all Chip could do as he sank on the couch next to Blue was try to catch his breath. "I can't believe your timing. Thank you so much."

Rebecca put a hand on his shoulder. "Don't thank me yet. The hard work is still ahead."

Chip leaned in close to Blue. His heart broke as her face again contorted in some sort of pain. "Hang in there. Stay strong. We're going to get you out soon."

———

AFTER WHAT SEEMED AN ETERNITY, Natalie's screen flashed the message: **Save Complete.** She pulled the mini-drive from the slot and dropped it into her laptop briefcase. "That's it, that's all of our work, up to the moment everything fell apart."

At Nat's words, Marda glared from where she sat in front of the computer screen. She was not at all happy at the prospect of having to flee. Nat understood, to some extent. They had all glimpsed their mistress, not a statue image, but real and in the flesh–after a fashion. Of them, Nat knew this would affect Marda most profoundly.

Marda had witnessed the mistress torment and torture the Shaefer girl, who had made her suffer. To Nat, it made no important difference at this point, but she knew Marda well enough to know she'd obsess over it.

Marda pressed, "Why can't we just re-create the SoulStaff?"

Nat slashed her open palm through the air. "They've locked me out. They've located my server, they know my port, and they know exactly where I'm coming in from. My last few attempts haven't even gotten past the login screen."

"Then do something else. Use your hacking tricks!"

"You don't know what you're talking about. I don't have any tricks left!" Nat was screaming now and past caring. "They're on to us, Marda, plain and simple. That's two computer geniuses, working within the program they themselves created, versus me. I had a chance as long as I could cloak my entry. I did it for a long time, but I just can't anymore."

"Then we call someone else."

Nat rolled her eyes. It was the never-ending curse of all engineers, having to explain computer tech to non-techies and their nonsensical mantra: *Spare me the details, just do it.* "No one's that good. We're done here. We just have to find another opportunity on another platform."

"You mean start over somewhere else? That could take months!"

"The mistress has waited thousands of years. One more year won't matter much."

"Watch your tone, Natalie!"

Natalie opened her mouth to reply, only to feel a pressure against her throat, followed by a sting. *Oh, my Goddess, what...*She pulled her head back to face a dagger extended out and pushed against her chin.

As a chill ran down her spine, Nat's gaze traced the hand, up the arm, to meet Cyn's expression of malice.

"I would be *very mindful* of Marda's advice at this point, Nat." Cyn leaned in close, her top lip curled in a snarl. "It's almost as if you want us to fail."

"What are you doing?" Surely, they didn't think...

She turned to look around her station. Cyn towered over her and to her left, she met Marda's dark, penetrating stare. Behind her, she felt a pair of hands grip her shoulders. *Van wants in on this, too. Figures. They all want a piece of me.*

Marda's eyes drilled into Nat's. Nat tried to look away, but Cyn's dagger pressed a warning.

Marda's voice sounded like ice. "Cyn's right. Why are you in such a hurry to fail?"

"Marda...please..." Nat understood what had happened. They'd failed, they wanted their scapegoat, and now they thought they'd found it. Her.

When she found her voice, Natalie tried to keep her tone calm, though she herself trembled. "Please...please, Sisters. Listen to reason. We can't succeed here. If we could, I'd be the first one to suggest how. Don't forget how I found our breakthrough after all that work. I got us in." The words tumbled out of her. "I recreated the SoulStaff, and I did it on my own. And it worked. Do you really think I'd do all that and chicken out now?"

Marda's eyes softened, perhaps just a bit. "Go on."

"Make it good," said Cyn.

Natalie closed her eyes and swallowed back phlegm. She knew the truth, the one she dared not say aloud. She wasn't willing to die for this cause. Yes, she thought women had been treated poorly throughout history, and she thought a reversal of the ruling order was a natural and welcome step to remedying the great wrongs of history.

But she didn't want to die for this cause, or *any* cause. She was a coward, and she wanted to live.

Right now, she just wanted to live past this moment.

She referenced the facts, trying not to think, just talk. "The police know some sort of attack, targeting other students, has taken place. Burton has awakened from her coma. She can, and she *will*, have the authorities convene on our location as soon as she can confirm it."

Marda's distorted features made her fury apparent. "No, you silly mouse, I won't accept that. There must be a way to put us back into the game and trigger the spell. Today was to be our day of victory and revenge. There must be a way."

"Marda, I can't even pull up the game world. The only reason we can still access the chaos-domain is because they haven't found our hack into it. It's also the only room that *we* can still lock *them* out of, but that doesn't do us any real good. All we can do is buy time to transfer Baalina back into the real chaos dimension and try again."

"The mistress will demand that someone pay."

Natalie closed her eyes, trying not to become ill where she sat. "Baalina has...a new playmate to torture...at least, for as long as the virtual room remains. We might even be able to take the blue-haired...adversary–" Nat couldn't bring herself to call the unfortunate soul a blue-haired bitch the way Marda did, "–along with her when we transfer them back. I'll oversee it personally."

"Yes, but..." Marda's eyes shone their malice. "Now that I think about it...why should the mistress have all the fun?"

Marda closed her eyes and seemed to swoon in the oppressive quiet that followed. "Yes...yes, mistress, I hear you. And we accept!"

Marda's eyes re-opened to look squarely at Natalie. "Can you still use the spell to conjure us back into the virtual chaos realm?"

It took a moment for Natalie to process the request. "Can I send us back in? Yes, but we can't really *flee* there. We'll be as trapped as–"

"Because the mistress has extended a gracious invitation for all of us to join her..." Marda turned toward the screen.

Nat had lowered the sound all the way down, so it currently showed Blue in the midst of a silent scream while a blazing fireball tore through her chest. "...to spend some quality time with her new playmate."

Cyn smiled. "Sounds delectable."

Natalie's stomach churned. Their house was collapsing around them, and all the goddess Baalina thought about was herself and her pleasures. She spared no thought for the danger she put the rest of them in.

Nat looked around the room and saw that the idea took hold, one to the other to the other, like a poison.

Matching looks of sadism crossed the faces of Cyn, Van, and Marda, but Natalie closed her eyes against the queasiness that threatened to overtake her. *God, no, I can't.*

Then she noticed that Cyn's knife had lowered, and Van's hands no longer restrained her.

They're not thinking about me anymore. In that moment, Nat made her decision. *They want the Shaefer girl, so let them have the Shaefer girl.* Nat spoke her decision with boldness. "Okay...I'll transfer the three of you."

Cyn's gaze locked on hers. "Don't you want to join us...Sister?"

She almost answered "no" but caught herself. "Someone...needs to make sure the rest of you can come back, and...I can finish packing in the meantime."

Cyn opened her mouth to reply.

But Marda answered first. "Excellent plan, Sister. Prepare us for the transfer." Her eyes locked on the screen, where Blue's body had once again expended itself and faded away. "As you say, time is short. I have much to pay that bitch back for, and not much time to do it."

CHAPTER TWENTY-TWO_

Again, the flames engulfed her.

Again, her hair incinerated, her skin burned. Again, the agony forced her to scream and thrash.

And yet...following those few seconds of pain, her avatar "died," which translated to over two minutes of a calm, more peaceful state of being—unreachable and untouchable by her tormentor, the so-called demoness.

It meant a chance to catch her breath, where the pain faded, and where she could regroup and consider her options.

After the time-out, she returned to her body, fully healthy, healed, and clear-headed.

For only a moment before the pain would begin again.

But the rest meant a new opportunity to turn the tables on her tormentor.

Good God. Could she adjust to this?

Many times already, she'd jumped at her attacker. Twice, she'd almost gotten her hands around the neck of the pompous bitch who equated making her life a living hell to some sort of distraction on par with taking up knitting.

She needed just one chance to grab that scepter and test its durability on the demoness' skull. Then she might actually keep the upper hand in this retarded exercise until Chip found a way to get her out of here.

It wasn't a great plan, but it was a plan. And it kept her sane.

She'd sacrificed herself, prepared to trade her life for Chip's, and she didn't hesitate in doing so. But even as she acted, she realized her sacrifice probably wasn't as final as all that.

Not by a long shot.

For all its trappings and for all her suffering, this wasn't really a hell. And she knew Chip was working on the other side, doing all he could to get her out.

In the meantime, she stood on the hot cement ground. She feigned to her left, the fireball just missing her. She pivoted, propelling herself directly at her laughing tormentor.

The demoness answered with a wall of flame spewed across her body that seared her eyes and set her aflame. Again.

"Prepare yourself, mortal worm. When next you return, I have visitors who are quite anxious to say hello!"

Blue's brief scream was cut off moments later by the relief of simulated death.

With each cycle, she noted the trauma of the experience took longer to shake off. *But I can endure...a while longer. Piece of...cake...Chip. But you can...come get me...any time now.*

———

As the mistress called to them, Marda signaled Nat to begin the incantation.

Marda filled the space between Cyn and Van. As they all faced Natalie, Marda's pulse quickened at the idea that they'd shortly be in the presence of...*her*! "Quickly, Natalie, our mistress awaits us! We should not leave her waiting."

It annoyed her, to an extent, to be forced to share this supreme moment with two of her underlings, a pair of muscle-for-hire who stood and waited in casual indifference, clearly oblivious to the honor they were all about to share.

Natalie, at least, responded to her command with the urgency required. She turned away from her laptop and held her hands over the three of them, muttering in the ancient language, pronouncing each sacred syllable almost as clearly as Marda would have if the honor had fallen to her.

The room faded and the three of them dropped into their video game avatar bodies, the transition, this time, much easier than before.

The heat closed around them, its presence oppressive and foreboding. Beneath her, Marda noted they stood on a huge cement slab of cracked and crumbled stone. Flames spewed from random cracks into the stifling air.

Closing the distance, in all her regal splendor and grasping the sacred scepter, Baalina...the mistress herself...stood before them in person! At long last!

"Mistress!" Marda called out and fell before her, prostrate at the Goddess' feet. She ignored the flesh of her face, which seared and burned as she threw herself down on hands and knees.

Marda sensed, rather than saw, Cyn and Van, who stood behind her. She called out her frustration, "Bow, you unworthy ones! Bow!"

Cyn protested, "But the ground is–"

"Get on your knees in the presence of the mistress, you lowly–"

And then...*she* spoke, and nothing else mattered. "Your demonstration does everyone present honor, Special One. But rise, Marda, and look upon the face of your most pleased mistress."

It took...she had no idea how long for the words to register. *She called me Special One. She is most pleased.*

Tears of joy spilled from her eyes and caused the stone to answer with a series of sizzles.

She looked up...into a grayish, thin-fingered hand lowered toward her. "Rise, Special One."

Marda could not hide the tremble in her voice. "I am not worthy to touch–"

"But you are. Take my hand, Marda. Quickly, my Special One. Cyn, Van, prepare yourselves. Our victim is due any moment now. I wish to see a demonstration of your skills. Entertain me."

————

"SURPRISE, BITCH!"

Blue appeared, seeing three people, one on either side, one in front of her. The scenario barely registered before the first blow landed from one of the giggling harlequins, a solid blow to her face before she saw it coming.

She spun into the second harlequin, who caught her before she could hit the ground.

Blue found her balance. As the second harlequin drew her knife, Blue thrust her knee up. She connected with the groin.

The crazy woman's giggles cut off and turned into a grunt of surprise. The harlequin doubled over.

"Surprise back!" Blue enfolded one fist into the other and struck the back of her opponent's head.

"Van, get her!"

Something slammed the side of Blue's face, and she went down.

"Hold her," she heard her wounded opponent cry.

Blow after blow landed. Soon, someone had her arms pinned back, and that's when it really hurt.

They took a long, interminable time at it—laughing, mocking, giggling. The blows fell. Not hard enough to trigger the release she sought, but enough to pile pain upon pain.

Finally, she collapsed.

"Looks like our playmate has stopped playing," a voice said.

"Fuck...you." *The simulated death is coming soon. It has to. Then we'll see. Ultimately, this is an extended ass-kicking. Sucks, but nothing special, especially since I'll come back healed.*

"Oooh, Sisters, sounds like she still has some fight in her."

She recognized Marda's crazy tone, which penetrated Blue's semi-conscious state.

"I don't see much fight, Cyn, she's going to sleep on us."

A hand gripped her hair and pulled her head up.

She stared into the face of the giggling, red-haired, crazed harlequin. "Oh, playmate, that's not very playful."

Blue grimaced. "We'll see how playful I am soon enough." She sensed, rather than saw, the red-haired harlequin address the others. "Do you hear that, girls? She thinks we're done."

Sharp pain stabbed her hand and jolted her fully awake. The excruciating agony forced her eyes wide open to view a dagger protruding from the back of her hand.

A foot came down on her wrist—not heavy enough to break it, but enough to pin it in place.

The harlequin bent, flexed the knife.

Her body's own attempts to pull away turned into another wave of blinding, excruciating torment. The fire, the burning, was mild compared to this.

"We've only just begun, sweetie."

Oh, God, what is she doing to me? Please, let it stop!

But it didn't.

CHAPTER TWENTY-THREE_

MINUTE AFTER MINUTE, the whimpers from Chip's love and soul-mate tied his stomach in knots, all the more distracting as they rose in both volume and intensity. Each new cry tore his attention from the screen, and he'd look over in time to see her features distort and her brow furrow. Then he'd turn back to the screen, nothing accomplished, frustrated and flummoxed.

He'd rise, abandoning the blank screen where his code needed to be. He'd return to her side on the couch.

Burton sat on the arm of the couch at Blue's head, her palm stroking Blue's forehead, occasionally touching her shoulder. Reading Burton's face, it looked to Chip that she halfway expected these actions to bring some sort of comfort.

"Can you...do anything?" he asked.

Burton glanced up at Chip, then returned her gaze to Blue. "No. I...thought I could, but...she's not there, Chip. I can't reach her."

"Then why is she–"

"I don't know. I'm sorry. I...just don't. But I won't leave her side, either. Until this is over."

Her unspoken words *one way or the other* hovered between them.

Chip sank onto the middle cushion. He could easily work his butt onto the edge, creating a spot for himself where he could reach out and take her hand.

Her limp, unresponsive hand. Warm, but lifeless. "We're going to get you back, Blue. I promise." Then he returned to his computer, stared at the screen, and fretted some more. And accomplished nothing.

———

"Aww, she's not playing anymore," said Cyn. She kicked out with a boot and rolled the limp figure over. Daggers protruded from one hand, the back of one thigh, a foot, and the back of her shoulder.

As she rolled onto the dagger in her shoulder, the body twitched.

"One more blow, and the cycle will start again," said Van, smiling at her partner and twin.

Cyn asked her standard question. "How long?"

Van considered. Normally, she consulted a stopwatch she kept specially for these sorts of sessions, but the computer character didn't come equipped with one. "Best approximation, maybe forty minutes."

Cyn met Van's gaze, and they exchanged volumes between them in their not-quite telepathic bond. *All in a day's work, my true Sister. And our new client is most satisfied.*

As we knew she would be.

"Impressive!" The Goddess gripped the royal scepter at her side as she strode across the broken ground, the train of her regal robes trailing behind her. "I haven't been so moved in centuries, Cyn and Van. I rarely play with my old toy anymore. He lies and whimpers, and every decade or so I make him cry and weep just to break the tedium. I'm afraid my heart's just not it anymore. But you two take it to a level of art!"

Baalina's gaze traveled from Van to Cyn, her admiration easy to read on her ashen features. "I knew, when I first touched your minds over a decade ago, that you would serve me well." Her gaze fell upon the three of them collectively. "After so long left in solitude with only one distraction, one forgets the sheer creative *fun* of torture."

Cyn bent slightly at the kind words from the mistress. Through her half-closed eyes, she spied Marda's face flaming a ruby red.

When Marda spoke, Cyn detected the tremor of jealousy in her tone, and wondered if the Goddess heard it, too. "They have served you well, mistress. In spite of Cyn's earlier mistake, she has–"

The Goddess waved her wrist. "Nonsense, all forgotten." The mistress extended her scepter toward Marda. "Come, it is time to demonstrate the leadership and trust I have placed in you."

Marda gripped the offered rod, both a weapon and a symbol of her status in the new order. Simple but deadly, with the sigil of Baalina etched into the blunt end, the spike weapon extended perhaps twenty-four inches and ended in a lethal metal point.

"Put an end to our mutual troublemaker!" commanded the mistress.

Marda's gaze fell upon their enemy. Her eyes glinted with fury and perhaps a touch of madness. Marda bent down over Blue and prodded Blue's neck with the point. "Wake up."

She pressed. The point vanished into her victim's neck. Blood spilled onto the stone.

A look of malicious cruelty crossed Marda's face.

Cyn was impressed. She didn't think the crazy bitch really had it in her.

To her surprise, Blue's eyes snapped open.

My God, she's still fighting!

Marda smiled. "You're still with us! Good. Remember when our positions were reversed, and you let me live?"

Blue's lips moved, but no sound came.

"You know..." Marda raised a hand to her chin, a mocking pose of reflection. "I wonder if you had killed me then, if my Sisters would have gotten this far on their own."

Cyn almost objected, then realized the jab wasn't really aimed at the three of them, but to make Blue feel worse.

Blue opened her mouth again.

Again, Cyn was taken aback by the strength of their foe.

Blue croaked out a single word, "Why?"

Again, Marda pretended to consider. "I would think that would be obvious. Because of how you humiliated me, we're going to keep playing with you. Then we're going to free our mistress, and the first thing we're going to do is find Eugene Farren and everyone else who stood in our way and make them all pay for defying us. Then we're going to proceed with our plans to conquer the world."

Blue spat another word. "Insane."

Marda laughed, a bitter sound.

A sound that made even Cyn uneasy.

Marda continued in her mocking tone. "I know, it sounds crazy, doesn't it? We're going to take over the world. But how many of us are really insane? We all start off with grand goals–maybe to become a brain surgeon, only we settle into real life as a pet doctor. And that's a bit short. But it's something."

Marda set the scepter aside, gripped Blue under her chin, and forced her to look eye to eye. "But it doesn't matter, really, in your case, does it? This little coven of insanity has destroyed you. Maybe we'll destroy your friends; maybe we'll never even leave here. Does that really make much difference to you, now? We'll aim for the world. Maybe we'll fall short."

She let Blue's head fall against the stone. "Either way, we'll destroy you. And that's something." Marda grabbed up the scepter and stood, drawing back to strike Blue's chest.

"Wait!" Cyn cried.

Cyn crouched near Blue's head, reached out, and pulled her arms back, exposing her belly. She pointed to a spot near the navel. "Aim there, Sister. It will hurt the most there."

With a cry of fury, Marda swung the scepter down, driving the spike into Blue's gut.

Blue's eyes snapped open, as did her mouth, but no sound came.

Marda offered a mocking wave. "Goodbye, Blue. We'll see you soon."

Tortured to death, Blue vanished.

Cyn held a hand out, and Van slapped it. "Just like Anthony Guinness."

At Marda's confused look, Cyn explained, "Owed a mob boss big bucks. Guy got tired of waiting for his money, so he asked us make an example of him."

Van giggled. "Anthony was such a tough guy, said we'd never get to him. Took six hours to die, but he cried like a baby the last three."

"And shit his pants," added Cyn.

Van grimaced. "Oh, gross, the mess! Thanks for reminding me."

Cyn considered Marda with new respect. "Should we get back to our apartment? We may be running out of time."

Marda shook her head. "No, this is way too fun. One more round, at least."

———

Release at last! But her "death" brought only dread. She had no strength left. But the regeneration took place without her act or desire. She lowered back toward her avatar body, a new body which would be healed of all its physical wounds, only to be wounded again.

God, no, I can't. I can't go back, please, someone...Chip?

———

"Chip!"

The angry woman's voice pulled Chip's gaze away from the computer screen.

Though all the computer screens lit up live and active, Chip looked around an empty basement computer room, empty except for himself and a middle-aged woman.

She stood dressed in a professional blouse and knee-length black skirt, long, dark hair pulled back. The edges of her eyes showed the beginnings of crows-feet, especially now, as they widened in distress.

Though he'd never physically met this woman, he recognized Leona Shaefer from Blue's photos and from the memorial service which remained forever burnt into his memory as one of the most miserable days of his life.

He wondered at her appearance, but then an obvious reason struck him. *After all these years, she's finally here to give me hell for the part I played in her death. But...why now?*

Instead, she cried, "Do something!"

"I'm sorry, Mrs. Shaefer. What?"

"They're killing her, Chip!"

He glanced over at the couch, shocked to see Blue still lying on it. He was certain she wasn't there a moment ago.

Blue's features distorted worse than ever, and she released another distressing moan.

"I'm doing everything I can."

"That's not good enough, mister!" The woman approached Chip and raised hands balled into fists.

To Chip, she seemed smaller in stature than he'd imagined, perhaps five-foot two versus Blue's additional couple of inches. Tiny next to Chip, who stood just shy of six feet.

But it still hurt plenty when she pelted him with her fists. "Ow! I'm going as fast as I can, it's just so–"

"They're killing her, Chip. She can't hold out much longer."

"But I don't know what to do!" A thought occurred to him. "Do you? I mean, from the other side, is there something you can do that we can't?"

She stopped swinging her fists, and her shoulders slumped. She squeezed her eyes shut, and tears streamed down her face.

Her body shook from the emotion, and Chip's heart broke at the sight of it.

"I told her...to trust you," she said between sobs. "I told her to come.

I said you were in danger, and she came. Now my baby's dying because of me."

God! He'd never felt so sick. But he couldn't shake off his helplessness. "I'll do what I can. I'll...somehow, I'll figure something out. Can you reach her? Can you tell her to hold on just a bit longer?"

"I can try, but...hurry, Chip, you need to hurry. She can't physically die where she is now, but...we might still lose her. Everything that we love about her is being stripped away by the second."

A loud moan, this one building to a cry, came from the couch.

He looked over, but now the couch sat empty.

Still, he heard her voice. "Chip. Chip!"

———

"Chip?"

He snapped open his eyes. The blurred face of a young woman wavered in his vision. "Blue?"

He lifted his head from the computer desk to bring into focus the face of the mousy, light-haired girl. Her name returned to him. *MacLeod. Burton calls her Skye.*

Skye's eyes reflected sympathy. "You fell asleep. We thought you could use a few minutes, but..."

Chip took in the room. Phil sat at the computer next to his, the chair pulled out where MacLeod had occupied the last console down. He could still hear Blue's moans. He looked over at the couch.

Burton, balanced on the arm of the couch, tried to restrain Blue's thrashings, more intense than he'd seen so far.

He rushed to her side, then helped Burton hold Blue by the shoulders while she placed a hand on her forehead. "Peace. Peace, be at–"

"No!" Blue twisted from under Burton's palm.

It was all he could do to hold her down.

Burton spoke out loud, though to whom, Chip wasn't sure. "I can't reach her. There's nothing to reach; this shouldn't be happening."

A desperate look marred Blue's face.

"Blue, we're coming for you. Hang in there, we're–" Blue's convulsion nearly threw Chip off her.

"Dammit, hold her!" cried Burton. "I'm going to try something else."

The agent enfolded her fingers over Blue's face and placed her other hand on top of Blue's head. "Hold her...still."

Blue continued to thrash.

But Chip just let his full weight press against her. She let out a grunt, as if struck, and then she went slack.

At the same time, Burton dropped to the floor, like her limbs had turned to jelly.

Blue lay beneath him, immobile, her face smoothed over with the peaceful look of deep sleep. *Thank God!*

Chip stood and reached down to the disheveled agent.

The agent took his hand and pulled herself to her feet.

Chip placed his other hand on her shoulder in a way he hoped reflected gratitude. "Thank you, Agent Burton. It worked."

But the woman shook her head. The concern on her face caused a sinking feeling. "I didn't. I didn't do anything, not really. I just...well, essentially tranquilized her. The natural equivalent of a muscle relaxant. I didn't want to do it, but she was going to hurt herself."

Sick to his stomach, Chip took in the sight of Blue's serene, relaxed face. He wanted to embrace the illusion, cling to it as the reality. "Then...whatever was happening–"

"–is still happening." Burton straightened her jacket and rubbed the back of her neck. "I hope I didn't cause more harm than good. But whatever action we're going to take, we need to do it soon."

Burton's words hit him. His head hurt, his vision blurred, and his concentration was almost gone.

Then he knew what he had to do. He looked at Burton. He hoped she'd hear his plea. "Listen, I need to go."

Burton blinked rapidly, but the expected dramatic response did not come. Her voice held a stone-cold calm. "Excuse me, Eugene, did you understand what I just said?"

"Yes, and that's why I have to leave. Just for a short time. I'll make a...food run. I can't think in here. Not here, not...around her."

Phil's voice reached them from his place behind the terminal. "A food run! You *are* joking, right?"

Chip understood the irony. The man who perpetually focused on food and snacks made it clear by the tone of his voice that today needed to be the exception.

"Listen, Bro, I'm all about taking time for a snack, but your timing kind of sucks."

Chip shook his head. "No, trust me, my timing's perfect. I need to get out of here, I need to clear my head, and I just..." He looked over at Burton. "I just do." He finished, even as he heard the lame tone of his voice.

Burton shrugged and turned back to Blue. "Do what you feel you have to do."

It felt every bit a dismissal. Feeling all eyes on him, Chip ascended the stairs and bolted out the door.

———

THE COOL AIR woke him up, but the descended darkness shocked him. Confused, he fished out his phone and tapped the screen light to trigger the backlight. The time flashed at him.

Seven-thirty? Really? So, his stomach hadn't tricked him. They'd skipped dinner. And, as a minor footnote, missed Thanksgiving all together.

He recalled, briefly, a thawing turkey and loads of fixings, food that still waited, split between the fridge and the pantry in their kitchen, in anticipation of the holiday dinner Phil and he had planned out days ago in order to play host to Blue today.

Now he just wanted to get her back alive and whole.

He wandered the darkened streets, the knots in his stomach still clenched tight. He'd never felt so helpless. Not even in the midst of their fight with Gunther, even when he'd tried to sacrifice himself so the ghost would leave her alone. At least then, he'd made that choice willingly.

And he'd nearly died for it, but he was content in his decision at the time he'd made it.

In the jumbled mess of his mind, the accusations flew, one by one, as he walked.

From Blue's mother. *I told her...to trust you. I told her to come. I said you were in danger, and she came. Now my baby's dying because of me.*

From Phil. *Your timing kind of sucks.*

From Rebecca. *Do what you have to do.*

From Blue, as she braced to enter the virtual realm, when she'd gripped his hand at the last moment: *I really don't want to do this.* And his response: *I'll take good care of you.*

Just one of many lame promises he'd made to her in the last few hours, beginning with his oath to win her back when she threatened to walk out of his life: *If you don't hear anything else I say, hear this. He will never love you the way I do. No one will. I would do anything for you. If you were ever in trouble, I'd lie, steal, cheat—I'd move Heaven and Earth to help you, and you know I would.*

He kept walking, his mind a million miles away, still mentally kicking himself. *Fuck. Nice one, brainiac. And here she is, waiting to collect on that promise you made, smart guy. The only thing is, there's nothing to lie about, nothing to steal, and you can't cheat your way to victory, either. So, you'd better find a way to move Heaven and Earth really fast. What's the plan, brainiac? Because you better come up with something, and fast.*

He realized he was approaching Smittie's. To his shock, the florescent red OPEN light still shone in the door, though looking through the pane-glass front, he could see Laverne and Smittie behind the counter chit-chatting with each other in an empty restaurant.

Well...he was hungry. Might as well grab some breadsticks and return with a few pizzas. He wasn't good for doing much else at this point. Might as well accomplish the one lame-ass excuse he gave to leave in the first place.

He opened the door, which triggered the bell alert, not that Laverne needed it to pounce.

"Well, bless my soul, Smittie, our favorite customer. Twice in one day, and on Thanksgiving, to boot!"

Not up to answering, Chip stumbled to the nearest booth and dropped into it. By the time he situated himself, Laverne was there.

She deposited a plastic cup of Coke on the table. "Where's your little honey, honey?"

The question hit him like a battering ram to the gut. He reached up and buried his face in his hands, trying and failing to control his hyperventilating.

An awkward silence followed, which Laverne finally broke. "Wow, was my joke that bad?"

A laugh escaped him, which caused his shoulders to shake.

Oh, God. He couldn't help it; he couldn't control it. He was going to have a breakdown right here in front of his waitress friend, and there wasn't a thing he could do about it, or any way he could explain it.

"Hey...hey, Chip! Are you okay?"

No, he was far from okay. He continued to gasp for air. His body shook, and he fought back tears he could no longer stop.

Blindly, he reached for the napkin dispenser in the middle of the table, fumbling for them a few seconds. Then a stack was placed into his hand.

Laverne.

Her voice reached him gently, softly, assuring. He realized, distantly, she'd placed her hand between his shoulders.

"Take it easy, easy, Chip, take it slow..."

He dropped his head to the tabletop. He was too tired to stand strong or do anything at all. He didn't know where to turn, what to do, where to go.

And while he floundered in this restaurant, lost and confused, Blue was back at the house, suffering.

"What am I going to do?" he called out.

"Easy, Chip. Take it easy."

He sat up and wiped wetness from his face. He looked around, taking in his surroundings.

The waitress sat across from him. Her dark eyes reflected only sympathy, not at all the freaked-out expression he expected.

"God, I'm...so sorry about that." He finished cleaning himself up.

Over her shoulder, he saw Smittie approach with a basket of breadsticks and sauces. He deposited them and stood at the table.

Laverne shot him a stern look.

He retreated to his station behind the counter.

Chip's stomach rumbled as the aroma of tomato sauce hit him. He reached down and tore a bite off the first one.

Laverne waited, seated next to him at the booth while he ate a few bites. She said nothing but sat without comment.

After he'd gobbled down two breadsticks, she asked, "Better?"

Chip blinked, hoping to clear the scrim that had settled across his vision. "Not really, but I think I'm done freaking out on you."

"Well, that's good. Let's take it from the top." She leaned forward.

Chip realized that she had her hand over his.

"Let's start with the obvious. Do I have to kick anyone's ass tonight?" Her dark-eyed stare seemed to penetrate the cloud of his fogged mind.

"Wait, what?" Then he realized. *She means Blue.* "No. No! She didn't do anything wrong, if that's what you mean, but...well, she's in trouble, and it's my fault."

Laverne paused. Her lips pursed. "Chip," she said, gently, as if speaking to a child. "Some people get into booze or drugs, and they do it to themselves. You can't let anyone guilt you into–"

"No, it's not that, either. Please. It has to do with my game." It was out there before he could stop it. *Crap!*

"Your game? Your–" He swore he saw a smirk flash across her face, just for a moment, before she resumed a stone-face stare. "Your video game? Did she, like, really hate it? I mean, some people just don't get–"

"No." He laughed at her conclusion. His head still spun, and he wondered what to tell her next. "It was a little more serious than that, but...I'm sorry, I'm not sure how to explain it."

"But, Chip, you were in tears. No video game is worth that. Why were you even working on it? And...did you all skip dinner?"

"I'm sorry, I can't really answer most of those questions." He added, "Well...yes, we skipped dinner."

To Chip's surprise, she looked hurt. "Do you think I wouldn't understand? Because I'm just a dumb waitress?"

Chip sighed. "No...it's more like, you wouldn't believe me. It would sound far-fetched." *To say the least!*

"Look, Chip, I know it's not my business, but can I tell you what I see when I look at you?"

Just to keep her talking while his head cleared, Chip agreed.

"I've been hearing you and Phil come in here every few days, talking about that game, since you first started programming it two years ago. I know you think I just kind of nod my head and I don't understand."

"Well, no, it's not that—"

Laverne held her palm out to stop him. "And that's fair. But I'll tell you something. I had no intention of bringing it up, but maybe it might help. A couple of months ago, you know, after I'd been hearing so much about it, I finally decided to go online and check it out. I mean, it was free, so I wasn't wasting nothin' but my time. Truth is, I don't play video games. I don't like them, so it was all new to me."

As Laverne talked, Chip smiled. The cobwebs were clearing as she spoke, and he grabbed a third breadstick. "That's nice of you, I didn't know that."

"Let me tell you something," said Laverne. "I was always pretty. Not so smart. I never did well in school, but I knew how to get along with people. I mean, look, I'm dumb, but I'm not stupid." She smiled at her own joke. "I know, back in the day, I was an eyeful for almost any boy."

"Still are, Laverne."

"Ain't you sweet." She patted his hand. "But my point is, I knew how to listen, and I knew how to get people to support me. I learned how to take the talents I did have, and I made the most of them. Now, Smittie and I are here, doing our small part to help kids get an education at a school I could never get into. So, the way I see it, we're making our own difference. But you two."

She held a pair of fingers out, indicating Chip's absent partner, Phil. "*You* two took your talents, and you created your own world! It's all there, on the screen, and none of it's real, but on the computer, it is. It was nothing, and you programmed it into existence from nothing. And you know what? That's a miracle to me."

Chip swallowed, giving himself time to absorb her non-advice. Last thing he wanted to do while she was opening up to him was snap at her for wasting precious time. When he spoke, he kept his voice even. "Thanks, Laverne, it's good to know you appreciated what we wanted to do."

"Hey, I *do* pay attention. I get it. You made something out of nothing-your own world, and you want everyone to come and see what you've created. And if that doesn't work, you just change parts of it, reshape it until you get it right. So whatever Blue's problem is–"

"Wait, what?" Chip held a hand out. *Something about what she just said. What was it?*

"What?" Laverne paused. "I said, you make your own world that you're sharing with others–"

"Yeah, but, the other part. If something doesn't work..." He dropped the breadstick and moved his hand in a circular motion to signal her to repeat her thought.

Laverne shrugged. "You just...change it. I mean, it's your world, right? You made the rules, I assume you can just change them, right?"

"We..." And then he realized what had been in front of their faces all along. "My God. How could I have not seen that?" *We're so damn caught up in the emergency.* Chip disengaged his hand from hers. "I need your pen and a piece of scrap paper. Please, hurry."

Laverne tore a page off her mini-notepad and handed him her pen.

Chip started to sketch. "Laverne, I have a house full of hungry programmers, and I need to get back to them as fast as possible. How fast can you get three pizzas to go?"

"We're closing, and we have four in the warmer we're getting ready to throw out. I'll box 'em for you, on the house."

Chip showed the sketch to Laverne, who made a face. "Looks kinda' cool, but I have no idea what that is."

"This..." Chip pointed to the page, "is the solution to my problem, and I have you to thank for it."

CHAPTER TWENTY-FOUR_

With time now a major factor, Chip talked Laverne into giving him a ride home. Without question, she'd stacked the four pizzas into her SUV and had him in front of his house five minutes later. He thanked her for helping more than she'd ever know, and, after accepting a quick kiss on his cheek, darted into the house.

Moments later, Chip stepped down the stairs into the basement, one arm balancing the stacked pies, napkins, and paper plates, the other gripping the railing.

All faces turned toward him.

Deep in conversation on the phone, Skye rolled her eyes but continued her dialog–something about electrical usage.

Burton turned her gaze from him a moment later, put her clipboard down on the desk, and walked to the couch to check on Blue.

Phil stopped his work, stood up, and closed the distance to meet him. He shook his head, his disappointment apparent. "I can't believe you went out and did that."

Chip grunted, flustered. "I didn't leave here specifically to get the pizza, but you know what? Eating helped. And it's going to help you guys. Whether you realize it or not. By the way, it's after dark."

Phil's look told Chip that Phil didn't know that, either.

"Exactly. Here, take this. The walk actually cleared my head, and I think I have a solution to our problem." He pulled the scrap of notepad from his pocket and slapped the page down onto the table.

Phil picked it up and took in the image, his eyes scanning the hasty notes to the side. His eyebrows slowly rose up his forehead. "This blows away our old maximum parameters that we set when we first created the game."

Chip nodded. "I know. And we've never changed them in the two years since."

"Well, no, there was no reason to. We wanted to contain the maximum power any of the characters can achieve."

"Not now, we don't." Chip waited for his words to sink in. "They're all in there. They can be just so strong, just so agile, and nothing more. Now's the time to change the basic parameters and introduce something new into the game."

Slowly, Phil sank into his chair and called up a new screen. "Jesus. Why the hell didn't we think of this sooner?"

Chip rubbed his hand over his own face, massaging his forehead to clear the cobwebs. "I know. I couldn't think earlier, and now it's obvious."

Skye wandered over. "What's up, guys?"

Chip answered, words flying out a mile a minute. "We have a plan that I'd like to bring you in on, if you can. Can you?" He drew a breath. "What are you working on for Burton?"

Skye shook her phone at him. "Damn holiday has us doing things the hard way. Normally, Rebecca could call the enrollment office, offer up some federal bypass codes, and we'd have access to classified student information in minutes. Then we'd know exactly where to find our little gang. But we can't. No one's on duty."

Chip fired up his 3D-rendering program on the computer in front of him. "So, instead..."

"I spent the last hour on the phone with the helpdesks of a couple of local internet providers, used those same bypass codes to talk to some people in charge, people who can analyze the raw data. I have them tracking homes in the vicinity with readings that indicate unusual usage today. Just waiting on some callbacks now." Skye's eyes looked down at Chip's sketch. "Wow, what's this?"

"That," said Chip, "might be the solution to our problem." He tried to mentally size her up and figure out her skills. "How fast could you render that? Phil's the graphic arts genius. But he's doing something higher priority, and it could go even faster if I help him."

Skye peered at the sketch. "I can draw a pretty mean action figure for you on the image renderer, if that's what you need."

Chip stood up and offered her the seat. "Make it fast, Skye, just make it fast."

———

"Fiona?"

Leona Shaefer stood in the center of the same living room where she and Fiona had lived over two years ago.

Of course, they weren't really in that living room. Leona had found her daughter only by pursuing her deep into the recesses of her daughter's mind.

Fiona huddled on the couch, hugging herself, her face ashen, her body dwarfed by the surrounding white leather.

Leona called out, this time using the "angry mom" voice that usually snapped her daughter to attention. "Fiona! Wake up!"

Fiona turned her head oh-so-slowly to center her gaze on Leona, dark circles under her eyes. "Mom?" The word croaked out of her.

Leona closed the distance to stand in front of the couch, still keeping her stern mother voice to hold Fiona's attention. "What do you think you're doing? Answer me, young lady!"

Fiona opened her mouth but then said nothing. She tipped her head toward her knees, and her eyes drifted closed.

Oh, no you don't, baby. Wake up. "I said answer me!"

Fiona's eyes snapped open, and she slurred out a reply. "I got away, Mom. They can't reach me here."

"Baby..." Tears welled up. "You need to go back."

Fiona shook her head. "No! They hurt. I want to stay here."

"But...you can't stay here, Fiona. Chip is on his way."

"No, Mommy. They hurt me...again, and again, and again."

"Baby..." Leona sank next to her daughter and wrapped her arms around her. "It's okay, baby, but you can't stay here. If you do, you won't be able to go back." Through her arms, Leona felt a shiver convulse through her daughter. "That's okay, Mommy. Okay. Chip can't get to me, anyway. So, I'll just stay here with you."

———

MARDA THRUST the knife into Blue's unresponsive body and heard her final cry before the body vanished entirely. She grinned up at Cyn. "How was that?"

Cyn applauded, and Van mock-bowed. "Bravo. I think we stretched that out over an hour that time."

"Still," mused Van. "She's almost gone. She barely made a noise for the last several minutes."

"So she's losing her mind?" Marda pressed the point of the scepter against her own open palm. "Glorious! One more round and she might end up an empty shell, whether her friends find a way to bring her back or–"

A new figure phased in front of her.

Marda started, then relaxed when she saw Natalie's familiar green-cloaked druid appear. "Nat, are you joining us after all?"

"Just for a moment, then I'll cast the spell to come back out. I wanted to let you know, I have the computers and our clothes packed and loaded into the car. Still no sign of the cops, but–"

"Great!" said Marda. "Then we can do this again."

Marda read the shock on Nat's CGI features.

"I was going to say, the longer we wait, the more time Burton has to gather her resources and come after us."

Marda pretended to consider. They had no evidence Burton had taken any action against them. "Or she might not be able to mobilize the authorities tonight. How do you get police to act on your word when there's no evidence that a crime has been committed?"

Nat averted her eyes and looked down at the fiery ground. "With all due respect, Marda, I strongly believe that's wishful thinking."

A burst of fury flushed through Marda. "Do you, now? Do you really? Well, maybe *I* think that your lack of interest in being in the presence of the mistress makes me question your motives to the cause."

The figure's eyes widened, then squinted in anger. "I am focused on getting us the hell out of here while we still have a window to escape. Frankly, Marda, it is you, and this obsessive excursion, that has put us in great peril."

"How dare you!" Marda pointed the tip of the spike at Nat.

Natalie met Marda's glare.

If the scepter intimidated her, Natalie hid it well.

"If we get out of here, and later succeed at bringing Baalina into our world, then we can enjoy being in Her Holy Presence every blessed day. But if we are captured, it will be at least, in part, because you three indulged yourselves with a minor distraction rather than staying focused on the goal."

"I'll show *you* all about our indulgence, you mouthy bitch!" She raised the scepter.

Cyn put herself between Marda and Natalie. "Marda, calm down. She's probably right."

Not you, too, Cyn. "Fiona has to pay for what she's done!" Marda scoffed.

Van stepped forward, next to Cyn. "What my partner means is that we should be grateful to Natalie for packing up for all of us while we deal with Fiona in the proper way."

Cyn picked up Van's statement. "A way that will send a message to the others. Even if they pull this girl out of here, right now, they will find nothing left of her but an empty, broken shell."

As if on cue, Marda heard the standard audio distortion of a new character phasing in. Fiona, the blue-haired warrior, reappeared in her usual spot, physically unmarked, standing erect.

As soon as the computer relinquished control of the avatar to its controller, the figure collapsed to the ground like a scarecrow pulled free of its wooden cross-frame. *She's not moving! Is she dead?*

Cyn and Van darted to her side.

Their victim had fallen on her stomach.

Cyn drew her dagger, targeted a specific spot on the back of Fiona's upper thigh, and thrust it in. She watched as it sank in several millimeters deep.

Fresh blood spilled from the wound.

The avatar uttered a grunt, a reflex more than an actual cry of pain.

Cyn and Van exchanged looks.

Marda asked, "So, she's not dead?"

Van shrugged. "I'm not sure we'd even know. The avatar might just keep coming back regardless of what's going on with her mind."

Natalie gagged and turned away. "I think I'm going to be sick."

Cyn picked up the thread. "If she's not broken, she will be soon."

Marda's mouth watered at the words. "Let's finish the job, then. Let's finish *her*." She reached down and pulled Blue's chin up.

The avatar's eyes remained closed and unresponsive.

Marda was not impressed. "We have the time. We can make it slow, to the end."

Cyn shrugged. "Fine with me."

Natalie broke in, "Didn't you hear a word I sa–"

Van cut her off. "Just a few more minutes, Nat. Go on back, we'll be there shortly."

Marda grinned. "Indeed, maybe you should let the big kids take care of this, Natalie."

Cyn chuckled. "Look at you. Get a little taste of blood for the first time, and all of a sudden *you're* the fearless one lecturing others."

Reflexively, Marda yelled, "Who said this was my first time?" The words escaped before she could stop them.

"*I* say!" snapped Cyn. "I have eyes, don't I? This entire 'session' has been an education for you. And that's...fine, so let's complete your education." Cyn motioned to the scepter still clutched in Marda's hand and bent at the waist in a mock bow. "Finish what you've started, Priestess."

Marda glanced at Baalina, who waited off to the side, a smile on her face. At Marda's acknowledgement, the Goddess nodded.

"You grow stronger by the moment, Marda. The final breaking of your enemy will make you my proper servant."

A flush thrilled Marda. She tightened her grip on the scepter and approached the prone body. *Where first...the hand? The eye? Will her body feel it if I gouge out an eye? I don't know. Perhaps that's where I should start.*

A new noise filled the air, a mixture of a hum and static, sounding a short distance away.

Marda turned to look along with the others.

A green, glowing line cut through the air in a vertical slash, as if a transparent scrim hovered a few feet away, and a surgeon now guided a deliberate slice into that scrim. It extended, slowly, a couple inches, six inches, now over a foot.

At the same time, the edges widened, pulling apart outward into a portal shape, which opened to reveal the large tree and the forest beyond, the area previously sealed off to them when Fiona's act had isolated the virtual chaos room from the rest of the game.

Only now, a new portal hung open before them, which would grant them access to the room they needed. *We can go...right now, we can go, and the mistress can be free!*

But even as the thought crossed her mind, a new figure flew and hovered before the mouth of the portal.

Flew? Yes, by the Goddess, it flew! Marda's eyes widened at the sight.

Marda's mouth dropped open, slack-jawed, as some sort of silver robot creature with a backpack jetpack and mini rocket-boots eased through the portal and lowered itself.

The robot-being extended one arm toward them. It pointed a metal nozzle positioned along the top of its wrist at them in a manner clearly intended as a threat.

The metallic-looking creature spoke through a booming, amplified speaker that blared a deep, angry male voice. "GET AWAY FROM HER! NOW!"

Natalie was the first to find her voice. "What in the hell! How did you–"

"DID YOU REALLY THINK YOU COULD CALL THE SHOTS IN MY OWN GAME? ARE YOU TRULY SO ARRO-GANT TO THINK I WOULD NOT FIND A WAY TO BREAK THROUGH INTO YOUR LITTLE HIDDEN ROOM?"

Marda stared, still unable speak.

But Natalie apparently had recovered first. "But...you can't create power-avatars of that sort. The parameters were set–"

"PARAMETERS I SET, AND PARAMETERS I CHANGED!"

"But we used the SoulStaff! Only the Divenium Crystal could get through–"

"THAT'S TRUE ON EARTH! BUT THIS ISN'T EARTH. THIS ISN'T A REAL PORTAL, AND IT DOESN'T LEAD TO THE REAL CHAOS REALM. THIS IS AN ADDED ROOM IN THE GAME MATRIX OF A VIDEO GAME WORLD. MY WORLD!"

Baalina grabbed the scepter from Marda. With a cry of fury, she unsheathed the blade and pointed it toward the robot.

Or rather, Marda realized, the suit of armor.

"You are still facing a demoness, boy! And I'll destroy you for your insolence." A stream of green fire spewed from the end of the rod, which blazed with an incredible heat that burned Marda's face, even as it sprayed over and engulfed the metallic figure.

Marda smiled. *The mistress has incinerated him where he stands! An appropriate end to all who dare stand before us.*

The green blast faded.

The robot remained before them, unharmed, not even singed. "I

AM THE GOD OF THIS WORLD. NOT YOU, DEMONESS! YOU CAN'T LOCK ME OUT OF MY WORLD!"

Uttering a fierce battle cry, Cyn charged, flanking the robot. As she passed, she thrust the dagger up against the robot's neck.

The dagger snapped, and Cyn bounced off the robot and tumbled across the stones, landing several feet away in an indignant heap.

The robot continued as if it hadn't noticed the attack. "YOU CANNOT HARM ME IF I DON'T WANT TO BE HARMED. YOU ARE A DIGITAL IMAGE OF A NIGHTMARE STANDING IN A BLUESCREEN SET! THIS IS NOT CHAOS. YOU ARE NOT BAALINA. YOUR DEMONESS MIND IS TRAPPED IN A SHELL LESS DISTINCT THAN INCENSE SMOKE!"

The robot pointed its wrist weapon directly at the demoness. "SAY GOODBYE TO YOUR LEADER, WITCHES. BAALINA, I RETURN YOU TO THE CHAOS FROM WHENCE YOU CAME!"

A red blast of energy shot from the robot's wrist.

Baalina barely had time to snarl her defiance before the beam struck her in the chest.

An instant later, her body disappeared.

Mistress! Seeing Baalina fall physically hurt Marda.

Natalie backed away. "My God, I...didn't expect this. They just changed the maximum parameters of the game while we were caught flatfooted inside of it."

"EXACTLY RIGHT, DRUID. I GIVE YOU SOME CREDIT. PHIL AND I WERE SO WRAPPED UP IN THE LEGEND, THE STORIES, THE POWERS, AND THE LIMITATIONS OF YOUR POWERS, THAT WE DIDN'T STOP TO THINK THAT *YOU* DON'T MAKE THE RULES HERE, *WE* DO. SO WE CHANGED THE RULES AND RENDERED THIS NEW AVATAR YOU SEE BEFORE YOU."

Marda turned to Nat. "What can we do?"

Nat's eyes met hers, round circles of shock. "Nothing. We've lost." Natalie raised her hands above her head.

Marda snarled. "Put down your hands, you little fool! You told me our avatars were the best the game could provide, that they could only *match* us, not *beat* us."

"That was true...at the time. But, he's...he's not a part of the same game anymore. We're a Civil War battalion, and he's a modern Marine with a machine gun and hand grenades. We just need to get out of here."

Van cried and drew her dagger. "We still have one move left!" She leaped toward Blue, the dagger raised to strike.

"GET AWAY FROM HER!" yelled the robot. The voice cracked, revealing the human anguish beneath.

A red beam struck Van in the back, and she disintegrated.

"Van!" Cyn barely had time to react before the robot fired and caused her to vanish.

Marda fell back to huddle with Nat. She had a sword strapped to her side that she knew would be useless. She no longer held the scepter. Her mistress had been taken from the game and forced back into the real chaos realm. "No matter!" She screamed her defiance. "We'll get you, yet. We hurt your lover beyond any hope of return. We'll find another way to raise the mistress. This isn't the end."

"ACTUALLY, IT IS."

The robot fired two more streaks of energy, which bulls-eyed both avatars.

———

MARDA HAD BARELY a moment to scream her anger, then the red blast engulfed her, and she awoke at the table, surrounded by her three co-conspirators.

Her vision snapped into focus in time to see Natalie powering down her laptop. "We need to go. Now."

"BLUE?"

Chip raised the robot's wrist. The power screen of his goggles centered Blue in his crosshairs. The converter gun, imbued with the same code that created the CGI Divenium Crystal to send the CGI spirits back to their bodies, signaled its ready status. "PHIL, AGENT BURTON, STAND BY. SHE'S COMING. AND SHE'S NOT MOVING." Through all the mechanics, Chip couldn't cover the shake in his voice.

He pulled the trigger.

Blue's CGI character vanished for what he hoped to God would be the last time. He'd released her tortured mind to return what was left to her real body.

God, please, don't let us be too late. He turned the gun on himself and fired.

CHAPTER TWENTY-FIVE

Chip found himself seated in front of his computer screen. *Back! And safe!*

His gaze traveled the room, at first seeing no one else, just empty computer terminals. He wondered, for a moment, if he was dreaming again.

Then he noticed everyone crowded around the couch where Blue's body laid, and he wanted to be at her side most desperately. "Blue!" He threw off his headset and bolted over. The people parted as he approached, all except Burton, who continued to kneel by Blue's head, reaching over the arm of the couch. One hand pressed, palm-up, on her forehead, her other hand on Blue's shoulder.

Blue lay, pale and unresponsive, like a corpse.

He dropped to his knees at her side, where he spoke his prayer at her. "Come on, Blue, come on, I know you're in there. Come back to me. Come back, Blue, come on!"

His attention darted back and forth between Blue's sick face and Burton, who sat, eyes closed, her face emotionless and trance-like.

"Blue...come on, I saved you. I told you I'd save you, and I did. I brought you back. Please, baby, come back to me, please."

He wanted to grab her and shake her. But he didn't know what

Burton was doing, and how much that would interfere with whatever spell or treatment or whatever the hell it was...he didn't care, as long as it worked.

"Oh my God!" Burton yelled, and her eyes snapped open. Her body fell away from Blue as if propelled by some force.

Chip watched, stunned.

Burton curled her knees up and folded her arms around her legs. "God...those monsters...those...my God..."

Silence filled the room. No one dared breathe.

Chip's gaze brushed over Skye, who had her hands balled into fists and pressed against her mouth.

Phil also waited, his eyes riveted to where Blue lay.

Burton, in the meantime, had removed her glasses. Her body trembled, and tears now flowed freely down her face.

Chip cleared his throat. "Is she..." The word stuck. He couldn't bring himself to say it. *Because she can't be. I won't accept it.*

Burton sobbed and shivered. "Please...give me a minute. Just a...minute."

"I'm sorry." From what Chip could tell of Burton, she went to great lengths to project herself as a woman of strength.

Burton found her voice. "She's...been hurt very badly, Eugene. They didn't just kill her once; they killed her over and over again. Slowly."

"But...they didn't, *really* kill her. Not *really*."

"Yes, *really*, Eugene. Mentally, the scars are there. One atop the other, and all fresh. God...she's..." Burton lost her voice again.

As Burton continued to sob, Chip's world dropped out from under him, and he closed his eyes against his own tears.

Burton continued, "She's...experienced something the human mind isn't meant to grasp and then return from. We all know we're going to die one day. It's the one unavoidable reality of existence."

Burton unfolded her legs and propped herself onto one knee. "That reality–when we approach that moment–is sometimes too much for someone to face...even once. They go into shock, or a coma, and then they're just *gone*. It's a biological imperative, and in most cases, it's a mercy."

Burton swiped the back of her hand against her cheeks. "But Blue...she held on. She was burned to death several times." An ironic laugh escaped from Burton. "The demoness. That's all she knew to do. It was painful, torture...but it was quick. And...what a sad joke. A demoness who lacks the patience to cause suffering."

Burton's green-eyed gaze took in Chip. "She had faith she would hold out until we could get to her. But then the others arrived."

Chip flushed at the thought of the brunette psychopath and the others.

"They...wanted to prolong her suffering as long as possible. And they did. And each time she returned, they did it again."

The words slammed Chip in the gut. "My game..." He brushed aside his own tears and blinked to clear his vision. He sat up, and this time, he grabbed Blue's shoulders and shook her. "But she's here now. She's here! We got her back." Now he addressed Blue's comatose body directly. "It's okay, honey! I got you. I saved you. Please, come back to me."

Burton put a hand on Chip's shoulder.

A strange tranquility flowed through him, along with a feeling of hope.

"Calm down, Eugene. Let me compose myself and try again. She's there, you're right, but she's protected herself, deep down in her head, the only place she could escape."

Chip blinked back tears. "Let you try what?"

Burton again positioned herself near Blue's head and placed her open palm against her forehead and her other hand on her shoulder. "I'm going to try to reach her."

FIONA?

The disembodied voice came at Blue from the walls. She looked around. *Is this another ghost?*

She cried out, "Go away!"

Fiona, where are you?

"I said go the hell away, Mom!"

Blue lay, curled up on the white leather couch, trying to lose herself in the corner. Her mother had finally abandoned her, angry or sad or disappointed in some way.

Well, too bad. So I've disappointed my mother, big fucking surprise, like that's never happened before.

She pushed herself farther into the cushions, just wanting to disappear. She willed the couch to swallow her. Make her go away forever.

Even as the room grew dark, she focused on the crack between the cushions, to make it darker, faster.

I got away from them. They kept hurting and hurting. They thought I couldn't possibly get away, but I did. She shivered against the cushion. *They can't reach me here. Ever. No matter what they're doing to me out there.*

Fiona...please listen to me. This isn't your mother.

Panic seized her. *God...no, they've found me in here, too. They'll find me and hurt me, and...*

Fiona, this is Agent Rebecca Burton. Eugene is out here. The people who hurt you are gone.

No, they're not! It's a trick! They're waiting for me. I'm only safe if I–

No, Fiona, they're gone. Eugene found you. You're back with the people who love you; you're safe. The people who hurt you can't hurt you any more, but you *have* to come out.

No! No, in the dark, they'll never find me.

Fiona, if the darkness encloses you, you'll never be able to come out again.

Good! Good, in the darkness they can't find me. No one *can find me here.*

Fiona, listen to me. Eugene... The voice hesitated. **Chip...Chip misses you.**

Chip? God, why didn't he protect me? Why did he leave me? He promised!

Fiona...You did well. You survived what no one else could endure. You created this space for yourself. And it's saved you. But you can come out. You *have* to come out.

No...no. They hurt me. They just kept hurting...and hurting. And when I couldn't take any more, they did it again.

Even now, she recalled the agony in her palms, the flare up of fire in her thighs, her wrists, trying to retreat to blackness, only to be pulled back to consciousness...

Fiona...I can help you deal. Please, trust me.

How, it's...the memory is everywhere.

Please, Fiona...you have to leave where you are and come to me. You have to decide that you want to live and that you want to return to Chip. The people who hurt you are gone, and if you come back to us, I can help you cope with the pain.

Chip's waiting for me? Chip? He...came for me?

She looked around the room, a place already fading away to near-darkness. *No, wait, I want to find Chip...*

She stumbled off the couch, and...

———

BLUE SCREAMED.

She convulsed as if she'd tried to go in every direction at once.

Chip barely deflected her swatting hand. *God!*

Blue thrashed right off the couch, onto the floor, face-first onto the rug, and half into Chip's lap.

"Hold her! Turn her over!" Burton yelled.

Chip grabbed one of her shoulders and rolled her over.

As soon as they'd gotten her onto her back, Chip had to fend off flailing arms and legs.

Someone fell across Blue's legs. Chip glanced at Phil as he pressed both of his arms across her thighs in an attempt to prevent her from kicking out.

Chip held up his arms and forced his way forward. Random blows battered his arms, a couple landed on the side of his face with stunning force.

Chip focused on Burton's imperative to hold her still, so he pushed forward anyway.

Blue lay, immobilized by the pair of bodies. *But, damn it, she keeps fighting!* Chip didn't know how long he could hold her.

She cried out. No! They'll hurt me again!"

Chip's ears rang, and his heart broke with every cry. *What did they do to her?* He turned sideways in time to see Burton place her hand, palm flat, against Blue's forehead.

In an instant, Blue's struggles subsided, but the whimpers continued. "No, no, please..."

Burton murmured in a soothing tone, "It's okay, Fiona. I got you, I found you, I found you. It's okay, peace, Fiona, peace..."

"No, please, I can't..." With a final tremble, Blue's body slumped and gave up the struggle.

Chip found himself face to face with his soulmate, her features twisted in agony. *Blue, please, come back to me.*

"She's back in her own head, Eugene. I think I can get her now."

Burton's response surprised him. *Did I say that out loud?*

"I got her...I got her..."

Chip's eyes snapped back and forth between Blue and Burton. The muscles in Blue's face relaxed, and a look of calm fell over her features.

At the same time, Burton's eyes rolled up into her head, and her expression twisted in some sort of distress. She started to slump sideways toward the floor.

Chip called out, "Skye!"

In a flash, Skye crouched at Burton's side, Chip figured, not a moment too soon, before Skye caught Burton's slack form and eased her to the floor.

Chip turned his attention to Blue and watched her eyes flutter open. He braced himself for another scream.

"Chip?" Her wide blue eyes took him in, recognition apparent in her features.

Her tone expressed her sanity.

"Chip! Oh, my God, you saved me!"

Before he could respond, she wrapped her arms around his neck and pressed herself against him.

He held on, speechless.

She trembled in his arms, her sobs escaping between her words. "Thank you, Chip, thank you so much, thank you for getting me out of there."

She's alive. And, more importantly, she's...intact. Sane. For the next few minutes, Chip let himself bask in his gratitude to whatever power had brought her back to him.

Over her shoulder, he spied Skye helping Burton sit up, who also looked disheveled but otherwise unhurt. Burton returned his look with a guarded face. *How did Burton do this?*

Blue spoke against his chest, still trembling. "Just hold me. Don't let me go, please. Don't let me go ever again."

Her words almost overwhelmed him. "You can't get rid of me that easily. But...you're going to be fine and back to yourself soon." His eyes met Burton's. "Right?"

Burton's eyes avoided his but looked toward the floor. "Well...she should be. But..."

Now that Blue had settled down in his arms, Chip spoke the thought top-most on his mind. "What did you do to her?"

Burton struggled off the floor and sat on the couch. She paused to drink from a bottle of water.

She looked somewhat like a football player resting on the sidelines after a big play.

"I told you. What happened to Fiona should never happen to anyone. Fiona was psychologically and physically tortured, more than any person was meant to endure, and after experiencing all those agonies, the memories have now been placed into her physical brain for her to try to process."

Blue's arms tightened against him. "It was horrible. So...beyond horrible. No matter what I tried to tell myself, to calm myself down, reason with myself, I was overwhelmed by what they'd already done to me."

Blue pulled her head up from Chip. She ran her hands through her sweat-dampened hair as another shiver passed through her. Her brows furrowed. "But...at the same time...for some reason now, I can think about it without those memories overwhelming me. It's like...watching some terrible hard-R movie. You know, you watch it, you cover your face, you can't un-remember it, but you're still distanced, because it's not really happening to you. But in my case, it did."

Blue disengaged herself from Chip, but her fingers entwined with his. Moment by moment, her face settled into normalcy. Her color returned, and life reflected through her eyes. "At first, I couldn't find anything to anchor to...and then I could."

Burton took another drink. "I found the source of the pain and blocked it. It wasn't easy, I had to..." She paused. "I experienced some of it. Not much, but...enough."

"Wait." Blue's eyes met Burton's. "What did you do? You've...*blocked* my pain? Is that healthy?"

"Normally, no, I would not take such an action. But in your case, you weren't going to recover on your own." Burton held up a hand. "As you know, I didn't block the memories, just the pain connected with them. And..." She hesitated. "It's temporary. Over the next few months, everything will come back to you. Slowly. Pieces at a time. Hopefully, in manageable pieces. We'll...try to help you with that."

Blue released a slow, trembling breath. "That explains it. I couldn't figure out how I felt so much like myself, but I'm so grateful that I do." Blue kept one hand clasped in Chip's and extended her other toward Burton.

After a moment's hesitation, Burton took it.

"Thank you," Blue said.

Chip looked back and forth and wondered what sort of communication passed between them. Something almost electrical transferred through Blue's hand when Burton touched her. He knew it because it carried through to him.

"Just tell me one thing," said Blue.

Burton's eyebrows rose. "What's that?"

"Tell me they didn't get away. Please, tell me we're going to stop them."

Burton looked at Skye, who piped up, "Officer Kirby's waiting for your orders."

The name of the cranky police officer caught Chip's attention. "What happened?"

Skye addressed Chip. "While you were going all Iron Man in the virtual world, the power company people got back to us and pinned our group down to a house address. Rebecca sent them off to watch the house and await further orders."

Burton released Blue's hand, stood, and straightened her leather jacket. "The arrests require my personal attention, but I couldn't leave without resolving this situation first."

Blue spoke up, a look akin to hunger on her face. "So, you're going now?"

"Yes."

Blue turned to Chip. "Help me up, please." She wasn't asking, and her face made it clear she expected no discussion, just obedience.

Uh-oh. "You might not be up to going anywhere."

But Blue no longer addressed Chip, but Burton. "Please, you've got to take me!"

Chip cut in, "That might not be a good idea. Burton, tell her."

Instead, Burton extended a hand to Blue. "Actually, if you want to ride with me, I anticipated your request." Her eyes swept the room. "There's plenty of space for everyone. Besides, Ms. Shaefer, I'd like to talk to you about a few things on the way."

CHAPTER TWENTY-SIX_

"I'll drive," called Cyn, and she settled herself behind the wheel of the purple P.T. Cruiser, its trunk open and filled with boxes organized and stacked by Natalie over the last couple of hours.

Van stood behind the car to review the packing job. "Shotgun," she responded.

Whatever. Natalie opened the back door and dropped herself behind Cyn. She supposed it made sense, as one of the smallest people. They had a couple-hour drive back to Kentucky, and everyone might as well be as comfortable as possible. The hard-shell carrying case to her laptop sat...well...on her lap.

But the idea of Cyn being at the wheel if a chase broke out scared the crap out of her.

One of Natalie's legs bounced with nervous energy, and the case bounced against her knee with each shake.

She didn't want to die. She didn't want to get caught, but with the time Marda had insisted on wasting, Nat had mentally prepared herself for the eventuality that they'd be caught. What she feared now most of all was the very real chance of getting killed in the fallout of their capture.

Behind her, also standing by the trunk, Marda called out, "Where's the Baalina statue?"

The words hit Nat like an accusation, one of many Marda had flung her direction since they'd been pulled out of the game. "We don't have the room. Someone can mail it to us later, *if* we get away. If we can't, it's moot."

In the silence that followed, Natalie wondered if, given a choice, Marda would swap the statue for Natalie and leave *her* down in the basement to be sent for later.

"Fine," Marda finally answered. Moments later, Marda joined her in the back seat but refused to meet her eyes.

Van sat up front with her twin.

Cyn reached up, readying to push the remote to the garage door opener.

"Wait!" Natalie called.

Cyn paused, her finger poised on the button.

"Listen," said Natalie, drumming her fingers on the computer case to further shunt off her nervousness. "Chances are, the cops have this house monitored already, and they're going to follow us. I hope not, but there it is. I don't like our chances of getting out of this, so I took some precautions on my own while you were all occupied."

"Go on," prompted Marda.

"I emailed all of our files and notes to the coven leader. That said, my computer and those files are the first thing the authorities are going to go after. The computer here is wiped clean, but they won't know that, either. If they pursue, we can run them on a wild goose chase, and it might be many hours before they discover they have nothing."

"I'm not so inclined to be captured," objected Cyn.

"That's fine. Maybe we get away, and maybe we don't. The point is, if they think they can get our plans from us, they'll stay on our trail and not think to track down the files online. We're now the decoys, giving our Sisters time to receive and assimilate the information, to pick up where we left off."

"What you're saying," Cyn finished, "is as of now, we're expendable."

There it was, out in the open, for all four to ponder.

"Wouldn't matter," said Marda. "If they capture me, I'd escape, sooner or later."

"So, we're in agreement," said Nat. "We try to get away. If we can't, we put on a good show, and we distract them as long as possible."

When no one responded, she added, "For the Sisterhood. For Baalina."

"For Baalina," the others muttered, though not with much enthusiasm.

Natalie sighed. Whatever happened, these would be the last actions she would take on behalf of the Sisterhood. If they avoided capture, she'd somehow vanish on her own, flee the coven, disappear, and start over.

If they captured her, she'd work from day one to show her captors her sincere intentions to reform herself. Because one way or the other, this was her final service.

And good riddance to them all.

————

BLUE FOLLOWED Burton to the large car parked in the street, light blue or tan or white, she couldn't tell in the dark. *Wow, a LaCrosse? That's a hell of a company car*, thought Blue, not sure if the "company" in Burton's case meant the Kelranians or the government.

The waiting darkness when they'd exited the house startled her. She'd returned from her misadventure at Burton's house sometime in the late afternoon, but a glance at her phone told her it was past ten o'clock. Did she really lose that many hours?

She didn't feel it.

She didn't really feel a *lot* right now. She was numb, tired, and her head buzzed like the aftermath of a rock concert. She remembered the sequence of events–the fights in the virtual world, the choice to take Chip's place, and being pulled into the vortex.

She recalled the *fact* of her helplessness, left in the hands of the sick psychopaths who worked her over. Again and again and again. But she couldn't recall the pain of it, or the agony. The excruciating details had vanished from her memory, at least, for now.

Didn't make her any less furious over what happened to her. She wanted payback, plain and simple.

Even still, "payback" didn't mean doing to them what they did to her. No, she could never be so cruel, even to someone she hated. Instead, it meant...

Well, she didn't know *what* it meant.

But, possibly, she'd find out tonight.

She piled into the passenger side backseat, cushioned by comfy fake leather.

Chip sat in the middle, while Phil overflowed the driver's side backseat.

In front, Skye sat shotgun next to Burton, looking perfectly comfortable, as if she did this every day.

Which, Blue reflected, she probably did.

Burton eased the car into the lane with perhaps more caution than necessary on the deserted neighborhood street. She wove in and out through darkened streets Blue had no clue about.

Burton raised an oversized police radio that looked as if it would be equally at home in a soldier's grasp. "Report," she called.

"Hey, Burton, if you had called thirty seconds earlier, I'd have said the house had been quiet all night."

Blue recognized the voice of Officer Kirby, sounding in somewhat better spirits than this morning, when they'd turned the tables on his bust.

Burton replied, "But now?"

"The garage door just opened. They're pulling out." Static, then a follow-up. "Wow, even from here, I can see they're loaded to run for it."

"Okay," said Burton. "Prepare to close the net. Hopefully, this will be quick and simple. Where are they?"

Kirby said the suspects were traveling north on...he rattled off a street name Blue couldn't make out, something French?

Jesus, she'd wasted over a year, floundering in doubt and confusion. Over eighteen months, and now she sat, carried along as a lost bystander down streets that Chip probably knew intimately, like the out-of-town tourist she was. Even Burton, who'd only been stationed here a few months, guided the car with confidence from one corner to the next.

"Where do you go to school, Blue?"

Burton's direct question broke her train of thought. "Sorry? Uh, NYU. English major."

"English?" Burton sounded surprised. "Not history? Anthropology? Occult studies? Or is this all fodder for your great American Horror Novel?"

She's teasing me, Blue guessed, not sure what to make of the line of questioning. "I don't go looking for this shit, but it just keeps finding me."

"Indeed, with a high rate of success."

Blue opened her mouth to reply.

Burton added, "By that, I mean, the ways in which you've handled yourself."

"Oh?" Blue wondered how much to admit. She trusted Burton. She wanted to trust Burton. Badly. The woman had saved her sanity, if not her life.

Burton continued, "You and I shared minds for several minutes. Stray thoughts, residue, if you will, leaked through our connection. I learned much about your encounter with Gunther that I didn't know before."

And with that, Blue's opinion of the situation soured. "I'm not sure I like that very much." In fact, she was sure she didn't.

"I understand." Burton let the comment hang while she navigated through the side streets. "It could not be helped. My point was not to discuss your secrets, but to praise your instincts."

"My instincts tend to get me in a lot of trouble."

"But they're correct most of the time. It's when you stop and think, and second-guess yourself, that you tend to err. For example, when you took the crystal from Chip, you knew he had a better chance of retrieving you from the chaos realm than you had of retrieving him. It was an act based on instinct, and you were correct."

Blue shrugged. "Call it what you will, I still stabbed him in the back."

Chip cut in, "I forgive you." His fingers found her hand and squeezed affectionately. "Agent Burton's right. You could never have deduced how to go back in the way I did. Phil might have, eventually, but it would have taken him a lot longer to figure it out."

Phil added, "Normally, I'd argue that as being snarky, but he's right. I had plenty to do, and I wasn't thinking anywhere near the ballpark of where Chip's reasoning took him."

Blue's eyes met Chip's. "You shouldn't let me off so easily."

In the darkness, a smile formed on his features. "It's okay, it's what I do."

Burton said, "Now, when you had time to ponder your relationship, you second-guessed those instincts. You wasted months because you used logic to counter your instincts and talked yourself into mistrusting him."

Chip answered, "You did?"

Blue could hear the hurt in Chip's voice. She snapped. "You said you weren't going to reveal my personal thoughts. Is there a point to all this?"

"I want to offer you a position in my organization, Blue. Or, more specifically, my team."

Blue's head spun. "What organization do you mean, exactly? Are you a federal agent, a state investigator, or a member of a druid cult?"

"Well...yes. Officially, you'd work with me for the government. Much of what you'd do would also benefit the Kelranian Order. The bottom line, Blue, is we'd be stopping evil people from committing evil. That's something you are already good at, and you'll be even better with the proper training."

A government agent. Me. It didn't seem real. The words came with James Bond music attached—a fantasy, nothing real. For years, Blue's ambitions were to work at a coffee shop and write poetry, with or without Chip by her side. As of twenty-four hours ago, Chip was now an irrevocable part of that deal.

Burton said, "There aren't many places that can make such a guarantee, but you know that I can. You can help me make a real difference in this fight."

"You want me to help you." Blue let the thought linger. "So, I'd report to you. I'm not even sure I *like* you. For one thing, you're very pushy."

If the comment offended Burton, she didn't show it. "I'm a leader, bred and trained. My tendency to take charge is only because I'm the most qualified to do so. You won't be able to say that about many people you might ever work for."

Blue grunted and mumbled under her breath, "And modest, too."

From the front, Skye spoke up. "She's not, you know."

Blue felt herself flush. *I didn't know she heard that.*

Skye continued, "You said she's pushy. She's not."

Oh, whew.

"I've been working with her for months. Rebecca knows what you excel at, hands that over to you, and at the same time, she's a good teacher. I've learned a lot from her during the last couple of months. If I were you, I'd jump at the chance."

Blue stewed and said nothing. More ghosts, demons, crazy people. She'd never wanted any of it, and she'd had enough of it.

Still, these sickos had caused her so much pain and so much torment. The Mardas of the world didn't care who they hurt, only *that* they hurt.

And now, Marda and her group were on the run, their plans thwarted, in part because of her actions. To make that kind of difference, to know that she'd taken these potentially disastrous situations and contained them, to contribute in some way to help others that truly mattered...how many people even had such an offer placed before them?

But, she could barely consider it at this time. "I need time to think about it. I just don't know."

Burton's voice reached her from the front. "The offer remains open. You don't have to decide anything tonight. You've been through a lot. But I can tell you, you'd be a hell of an asset to us."

Keep talking. You sure can be smooth when you want something. She had to admit, the words did much to bolster Blue's spirits. She'd spent her childhood beneath the dominance of a strict mother who tended to emphasize disappointment over approval. She didn't know if she could ever work for Burton, but it was damn nice to hear the words. "I'll think about it."

Burton's radio crackled to life. "That's it, they're bolting. They saw me. They've abandoned the car in front of the student center, and they're making a run for it."

"Get it surrounded!"

"Already on it. All units converging to cover the exits. If they go in there, we can box them in."

As Burton raised the radio to her mouth, the car picked up speed. The Buick tapped cylinders to thrust to highway speed in seconds.

Blue gripped the seat and held on for dear life.

From the front seat, Burton offered assurances into the radio. "We're right behind you. On our way. Proceed with caution. I want them taken down."

CHAPTER TWENTY-SEVEN_

Cyn turned the vehicle down Lafollette Street and pressed the accelerator.

Natalie braced herself as the Cruiser opened up and raced down the road, clear except for the stoplights at every corner. A couple miles up, they'd reach the on-ramp to State Road 37, where they could floor it the whole way north toward Indianapolis.

She caught two green lights.

Nat turned and looked.

The unmarked police car stuck to their bumper. *Dammit!* A second and third car pulled past. *More cops. They're surrounding us.*

Cyn swore and called out, "We can't make it, guys. We're going to have to run for it. Hold on and get ready."

The next light turned red, and Cyn ran it.

Like a physics project demonstrating action and reaction, the sirens blared from the car behind them. The cars on either side joined the chorus of screeches.

Up ahead, the student center drew close, windows lit up to show the empty interior of the community study hall.

Natalie had spent several hours there to study, read, surf, enjoy the coffee, and support the local vendors. Her mind worked out the possibilities. None of them were good, but they could potentially split up three ways, make it difficult for their pursuers, and maybe someone could slip away.

The police boxed them in and forced their car into the far-left lane. The two-story limestone building now loomed above them.

"Hang on, brace yourselves, and be ready to run like hell!" Cyn jerked the wheel and sent the car careening onto the sidewalk and across the lawn.

The building closed in, and Cyn hit the brakes.

Marda's scream filled the car.

The cruiser impacted the side of the building, crushed in the hood, and came to a jarring stop. "Go! Go now!"

Van popped the passenger door, stepped out, reached in, grabbed Cyn, and pulled her through to her side. As a unit, they darted for the glass doors.

Nat wanted to crawl over Marda and just get the hell out of there, but she waited. In her peripheral vision, she saw the red and blue lights. Vehicles pulled up and surrounded them on all sides but the car doors that faced the building.

Marda had finally struggled out of the car, which cleared the path for Natalie to exit. She pushed her laptop case in front of her and fled, focused on the sets of glass doors dead ahead.

Cyn and Van made for the doors to the right of her.

Natalie overtook Marda and closed in behind the twins. At that point, what happened to Marda was of little consequence to Nat.

"HOLD IT RIGHT THERE!" the police called out over a megaphone.

The sheer volume and authority of the voice made Natalie crouch as she ran.

"YOU ARE UNDER ARREST! YOU ARE ORDERED TO STOP RUNNING AND LIE ON THE GROUND WITH...DAMMIT!"

Natalie pushed through the doors.

In the foyer, straight ahead, a second pair of glass doors led to an open study room. If Nat broke to the left, she'd descend stairs down to the basement cafeteria and common area.

Cyn and Van continued ahead. They burst through the glass doors and darted straight back as far as the room would take them.

Okay, fine. So Nat moved left toward the stairs. She grabbed the metal rail and pumped her feet down the stairs, descending to the basement as fast as her legs would take her.

She heard a second figure behind her. *Marda! Dammit! Don't follow me!*

Nothing she could do about that now.

She just kept running.

———

Officer Kirby watched the four perps ignore his warning and run into the student center. He stopped in mid-sentence. Why waste the breath?

"DAMMIT!" His curse blasted out of the megaphone at 120 decibels. *Nice one, Kirby.* He released the broadcast button and swore a couple more times.

He checked his piece and nodded toward his partner. The police-issue Glock rested in his hands. He had become an expert at using it–if you counted patting the handle for emphasis, or occasionally waving it in the air when a drunk college student got some really dumb ideas.

When the situation called for action, most of the time, pepper spray did the trick. The Taser helped him handle more intense scenarios.

For most of his career, his gun remained holstered to his hip. The only human shape he'd aimed it at were targets on the shooting range. Tonight, he sensed, that could change. *If I have to, I have to.* The thought didn't bother him overly much.

Burton had kept him in the dark, but he knew these four were bad news—the real deal. They had to be stopped one way or the other, and he was more than up to it.

His gaze met his partner's. Selena Gonzalez had been assigned to him two years ago, a new recruit out of the academy. She'd served with distinction. As far as he knew, she'd never pulled the trigger, either.

"You up to this, partner?" Kirby felt a surge of pride at the stone-steady look on her face, the confident nod she offered.

"Don't you *dare* think of keeping me out of this one, Boss."

Kirby smiled. "Let's go get us some bad guys."

He scanned the second car, where Caliburn and Franklin stood, poised and ready. Good men. Veterans. He'd need them. "You're with us. They're going to try to split, I can feel it. We go forward, catch who we can, and flush the rest into the guys waiting out back." He nodded to Caliburn. "You two cover the café."

The four of them burst through the front entrance, and they split into pairs.

Kirby and Gonzalez continued forward through the second set of glass doors. Kirby's Bluetooth informed him that a fourth and fifth car had already set up the roadblock in the back alley. *Either way, we've got these bitches. Only thing to find out is if this goes down easy or hard.*

His gut told him it would go down hard.

———

NATALIE DESCENDED THE STAIRS, scanning the abandoned cafeteria, and looking for any exit.

She took in the side counter and entrance to the kitchen. Her first thought was to make a break for it, but the flexible metal gate bent around the register and extending to the door stopped her cold. *Dammit!*

Then she noticed, for the first time, a fire exit toward the back of the room. A metal bar ran along the front of the door.

Marda joined her. "Quickly, give me the metal case."

"Why?"

Marda reached out and pulled the laptop case from her unresisting fingers. "Because I'm getting away from here, and I want a weapon!" Marda bolted toward the fire exit.

"Wait!" Natalie started after her.

"Freeze!"

The barking command of police authority froze Natalie's blood. She swore her heart stopped in her chest.

"Hands above your head! Now!"

Natalie squeezed her eyes shut. She knew her life would end at any moment. "Don't shoot!" she cried. She waved her hands over her head. "Please, don't shoot!" *God, please no, don't kill me!*

Nat heard the door open, and the fire alarm go off.

"On your knees!" screamed the officer.

As if she could help it! Natalie's knees gave out, and she fell on her face, still crying. "Don't kill me, please. Please, I'm unarmed."

"Hands behind your head!"

She opened her eyes, vaguely aware of the linoleum pattern before her face.

Another figure ran past her and mumbled something about not being worth the bother.

Tears fell freely down her face. One officer held a gun pointed at her prone form; a second officer pulled her wrists behind her back and slapped on the cuffs.

That's me, not worth the bother. Helpless, cuffed, and I'll never have to run again.

On the floor, she trembled and muttered thanks to whatever entity had looked after her in this moment–certainly not the Goddess-bitch Baalina. *And I'm alive, alive, they didn't shoot me. Thank you, thank you, they didn't shoot me.*

As her police captors gathered 'round, Natalie wept tears of gratitude.

———

KIRBY AND GONZALEZ burst through the glass doors into the student common study area. Spread out before him in three directions were small computer library kiosks, armchairs, loveseats, side tables, study nooks–a plethora of hiding spots and attack points–laid out in a night-mare maze of opportunity for the two fleeing perps.

Kirby had patrolled this area for years and knew it well. It stayed open 24/7. That was one advantage. He noted two others—the area remained well lit at all times—and most nooks were designed for seated studying.

He and Gonzalez could see across the entire room as they stood side by side. One of the perps was crouched behind a study nook. She thought, or perhaps only hoped, she was out of sight. Kirby motioned toward the perp.

Gonzalez nodded.

They heard noise from some distance away, deeper into the building.

Crouching and sweeping, Gonzalez and Kirby closed in on the fugitive they'd identified from two angles. Kirby knew, if either of the perps tried to double back for the entrance, he and Gonzalez would stop them long before they made it to the door.

And stop the perps they would. One way or the other.

CHAPTER TWENTY-EIGHT

As the car sped ahead, Blue held on to the grip strap for dear life.

Up front, Burton had gunned the engine and centered the bumper to close in on the building surrounded by the police cars. Red and blue flashing strobes lit up the two-story limestone building like a rocket ship ready to launch.

The car torpedoed the last few hundred yards, then screeched to a stop of smoking rubber, pulled up just behind the bumper of the last police car in the lineup, and settled into place. The sidewalk that led to the building lay just outside Blue's door.

Blue threw open the door and darted up the sidewalk. Her vision targeted the glass doors dead ahead, and her feet pumped fast on the cement to close the distance. One train of thought dominated her: *Marda's in there! She's not getting away. I'm making damn sure of it this time.*

Chip called after her, his voice already some distance behind.

She pulled the dagger from her denim jacket and approached the double doors.

Behind her, Burton shouted, "Lower your weapons, dammit! Stand down! She's with me."

Blue didn't think they'd shoot a teenager in the back.

She burst through the doors and stopped in the foyer to consider —*straight ahead through the second set of glass doors, or take the stairway to the left?*

Through the glass, Officer Kirby and another officer—the Hispanic policewoman—closed in on someone who'd just given up their hiding place behind a loveseat.

Blue pushed open the doors just as the woman stood and raised her own dagger in a clear threat.

"You're not taking me! Cyn, run!"

Another voice, some distance off, called back, "Van, wait, what are you—"

"DROP THE KNIFE!" The policewoman raised her gun to target the woman braced to charge. "I *WILL* SHOOT YOU! DROP IT!"

She crouched in a battle stance. Her lips set back into a grin of malice. "Run for it, Cyn, just go. I've got this!"

The scene blurred, and Blue gripped the handle of the door to keep from falling. *My God, I...I know her!*

She recalled the sadistic grins of the two CGI harlequin sickos who oversaw her torture, the two who kept rousing her whenever blackness threatened to end their fun. *That's one of them. And the other one is up ahead.*

Blue reeled as if kicked in the gut. She blinked to clear her vision. Up ahead, she saw the woman with the short red hair step out of her own hiding spot and beckon to her partner.

"You're not taking me to prison!" And with a strangled cry, the closer woman charged to rapidly close the distance on Officer Kirby.

Three rapid, explosive pops made Blue cover her ears. *My God, they shot her.*

When Blue looked up, the dark-haired body lay prone; liquid red already stained and spread along the tan rug.

"No!" The redhead stumbled. Her knife dropped to the ground, and she fell to her knees. "No, Van, no, baby, no..." She crawled toward her on all fours.

"Stop where you are!" The policewoman shouted.

Her pistol followed her target as the woman pulled herself along the floor.

"Stand down," Kirby called out. "Stand down, she's not a threat."

The redhead reached her partner, grabbed her by one shoulder, and turned her over. She cradled the bleeding woman in her arms. "No...no, Van, stay with me, Van, please..."

The brunette sputtered some words.

Blue took a few steps forward, transfixed by the drama.

"...should have run, Cyn...I wanted you...get away."

"It's both of us or nothing, do you hear me? Van?"

The policewoman stepped forward, handcuffs out. She grabbed the redhead from behind and pulled the women apart.

To Blue, it looked like handling a life-sized beanie doll.

The officer pressed her unresisting prisoner to the floor and snapped on the cuffs.

The prisoner simply cried and stared through the process.

Behind Blue, the door opened, and a team of medics closed in on the scene, but Blue knew they were too late.

Then she realized. Kirby and his partner were at ease. As far as they were concerned, the main floor was all clear.

And they would know.

So Marda wasn't here.

And whatever else happened, Blue had to make sure that Marda would not get away.

She slipped back through the glass doors and headed toward the stairs. She descended, her legs pumping over each step. It was everything short of throwing herself down the stairs.

She descended upon the commotion of additional police action playing out, and in the background, an insistent, clanging bell.

A terrified girl's voice droned on, getting louder as Blue approached. "They didn't shoot me, they didn't shoot me..." As Blue dropped down level with the basement, she heard a continuous monotone of pleading, a voice familiar to her. *The whimpering, green-*

cloaked druid, the one I felt sorry for just before she stabbed me in the back.

Blue took in the scene. Two police officers looked down at something. One put his finger to his Bluetooth earpiece.

Where is she?

One police officer pulled the mousy, tearful woman to her feet.

The woman's eyes met Blue's, and she slumped, giggling. "They didn't shoot me! And you got away, too. Good for you. I'm so glad."

The other police officer turned his attention to Blue.

And as far as Blue could see, no one else was in the room. *Where is she?*

"You!" The officer pointed at her. "You're Fiona Shaefer? The one with the federal agent?"

"Yes. How did you—"

"They radioed your distinctive feature." The officer patted his own hair to indicate hers.

Oh.

"How'd they do upstairs?"

"They got 'em, and it's secured," Blue answered automatically, and to her shock, the officer nodded and opened a channel on his radio.

"Where is she?" Blue asked.

"The fourth perp?" The officer motioned to the still-open emergency door across the room.

Through the opening, Blue saw darkness and a far limestone wall. Blue realized the fire alarm was the source of the distant bell. "She's in the alley. She can't go anywhere. She's either going to step out or come back in. There's nowhere to go. Either way, she's done."

Blue closed in. She braced herself to step outside, past the doorframe. She tightened her grip on the ceremonial knife and held it at the ready. "You're right. Because I'm making sure of that."

———

Chip watched Burton's face flare red as her radio crackled to life. He recognized the voice of Officer Kirby. "Shaefer peeked in, and then I think she went downstairs."

"Ms. Shaefer was just here," cut in another voice. "She just followed perp four out the emergency exit. I...told her she didn't have to do that."

"Damn it!" Burton started toward the glass doors.

Chip followed. *Oh, God, Blue, what are you doing?*

Burton raised her radio. "Get out there and stop her."

"Too late. She's engaged perp four. I can hear them fighting."

Burton broke into a run. Chip shadowed her as she ran through the doors and descended the stairs.

———

Blue stepped into the cold night air. Strobes of red and blue lights bathed the walls of the tiny alley and loading dock. The back wall of the next building extended several yards along the alley. The stench of fast food reeked near a large brown dumpster from where it sat in the alley between the buildings. Police cars blocked the exit to the left; more police cars blocked the right.

Something banged against hollow metal. The echo drew Blue's attention to the dumpster. She detected a hint of movement on the side farthest from her vantage point.

Her heart thumped in her chest. As she closed in on her target, adrenaline fired her senses.

She considered sneaking up. *Fuck that.* Instead, she called out, "You're surrounded, Marda." She eased toward the dumpster. "Come out. You're beaten."

"Why should I?"

Blue grinned. *Too stupid to resist answering even an idle threat. Just like Gunther.* Now she knew exactly where Marda waited. "Because, if I come in after you, bitch, it's going to hurt a lot worse."

"Maybe. Maybe not. Maybe I'll take you with me."

"Not on your best day. We're not playing video games anymore."

A commotion of voices echoed over the walls, and then the alley erupted in bright spotlights of white.

As spots blurred her vision, Blue raised a hand and squeezed her eyes shut.

A megaphone-amplified voice called out, "THIS IS THE POLICE! RAISE YOUR HANDS AND COME OUT WITH YOUR HANDS UP!"

"Got you now!"

Fuck! Footsteps closed in, and then blunted metal slammed against her arm.

Rather than resist Marda's charge, Blue back-pedaled and let Marda push her against the wall. Already, her vision was returning.

Marda drew her arm back to swing the metal computer case at Blue a second time.

Blue charged, knocked Marda back, and forced her to drop the case.

Marda growled and swung again.

Blue elbowed her in the chest, grabbed her by the front of her blouse, and flung her bodily against the wall. "I said...NOT on your best day!"

Marda hit the wall but pushed off to turn her momentum into a charge. "I'll kill y–"

Blue cut off the threat with an open-hand punch to her chin.

Marda's jaw jerked backward, and her head hit the wall.

She tried to fall forward, but Blue thrust a forearm up and pinned her against the wall.

Blue raised the knife and pressed it under her chin.

Marda spat blood into Blue's face and tried to squirm away.

Blue held on tight and pressed with the knife tip. "You're not going anywhere!"

Blue held the edge of the knife against Marda's neck, hard. "Slip sideways now!"

Marda stopped her struggles, but a crazed glistening reflected in her eyes. Her voice called out hoarsely. "Mistress...help your servant..."

Enough of this! Blue folded her fingers into Marda's hair and yanked. "Stop it!"

Marda's eyes focused on Blue. Sanity–or, at least, coherency–appeared to return.

To Blue's shock, Marda smiled, then pushed forward against the knife.

Her heart pounding, Blue shoved her arm against Marda's chest, trembling. "Stop it. Just give up. Your mistress is defeated. You've lost."

"Then kill me." Marda's voice reached her, hoarse, barely a whisper. "Because I haven't lost. I won't *ever* give up, Blue. You know it."

"Shut up!"

"They'll lock me away. They'll try to reform me. They'll let down their guard, and then one day, I'll break free."

Blue heard movement behind her, but her gaze remained locked on Marda's. "I said shut up!"

"One day, sooner or later, I'll find my mistress, and then...we'll find you."

"Never. Not ever again."

From behind her, Burton's voice called, "Blue, put the knife down. Blue, we've got her."

Marda emitted a crazed laugh. "Do...you hear that? She's got me. Burton's going to take me. Show me the error of my ways."

Burton continued, "Blue, lower the knife. Now, Blue."

Marda looked away to a vision only she could see. "And I'll find you. First, I'll kill Chip. Then Phil. And then we'll have our fun with you. For real."

"Shut up."

"And if you think it was bad before, that's *nothing* compared to what lies ahead. I can't wait."

Marda smiled and spoke, her voice roughened by the knife pressed against her throat. "Now, lower the knife, Blue. Turn me in. Because that's what you do."

Fury flared through her, then past her. Blue closed her eyes and considered.

Then she knew. "You know what, Marda? I believe you."

Blue swiped the blade across Marda's throat.

The skin ripped open, and red sprayed out. Then it spilled out a gaping gash in Marda's neck. Marda's eyes bugged out, and her jaw worked soundlessly.

She slumped in Blue's arms, but Blue pulled her hair and forced face-to-face contact. "You're dead, Marda!"

Pandemonium broke out behind them.

Burton's voice. "Oh, my God, get her off, now!"

Chip cried her name.

Marda's eyes turned glassy and staring.

"Tell your mistress how you failed, Marda. Tell her she'd better hope no one kills *me* anytime soon, because I'll come for her next! Do you hear me? Do you?"

Multiple arms and hands grabbed Blue and pulled her away.

She struggled against the bodies. "You're dead! Dead!"

Burton's command shouted over the others. "Get Shaefer out of here and into custody, now! Do not let this woman die! She is *not* going to die. Hold her!"

Blue cried out, struggling against the arms pulling her away from the scene. "She deserved to die, Burton! She was evil! I know evil when I see it, Burton. Don't you dare save her now!"

"There's so much blood," Skye cried.

Arms and bodies dragged Blue away toward the blue and red lights.

Blue heard a mad giggle. *Wait, that was me.*

The world turned topsy-turvy, dissolving into more yells and arguments.

"Why didn't your men try to stop her, Kirby?"

"You took my radio from my hand and told my men she was with you, Burton! Hands off, you said. I heard you. Don't you *dare* pin this on me! She's *your* loose cannon, not ours!"

When she found her bearings, her hands were cuffed behind her, and someone was lowering her into the backseat of a squad car.

"Shut up, Shaefer!"

The fog cleared enough for Blue to recognize the voice of Officer Kirby.

Kirby peered into the open window and snarled, "Shut up, now, or even your fancy relative attorney friend won't be able to help you."

Blue sat and waited, but her head still spun. *What just happened?*

Kirby's voice droned in her ears, a monotone, part sympathy, part business. "Look, Shaefer, I'm not entirely sure what just went down, but I know enough to understand that the right person is lying on the ground, bleeding out. And I suspect that if it had been me, I probably would have done the exact same thing."

Blue tried to focus, but Kirby's words hadn't penetrated. She just listened to him talk.

"Now, I am breaking a dozen regulations telling you this, but you need to sit tight and say nothing. There's a reason Miranda reads 'anything you say can and will be used *against* you.' The police are not here to be your friend. Do you understand that?" With that, Kirby recited her Miranda rights.

A detached part of her was bemused that the wording in real life was exactly the same as a lifetime of TV cop shows. The rest of her was still in too much shock to care.

"...Do you understand these rights as I have read them? Shaefer?"

By now, she was coming down off the adrenaline, which left her tired. Her breathing normalized. The impact of what she'd done closed in on her. "I understand I killed someone."

"Shaefer, dammit!" Kirby stepped away from the car. He called back, "I don't want to hear that."

It was true. She couldn't undo it. She'd stared someone down, drew the knife, and made her bleed to death. Because of her, a human life had been snuffed. She felt the shakes come over her.

"Blue?"

She turned toward the familiar voice. Chip's face was now framed in the window. "Oh, Chip, I blew it *bad* this time."

"Shhh!"

Chip looked every bit as if he wanted to reach in and comfort her, but he didn't dare.

"Don't worry, we'll...we'll think of something." He couldn't disguise the futility, the emptiness, of his statement.

"I'm sorry, Chip. You waited so long for me, and now–"

"Hey, I'll wait for you forever." Emotion cracked his voice. "Don't you give up."

She blinked through fresh tears. Remorse for her actions settled over her and constricted her like a straightjacket. She had taken another life, and that fact disgusted her. Her actions went against everything she held sacred. *What in the hell was I thinking?*

And it scared her. Because she also knew, with conviction just as deep, that Marda Mercedes deserved to die. And if Blue were free to change the last few minutes, she wouldn't.

She'd do the exact same thing again, without hesitation.

CHAPTER TWENTY-NINE

Skye MacLeod turned from the body lying in the gutter. Blood spilled over the concrete, in spite of the efforts of the paramedics. *There's no way they're stopping that. No way.*

Having seen the carnage, her stomach flip-flopped. She stepped away and drew deep breaths. Her lungs craved fresh air, even though she already stood outside in the brisk cold.

Her sometime commander and mentor barked out demands for a miracle. Another miracle. In this case, one too many miracles.

"Clamp down. Clamp down. I need to find her mind. Hold her still. I'm *not* going to lose her. I'm not!"

Even several paces away with her back turned, Skye saw in her mind's eye (somewhat less gory than the real thing, perhaps) Burton crouched over the body; she probed with her hands on the woman's hands, her forehead, her ankle, any accessible exposed skin where Rebecca could try her "lay-on-hands psychic trick", as MacLeod thought of it.

But she knew it didn't matter. Theoretically, when someone lost their mind, a body could be kept alive indefinitely, in or out of a coma-like state, hard to reach sometimes for years, but not impossible for some gifted people like Rebecca.

But the opposite was just not true. If the body died, the mind slipped away moments later. And Marda's body would most certainly die.

Blue had seen to that.

Skye waited for the inevitable.

Burton cried out in borderline hysteria. "No! No!"

An unfamiliar man's voice answered, "Agent Burton, if we're going to have any chance, we need to go now. I'm sorry."

She could hear chaotic shifting and scampering, what Skye knew was wasted effort on the part of the EMTs. But they would do what they were trained to do.

God. God, how had this gone so horribly, horribly wrong? What was happening? Skye couldn't wrap her mind around it. The clarity about what was good and bad, and who those players were, all blurred together.

And yet, nothing's really changed. At least, not in my mind.

But that wasn't true. Things had changed a *lot* and would change even more in the next few minutes, unless...

Skye drew a deep breath and steeled her courage. In the three months they'd worked together, Skye had followed orders and learned a lot. She was often praised for her work. For all her mystical powers, Burton was rather ignorant of modern technology and had little patience for it. Skye had been proud of her contributions in that regard.

The chaos had settled. How long had she been sitting here daydreaming? She wasn't sure. She turned and saw Rebecca standing alone, gaze focused on the gory puddle of blood. As the police closed in to tape off the area, Rebecca moved toward Skye.

Before Skye could speak, Rebecca spoke first. Anger seethed through every word. "I want her locked away *under* the prison! She slaughtered our biggest lead into the Sisterhood after I'd *explicitly* told her to back down."

"Rebecca, please—"

"I'll see her in the gas chamber if I have to! She slit someone's throat with hardly a thought about the consequences. She ran into—"

"That's not true, Rebecca. You don't think she thought hard about the consequences? She knew *exactly* what the consequences were."

Rebecca glared. Her eyes flared a hint of red in her pupils.

Perhaps it was just a trick of the flashing sirens, but the effect made Skye pause.

"Do you have a point, MacLeod?"

Her condescension broke the spell. "You can't do this."

"Watch me!"

"Listen to yourself. What are you most angry about, really? That Blue killed a raving psychopath who'd attacked her several times, and threatened her life and the lives of the people she loved? Or that she disobeyed your orders?"

"Murder is murder, and you can't justify–"

"Marda Mercedes tortured Blue nearly to death, and she made it quite clear that she would not hesitate to finish the job, given half a chance!"

Rebecca scoffed, but she hung her head and walked away.

Skye shouted at the back of Burton's retreating form, "Jesus, Rebecca, you said it yourself. Blue suffered more than any person ever has a right to suffer. More than the mind is normally capable of handling. If not for your intervention, she'd be catatonic still. You don't know what that's like. How can–"

Rebecca spun to face her. "If I were you, I would not presume to tell me what you think I know about suffering, little girl!"

No doubt about it. Rebecca's eyes gleamed red.

But Burton wasn't the only one riled up. Skye had to get her point out, and she would not let Rebecca bully her. "You're not being reasonable. You're angry at this failure, and you're lashing out."

"And I suppose you know what's right for everyone concerned?"

"Maybe I do, maybe I don't, but *you* did. Just a few minutes ago, on the drive over here. You sat there in front of everyone and told Blue how impressed you were with her instincts. You told her that those instincts were usually right, and you advised her to trust them! And you know what? She just did!"

The fury fled Rebecca's face, and, in an instant, changed to shock. "I didn't mean–"

Skye pressed, "You were so impressed with her ability at that time that you offered her a future spot on your team. What makes you so wrong then, when you could see the situation impartially, and so right now, when you're so angry that things didn't go your way?"

Skye panted from the emotion of her argument. To her credit, Rebecca now looked abashed rather than angry and answered with level tones.

"She still killed someone, Skye. There are consequences for that."

Skye pointed at the police car where Blue sat, awaiting her fate. Skye's voice quivered with emotion. "That young woman saved us from an impossible situation. We were stuck in a place with no idea how we were going to get out. She got us out of there, and then she trusted us. She trusted *you*, and she trusted her boyfriend. That trust landed her in a terrible, terrible place she barely pulled herself back from. You can't compare her to Marda. Blue was *more* than provoked. You can't possibly consider this a pattern of behavior. You can't..." Skye's voice cracked. She tried again. "You can't let this happen. It's wrong, and in a couple of days, when you've had time to collect yourself, you're going to know it."

Skye waited. Rebecca no longer appeared to fume. Instead, she met Skye's gaze with her standard stoic expression.

Rebecca wiped her bloodied fingers with the handkerchief. "Very well. Come with me."

With Skye at her side, Rebecca stepped up to one of the fire trucks. She flashed her badge to a pair of firefighters. "Gentlemen, your country needs you. I require your assistance on an errand about which you can speak to no one."

The two firefighters exchanged a look, and one of them said, "What can we do for you, Agent?"

"I need to break a window. I need a fast, efficient way without hurting myself."

Skye's head spun at Rebecca's words. *Are we going to bust Blue out? Oh, my God.* She thought Rebecca could just flash her badge and order her freed. *What are we going to do?*

The other firefighter reached into a tool kit, and, after a quick search, held out a small, screwdriver-shaped rod. "Point the plunger, then press the button. Can I help you with that, ma'am?"

"No, I just need it a moment." Rebecca had already fished an evidence baggie from her pocket. She palmed the tool. "Thank you, gentlemen. This didn't happen." She met and held the gaze of each fire-fighter.

"Understood, Agent. We've just been standing here."

She turned to Skye. "Follow me, please."

Skye followed Rebecca past the squad car where Blue still sat, sulking.

Chip and Phil's gazes followed them as they strode past and out of sight.

Rebecca led Skye to the front of the building and stopped before Rebecca's car. She extended the evidence bag toward her. "Hold, please."

Skye took the proffered baggie.

Rebecca pressed the tool against the center of the window.

There was a "pop" that made Skye flinch.

When Rebecca stepped back, the window had spiderwebbed, and slivers fell away over the door. Shards of glass sprayed the passenger seat and the outside.

Rebecca's eyebrows rose and she flashed Skye a smirk. "Overkill, but it will do." Rebecca scanned the glittering shards. She reached into a pocket and withdrew a white handkerchief, reached down, and retrieved a sharp, jagged piece of glass.

Skye stared, dumbfounded.

Without another word, Rebecca led Skye back around the building and toward the crime scene. She flashed her badge at the police officer on guard, bent down, and dipped the shard into the gory puddle.

Rebecca's eyes met Skye's. "Baggie, please?"

Skye understood. She extended the baggie, top pried open.

Rebecca dropped the shard in. Rebecca rose. "That is the piece of glass Marda used to slice her own neck after she broke free from me as I struggled to get her into the car. Do you understand? She broke free from me."

"Wait," Skye objected. "It was my idea. Maybe you should say she broke away from–"

Rebecca shook her head. "If you let an important witness slip away from you and kill herself, Skye...frankly, your record isn't established enough to survive the black mark."

"But...wait, it's okay if *you* did something that incompetent?"

An ironic smile crossed her lips. "If anyone in the Kelranian Order has job security, it's me."

Skye nodded as if she understood. She didn't. Not really.

Now tired and drained, the chill in the air penetrated Skye's thin fall jacket, and she shivered. Her thoughts turned back to Blue. She opened her mouth to ask, but Rebecca beat her to it.

Rebecca's police band radio beeped. She raised it to her ear. "Burton."

Skye waited out the several-second pause as Rebecca received a message.

"Thank you." She looked at Skye. "Well, that's it. They called it as soon as the body arrived at the hospital. Marda's dead, and Shaefer's actions caused it."

Though she expected it, Skye still hated to hear the news. *What happens now?*

Rebecca met her gaze and held it for several seconds. "Now, please tell Kirby to let Fiona go. Tell him the Special Investigations Unit will not be pressing charges. Later, I'll talk to Kirby about how to handle this incident with his men. For now, just tell Shaefer that, officially, I wish her the best, but she is not to try to contact me. And she should not hold her breath for me to contact her." Rebecca held out her hand.

Skye deposited the evidence bag into it. "I'm sorry," Skye mumbled.

"For what?"

"For how it turned out. The cult's still active. Baalina slipped away. There's still a real danger the Sisters could bring her back."

Rebecca walked up the alleyway. "Leave that to me. I need you to catch a ride with a patrolman to a nearby hotel. Reserve two rooms. I trust you don't want to spend the night in our trashed house?"

"Not really, no, but where are you going?"

"To end this. Just text me the hotel name and our room numbers. I'll see you in a couple of hours." Rebecca turned and walked away without another word or glance back.

CHAPTER THIRTY

Officer Kirby pocketed his phone and turned toward Chip and Phil. They stood on either side of the window to give the Shaefer girl a view to the outside world. They also stood too close to the car for regulation, but in for an inch, take a few feet, at this point.

His head reeled over the news that he and Gonzalez had bagged one of the Terror Twins, infamous assassins from Chicago, and that they held the other one in cuffs. The two of them filled a slot on America's top five Most Wanted for as far back as he could remember. But they had shoved the surviving twin into a squad car, and that car now raced to the county lockup. For that alone, tonight would officially go "front page." There was no cramming this genie back into the liquor flask.

He knew the regs, but he couldn't bring himself to shoo the kids away from the car. The Shaefer girl had a tough road ahead, and opportunities for little kindnesses would soon be few and far between.

He hated it. He hated the whole thing. He'd been wrong about these kids, and in many ways, it sorted itself out exactly right. But also, very wrong. He wouldn't cause them any more grief, at least, no more than he had to.

He also hated to repeat what he'd just been told on the phone, but he had no choice. It wouldn't surprise anyone, but it needed to be said. "I'm sorry, Shaefer...and Farren." He nodded toward the large fellow whose name escaped him. "Marda Mercedes was declared dead on arrival at IU Bloomington hospital. I'm sure it's just a matter of time before the feds make it official, and–"

And here she came, the tall, skinny assistant to the agent, the girl he'd seen all but literally attached to Burton's right elbow this entire case. The feds were usually fast, but this was a blitzkrieg. *Burton really means it. She's going to bury the poor girl. She doesn't stand a chance.*

———

CHIP HAD CONTINUED to offer words of support, words Blue couldn't cling to or have faith in. She already saw a vision of herself, thirty years later, squinting at a mature Chip on the other side of the glass partition, having wasted his life attached to his wife, the killer. Do they allow conjugal visits for convicted murderers? She somehow doubted it, but she would find out soon.

I should tell him to go away, and to never come back. But I've done that too many times, and it never did any good.

Besides, I need him now. That's the truth of it.

Chip cut an empty platitude off and stepped away from the window.

Blue peered through the window in time to hear Kirby's announcement. To his credit, he sounded terribly sorry about it. Then he stopped mid-sentence.

Skye approached.

Blue's heart sank.

Phil took a half-step forward and stopped.

Skye smiled, apparently flattered that her presence came off as so important. "Officer Kirby, Rebecca Burton of the Special Investigations Unit wanted me to tell you that the Unit will not be pressing charges against your suspect, Fiona Shaefer. The Unit considers this matter settled and furthermore insists that you release the suspect immediately. She will also contact you in the next few days about counseling your officers on what they might or might not have heard during these last few minutes."

Blue waited. She heard the words, but she couldn't process them. Apparently, neither could anyone else. She realized, from a distance, that Skye wasn't delivering the news they'd braced themselves for, but she couldn't wrap her overtaxed brain around what it meant.

Kirby broke the silence first with, "You've got to be kidding me," followed by, "My people will back my play."

Blue detected sarcasm in his next words. "Please tell Agent Burton that I look forward to reading her report."

It started to penetrate. *It's over, it's over...it, no, it can't be over.*

"Blue, did you hear that?" Chip's voice.

She did, but she didn't. She bent down, nauseous and overtaxed; the last twenty-four hours caught up with her and weighed her down.

Vaguely, she became aware that someone opened the car door. Hands, not rough but insistent, pulled her out of the car.

"Easy, Shaefer, easy," Kirby coaxed.

Blue stood before Chip, who waited with a look of expectation. She wanted to step forward, but her wrists were still bound.

And then, they weren't, and she fell into his arms. Drained and spent in every possible way, Blue could no longer focus on what had happened or why. "I want to go home. I just want to go home, Chip, please, just take me home."

Home is in New York, a part of her protested.

No, home was with Chip, and she'd finally come home after a long time away.

SKYE MACLEOD SAT on a metal bench outside the glass doors of the student center. She'd confirmed that Kirby would arrange a ride for wherever she wanted, when she wanted, but she needed some time to collect her thoughts after such a crazy clusterfuck of a day. After all the intelligence gathering and tactics, after all the plans and schemes, today had erupted into another climax of chaos, as so much of her life tended to do.

Still, it had turned out okay, at least, today.

She just needed to sit and let everything percolate for a minute before she started to surf for hotels on her smartphone. In a couple of days, she guessed, they'd head home, and she could bring this chapter of her life to a close.

Skye was proud of herself and her accomplishments. She'd stayed sober, and, until tonight, rarely felt the need to sneak a drink. Now, however, she missed Minnie. Later, in the privacy of her room...well, who knew?

Soon, she'd be heading home to Broad Ripple, where–

A figure approached her, slowly, tentatively. She couldn't actually see him in the dark, but she recognized Phil's distinct silhouette, large, tall, and bear-like, but in a cuddly way more than a threatening way. She recalled the last twenty-four hours, how he had sort of taken her under his wing–his considerable wing–and had watched out for her.

She'd kind of miss that.

She waited him out as he approached and sat on the other side of the bench. *Did the bench shift? Surely, that's my imagination.* She smiled at him.

He smiled back. "Hey," he said.

"Hey."

Phil's gaze flicked back and forth between Skye's face and a spot on the ground. "Um...we're leaving soon. I'm guessing you are, too, but I imagine in your case, that means you're leaving...town."

"Broad Ripple," she answered his unasked question.

"Ah. I love Broad Ripple." Then, a moment later, "Actually, I've only heard Blue *talk* about Broad Ripple, but it sounds like I'd like it."

Skye giggled.

"Listen, I was wondering, is it okay for...you know, agents to stay in touch with people?"

Oh, God. She realized. *He's hitting on me.* And everything clicked. The protectiveness wasn't just protective. He liked her. *Oh, God, now what?*

Phil continued, "I mean, after a case is over and stuff?"

Skye licked her lips and let the silence draw out as she considered. "You mean, like, as friends?"

"Yeah."

Even in the dark, Skye saw Phil's face flare beet red.

"As friends, or whatever. That is, if..." He let the question linger, unasked.

Skye reached into a pocket and drew out a fold-over business card holder. "I'm not an agent, I'm a contractor. I don't work all the time. Yes, I'd like to stay friends with you." She extended the card and added, "But...yes, there is someone else. Her name is Annabelle."

Phil's eyes fell upon the offered card. "Oh. Oh, no, I'm sorry. I didn't realize..."

Skye giggled. "Don't be. I'm not..." She considered her next words. "I guess you could say I don't let gender get in the way of who I fall for. I had a boyfriend just before...well, that's a long story." She gave the card a shake. "It's a story I'd like to share with you some time, if you still want to hear it."

Phil took the card. "I think I'd like that."

Skye nodded at the entwined couple standing on the sidewalk. Not making out, in fact, just barely moving. They just held and held and held each other like they'd never let each other go. "How are they doing?"

Phil considered. "Good. They've still got a long road ahead, but this is the first time in quite a while I feel good about their relationship."

"They seem sweet. You keep an eye on them, and keep me posted." Skye reflected on the embracing couple. *Maybe someday, I'll have that, too.*

Skye and Phil sat in comfortable silence. She enjoyed this quiet finish to a terrible day.

———

THE SQUAD CAR pulled up to the house.

Blue, Chip, and Phil huddled in the backseat, exhausted. They thanked Officer Gonzalez and stumbled out of the car. Chip held tight to Blue as if holding her up. And maybe he was.

After a precursory goodnight, Phil retired to the basement, leaving Chip and Blue to settle on the living room couch, where they held each other in grateful silence for many minutes.

Chip seemed to instinctively understand Blue's need for quiet and comfort.

Finally, obeying some psychic cue, he spoke the first words between them in over an hour. "Hungry?"

"Yes, very much."

Chip vanished into the kitchen.

From where she sat, Blue heard the telltale beeping and hum of a microwave, and, a couple minutes later, Chip returned with two steaming platefuls of pizza.

As he seated himself next to her, a thought made her giggle.

Chip smirked at her. "What?"

Blue held up the slice of greasy goodness. "Thanksgiving dinner." She laughed, the simple release so much more than she could have expected just an hour ago.

"Oh, hell no, it's not," said Chip. "The turkey and fixings are still defrosted in the fridge. Phil and I had plans to do dinner up big, and that's still going to happen. It's just going to be a day late." Chip's hand enfolded hers briefly before returning to his plate. "Besides, now I have a lot more to be thankful for."

Blue bit down on the pepperoni slice. She had to admit, as pizza went, Smittie's was pretty yummy stuff, even if the waitress liked to dance on her last nerve. She devoured four pieces without pause, making up for a twelve-hour gap in meals with a quick gorging. With each bite, her stomach calmed and settled.

After two pieces, Chip put his plate aside.

Blue leaned her head back against him.

He shifted and allowed room for her to put her head on his shoulder. Chip checked the time on his phone. "Well, it's officially after midnight, and the Black Friday lines are starting. I was going to go stand in line at Best Buy, but I guess I can skip it this year."

Blue giggled, put her balled fist up to her mouth, and stifled a burp. *Gorgeous and classy! I am the complete package.* "You'd be out there alone, my man." She let her head fall back into his lap.

"Alone, right." He elbowed her. "Just me and hundreds of other bargain hunters—"

"Cheapskates."

"Bargain hunters," he emphasized, "who want to spend the night shopping."

She enfolded her fingers through his. With his free hand, he traced her eyebrows with a finger as if trying to memorize her features. When he spoke, all trace of humor had vanished.

"How are you? Really?" His finger trailed, feather-light, over her lips.

As a shiver passed through her, Blue smiled. "I'm fine. Really. As good as I've ever been in a long time."

"I'm worried," Chip admitted. "Agent Burton said she'd blocked out a lot of what happened to you, but that over time, it's going to start coming back."

"I remember enough." Blue let the words hang in the air. "Nothing's forgotten. I remember the pain, and the anger, and the...helplessness. But right now, it's like it happened a long, long time ago. So..." She shrugged. "I'm okay."

"I'm so sorry," Chip said. "You trusted me, and I let you down."

"Don't say that!" Blue grabbed his hand. "You came for me. You found a way to me, just like you said you always would." She squeezed her eyes shut against fresh tears.

"But I couldn't get to you fast enough. If I had figured out–"

"You're the only person who could have gotten to me at all, Chip. They...they weren't done. If Marda had it her way, she and her posse would have been found in a coma, spending all of eternity torturing me just because she got a kick out of it. You stopped them. And I will never forget that." The memory, even blunted, disturbed her.

She disengaged her hands and sat up. She resettled on his lap so they lay face to face in an embrace on the couch. "You came for me. And I'm never leaving you again."

Chip kissed her, his passion cushioned in infinite gentleness.

Before separating, she brushed her lips over his one last time. She sensed his tentativeness. He handled her like delicate China.

And right now, that's what she needed.

She lowered her head to his shoulder. "I mean it. I'm never leaving you again. I mean, I'll finish the semester at NYU, but then I'm transferring all my credits to IU. If I can get enrolled for January, I'm moving to Bloomington." She met his gaze. She could feel him tensing beneath her. "Scared yet?"

"Scared? No, that's...that's amazing. The writing program here is first-rate. I'd been trying to..." He trailed off.

Yes, he'd been trying to. Trying to get her to enroll, trying to bring her closer to him for months, frustrated at her hesitancy to even consider it. Clueless as to why, until a few hours ago.

He kissed her again, still tentative.

Another shiver of excitement passed through her. When they separated, she looked down, not meeting his eyes. "Chip...look, I...I know it's been a long time. For both of us. I'm going to need you to be a little patient. Do you understand?"

Chip nodded, his face impassive. "Look, no one could have expected this. I'll wait as long as it takes. Weeks, months...take whatever time you need."

Blue laughed. Her eyes met his. "Months? You're talking *crazy*, you silly man!" She pressed her lips against his, her desire loud and clear in her kiss. "I meant more like a couple of *hours*. Just...handle with care, okay?"

He pulled her into a loving embrace. "Always, Blue. Always and forever."

EPILOGUE_

Rebecca Burton snapped on the lights and descended the wooden stairs to the basement. She took in the circle and faced the statue of the chaos demoness, self-labeled "Goddess" Baalina–erect and proud, captured with her standard trappings of scepter and robes. Just one of her many lies.

Baalina specialized in luring strong, damaged women to her side, women with high intelligence but who had been scarred by society in some way.

Today's world offered a plethora of victims for Baalina to exploit–perhaps more than ever because more women than any other time in history faced their future with high expectations and set themselves up for so many crushing disappointments.

Baalina used these women to further her ends with promises of power and revenge–promises she never intended to keep. Chaos, destruction, and torture were Baalina's primary interests, with deceit her currency to lure and hold her followers.

Rebecca had hoped to save four of those victims, to counsel them, to guide them, and to hone and reshape those talents so terribly misplaced and misused, in the service of the Kelranian Order.

She'd have to settle for two.

As Skye had predicted, the more she reflected on the fate of Marda Mercedes, Baalina's "special one," the more she saw Marda as a hopeless cause. She realized Blue's actions saved everyone a lot of wasted time.

Several minutes earlier, for reasons unclear even to her, Burton parked the car a few blocks from this address. As she walked, Rebecca tasted the streets, and she absorbed the life of the students who lived here. She closed in on the student house, rented and re-rented for mundane study, the kids around them blissfully unaware of the horrible plots and schemes that took place here. How close they'd all come to losing this university, perhaps the city or beyond, to the delusions of a demoness and her minions.

And that would have been it, Rebecca mused. An entire city was not an acceptable price to pay. But world domination was never a possibility. Between the weapons, technology, and the magic that so many others stood by, ready to wield, world domination would never have been in the cards for this demoness.

But this neighborhood, for certain. Bloomington, perhaps. With thousands dead in the process. And that would have been more than enough to leave a scar that could never be removed. Interpreted as perhaps a terrorist attack, a student uprising, or some extreme weather event, the world would never know the true threat from the spirit dimension.

Left on their own, the Sisters would try to raise their Goddess again. And again. And again. There was only one way to stop them forever.

Rebecca stood in the center of the communing circle and raised her hand toward the statue. The ancient words of summoning came to her easily, her voice an angelic call, a siren that commanded the magic to bend to her will.

The portal formed before her along the curve of the circle; it opened upon the fiery pit of the chaos realm where Baalina stood, arrogant and angry as ever. Red lips pulled up over jagged white teeth.

Burton read the dismay on the face of the demoness at this summons.

"Tesh Ka Ra bitch, where is my devoted servant? What have you done with my Special One?"

Unruffled, Rebecca faced the scoffing image. "She needlessly lost her life in your service and is beyond anyone's reach, including yours."

"And the others?"

Rebecca shrugged. "One of the so-called Terror Twins is dead. Neither the other twin nor the other survivor will acknowledge your call."

"They were weak. I would have granted them anything they asked of me, once I freed myself."

"You believe your own lies, demoness. You have no gifts to bestow upon your followers. You cannot lie to *me* unless you lie to yourself."

Baalina snarled. "Where two fall, three will take their place. I sense a strong soul. New, yet familiar. It calls to me, even from here in the depths, someone to whom I have already called out, and she has heard me. I tempted her to kill, and she obeyed. Who else is more worthy to be my new Special One?"

"Fiona Shaefer was tortured by your hand. She would never follow you."

"She might."

Rebecca slashed her hand in dismissal. "She won't."

Baalina cocked her head like a slow child only beginning to suspect what their peers had already deduced. "Why do you summon me, Tesh Ka Ra? Do you simply wish to stare at me and gloat?"

Rebecca looked back and said nothing.

Baalina's annoyance grew. "Begone! Your mission to pass final judgment upon the fallen angels is yet decades away. I've plenty of time to escape from here before your powers mature."

Rebecca braced herself. She'd delayed long enough. "Is that how you understand the ancient writings?"

"I said begone!" Baalina reached out as if to cross the portal into the physical realm. The opening sparked as the demoness swiped the magical energy barrier.

"Your powers cannot penetrate the shield, demoness."

"Then leave me to my suffering," Baalina mocked, "so that one day I may learn my lesson and repent of my evil ways before my judgment arrives." Baalina spat. "That will never happen, Tesh Ka Ra bitch!"

Rebecca raised her hand. "You've been mistaken about many things, Baalina, but you're correct on that one point."

"You are a servant to a power that is less than nothing to me, Tesh Ka Ra. I laugh at Him as I laugh at you. Begone. I am done with you."

"But *I* am not done with *you*, demoness. My mission begins today, with you. Now. Judgment has arrived for you, demoness Baalina. Prepare to receive final punishment."

Rebecca started a new chant. Both the words and the associated magic penetrated the portal to reach the creature beyond.

"What? No!" Baalina screamed. "You cannot do this! You have no right to judge me."

Red flame flared across her robe. Baalina swiped a hand to snuff it. "No!" The flame caught, and the robe blazed.

The flames engulfed her, and the beast thrashed. Baalina's cries turned from anger to a howl of torment. "No! Damn you, you can't."

As Burton bore witness, fire burned the demon's face. The scepter dropped from her hands, useless and discarded. It fell against the stone, where it also caught fire.

The flames ripped away skin to expose muscle and bone.

Burton watched the punishment draw out its predicted course. The creature's cries halted mid-scream, the ghastly spectacle ended, and the flames burned out into a red pyre.

Baalina was no more.

The sting of hot tears streaked Rebecca's face.

The Tesh Ka Ra had taken her first life–the first of many lives that would be lost before her righteous judgment in the years to come.

Rebecca Burton–the Tesh Ka Ra–waved her hand to close the portal.

A voice reached her, a pitiful sound, yet strong enough to override the chaos of the flames. "Wait..."

Rebecca stopped. *How is it possible the demoness survived the purification?*

"Release...me..."

No, not the demoness. A man's voice, overwhelmed with pain and torment.

The answer struck Rebecca like a cold flame. "Krane?"

"Yesss..."

Oh, my sweet master, no! Brother James Krane of the Kelranian Order called out to her. Even now, *after* centuries of torment from where his spirit lay in agony, never released.

Her hand trembled, but Rebecca again extended her magic through the portal. "Brother Krane, by the power of the Tesh Ka Ra, I release you to find the peace too long denied you. Go with God."

"Thank you..."

She waved her hand, and the portal closed.

Rebecca stumbled out of the circle and sank into a chair. She'd never felt so alone. So truly alone.

And in that quiet room, Rebecca Burton wept.

She wept for Marda, for Fiona, and for Brother Krane. She wept for the demoness Baalina and for all of her deluded followers.

And as the Tesh Ka Ra contemplated her destiny, she wept for herself.

The End

About the Author

R.J. Sullivan's novel *Haunting Blue* (2010) is an edgy paranormal thriller and the first book of the adventures of punk girl Fiona "Blue" Shaefer and her boyfriend Chip Farren. *Haunting Obsession* (2012) and *Virtual Blue* (2013) continue the paranormal thriller series. R.J.'s short stories have been featured in such acclaimed collections as *Dark Faith Invocations* by Apex Books and *Vampires Don't Sparkle*. These stories were compiled in R.J.'s 2015 collection *Darkness with a Chance of Whimsy*. Revised editions of these titles were released by Dark-Whimsy Books in 2020.

Commanding the Red Lotus (2016) collects three space opera tales in the tradition of Andre Norton and Gene Roddenberry. New titles to the series are forthcoming from Hydra Publications.

rjsullivanfiction.com

The Original Paranormal Thrills by R.J. Sullivan...

... Revised Editions by 

RJSullivanFiction.com

Also Available in Audiobook

Narrated by Danielle Muething

DanielleMuething.wixsite.com/mysite/about

Travel Through Time and Space with R J Sullivan

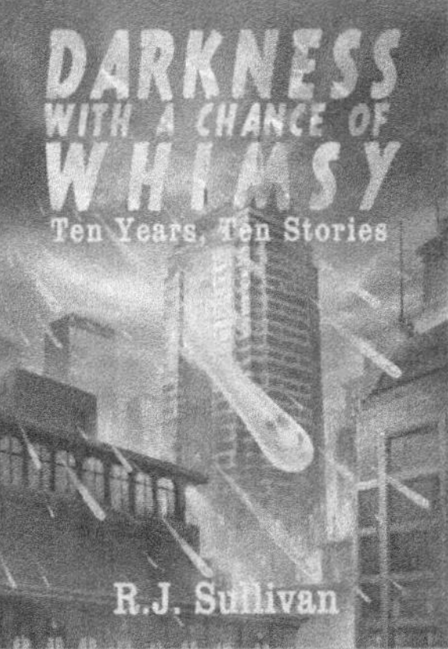

**RJSullivanFiction.com
or Amazon.com**

Haunting Obsession
Elegant Paper Dolls

Maxine and Loretta
gorgeous glossy color book
4" figures, 10 costume changes!
$5! Sexy and Cheap!

Order exclusively from
RJSullivanFiction.com or
at personal appearances.

Renderings by Nell Williams,
NellWilliams.com

This book is part of an author-cooperative urban fantasy universe. Characters created by E. Chris Garrison (including Skye MacLeod and the Transit King) and R.J. Sullivan (including "Blue" Shaefer and Rebecca Burton) interact in a shared world. For example, Chris's Transit King appears in R.J.'s Haunting Obsession, while R.J.'s Rebecca Burton lends a hand in Chris's Mean Spirit. So if you love what you just read and want the entire story, here's a handy guide and timeline to:

The Skye-Blue-niverse

Haunting Blue by R.J. Sullivan *
Four 'Til Late by E. Chris Garrison**
Haunting Obsession by R.J. Sullivan
Sinking Down by E. Chris Garrison**
Blue Spirit by E. Chris Garrison
Me and the Devil by E. Chris Garrison**
Virtual Blue by R.J. Sullivan*
Restless Spirit by E. Chris Garrison
Mean Spirit by E. Chris Garrison

*Also part of The Collected Adventures of Blue Shaefer by R.J. Sullivan
**Part of the Road Ghosts Omnibus by E. Chris Garrison

Enter the Skye-Blue-niverse at:

**https://sillyhatbooks.com/
and
https://rjsullivanfiction.com/**

9 781953 763044